ANG.

DEA1 .1

Book 1 of the Inspector Sheehan
Mysteries

By

Brian O'Hare

GLOSSARY

Police Service of Northern Ireland Acronyms.

Northern Ireland is part of the United Kingdom (Britain) and its police service has broadly similar ranks to its counterparts in England. The short glossary below, while not exhaustive, is offered to clarify for American readers the abbreviations used in this book.

RUC—The Royal Ulster Constabulary now redundant and replaced, in 2001, by:

PSNI—The Police Service of Northern Ireland which is peopled by:

CC—Chief Constable

DCC—Deputy Chief Constable

ACC—Assistant Chief Constable

CS—Chief Superintendent

Superintendent (tends not to be abbreviated)

DCI—Detective Chief Inspector

DI—Detective Inspector

DS—Detective Sergeant

DC—Detective Constable

SOCO—Scene of Crime Officer

Table of Contents

ONE

Detective Chief Inspector Jim Sheehan studied the mutilated corpse. "Something about the body doesn't seem right," he muttered.

Detective Sergeant Kevin Doyle looked at him askance. His inscrutable face almost registered surprise. "It's naked, sir!" he said. "The tongue is pulled some three inches out of its mouth. It's lying sprawled on the floor on its back. It's got knife wounds all over the place. Why wouldn't it look not right?"

The chief inspector stared again at the dead body of the Most Reverend Charles Loughran, until today Bishop of the Diocese of Down and Connor. His sergeant was right, of course. This was a brutal murder. The wounds had been inflicted with considerable ferocity but, while there was plenty of blood, it was clear that the victim's clothes had been removed post-mortem. The bloodied garments were

1

lying in an untidy heap against a far wall, slung there as if to distance them as far as possible from the body. But how did the bishop finish up lying on the floor on his back, his right knee bent, twisted almost, and tucked under his left leg, his hands stretched backwards above his head? Did he simply fall like that after the killer had undressed him or had he been posed like that? And the tongue? How did that happen?

Dr. Richard Campbell, Deputy State Forensic Pathologist, a stout man, balding, was kneeling by the body. He had rolled it half-over to examine the back and sides, feeling around the back of the head for bruising or lacerations. Returning the body to its original position, he struggled to his feet, almost losing his balance. He righted himself, breathing rather more heavily than he should. He flicked a glance at Sheehan's trim, efficient shape as he peeled off his latex gloves and said, somewhat testily, "I really am going to have to start going to the gym."

The corners of Sheehan's lips twitched but he simply said, "Well, what's the story?"

"I won't be sure until I see the body back in the mortuary but I'd say the knife wounds did it."

"Y' think!" It wasn't a question.

"Come now, Jim. I've learned a long time ago not to jump at the obvious. But this time, yes, I think!"

"Any other injuries? Signs of a struggle?"

"None that I can see. The infra-red photos might show some latent bruising but I can't see anything at the moment"

"No trauma to the head anywhere?"

"No."

"He's a big man. Gave in without much of a

struggle, did he not? How did the killer overcome him so easily?"

"Hard to say right now …"

"Ah, come on, Dick. You can hazard some sort of a guess. It'll be at least a couple of weeks before I see your report."

"Well, don't hold me to anything, the autopsy could change things entirely, but I'd say the first blow from the knife probably came as a surprise. If it didn't kill him right away, it certainly would have immobilised him."

"Pretty lucky, what? I mean, the heart is well protected by the sternum and the ribs, isn't it?"

The doctor nodded but said, "Might have been more than luck. There's a severe wound in the middle." He pointed. "There, just at the top of the abdomen. Looks like it might have done the trick. If the blade was aimed at just the right angle, it could have hit the heart immediately. If you knew what you were doing, it wouldn't be that difficult."

"Medical knowledge?"

"Maybe, or combat training, perhaps."

"Time of death?"

The pathologist consulted his pencilled notes. "Liver temperature relative to room temperature, rigor mortis well started, one and a half degrees an hour …" He muttered some figures, brows furrowed as he did some mental calculations, and said, "I might have to change my mind about this but I'd guess roughly between ten pm yesterday and four o'clock this morning." He clicked shut his brief case and looked at his watch. "Nearly ten o'clock and I haven't opened the office yet. I'm outta here."

"What about the tongue? How did it get like that?"

"Oh, it was obviously pulled out deliberately. Judging by the bruises I'd guess a pair of pliers."

"Why?"

The pathologist shrugged. "Absolutely no idea."

"Okay! I might call in to see you in a day or so."

"Ah, come on, Jim. I'm already up to my eyes. Any suspicious deaths near the Royal always have me doing a Force Medical Officer's work as well as my own. Gimme a few days."

"I know, Dick, but this was a bishop."

"All right, all right." He spent a moment in thought. "This is Thursday. Call in to the mortuary at the Royal Victoria sometime next week. I might have something."

As he left the room, Sheehan called after him, "Thanks, Dick." He turned his eyes once more to the crime scene, focusing particularly on the crime scene unit, dressed in tyvek white hooded coveralls and facemasks, as were he and Doyle. Some officers were dusting doors and windows for fingerprints, some crawling on the floor searching for fibres or any small item that might later prove significant. He spoke to one of the officers on the floor.

"Anything?"

The man shook his head, "Nothing, sir."

"Nothing?" Sheehan said.

The man shrugged. "Apart from the blood spatter, sir, clean as a whistle. Even the ordinary stuff you'd expect to be lying around; nothing."

Sheehan turned to the man dusting the edges of

the door. "Fingerprints?"

Again a laconic shrug. "Some, but they're not fresh. I'd guess the victim's, maybe some staff."

"Bloody hell!" He turned to the photographer who had been flashing for several minutes. "All right, that'll do." He glanced at his sergeant who was standing above the body. Doyle was a large man, early fifties, a confirmed bachelor like himself. Normally dressed in a dark sports jacket, he looked huge and awkward in the voluminous biohazard coveralls. Awkward? Strange how misleading impressions can be. Nobody was more effective or more reliable in a tight corner than Doyle. But right now he was being neither effective nor reliable. He was just standing there, staring down at the corpse. "What are you doing, Doyle?" he called to the sergeant.

Doyle seemed nonplussed. "Uh ... saying a wee prayer for his immortal soul."

Sheehan felt a stab of guilt. Concern for the victim's eternal destination had not brushed, even remotely, against the fringes of his own mind. Doyle, of course, was probably still thinking about his father. He had asked for a week off a couple of months before to bury him. Somewhere abroad. His parents had moved abroad after they retired. But where? Who knew? Somewhere in Europe, probably. Doyle was not profligate with information.

Sheehan dismissed his feelings of guilt and said, "Aye, right. There's time enough for his immortal soul. Right now we have to try and find out what's happened to his mortal body. Go and find a sheet somewhere and cover him up. That's no way for a bishop to be lying."

He stared around the crime scene. He was in a

large, well-appointed sitting room, or study perhaps, leather armchairs, bookshelves from floor to ceiling, a heavy, polished oak desk facing away from the window, a fireplace with the embers of the previous evening's fire still warm. A large crucifix hung on the wall over the fireplace. Sheehan's eyes rested on it before flicking guiltily away. His Catholicism, unlike Doyle's, had lapsed some years before but he still had trouble confronting the images of his childhood faith.

His eyes ranged the room once more. Everything seemed normal, in place.

Nothing to indicate a struggle. No forensics. No weapon. *This perp seems to know what he's doing.* His eyes strayed back to the body. "Who would want to kill a bishop?" he muttered.

Doyle *had* just re-entered the room with a sheet from the forensics van. "An atheist?"

Sheehan gave him a withering glance. "Aye, right. How did the perp get in?"

"Don't know," Doyle said. "Doors all locked. Windows securely fastened. No sign of a break-in. Maybe the victim knew the killer and let him in?"

Sheehan didn't respond. He was looking at the CSI officer who was fingerprinting the desk. The man was focused on something at the side of the desk, staring at it, rubbing it gently with his thumb. Sheehan strode over to him. "Found something?"

The officer made a 'maybe-maybe not' waggle with his right hand and pointed to some small scratches on the side of the desk. "There's a letter and some numbers here. They feel fresh, scraped in with a pin, or something with a sharp point."

Sheehan, and Doyle who had followed his boss, peered over the investigator's shoulder. Sheehan said,

"Can you make them out?"

"Yes, sir," the officer replied. "It's a capital E followed by some numbers … 3 … 4 … 1 … 0."

"Have you any idea what they mean?" Sheehan asked.

"Not a clue. Probably nothing."

"Maybe it's an auctioneer's lot number," Doyle suggested.

"Bit vandalistic that, on that lovely desk," Sheehan mused. "They usually put wee stickers on their lots." He exhaled a frustrated breath. "Photograph the numbers anyway. And Sergeant, just to be sure, check out where the desk came from."

The CSI officer stood up and began packing up his gear. The other members of the unit were doing the same.

"You guys finished?" Sheehan said.

The officers nodded.

"Okay, Doyle," Sheehan said. "Have the body removed." He began to struggle out of his own coveralls, having trouble, as always, with the zip. "Hate these bloody things," he muttered. He handed the coveralls to Doyle who had just divested himself of his own. "Here! Get rid of these." He looked at his watch. "After ten. Most of the staff will be in by now, I expect. Round them up. Maybe one of them can throw some light on this. I'll start with the woman who found the body."

TWO

When Doyle returned with Mrs. Bell, Sheehan was already seated behind the bishop's desk. Mrs. Bell, a woman in her late fifties, looked terrified. Naturally small in stature, she was reduced to waiflike proportions beside Doyle's substantial bulk. Doyle stood to one side and pulled out a pen and notebook. Sheehan examined the woman. Her hair was pulled severely back and fastened with a piece of elastic band and her face bore the pinched, defeated look of one who had known little in the way of joy in her life and far too much in the way of hardship. Her hands were clasped in front of her abdomen, trembling, as she stood at the door waiting for instructions. Sheehan felt a twinge of sympathy. *The poor woman is scared out her mind and she's probably done nothing wrong.* Trying to put on a welcoming expression, he indicated a chair he had placed before the desk and said, "Come on in, Mrs. … Ms …?"

"Mrs. Bell."

"Mrs. Bell. Please, take a seat."

The woman edged towards the chair, sitting on the extreme front end of it, her hands now clasped in her lap. Sheehan wondered if she'd keep her balance or slide off the chair at some point during the interview. He cleared his throat. "There's no need to be worried, Mrs. Bell. I simply want to know how you came to find the body."

The woman's lips moved as if she wasn't accustomed to talking. Nothing emerged. Then she said, hesitantly, "I'm the housekeeper here. I come in three mornings a week to clean up. This is one of my days. I came in at eight o'clock this morning and …"

"Excuse me," Sheehan interrupted her. "How did you get in?"

She looked at him, puzzled. "I came in the front door."

"No, I mean, did someone let you in?"

"No, I have a key, two keys, one for the ordinary lock and one for the big lock."

"A mortise lock, sir," Doyle volunteered.

"Do you keep these keys all the time?"

"Yes."

"Where?"

"In my handbag."

"Where do you normally keep your handbag?"

"In a drawer in my bedroom."

"Would anyone have access to it?"

Mrs. Bell peered at him. "What?"

"Can anyone ever get at your handbag apart from

yourself; children in the house, perhaps?"

"Oh no, sir. Tommy has went away to work in England and Mary's married and living in Dungiven. I never hardly see her. Nobody else is in the house. My husband's dead."

"Oh, I'm sorry to hear that. All right, tell me how you found the body. Take your time, no need to rush."

"Well, I usually do the hall and the downstairs before I go up to the bedrooms. I was on'y just finished in the dining-room and I came in to do the bishop's study and …. And …"

Her face began to crumple and Sheehan said: "It's all right, Mrs. Bell. Take your time."

The woman composed herself and went on. "I opened the door and he was … I seen him right away. I … I was so shocked. It took the breath out of me. I couldn't get a breath. And all I could say was, 'God save us! God save us!' over and over again." She stared at Sheehan, her expression confused. "On the television when they find a body they just scream and scream, but I never had the breath to make a squeak, I was that scared. I ran down to the monsignor's office to phone 999, but my hands was shaking that much I dropped the phone and I couldn't hardly find the numbers, and I had to try again."

It seemed that Mrs. Bell could talk very well once she got started. Sheehan raised a hand, palm outwards. "That's okay, Mrs. Bell. Did you examine the body or touch it in any way?"

Mrs. Bell shuddered, turning to glance quickly at the space recently occupied by the body. "Good Lord, no. And him like that? I never got past the door. The second I was able to move, I was away out of there, to the monsignor's office."

"Who exactly is the monsignor?"

"Monsignor Byrne. He lives here, too. He's the bishop's secretary, but he's not really a secretary. There's two other secretaries works here, in the front office. They do the typing and answer the phone and, oh yes, one of them does receptionist duties as well. Monsignor Byrne just works along with the bishop."

"All right. That'll do for now. Oh, just one other thing. When was the last time you vacuumed the bishop's study?"

She squinted towards the ceiling. "This is Thursday. I work Mondays, Thursdays and Saturdays. It was Monday morning."

"Did the bishop ever do any vacuuming?"

Mrs. Bell gave him a disparaging look. "The bishop? Noooo, goodness. I get paid to do all that."

"All right, Mrs. Bell. Thanks very much."

Doyle led the woman out and turned back to his superior. "Do you want to see the secretaries, sir? I had a brief word with them. They don't seem to know any more than Mrs. Bell."

"Did you sense that either was acting a bit guilty or unusually nervous?"

"Looked for that, sir, of course," Doyle replied, miffed. "I guarantee that neither of them has a clue about this."

"All right. All right. Is there anybody else?"

"Just the cook, sir. She's down in the kitchen bawling her eyes out."

"Is there anyone with her?"

"Yes, a WPC. She's not getting much sense out of her at the minute. Every time the cook opens her mouth to say something, she starts blubbering again."

"You're happy there's no guilt there?"

"Wouldn't think so. I think her tears are more from fear about losing her job than any real grief for the bishop."

"Okay. What about this monsignor?"

"There's no sign of him yet. Do you want …?"

A knock on the door interrupted him. A uniformed constable stuck his head in.

"There's a Monsignor Byrne just arrived, sir," he said to Sheehan. "He's insisting that he be allowed to speak to you."

"That's all right, Constable. Send him in."

The man who entered was tall, well over six feet, heavily built, wearing a charcoal grey topcoat over a black suit and clerical collar. His expression was registering shock but he was in control of himself when he spoke. "Sorry for insisting I be permitted to see you, Chief Inspector," he said, extending his hand as he approached the desk.

Sheehan stood up and accepted the handshake.

"Monsignor Byrne, I live here. I work as the bishop's secretary." He shrugged his shoulders self-deprecatingly. "Kind of a right hand man." He sat down as the policeman indicated the chair. "I was at a wedding in Fermanagh yesterday. Stayed over. Just got in a few minutes ago." His face filled with questions. "What on earth has been happening?"

The inspector studied the priest. He saw an affable man, late forties, greying hair thinning on top. Despite the distress on the man's face, the inspector saw something there that he immediately liked. He couldn't quite put his finger on it; a naturalness, an easy warmth, perhaps.

"I'm sorry to take over your house like this, Monsignor. I suppose you heard about ..."

"Just that the bishop has been found dead. Your man at the door told me. But why are PSNI detectives here? How ...?"

"I'm sorry to have to tell you, Monsignor, that the bishop has been murdered."

"Murdered?" The monsignor was stunned. He stared at the chief inspector and then said again, "Murdered?"

Sheehan nodded, giving the man time to process this shocking information.

The priest then said, "Do you know who, why?"

Sheehan shook his head. "No. We're just starting the investigation. Are you up to answering a couple of questions now?"

The monsignor seemed to gather himself up in his seat. "Yes! Of course, of course."

"Good. Might as well get this out of the way. I take it someone can confirm your whereabouts between midnight and four this morning?"

The priest looked up, a brief spark igniting his intelligent, grey-green eyes. Sheehan held up a placating hand. "For the record. Elimination purposes."

"Of course. I see." He seemed to collect his thoughts, then said, "At midnight I was still chatting with the parents of the bride in the Lough Erne Resort hotel in Fermanagh but, as I recall, I went to bed shortly after that. Alone, I'm afraid." This with a faint grin. "I did have an early call, seven-fifteen, the switchboard can verify that. A shower and a quick breakfast, then I drove straight here."

"What sort of man was the bishop?"

"Oh, he was quite well liked, quite progressive and modern in his thinking. Perhaps a bit too modern for some, but clever. Always writing articles for theological journals."

"Had he any enemies, people with a serious grudge against him?"

"Not that I know of. Bishops, of course, can rub plenty of people's sensitivities the wrong way. Comes with the territory, I'm afraid. You can't organise and control a whole diocese without annoying somebody in the process. But I must add, I cannot imagine he would have annoyed anybody enough to make them want to murder him."

"How did you get on with him yourself?"

Again the faint grin. "Well enough not to feel that I wanted to kill him. He was my boss but we had a good relationship. We share doctoral qualifications in biblical studies and that makes for an interesting, if sometimes, argumentative relationship. But I would not be in this post if he didn't like me."

Sheehan rubbed his hands along the surface of the desk. "This desk here, have you any idea where it came from?"

The monsignor shook his head. "No, it was here before I came. Probably came with the house when the diocese purchased it. It's been there for years, I'm sure. Why?"

Sheehan pointed. "It's just that there are some letters and numbers scratched here on the side." Both officers watched the priest intently as Sheehan said this but all they saw was innocent mystification. The priest peered at the scratches and shook his head. "No, never saw them before."

"Do they mean anything to you?"

"Sorry. No idea."

"Was the bishop involved in anything lately, I don't really know what, a service maybe, some sort of symposium, or something that might have caused someone to resent him?"

"Sorry, Chief Inspector, I really don't know. I'll go through his papers for you and if I find anything of interest, I'll contact you."

"That would be very helpful, Monsignor. Thank you."

The monsignor began to rise from his chair. "If that's all, Chief Inspector, I'm going to have to make calls, get the funeral preparations organised."

"Could you stall on the funeral, please, monsignor? I don't know quite when we'll be able to release the body."

"Oh, of course. But could you try to speed things up, please? A bishop's funeral is a huge thing. So many dignitaries and prelates have to reorganise their diaries, you know the sort of thing."

"I'll do what I can, Monsignor," Sheehan replied. "Thank you for your time. I'll contact you if I need to speak with you again." He nodded to Doyle who showed the priest to the door. Doyle shook hands with him as he left and turned back into the room.

"What do you think, Doyle?" Sheehan said, eyebrows raised.

"One never knows, but he seems genuinely shocked."

"Uh huh."

"Besides," Doyle went on stolidly, "if he was in Fermanagh at midnight, it'd take some driving to get to Belfast, bump off the bishop, clean up the scene and get back again in time for the seven-fifteen call. It might just be possible, but I have my doubts."

"Of course you do. No way would a Catholic priest do something like that." He grinned at Doyle's dour expression. "Joke. Joke. Roughly how long from Fermanagh to here?"

Doyle gave the question a minute's sedate thought. "About a couple of hours."

"Leave maybe before one, arrive around three, three-thirty," Sheehan mused, "do the deed, clean the place forensically, that'd take a while, leave around five, just back in time for the wake-up call, that is, if he was able to get back to his bedroom without the receptionist or night clerk noticing him. It'd be tight all right."

He got out of his chair, stalled briefly before forcing himself to turn towards the window. Doyle noticed the sudden wince and the brief favouring of the right leg but he knew better than to comment. He confined himself to the internal observation, *Winter's coming.*

Sheehan's eyes had shut at the sudden pain in his hip but he dismissed it angrily. He opened his eyes to look out on a garden that was attractive without being fussy, plenty of lawn, a few fruit trees and a little winding path leading to a substantial potting shed at the far end, almost hidden behind a huge damson tree. There was a significant October wind blowing, creating plenty of movement. A wooden table, with four wooden chairs, covered one end of the substantial patio. A few plastic recliners and chairs were spread over the rest of it. A pleasant place to relax in during the summer evenings, Sheehan thought, but not today.

He turned to Doyle. "So what have we got, Sergeant? A dead bishop, squeaky clean crime scene, no murder weapon, no suspect, no obvious motive, locked doors and windows. Does that about sum it up?"

Doyle stared at his superior, then shrugged. He offered no comment.

Sheehan sighed. This one was going to test the best of them. "Get some uniforms canvassing the neighbourhood, Doyle. Maybe somebody saw something in the middle of the night. Search for the weapon, too, although I wouldn't hold out much hope for that. This guy wouldn't be that stupid." He took one last look at the crime scene. "Organise background checks of the staff and get them written up for the case files. I'll go back to the station and get an incident room set up."

THREE

Seven days had passed since the discovery of the bishop's body, seven days and seven long nights. It was a frustrated group that had gathered the following Thursday morning in the incident room at Strandtown Police Station, Belfast B District. Precious few leads had presented themselves and the extensive investigations into the backgrounds of the bishop's staff had led nowhere. Sheehan stared at his team, not yet a particularly large team. They were easily accommodated in the substantial incident room. Desks with phone lines had been provided for the lead sergeants and a couple of other desks had been added for general use. There were plenty of photographs on the white board but they were more decorative than useful at this point. The men looked bored, restless, inactive. Sergeant McCullough, who led one of the three investigation teams, was attempting to balance his flaccid bulk on the back legs of his chair as he tried to lob paper balls, made from the remains of a carry-out container, into a tin basket in a corner.

Tom Allen, a young detective, tall, well built, newly promoted to Crime Branch, said into the air, "Maybe something he said annoyed the actress."

There were a few grins. Sergeant Fred McCammon, long familiar with the gallows humour of these dead periods, suggested, "Maybe something he *did* annoyed the actress."

More grins.

"Maybe it was something he didn't do that annoyed the actress," amplified Sergeant Bill Larkin, immediately recognisable because of his bald pate and heavy black glasses. He was currently responsible for running the incident room but was also temporary liaison with Forensics. That was to change and he would soon be in charge of his own forensics team. His comment elicited a few ribald guffaws.

"Thinkin' about yourself, Larko?" somebody shouted, to more laughter.

To Sheehan's ears, the merriment was forced. The team had hit too many dead ends. Days of intensive enquiries with costly weekend overtime, long hours of futile interviews with neighbours and individuals connected with the victim, had produced the usual piles of paper but little of substance. As Senior Investigative Officer he had spent hours reading and digesting all of the statements coming in for logging in the Policy Book. They made dismal reading. Usually there were some enthusiastic comments about the value of leads, possible lines of future enquiry. These statements were flat, terse, uninspired. Mood they're in, Sheehan was thinking, *this case could easily run out of steam. Better get them up and at it again.*

"Okay, listen up," he shouted over the laughter. "We're getting nowhere with this case. But that might just mean that we haven't been looking in the right places. Our best hope of cracking this thing is to find the motive. Find that and we're up and running."

"Sir." It was McCullough. Sergeant McCullough, fat, unfit, had plenty to say but rarely anything insightful. "We grilled everybody connected with the case. There's no sign of a motive anywhere."

"Aye, right. Just a random killing, is it?" Sheehan leaned forward on his desk. "Nobody just pops in and murders a bishop and then goes to all that trouble to clean up the crime scene. This was deliberate. This was planned. No matter how crazy the killer seems, there is a motive in there somewhere. Our best bet is the bishop himself. If we search his background thoroughly enough, we'll find something. I'm sure of it. Check his friends, his habits, his bank statements, anybody remotely connected with him. Look for something in his private life. Maybe there's something murky there. We'd need to be thorough. I've never see a case so devoid of leads. Search for any scandals, affairs, homosexual rumours, anything. Was he involved in a cover-up of the activities of any paedophile priests? You might find a woman, or another man, or a boy ..." He raised his hands in apology to Doyle. "I'm not saying we will, but we might. So look, keep looking. The answer is in the bishop's life." He pointed a finger at Sergeant McCammon. "Fred, you and Allen draw up a list and divvy it up. Doyle, you and I will go to the Royal Victoria Hospital and see if Dick Campbell has anything more to tell us."

FOUR

D r. Campbell looked up from the body of a young woman whose abdomen was sliced open and almost emptied of organs. Sheehan averted his eyes as he came further into the mortuary.

"Ah, right on time," the pathologist said. "I've only just finished with your bishop."

Sheehan, head still turned aside, waved a hand and said, "Cover that up, will you."

The doctor grinned at Doyle, pulling a sheet over the cadaver. "Is he always going to be a big girl's blouse?"

Something faint flickered on the sergeant's staid expression but it disappeared as quickly as it had come. Apart from a quick glance at his superior, he showed no reaction.

"We've been busy chasing our tails all week and

getting exactly nowhere," Sheehan said, "Anything new on the body?"

The pathologist went to a sink and washed his hands. As he was drying them, he moved to a large refrigerated drawer in the wall and began to pull it out. "Yes, a couple of things." He pulled the drawer out to its full length and pulled the sheet from the bishop's corpse. The abdomen's new stitches vied with the knife wounds for attention. "The knife wounds. Now that they're cleaned up, you can see that the pattern they make is cruciform."

"A cross?" Sheehan stared at the wounds. A fairly straight vertical line of three stab wounds from the sternum to the abdomen was bordered by two further wounds on either side, making a detectable diagonal line. "What do you think it means?"

"You're the detective, Chief Inspector. I only find this stuff."

"Maybe he hates bishops, or Catholics," Sheehan said, sounding frustrated. "Maybe he was hammering the knife into the bishop saying, 'You like to wear crucifixes. Try this one for size.'"

The pathologist grinned. "You never know," he said. "There was a definite frenzy about the strikes. I've come across crazier explanations."

Sheehan stared at the body, tracing the wounds with his eyes. "Five wounds. The five wounds of Christ, do you think?"

"Oh, biblical scholar are we now?" the pathologist said.

Sheehan glanced at him, offering a reluctant grin. "It's my Catholic upbringing. Hard to escape this kind of thinking. It does look like some form of religious symbolism, however. A bishop, wounds in the shape of a crucifix." He glanced up at his sergeant. "What do you think, Doyle?"

"I'd have to agree, sir," Doyle nodded, "although I'm not sure where that gets us."

"It's a lot more than we had an hour ago." Sheehan grunted. He turned to the pathologist. "Did you find anything else on the body that shouldn't be there?"

The pathologist looked at him blankly and then brightened. "Oh, you mean hairs? Fibres? Dust? Somebody else's blood?"

Sheehan stiffened. "Yes, well?"

The pathologist shook his head. "Nope. Nothing. The body was clean. The killer was careful." Then he grinned as Sheehan raised his fist. He put his hands up defensively and laughed. "Just a wee bit of mortuary humour. We have to do something to liven up the place."

"Not funny," Sheehan growled. "What about the knife? Can you tell us anything about that?"

The pathologist held up the forefingers of each hand, with an upwards little gesture indicating that yes, he had something, and yes, he was quite pleased with himself. He looked like a magician about to perform. He ambled over to his desk and lifted off a couple of printed A4 sheets. "With five wounds to examine, I had plenty to work with," he said. "It soon became clear that the knife was not your ordinary kitchen knife. Initially I thought it might have been a hunting knife, but the wound clearly shows a double-edged blade, sharp edges and a sharp point as well. More like a fighting knife. I would also estimate the length of the blade to be six or seven inches ..." He started shaking his head and waving the papers back and forward. "Have I not enough to do, examining corpses all day? No, I had to do your job as well and start looking up knives on the internet."

"Gimme a break," the chief inspector said. "You love that sort of stuff. What did you find?"

"Well, you can do a wee check yourself but I found a combat knife here that might fit the bill."

He showed the policemen the pages, the first of which was filled with text and headed, "Combat Knife". He turned to the next page which contained photographs of two different fighting knives. "I think I have narrowed the search down to two knives, the Gerber LHR Combat Knife and the Fairbairn-Sykes Fighting knife."

Doyle moved forward to look at the sheets. "A lot of us had knives like that in Afghanistan," he said.

The pathologist looked quizzically at the sergeant's expressionless face. Then his own face cleared. "Of course, I remember now. Two tours, right?"

Doyle nodded.

"Yes, of course. You probably know, then, that this was a favourite knife of the British Commandos?"

Doyle shook his head. "They were just knives to us. We didn't give them a whole lot of thought." He glanced at the pages. "Seems you know a lot more about them than I do."

The pathologist beamed, as did his balding pate under the bright mortuary lights. "Actually, the Gerber is an updated version of the Fairbairn-Sykes, designed by a US Army Captain, Bud Holzman. You can study these. Either blade seems suited to the wounds."

"Who would own such a knife?" Sheehan asked.

"Well, it is mainly of interest to collectors …" He paused and pulled himself upright. "What? You want me to go out and start checking out knife owners for you?" He shoved the papers at Doyle's chest. "Here, take these and get outta here. Check them out yourself. I'm busy."

Doyle accepted the papers awkwardly, staring at his boss. Sheehan nodded. "Take anything you can get off this guy. He never gives us much." He grinned as the doctor bristled. They turned to leave but at the door he stopped again and said, "Oh, by the way. Are you ready to release the body yet? The monsignor is anxious to get on with the funeral."

"Yes, tell him he can have the body for burial any time."

As they left the morgue, Sheehan said, "Doyle, go back to the incident room. See what else you can dig up on the internet about the knife. I'll go and have another word with the monsignor."

"Right, sir. What do you think this new information tells us?"

"Hard to say. Maybe we're looking for a commando who hates Catholic bishops."

FIVE

Sheehan drove along the Antrim Road in a northerly direction to the city outskirts. The bishop's house, in an area that was largely residential, was an elegant townhouse, set on a generous plot with mature landscaping. The inspector's ring was answered by one of the secretaries who informed him that the monsignor was at home but that he was with someone.

"Could you check if he's able to see me in the next little while?" Sheehan asked her. "I'd be happy to wait if he's not going to be too long." The girl, not much more than twenty, nodded her pony-tailed head and invited the inspector to sit on a chair in the waiting room. She came back in a few seconds and said, "The monsignor will see you shortly."

Even as she spoke, Sheehan could hear the

monsignor talking to someone as he walked along the wooden-floored hall. He rose to meet him and saw that the priest was accompanied by a very attractive, dark-haired woman who was carrying a bundle of papers.

The priest stopped and said, "Good afternoon, Chief Inspector. May I introduce Margaret Sands, our Cathedral organist. We were just talking about some music for the bishop's funeral."

Sheehan moved forward and offered his hand to the organist. Shrewd brown eyes met the inspector's gaze as he said, with a smile on his lips that he was unaware of, "Pleased to meet you." He shook her hand with a slight bow. "Jim Sheehan."

The woman returned his smile with a faintly amused smile of her own. The policeman's greeting was somewhat old-fashioned but she could easily forgive that in a man whose dark, handsome face possessed two of the most intense blue eyes she had seen in a long time. She responded warmly to his handshake and said, "Very pleased to meet you, too, Chief Inspector. The monsignor has been telling me all about you."

Sheehan could not restrain a startled, "What? Sure he knows nothing about me."

The monsignor laughed. "I think she's playing with you, Chief Inspector. I merely told her you were investigating the bishop's demise."

"Oh, right." Sheehan glanced at the woman and discovered that he was still holding her hand. "Oh," he said again, and laughed sheepishly as he let the hand go. *Good man, Jim,* he was thinking. *A dab hand with the ladies, aren't you? You're totally outta practice, man.*

The monsignor continued to speak. "As I said, we

were choosing music for the funeral. I don't suppose …?"

"Yes," Sheehan interjected, "that's one of the things I'm here to see you about. You can arrange to have the body removed from the mortuary any time."

"Thank you, Chief Inspector," Monsignor Byrne said. "That's good news."

Margaret turned to the priest. "Well, I'll go on, Monsignor. Call me when you have a time and a date for the funeral." She turned to Jim, her smile full now. "Nice to have met you, Chief Inspector! Perhaps we'll see you at the ceremony?"

Sheehan had given no thought to attending the funeral Mass but he said, "Yes, I … I hope to be there." Sitting through the long obsequies seemed a small price to pay if there was an opportunity to meet this woman again, and this time he'd be better prepared.

The monsignor opened the front door to let his visitor out. "I'll be in touch shortly, Margaret," he said as she passed him. "Now that the body has been released, we should be able to hold the funeral in a couple of days. 'Bye."

"'Bye, Monsignor." She cast a quick glance back at Sheehan. "'Bye, Chief Inspector."

"Nice to have met you," the detective shouted after her as the door closed.

The monsignor said, "Shall we go to my office?"

As they walked down the corridor, Sheehan said, "Seems like a nice lady, that."

"Lovely woman," the monsignor agreed. "She teaches in the local girls' grammar school. Her husband died some eight or ten years ago. No children, sadly. She devotes a lot of her spare time to the

Church, training the senior and junior choirs."

Sheehan could not explain why his heart lifted when he heard that Margaret had no ties. Although he was past forty now, it had been a long time since he had pursued any kind of relationship. Perhaps he had accepted that bachelorhood was a natural state for him; perhaps he had never met the right person; perhaps his work didn't give him a chance to meet the right person. Yet now, there was something about Margaret Sands. When she had stared into his eyes like that, he had been ... unmanned.

Nothing of this showed in his face, however, as he sat in the chair the monsignor offered him. Businesslike now, he said, "We're still no further to finding the motive for the bishop's murder. I was wondering if anything turned up in your search of his papers?"

Monsignor Byrne shook his head slowly. "We've been pretty busy this past week but I am gradually working my way through his files. I'm sorry, Chief Inspector. There's not much there that would help you in your search for a motive."

"Sorry to push this, Monsignor, and I don't mean to be indelicate, but is there anything in the personal life of the bishop ...?"

The monsignor said, "Oh, no, no, no, Inspector. You're wasting your time going down that road. The bishop's personal life is ... was impeccable."

"What about covering up for priests who might have got into some sort of trouble?"

"I would doubt that, Chief Inspector. Certainly not any paedophile priests. I'm sure I would have heard of that."

Sheehan pursed his lips, frustration beginning to

take hold of him again. "What about his correspondence? Anybody annoyed with him about anything, anything at all?"

The priest raised his shoulders. "There was one thing but I don't see how it could be relevant. He did get more than a few letters this past while about a recent article he had written for *The Tablet*. But the letters were in the nature of argument and debate, not threatening in any way."

"What was that about?"

"Actually, I'm a bit annoyed with the bishop myself about that article. Usually he seeks my opinion before sending anything off but the first I heard of this particular article was when it appeared in *The Tablet*."

"Why did he do that?"

"I suppose he knew that I would have disagreed with what he wrote and there'd be an almighty argument about it. I guess he just decided to avoid the confrontation."

"What was wrong with it?"

The monsignor stared at him. "I don't know how to answer that in a couple of sentences. It's a theological thing, and it's as much to do with tone as with content."

"I am a Catholic," Sheehan told the priest. "I might be able to understand something of the problem."

"Okay. I suppose you can hardly have missed the constant media conflict that almost daily flares up between the Catholic Church and the increasingly secular society we now live in."

Sheehan nodded.

"We're accused of interfering with people's

liberties," the priest went on. "We're responsible for terrible confusion in the minds of ordinary people about their sexuality. Our dysfunctional approach to divorce is causing endless grief to good Catholics who seek to escape abusive marriages. Our stance on homosexuality is utterly at odds with the rest of society, you know the kind of thing?"

Sheehan nodded again. Lapsed Catholic though he was, he had had his share of people throwing these same accusations in his face. "I do, Monsignor. I've come across them myself plenty of times. To be honest, I'm not really well enough up in theology to know what way to respond."

The monsignor signalled his understanding and said, with some bitterness, "You and a whole lot of others, Chief Inspector. And the constant dribbling of accusation is beginning to wear an awful lot of Catholics down. Many are beginning to wonder if there is not some basis of truth in the modern way of thinking." He stared at the policeman. "I mean, how many young people of your acquaintance are living together in … unmarried bliss? It's practically the norm now, for Catholics as well as Protestants, or atheists. How many Catholics are divorcing and remarrying? Modernism. It's having a brutal effect on the faith of the new generations."

Sheehan couldn't quite see where this lecture was going. He wondered if he had simply triggered one of the monsignor's hobby horses. "I hear what you're saying, monsignor, but I don't quite see …"

The priest smiled. "Sorry, Chief Inspector. Perhaps I got a bit carried away. The point is that, in an effort to try to empathise with what modern Catholics are going through, some theologians, priests, even bishops, are beginning to blur the hard edges of

31

the specific laws and commandments that we Catholics have to live by. They are beginning to promote ideas such as a new spirituality for divorced couples, a spirituality for gay people, a spirituality for co-habiting adults in a loving relationship …" He expelled a heavy breath; "… as if there could be more than one spirituality. That is causing a lot of dissension within the Church. And, unfortunately, Bishop Loughran seems, uh, seemed to have liberal leanings in the direction, almost, of moral relativism. Nothing specific that he has said; he's been very careful about that. But as I say, the tone of his recent writings has been causing concern in some quarters."

"And the letters he received, they just …?"

"They're from a range of Catholics, clerical and non-clerical, attempting to argue with his stance, but there's nothing threatening in any of them. I can make them available to you, if you wish."

Sheehan said, "I might take you up on that, but it's hard to imagine that …"

"My own thoughts exactly, Chief Inspector. But I'll keep searching."

Sheehan rose from his seat, fought to conceal the sudden twinge of pain from his right hip, and offered the priest his hand. "Thank you, monsignor. We've got a couple of new leads that we're following up but, please, if you come across anything even slightly suspicious, don't hesitate to contact me." He was about to thank the monsignor again when his mobile phone rang. He reached into his pocket. "Excuse me, Monsignor!" He pressed a button on the phone. "Sheehan."

"It's Doyle, sir."

"Yes?"

"There's been another killing, sir."

"What? Where?"

"Easton Crescent, sir, just off Cliftonville Road. Not far from where you are now."

"I know it. Why are you calling me?"

"Assistant Chief Constable's just off the phone, sir. He says we've got it."

"Bloody h … uh …" He glanced an apology to the monsignor. "Didn't you tell him that we're already up to our eyes?"

"Yes, sir, but he says there might be a connection. He says we have to take it, sir."

"Connection? What connection?"

"This body's naked, too."

"That's all? That could mean anything."

"I know, sir. But we've got it anyway."

Sheehan sighed. "Where are you now, Doyle?"

"I'm at the scene, sir."

"Right, I'll be there in about fifteen minutes."

"Uh ... sir?"

"What is it?"

"The ACC says we're not to let up on the bishop enquiry. He's getting flak from upstairs and wants an early result."

"You know what you can tell the assistant chief, Doyle?"

"What, sir?"

Sheehan hung up. He looked at the monsignor who had also risen to his feet. "Sorry about that. There's been another murder."

"I gathered as much. Is there anything I can do?"

"No thanks, Monsignor. I'd better get on." He glanced back over his shoulder as he hurriedly left the room. "You'll keep me informed about the funeral arrangements?"

"Of course, Chief Inspector."

SIX

As Sheehan turned into Easton Crescent, he had no difficulty in identifying the house he was looking for. There were several police cars parked outside it, including that of the Deputy Forensic Pathologist, and a knot of curious onlookers outside the police perimeter tapes. The house was a large, red-brick two storey villa, clearly built in a different era. Elegantly proportioned bay windows protruded on each side of an impressive front door at the top of a small flight of steps. Looking for somewhere close by to park, Sheehan found his mind wandering to two lustrous brown eyes and one of the most attractive smiles he had ever seen. He shook his head. *Not now*, he muttered to himself, exasperated. *Man, you're acting like a love-struck schoolboy. Who's to say she hasn't already got a steady relationship or maybe ten other guys running after her? Focus, man, you've a body to examine and a murder to solve.*

Doyle, suited out in coveralls, was waiting for him when he reached the top of the steps. "The body's in the lounge, sir."

"SOCOs finished?" he asked.

"Yes, sir."

"Right, I don't need this, then," he said, pushing away the plastic coverall that Doyle was holding towards him. "Where's the body?"

Doyle led the chief inspector down a hall into a substantial lounge. Sheehan did not immediately see the body. His gaze was arrested by the deep red colour of the wall that housed the white marble fireplace. *Good grief*, he wondered, *how do they live with that?* The other walls were beige, matching the pale leather suite. The floor was wooden, with mats rather than the carpet he expected. One of the armchairs had obviously been knocked out of place as had the small occasional table that normally stood in front of the sofa.

As Sheehan walked around the sofa, Doyle said quietly, "Prepare yourself, sir."

Lying on the floor, between the disturbed items of furniture, was the naked body of a large man who looked to have been in his early to mid-fifties. There was a short rope, perhaps four or five feet in length, tied in a noose around his neck. The body was lying on its side, left leg bent and raised towards the abdomen. The right leg was also bent but drawn down and away from the other. None of this, however, was immediately evident to Sheehan. What caught his eyes and made him almost gag was the huge rip in the man's stomach, the bloodied entrails half dragged out on to the floor beside him.

"My God," he said. "What's this all about?"

"Thomas O'Donoghue, sir," Doyle stated. "Principal of St. Matthew's Boys' Secondary School, near Bearnageeha."

Sheehan wanted to go back out into the air but he forced himself to study the body. After a few moments he said, "Apart from the guts lying all over the place, do you think this body might have been posed like the other one?"

"I suppose it's possible that he could have fallen like that," Doyle responded, "but look at the way the victim's head is resting, face down, on the crook of his bent left arm. And his right arm is out straight but the left hand is clutching it. And the bowels, sir, they're sort of placed there. Hard to imagine that they'd land like that if he was just thrown there."

"The entrails or bowels or whatever they are, might have spilled out a bit but they do look like they had some help. They've definitely been pulled out." He looked at the rope. "What's with the rope? Was he hanged?"

Doyle pointed at the ceiling from which hung only a small candelabrum with three brass prongs, each holding a bulb. "If he was, it wasn't here. He'd have pulled that light out of the ceiling as easy as anything. Even if he'd been unconscious, it wouldn't have held his weight."

"Not much sign of a struggle, apart from that chair and the wee table. You think he might have been hanged somewhere else and brought back here?"

"I'm not saying that, sir," Doyle said. "I'm saying there's nowhere in here where he could have been hanged."

Sheehan stared at the rope. It was a well-used, ordinary piece of rope that one would find in most garages or gardens. "It's probably a waste of time but get some forensics on this bit of rope as well."

Doctor Campbell, who had been washing his hands in a small cloakroom off the hall, entered at that point. "Ah, there you are, Chief Inspector. Have I not enough to do without always getting called out to these suspicious deaths? Where are your FMOs?"

"Dead bodies, Dick. Your line of country. Forensic Medical Officers are not in your league. And you're only next door, or near enough, so quit griping and tell me how this man died." Sheehan's half-grin belied the sting in his words. He could empathise with Dick's mock-vexation but the pathologist's quick eye at the scene often saved a lot of time and with the Royal Victoria Hospital within accessible distance from most parts of the city, protocols sometimes got by-passed.

"Well now, here's the thing," the doctor said, turning towards the body. "The noose has been pulled tight, no doubt about that. And it has left abrasions on the victim's neck, but they look post-mortem to me. I rather think the rope is only decoration, a prop, if you like, for some theatrical image the killer had in his head."

Sheehan stared at him, waiting for him to continue. The doctor smiled at him, pleased with his deduction.

"You're going to make me ask you again, aren't you?" Sheehan said.

The pathologist rubbed his hands together, grinning. "No need, Jim. No need. I'm happy to tell you, subject, of course, to confirmation by an autopsy." He lowered himself awkwardly to kneel beside the corpse. "At first glance, it would appear that the disembowelment is the cause of death. But like I told you last week, you can't always jump on the obvious." He raised a finger, inviting them to follow his reasoning. Pulling the rope aside, he pointed to a number of small bruises on the front of the throat. "Just here, on the lateral side of the neck, level with the tip of the laryngeal prominence …" He looked up at the inspector over the rim of his glasses, "… Adam's apple, to you; just between the sternal head and the clavicular head of the sternocleidomastoideus muscle …"

Doyle's ballpoint hovered above his notebook, static. His stolid face remained expressionless as he stared first at the doctor and then at his superior. Sheehan said, "For crying out loud, Dick, will you speak English!"

The doctor beamed. He pointed again. "All right. Just here is one of the most deadly points you could strike someone. Tips of the fingers, rigid fingers, I would guess, looking at the nature of the bruises. No chance for defence after that. No possibility of revival. That, I believe, is the cause of death."

"Some kind of martial arts expert?"

"I don't know about expert. It's not that difficult a blow to deliver. But he would have to have some idea about what he was doing, no doubt about that."

"So he definitely wasn't hanged?"

"No, the abrasions are not severe enough."

"And the entrails?"

"Definitely some sort of post-mortem statement. Not sure what your killer is saying though."

"Was he killed here, or somewhere else?"

"Well, judging from the hypostasis ... the lividity

…" He moved the body to show the underside to the two policemen. "See, lividity is evident here, and here. Gravity, you know? If he had been moved post-mortem, it is unlikely that these parts of the body would have these signs."

"So you saying he was killed here?"

"That would be my guess, subject, of course …"

"All right, all right," Sheehan interrupted. "Since when are your guesses ever wrong?"

The doctor beamed again. "Well, now that you mention it …"

Sheehan grimaced and shook his head. "What about time of death?"

"I'd say it was pretty similar to the last killing you had. Somewhere between ten yesterday evening and four or five o'clock this morning."

"Same guy?"

"Oh, I've no way of telling you that. Could just as easily have been somebody else."

"All right, Dick. Thanks."

After the pathologist had left, Sheehan said to Doyle, "What do you think? Same killer?"

Doyle shrugged. "There are similarities certainly in the MO, no obvious break-in, windows locked. Killer may well have been let in by the victim. Roughly the same time of death, although I don't think we can read much into that. It's a time that most killers would prefer, the hours of darkness." He stared sombrely at the body. "But the method of killing is totally different. That's a bit unusual. Perps tend to like their tried and trusted. But then, the body's naked."

"The bishop's death was widely reported in the

press. Possibility of a copy-cat, do you think?"

"No idea, sir."

"SOCOs get anything?"

"They found a few sets of prints, sir, but nothing much else."

He pondered that. "There were no prints the last time." Then he asked, "Who else lives here?"

"The victim's wife. She's a teacher, too. She was at an overnight conference in the Slieve Donard in Newcastle. Just got back this afternoon. Found the body as soon as she got in."

"SOCOs got her prints?

"Yes, sir."

"Anybody talk to her?"

"I had a word with her myself, sir, but she's in a state. Wailing all over the place. I couldn't get much sense out of her."

"Hardly surprising. I'll try her myself in a few minutes. No children?"

"Got that much, sir. Two. A boy and a girl. Both at university across the water, one at Dundee, the other at Manchester."

Sheehan went to the window and looked out on to the street. The curious were still there. *What on earth do they expect to see?* he wondered, irritated. Some members of the press were gathering as well. He turned to Doyle. "Press are out there now. Tell them the bare minimum."

"Okay, sir."

"Right. So we have another naked body, no break-in, clean kill, like we had before. But this time we have prints, the body is lying in a different pose and the method of killing is different. And there are no letters or numbers scraped into the walls or desk anywhere either. Keep that little tidbit to ourselves, Doyle, although it may have no significance whatever. So, it's like somebody tried to copy the first killing but didn't have enough information to replicate it exactly." He went back to the window to think. After a while he said, "We'll pursue this investigation as a separate killing unless we find reason to think differently. And Doyle, make that clear to the press."

"Right, sir. I'll get the usual team to do a door-to-door of the neighbourhood. Do you want some of our own team to go over to the school?"

"Yes. Send Connors and Miller. I'll go and have a chat with the wife ... widow. Where is she?"

"She's with a WPC in the kitchen, sir. The WPC is making her a cup of tea."

When Sheehan came into the kitchen, he found Mrs. O'Donoghue and the WPC sitting at the table drinking tea. The woman police constable rose to her feet as the chief inspector entered the room. He nodded at her and said to the slim, greying woman who was no longer weeping but seemed to be in shock, "Mrs. O'Donoghue, I'm Chief Inspector Sheehan. I'll be investigating your husband's ..." When he saw her face begin to crumple again, he sped on. "I'm sorry to have to ask but would you be up to answering a couple of questions? The sooner we get the investigation started the better our chances of finding the perpetrator."

The woman simply stared at him but Sheehan pressed on. "Can you think of anyone who might want to harm your husband?"

Again the blank stare.

"Do you know if you husband had any enemies?"

This time there was a spark in her eyes. "Enemies? Thomas? Of course not!" She hesitated. "Well … No, definitely not."

Sheehan did not miss the hesitation. "If there is anyone at all who had any kind of grudge against your husband, it would be best to tell us now. If it is not serious, we can eliminate the person from our enquiries."

"Well, his deputy, Norman Henry, is forever giving Thomas a hard time. I don't know how many times Thomas came home in the evenings stressed out because of fights with this man."

"What do they fight about?"

"Everything, it seems. Henry doesn't like the way my husband wants …" Her eyes teared, "… wanted to run the school. I think he wants my husband's job. He's very ambitious."

"Can you think of anyone else who might resent him?"

"No."

"Does your husband owe anyone any money? Has he any significant debts? Sorry to sound impertinent, but does he gamble or anything?"

Her eyebrows went up. "Thomas? He's so straitlaced. He'd never do anything like that. And we both have good salaries. We don't owe anybody anything. We've even got the mortgage paid off."

"What did he do in his spare time, for recreation?"

"He plays golf. He is … was … a member of Belvoir Golf Club." She pronounced it 'Beever'.

"Was there anyone in particular that he would play with?"

"Yes, he had a steady fourball for Saturdays." She thought for a moment. "Gerry Kelly, Noel Boyle and … and Kevin Durkin."

"Okay. Thank you very much, Mrs. O'Donoghue. You've been very helpful."

He nodded again to the WPC and left the room.

SEVEN

The incident room was packed, barely able to accommodate the total investigation force. Extra chairs had been drafted in and were placed around the desks. Sheehan was sitting on a chair at the top of the room, Doyle leaning back against the wall beside him. The three teams working the two cases, the Office Manager, Bill 'Larko' Larkin, and a couple of SOCOs were all attending Sheehan's latest debriefing. Larkin was adding some photographs of the O'Donoghue scene to the white case-board. "Put up a new board, Bill," Sheehan called to him. "We're treating these as two separate cases."

Larkin sighed heavily and went out to look for another board.

"Right, okay." Sheehan called the teams to attention. "Eight days and two murders later, how far on are we? Connors, what did we get at the school?"

"Everybody's shocked, sir," the big detective said. "They'd been wondering all day where the principal was but you could tell that they didn't expect this."

"Anything stand out?"

"Well, generally no." He glanced at Simon Miller who had accompanied him to the school. "But a few did say that there was some bad blood between the principal and his deputy, a man called …"

"Norman Henry," Sheehan finished for him.

Connors stared at him, impressed. "Yes, sir, how did you …?"

"What sort of bad blood?" McCullough asked.

"Seems they were always arguing, even in front of the staff."

"We should be talking to him then," McCullough said. "What were they fighting about?"

"Consensus is," Miller stated, "that they were at opposite ends of the spectrum with regard to management styles." One or two smiled at his choice of phrase. Miller, slight, neat, was definitely at the opposite end of the body-shape spectrum from his large, rugby playing partner. Oblivious to the smiles, Miller went on, "O'Donoghue wanted to tell nobody anything and Henry was all for an open, consultative style of working."

"Staff would be behind Henry, then?" Sheehan asked.

"I wouldn't be so sure about that," Connors replied, shifting his solid body on the small wooden chair that looked altogether too fragile for his weight. "He is very ambitious. Gets up a few noses the way he's always ingratiating himself in here and in there, with visiting inspectors, board of governor members, influential parents, and so on. But they did not care much for O'Donoghue either. He was very aloof and nobody ever knew what he was thinking."

"What about the students? Anything there?"

Connors glanced at Miller for support. "We might have to go back tomorrow and look into that. But I got the impression that the principal was so distant from the students that he wouldn't have upset any of them enough to want to harm him. Henry dealt out all the punishments and so on. They'd be more likely to take offence at him."

"Okay. Lab boys have just informed me that they got three sets of prints at the scene. Two sets match the victim and his wife. See if the other set matches Henry's. If they do, bring him in for questioning." He stared for some minutes at the notes on the desk in front of him. Then he looked up. "Any forensics on the rope?"

"Nothing much, sir." It was Doyle who answered. "It's just a piece of traditional sisal rope. Very common. Can be bought in most hardware and gardening shops. This bit was quite worn. Forensics say that it would be impossible to trace. It could even have been hacked off a rope in anybody's garden and would probably not even be missed."

"Great. Why am I not surprised?" He shook his head in disgust and then said, "What about the golfing buddies?"

Fred McCammon fielded that one. His gaunt face had grown even more gaunt than usual during the past few months. His son had been caught peddling drugs in London and had been sentenced to two years. Fred spent his nights bordering on panic instead of sleeping, wondering what was going on for his son in that jail. He was managing to hold things together at work, however, and said, "They seemed genuinely shocked, sir, upset, you know? We're looking into the relationships, but I don't expect we'll find much untoward. They are all respectable businessmen."

"Business is hard these days," Sheehan mused. "Anything giving any of them problems?"

McCammon's face wrinkled as he grimaced. The thought had not occurred to him. "I could find out, sir, but even if there was something, their only connection with O'Donoghue was their weekly golf game."

Sheehan nodded. "All right." He stared around. "What news about our bishop?"

The uneasy glances passing backwards and forwards between the members of his team gave him little encouragement. Sergeant McCullough was the first to speak. His self-serving whining had been getting on Sheehan's nerves as the investigation stumbled and stuttered vainly in different directions, but his face remained impassive as the flabby detective said, "This guy's impossibly clean, sir. I don't know how we're going to find any motive. He does his job, works out of his house, seems to be nice to everybody. It's a real dead-end, this." There was a muttering of assent. Others had dead-ended as well.

"Thank you, Sergeant," Sheehan said, dead pan. *Useless jerk,* he was thinking. He looked around the room. "Anyone else?"

"He's apparently s … s … something of an intellectual," volunteered Geoff McNeill from the back of the room. McNeill, curly dark hair, thirty something, quite bright, contributed to discussion only occasionally because of his stutter. Normally it gave

48

him little trouble but it often manifested itself when he was subject to scrutiny from several pairs of eyes. "Highly regarded by his p ... p ... peers ... although there's some talk about his ... uh ..." he looked down at his notebook, "... liberal tendencies, as if they, whatever they are, got up people's n ... noses a bit. Other than that, he's c ... clean, sir. He's been over to London a couple of times but it all looks innocent enough. Visited with the archb ... b ... bishop there, went to a couple of Masses. Haven't found anything else ..." Catching Sheehan's glare, he added hastily, "... but T ... T ... Tom and me are still working on it."

Tom Allen, the youngest detective in the squad and probably the most enthusiastic, raised a tentative finger. Sheehan raised an eyebrow. Allen said, "Sergeant McCullough's right about the bishop's lifestyle and Tim's findings at the school correlate with Geoff's and mine. But there are a couple of other things we should mention, though I am not sure that they will lead us anywhere." He studied his notes. "I heard that the bishop wrote articles for *The Tablet* and I looked up some back issues in the library ..." McCullough made significant play of leaning back in his chair, clasping his hands over his bloated belly, and raising his eyes to the ceiling. Allen ploughed on, trying to ignore him. "The letters pages are quite interesting. It seems that the bishop has raised the ire, and judging from the letters, quite a considerable amount of ire, of a lot of ordinary Catholics as well as clergy."

"What did he do?" McCammon asked.

"Nothing terribly serious, from our point of view. But I just thought I'd mention it." He looked down at his notes. "The bishop's been writing articles that seem to pander to the more liberal and secularist elements of society instead of, as one correspondent said, 'holding the line as is his bounden duty.'"

"So this is your big investigative breakthrough, is it?" sneered McCullough. "You think one of these letter writers bumped him off because they didn't like his … whatever you call it?"

"Theology." This from Doyle. It was as if a statue in the corner had suddenly spoken.

"Theology, right," repeated McCullough, still staring at Allen.

The young detective looked uncomfortable but stuck to his guns. Sheehan chose only to observe the interplay. Allen, despite his size, still retained boyish good looks but was trying for a more mature appearance by growing, without any great success, a scraggy mustache. *Don't try for designer stubble*, Sheehan was thinking, while at the same time reminding himself not to judge the book by its cover. Allen was bright and could hold his own in the squad room.

"I'm not saying that," Allen said, striving to remain composed. "I'm simply pointing out that there are some people who feel resentment towards the bishop. And religion is a funny thing. Look at all the wars and devastation it has caused over the centuries because people took notions. Who's to say that some of these people can't take notions?" He searched through his notebook. "And there's another thing. The bishop's caused a bit of grief among some of the parishioners because he blocked steps to set up Tridentine Masses. One or two people I've been talking to tell me that some of these wee Tridentine groups are quite bolshie about it."

"Set up what?" This from Oliver McCoy, a beefy

twenty-five year veteran.

"Tridentine Masses," Allen repeated, looking at his notes. "I think they are older forms of the Mass …"

"They're just the old Latin Mass," Doyle interjected. "The way Mass used to be celebrated before Vatican Two."

"So what's the big deal?" McCullough asked.

"Read the odd newspaper, McCullough," Sheehan snapped. "There are bishops and cardinals all over Europe, and America too, breaking away from Rome over this very issue. It's an issue of grave concern to many people in the Catholic Church." He turned to Allen. "Do you think you can check out some of the parishioners who are aggrieved at the bishop's stance? There might be some hard-lined fundamentalists among them who felt het up enough to do something about it."

Allen looked pleased. "I'm already working on it, sir."

"Good man." He fingered his notes again. "Who was checking the Monsignor's alibi?"

One of McCammon's team, Gerry Loftus, mid-thirties, curly red hair, open freckled face, raised his hand.

"Well?"

"It's solid, sir," the detective said, nodding his head vigorously as if to emphasise the truth of what he was saying. "No way he coulda done it. Plus the fact that the night man says that there is only one entrance open at night and there was no way anybody coulda got past him. You can definitely cross him off, sir."

Sheehan nodded, not displeased. He liked the monsignor. He looked at Doyle who for some reason always chose to stand against the wall near his boss. "Anything more on the knife, Sergeant?"

Doyle straightened, his height and bulk all the more impressive as he looked down upon his seated colleagues. He pulled his notebook from his jacket pocket. "The doctor had it more or less pinned down," he recited in his customary monotone, "but the scenario is far less positive than we first thought. I studied the knives like you said. The Gerber Mark 2 is a possibility. It replaced the Fairbairn-Sykes because that had a weak blade and the grip design made it difficult for the person wielding it to determine blade orientation. The Gerber Mark 2 sorted that. And since our perp seemed to have no difficulty with aiming that first blow, I'm assuming that he would more likely have used the Gerber. So, like yourself, I thought that if we could track down these knives we could get ourselves a list of suspects."

"And did you?" Sheehan felt some hope.

"I tried, sir," the sergeant said, "but then I discovered that the Gerber was first manufactured in 1966 and the line continued until about 1999. Over quarter of a million were made. I rang an army friend of mine, a quarter-master …"

"You have a friend?" This witticism from McCullough. No one, however, appeared to appreciate it.

Doyle ignored him. "My friend tells me that a lot of the guys kept their knives, hundreds of them. And any civilian can simply purchase them from retail outlets that deal with Wilkinson Sword. Collectors are even finding them in pawn shops. It's a needle in a haystack, sir. It'd be impossible to get a handle on that knife, especially when we don't even have it."

"Good one, Doyle," came a voice from the crowd. "'Get a handle on the knife.' Good one!"

This elicited a few chuckles, quickly quashed when Sheehan's glare tried to identify the culprit. Sheehan's hard gaze dimmed as he focused aimlessly at the back of the room for a few minutes, the others simply watching him. He was capable of flashes of brilliance and many of those present had witnessed his sudden insights in the past. No brilliance this time, however. Sheehan was as confused as they were. He simply said, "That's a pity, Doyle. I thought we might have had something there."

He shook his head in frustration as he looked again at his notes. Then he looked up. "Anybody think it's time for a media appeal? You know, the usual questions. Did anyone see anybody at or near the crime scenes at such and such a time on the nights in question? Does anyone know anything that might shed light on these killings? And so on."

"I think that would be essential, sir," McCullough responded, adopting an earnest look. "We really don't have any useful evidence at this point and we're going to need something soon or the whole thing's going to slide away from us."

Sheehan compressed his lips and then he said, "Okay. I'll get the Assistant Chief Constable on it right away. He likes that sort of thing. And when people start ringing in," he added, looking pointedly at McCullough, "listen to what they say. Don't fob them off because what they say sounds nutty. Take notes and we'll decide at the debriefs what's nutty and what isn't."

"Are we sticking with the religious angle, sir?" Allen asked.

Sheehan nodded. "I can't see where it's going to lead us but everywhere we go it seems to crop up. So, yes, until we get something else more promising, that's where we stay."

Sergeant McCullough, hands behind head, his chair balanced precariously again on its two back legs, said, "What about going to the funeral service and scoping the faces of the people there? We might see somebody acting funny."

Doyle looked at him. "Are you serious?"

"Why not?" McCullough said peevishly, sitting forward on his chair.

"Have you ever attended one of these things?"

McCullough had picked up a ballpoint pen from his desk and was fiddling with it. Now he pointed it at Doyle, "No, I'm not Catholic like you. I'm sure you've been to dozens."

McCullough had come up through the old RUC, the Royal Ulster Constabulary, and still had trouble coping with the new positive discrimination regulations that had brought significantly more Catholics on to the force. He seldom tried to hide his prejudice but he had little support from the team. If Doyle experienced any irritation, however, it was not obvious. He said, in his customary measured tone, "Only one bishop has died in this diocese in the last twenty years, so I've only been to one."

"So why would you know a whole awful lot more about it than me, then?" McCullough countered.

"Can it, McCullough," Sheehan snapped. Then to Doyle, "So why not have somebody there, Sergeant?"

"First of all, the altar will be crowded with all the priests of the parish, the auxiliary bishop, various guest celebrants. For that reason, three quarters of the clerics to the rear of the altar will normally be hidden from view during the ceremonies." All eyes were now upon him. For once, something akin to an expression appeared on his impassive face. It was as if he was surprised that he should be holding their undivided attention. "Then the first several rows of the cathedral will be filled with visiting dignitaries," he went on, "representatives from dozens of agencies and God knows who. And that's not taking into account hundreds of people who would be significant some way or another in the diocese. And then there's the ordinary faithful." He stared at McCullough. "Who's going to be able to scan that lot?"

McCullough threw his ballpoint on to his desk. "Okay, okay," he said in surrender. "Bad idea."

Arthur Smith, a washed-out detective nearing retirement who rarely spoke at the briefings, now filled the awkward pause with a quick question. "Do we look for any religious angle with the O'Donoghue murder?"

"No. Until I get any info that makes me think differently, we treat these as two separate cases. I've a feeling that we've got a good suspect in that VP. Let's wrap that case up, and quickly. It'll keep the assistant chief off our backs for a few days" He turned to Doyle. "Doyle, you and Allen make out a list of the Tridentine … soreheads. Share them out with the rest of the team. See if anyone stands out." There were some groans. Sheehan glared at them again. "So what? You got any better ideas?"

"No, sir," McCammon said. "It's just that this Tridentine stuff … it's alien to us, not our area of expertise."

"Well, make it your area of expertise," Sheehan growled. "By the time you get back here I want every

one of you able to say the Tridentine Mass backwards.
Now, do your jobs."

EIGHT

Sheehan's head was buzzing. He had not felt like going back to his empty flat, to sit there tortured by one of the most frustrating cases he'd had in years, but he wanted to watch the local news on television to see how the ACC would handle the appeal for witnesses. He checked his watch. Twenty-five past six. Just time to put the kettle on for a cup of tea before the news.

He went into the tiny kitchen, no room there for much more than a small table and two chairs. When he came back into the main room the Ulster News' introductory music was already starting. He sat on one of the two armchairs that represented the bulk of the room's furnishings and listened with half a mind to the usual litany of road deaths, a piece on a new art exhibition in the City Hall, something about a farmer who had starved twenty animals to near death. He sat up a bit and watched with more interest when Edward Corrigan's face suddenly filled the screen. Corrigan, dark haired, who might have been handsome if it wasn't for his perpetually combative expression, was a Member of the Legislative Assembly (MLA), a nationalist politician who loved to spend time in front of the TV cameras and was often prepared to court controversy in order to do so. A couple of weeks earlier he had sparked a furore because of his vocal support for gay rights and civil partnerships, a stance that earned him disapprobation both from the fundamentalist Democratic Unionist Party and many of his own Catholic brethren on the Nationalist side.

Sheehan had met him a few times. He found the man cold and insincere and could not warm to him, particularly because of his penchant for pursuing fashionable causes at the expense of personal principle. He stared at the talking head. *What's he been up to now?* he wondered and tuned his ear to what was being said.

"The Catholic bishops are going to have to learn that there has to be a distinct separation between Church and State," Corrigan was saying, striving for a statesmanlike demeanour. "Church schools not only place unbearable demands on the province's education budget but they continue to perpetuate the segregation that has contributed so massively to 'the troubles' in Northern Ireland."

"But surely the right of parents to choose a faith-based education for their children is guaranteed by the European Convention for Human Rights?" the interviewer argued.

Corrigan gave him a scathing glance. "The European Court for Human Rights? There's an argument for another day. Prisoners, rapists, paedophiles, the dregs of society, all running there to have their human rights upheld … and succeeding? We're going to have to take a serious look at that."

"But ..." was as far as the interviewer got before Corrigan continued.

"But regarding faith-schools, we are now a pluralist society in Northern Ireland. There are thousands of immigrants from many countries and faiths whose human rights are being trampled all over if their children are forced to submit themselves to an ethos that is alien to their own belief systems."

"But you yourself are Catholic," the interviewer interrupted. "Are you suggesting that your schools lose their own culture and identity to accommodate foreign cultures?"

"Don't be putting words into my mouth, Eamon," Corrigan said. "I'm simply making the point that the Church has its work to do and the Department of Education has its work to do. Each has a separate function and therefore each should be kept separate. Future generations will judge us, and rightly, if we fail to address this issue now."

Aye, right! Sheehan tuned out and went to leave the empty cup in the kitchen sink. When he was there, he heard the anchor-woman refer to the two recent murders in East Belfast and say that there would now be an appeal for witnesses from Peter Harrison, the Assistant Chief Constable. Sheehan came back into the room and sat down. The ACC was photographed standing in front of a battery of microphones held by a throng of radio and television reporters. He was dressed, as always, in full dress uniform, newly cleaned and pressed, carrying himself with what he imagined to be a military bearing although, as Sheehan well knew, he had never experienced military service.

Sheehan listened as the ACC outlined the basics of the two killings, stressing that the murders of two such prominent citizens were an affront to all decent and right-thinking people. He looked earnestly into the TV camera that zoomed in on his face and intoned, "There are many people in those areas who may have been leaving or returning to their homes at those times. If you have seen anything, anything at all, regardless of whether you believe it to be of significance or not, or if you perhaps know something about either victim that might have contributed to their deaths, I implore you to contact your local police station and tell them what you know. We have had too much lawlessness in Northern Ireland for too many years. We cannot allow it to continue." He paused to offer the camera one final, soulful gaze. "Only you, members of the communities themselves, can help us put a stop to it. Thank you."

The camera panned back and the ACC could be seen raising his hands and moving backwards from the reporters and their microphones, signalling the end of the appeal. Sheehan leaned forward and turned off the television. *I came home for that?* He sat back on his armchair, restless, still staring at the blank screen. "Ah, t'hell with it," he muttered aloud. "I'm not sitting here all night. I'll give myself a wee wash and head out".

It was just after seven-thirty when he left the flat. He climbed into his car and drove towards the city centre, struggling to get his butt more comfortably settled on the seat. *Bloody sciatica.* As soon as the cold weather comes, and him nowhere near fifty. Bad enough the pain but he hated his men to see any sign of weakness in him. He dismissed the discomfort and went back to the murder of the bishop. *Are we right in following the religious angle? Isn't sectarianism an equal possibility?* But even at its birth, the thought was killed. In the thirty-odd years of 'the troubles', there had never been a serious threat to any Catholic prelate. And anyway, there was just nothing pointing in that direction. He stopped at a red light. *Religion? That was astute of young Allen, reminding us what damage religion has done to humanity.* Something tugged at his conscience and he amplified the thought. *Well, perhaps not religionper sebut some mad adherents' notions of what religion was without any real understanding of what it should be.* He flashed at the guy in front. *Lights are green. What's wrong with you?* But Allen's point was still a good one. The youngster had not been implying that a good Catholic or some ordinary traditionalist offended by the bishop's liberalism was the killer. He was, perhaps intuitively, wondering if there was some sort of fundamentalist nutter on the loose. Sheehan's lips tightened. He was beginning to tend in that direction himself. *But where the heck do you start looking for someone like that?*

He eased his car into the large parking complex in Chichester Street and made his way up through the levels until he found a spot. As he locked his car, he stretched sideways to pull a bit on the sciatic nerve and headed for the street, wondering exactly what he had meant by 'someone like that'. Not some wild-eyed, manic individual running around with 'The End is Nigh' on a stick, that's for sure. Our man shows a serious streak of intelligence and awareness. The bishop's crime scene was unusually clean, the manner of execution skilful. And there was the ease with which the killer had entered and exited the premises. *Like a flamin' phantom.* His mind went again to the number on the desk: E3410. Significant? Not significant? He could not begin to fathom what it might mean or whether, indeed, it meant anything but his mind kept gnawing on it.

He turned into Royal Avenue and headed for Castle Lane, not far from the Castle Court Shopping Centre. There was a Starbucks there that he liked. It was a good location in the city centre for 'people-watching' and he always enjoyed the pleasant atmosphere in the area upstairs with its comfortable seats. Although he had nothing since lunch, he didn't feel much like eating. There was a turkey panini there, with brie and cranberry, that would more than meet his prandial requirements.

A late October wind was blowing and there was a chill in the air. Some trees on the pavement were losing leaves but their reds and golds and browns provided the grey evening with a splash of colour. Sheehan pulled the collar of his overcoat up around his neck and turned into Castle Lane. What he did not notice was that some yards away, carrying several shopping bags, was Margaret Sands, the woman he had met at the bishop's house. She, however, saw him and would have given him a wave of acknowledgement had he not already turned his back on her to go into Starbucks. She stared at the café's entrance for a moment, a small smile forming on her lipsas she reflected that she'd had a long evening's shopping: the idea of a Starbuck's seemed suddenly inviting. She went into the café and up the stairs. There was a lengthy queue there but the detective was at the end of it. She joined the queue behind him but Sheehan did not notice her arrival. He had been listening, somewhat awed, to the skinny, shaven-headed youth at the front of the queue ordering 'a triple shot, extra hot, skinny, sugar free hazelnut latte'. *Bloody hell,* he was thinking, *I was just going to order a cup of coffee. They probably won't have a clue what they should give me.*

Behind him Margaret bent down, making plenty of noise with the plastic shopping bags as she set them on the floor beside her. Hearing the noise, Sheehan automatically glanced round. "Oh, hi!" he said.

Margaret was still pretending to balance the bags close to her feet. She looked up with an expression of uncertainty and then allowed her face to clear. "Oh, hi!" she replied, registering surprise. "Chief Inspector …"

"Sheehan," the policeman offered. "Jim."

"Of course. Jim. How are you?"

"I'm fine. Are you here for a coffee?"

She threw an amused glance at the huge coffee menu on the wall behind the counter and said with a grin, "My goodness. Nothing gets past you detectives."

"Oh, God!" Sheehan emitted an embarrassed chuckle. "I'm sorry. What a stupid question. What I really meant was that if you were, would you mind if I joined you?"

"That'd be nice," she said with a smile that nearly stopped his heart. She pointed at the shopping bags. "I don't really like sitting on my own but I've been shopping and felt like a break."

Sheehan was delighted. "Good." He noticed a couple vacating a spot beside one of the windows. "Look, there's a table becoming vacant over there. Why don't you sit there and hold it for us? I'll get the coffee. What would you like?"

"Thank you. A Cappuccino would be nice."

"I'm going to have a bite to eat. Can I get you something?"

She looked at the pastry counter. "Maybe one of those Danish, if you wouldn't mind."

"Not a problem. Grab the table and I'll be over in a few minutes."

When he joined her at the table with a tray containing their orders, she sensed a subtle shift in his demeanour. She thought he seemed more settled; he seemed to have collected himself while he was standing in the queue. Sheehan placed her coffee and pastry before her, set out his own, put the tray to one side and sat down. He looked up and smiled as he was unwrapping his knife and fork from a paper napkin. She detected something in the depths of those blue eyes, a solitariness, perhaps a sadness, that gave him a degree of vulnerability. Interesting man, she thought. "Thank you," she said, preparing to sip her coffee.

"That's okay." He glanced at her bags. "Shopping long?"

"Couple of hours. Glad to get off my feet." The café was warm after the chill outside and she stood up to divest herself of her top coat. As she placed it over the back of her chair, she nodded at the window. "Crowds are thinning."

Sheehan, who had stood to remove his own coat, looked out into the dusk. The street lights were on. Shoppers and workers were heading home. Store windows were now dark, blocked off with iron bars or roll-down aluminium protective blinds. "Streets no longer look nice with all that stuff blocking the windows," he said. "I can remember my childhood days when a walk down Royal Avenue at night was all brightness and window magic. Now look at it." He smiled at her again as he sat. Outwardly calm, inside he was panicking. *Say something half sensible, for heaven's sake, or you'll bore the living daylights out of her.* He couldn't think of a thing.

While he was forking a piece of panini into his mouth to cover his confusion, Margaret said, "How's the case going?"

He swallowed the food and said non-committally, "We're following a few leads but it's early days yet. I think this one is going to be slow."

"You can't talk about it, can you?"

He shook his head. "Afraid not."

"That's okay. Let's talk about you instead."

He raised his eyebrows. "Me? That'll be a short conversation."

"Do you always chatter so incessantly when you are with someone from the opposite sex?"

He looked into her mischievous brown eyes and thought, *what the heck, I'll just say what's in my head.* "I suppose you could say that I'm out of practice," he said. "I haven't been in any kind of relationship for several years." He looked at her with more earnestness. *Might as well find out right away where this can go*, he thought. "What about you? Are you in any kind of steady relationship?"

She was somewhat startled at his directness. "Wow! That came from left field. What would you say if I told you I was?"

He thought about that for a minute, holding her gaze easily now. He was aware of the hum of conversation around him, the clink of utensils, but he was focused only on those eyes. "Well, I'd probably just enjoy your company for the next hour or so," he said, "and then say goodbye."

"Oh? So you wouldn't think I'm worth fighting for?" she said, head to one side.

"I wouldn't say that. No reflection at all on you. It's just that, I did get into such a fight some years ago …" She saw a flash of intense hurt cross his eyes. He smiled, a pretty wan effort. "I fought and I lost. I didn't like what it did to me, so I wouldn't want to go through that again."

She was no longer smiling as she looked back into his eyes and said, "I'm sorry to have forced that out of you. The fact is, I lost my husband ten years ago and I threw myself into my work, teaching, training the Cathedral choir. I haven't had any relationships since, nor am I having one now."

They both sipped their coffees. Then she said, "Have you?"

"Have I ...?"

"Ever been married?"

"You mean, other than to the job?"

"Of course."

"No."

"No?"

"No."

She threw her eyes to the ceiling. "Again with these effusive and convoluted explanations," she said, feigning exasperation. "I just can't get a word in edgeways with you."

Sheehan grinned. "You do all right."

They sipped their coffees again, staring quietly at each other. *She really is beautiful,* Sheehan was thinking. Then he said, "My goodness, this has become suddenly very intense."

"I know," she laughed. "I can't believe I just asked you that."

66

"But I can't pretend that I'm sorry you did. Let's just chat and enjoy the view and the ambience."

She raised her cup. He raised his and clinked it against the side of hers.

"Sláinte!" he said.

"Sláinte!" she replied.

An hour and two cups of coffee later, Margaret looked at her watch. "Well, I suppose I'd better get home."

Sheehan experienced disappointment. Conversation had flowed easily and, while both of them had carefully avoided revisiting the earlier personal exchanges, they found themselves comfortable in each other's presence and the hour had passed quickly. As she gathered up her bags, she asked, "Where are you parked?"

"Chichester Street."

She gave him a doleful look. "*Dommage*! I'm going in the opposite direction." She was thinking that she would have liked to have learned more about the 'fight' he had referred to but she was certain that there would be other opportunities in the future to broach that particular topic. She refused the detective's offer to carry her bags and as they walked down the stairs to the door, Sheehan cleared his throat and said, "I don't suppose you'd like to do this again; on purpose, I mean?"

"Why?"

"Why?" He looked at her, puzzled. "Why what?"

"Why don't you suppose that?" She smiled at catching him on the back foot again.But that was a part of his personality that she found attractive. She had had more than her share of self-assured Lotharios hitting on her over the past few years. Jim's awkwardness, especially in a man so good-looking, was refreshing. She put the bags down and said, "Have you a pen and a card or a piece of paper?"

Wordlessly he handed her his card and a ball-point. She wrote something on it and handed them back. "There's my number. Call me sometime." She gave him a last smile, gathered up her bags and left. Jim stood staring after her. After walking a few yards, she stopped at the edge of the pavement, checking the traffic flow before attempting to cross the street. She glanced back at the café and saw him still standing in the lighted doorway. She lifted one loaded arm in a goodbye gesture and disappeared into the street's shadows.

NINE

Miller was sitting in front of a laptop with Connors' large bulk bending over him when Sheehan entered the incident room the following afternoon. Connors straightened, his normally haunted expression replaced by something akin to pleasure. "Just writing up a wee report here, sir. Bit of good news I … we … think."

"Time somebody got something," Sheehan growled but every fibre of his being jumped to attention. He waited while the two men continued looking at him. "Well, am I supposed to guess what it is?"

"Sorry, sir," Connors said. "That vice-principal … there's a young lad outside in reception who says he saw Norman Henry coming out of O'Donoghue's residence at nine o'clock on the evening of the murder."

Sheehan tensed. This was good news but ... "Is it reliable?" he asked, probing both men's eyes. "We're not talking some pissed-off ex-pupil trying to create trouble?"

"Well," Miller was hesitant, "you're right about him being an ex-pupil, sir, but he looks scared out of his skull and I'm prepared to bet that he's sincere."

"What's his story?"

"He's here because of our appeal on the television for anyone with information on either of the two killings. He says he was walking down Easton Crescent at nine o'clock on Wednesday night last to call for his girl friend."

"Wednesday, the twentieth?"

"Yes. She lives only a few doors from O'Donoghue. When he was passing the victim's house, he noticed Henry coming down the steps. He knew him because, as I said, he had been a pupil at St. Matthews only a couple of years ago."

Sheehan remained cautious. "How can he be sure that it was the night of the twentieth?"

"We asked him that, sir," Miller replied. "He says he can only afford to take his girl out two nights a week and Wednesday night is one of them, and he always picks her up at nine o'clock."

Sheehan nodded. "It's something, I suppose."

"But there's more," Connors interjected, grinning as he bumped fists with Miller.

Sheehan observed the interaction and wondered if Connors was now getting over his divorce. He had married a Protestant and, as a Catholic, had found the whole idea of divorce traumatic and an affront to his sincerely-held beliefs. Sheehan had heard that the split had been acrimonious and that for the past few months Connors had been living in a small flat on the Antrim Road in unhappy solitariness, leaving the flat only to go to work. *Police work was hell on marriage,* Sheehan mused. *Perhaps I'm the lucky one.* None of this showed on his face, however, as he said, disguising the hope he suddenly felt, "Well, what is it?"

"That third set of prints, they match Henry's."

Sheehan, too, felt like bumping fists. He restrained himself to a, "Well, now, that is interesting. Good work, the both of you. Get the kid's statement and pull Henry in for questioning."

All looked up as they heard Doyle come into the room. Doyle's dour expression appeared even more disapproving than usual. "What's up, Sergeant?" Sheehan asked.

"Did you see the papers this morning, sir?"

Sheehan shook his head, wondering what was coming.

"They've linked the two killings and they're calling them, 'The Naked Murders'."

"Bloody crap!" Sheehan exploded. "I warned the chief to make it clear at the press conference that we are treating these as two separate cases."

"Didn't do a great job," Doyle said with cheerless disrespect.

Sheehan ran a frustrated hand through his hair. "Now we're almost certainly going to get some disaffected republican or disgruntled loyalist or aggrieved drug baron jumping on the bandwagon."

"What do you mean, sir?" asked Miller.

"You know what this bloody country's like.

There's every likelihood that some of these guys will use this opportunity to settle old scores or grievances, stripping the victims naked in the hope that the bishop's killer will be blamed." He paced away from the desk in frustration. "Bloody reporters. What is their problem? Doyle told them at the second scene that we were treating these crimes as separate. God!!" His exasperation was plain. "You can't watch the so-and-sos." He sat on the corner of McCullough's desk, his feet spread for balance, hands in his trousers pockets, as he glared at the floor. The others watched in silence.

Then he looked up. "Doyle, call the papers and make it clear that we do not see any connection between the killings. Tell them to print a retraction." He rose from the desk. "Then get back here. We're pulling Henry in for questioning. I want you with me for that." He jerked his thumb at the door and looked at Miller and Connors. "So why are you two still here? Drag him in. And don't take all day about it."

TEN

When Sheehan and Doyle entered Interview Room Two, Connors was leaning against a wall examining his fingernails while Norman Henry sat on a chair at the table, arms folded, one leg crossed over the other, fuming. His plans for that Friday afternoon did not include wasting pointless hours in a police station. The Deputy Head was a slight man but dressed in an elegant pin stripe suit with matching shirt and tie. His hair was long but carefully groomed. The phrase 'tailor's dummy' flitted through Sheehan's mind as he sat at the table opposite the teacher.

The teacher jumped up from his seat and began to remonstrate with the chief inspector. "What right have you to drag me in here like this? I …"

"Sit down, sir," Sheehan said.

"I will not," the teacher snapped. "I demand …"

Connors, built like a rugby player, stepped forward and placed a hand the size of a baseball mitt on the man's shoulder. "The chief inspector would like you to sit down." He exerted what seemed like minimal pressure but Henry's legs buckled and he slumped back into the chair.

Sheehan nodded at Connors. "Thank you, Detective. We'll take it from here."

As Connors left the room, Sheehan and Doyle sat on the two chairs opposite the suspect, the only other furniture in the room. Sheehan placed a small recorder on the table between himself and Henry.

"Why am I here?" the man continued to bluster, eyeing the recorder. "Why are you recording this interview?"

Sheehan held up a silencing finger, face expressionless, while he switched on the recorder and intoned, "Twenty-third October, two thousand and ten. Interview with Norman Henry, Interview Room Two, at …" He glanced at his watch. "… three twenty-two pm. Chief Inspector Sheehan conducting the interview with Sergeant Doyle present."

"What's all this about? Do I need a solicitor present?"

"Why? Have you done something?" Sheehan said.

"I haven't done anything. I demand to know why I am here."

"If you haven't done anything, why do you want a solicitor?" Sheehan said.

"I ... I don't want a solicitor."

Sheehan nodded. "Very well. We will proceed on that basis." He bent over the recorder and intoned,

"Mr. Henry has waived his right to have a solicitor present during this interview." He folded his arms on the table in front of him and leaned towards the suspect.

Henry sat more upright on his chair. He looked extremely nervous but he continued to bluster. "You still have not told me why I am here. Am I under arrest or something?"

"No," Sheehan said. "You're not under arrest. We simply want to ask you one or two questions about Mr. O'Donoghue's murder."

"I had nothing to do with that. I told everything I knew to one of your detectives."

"Yes indeed, Mr. Henry, but we have one or two follow-up questions." He looked down at some sheets of paper and spread them slightly. Without looking up, he said, "Would you tell us again your whereabouts on the night Mr. O'Donoghue was murdered, say between nine-thirty and two am?"

Henry shifted in his seat. His eyes darted from Sheehan to Doyle. Something furtive entered his demeanour. "I am sure your detective has already noted this," he said, attempting to inject a note of irritation into his voice. "I worked at home for a little while and went to bed."

Sheehan nodded. "I don't suppose anyone can confirm that?" he asked.

Again that furtive look in the suspect's eyes. *This guy is lying through his teeth,* Sheehan thought.

"No," Henry snapped. "I already told your detective that I was alone."

Sheehan shuffled the papers on the desk again and then stared directly and forcefully into the teacher's eyes. "Would you care to explain how it is that we have a witness who places you at the scene of the murder at nine o'clock on the night in question and forensic evidence that puts you inside the house on that same night?"

Henry paled. *Got you, you bastard,* Sheehan exulted.

The teacher had difficulty in replying but managed to say, "I was at Mr. O'Donoghue's house before nine o'clock but it was only ... only to deliver some statistics that he had me working on. He wanted them that night."

"Oh? What statistics exactly would you be talking about, sir?"

Henry began waving a hand about. "It's complicated ..."

Sheehan sat back, waving a magnanimous hand of his own. "That's okay, sir. We've got all night if you need it."

Henry expelled a shallow breath and said, "We're preparing a budget analysis for the heads of department for the new academic year. Mr. O'Donoghue always top-slices the annual income for various capital and recurrent expenses before allocating budgets to the heads of department. He wanted an exact student count. Their numbers and ages bring in varying allowances from the South-Eastern Education and Library Board." Henry spread his hands. "It was these funding allocations that he had me working on. He wanted the figures as soon as possible. I didn't have them finished at school last Wednesday so he instructed me to bring the completed statistics to his house that night. The head of departments' meeting is on Friday afternoon and he wanted a couple of days to work on the budgets."

Sheehan was puzzled. All of this had the ring of truth, yet he was convinced that the suspect was lying about something. He had sat too many times in this room not to have developed a sixth sense about this.

"And when did you give these figures to your boss?"

"Somewhere between half-eight and nine. He is a very stubborn man. When he ordered me to bring them that night, he would not have accepted any refusal." Henry's expression became petulant. "I had to work on the darn' things all day."

Again Sheehan was puzzled. Henry was showing no signs of stress as he said this. Could he be telling the truth? He pressed on. "And he was alive when you left him?"

"Of course he was," Henry almost shouted. "You think I killed him?"

"Why didn't you tell us you were there that night? You must have known it was germane?"

Again Henry showed signs of unease, trying to cover his discomposure by waving his hands about and making negating noises. "It was because ... because, well, you probably have heard that the Principal and I didn't get along. I was terrified to hear that he had been murdered sometime after I had left and I was afraid the police would think I had done it if they found out that I had been there." He stared at the two policemen, almost beseechingly. "I'm sure you can understand that?"

"Oh, yes, Mr. Henry, I can understand that exactly," Sheehan nodded. "And I'm sure that you can understand exactly where we are coming from. Forensic evidence places you in the house. A witness has you there close to the time of the murder. You have no alibi and I don't believe you're telling me the full truth."

Yet again the furtive unease flashed in the suspect's eyes and Sheehan was more then ever convinced that the man was hiding something. "Everything I have told you is true," Henry shrilled, almost in tears. "I mean, he was a very autocratic man and I agree that we did not see eye to eye about how the school should be run. But that is hardly a motive for murder. What more can I tell you?"

"You can tell me what you're hiding," Sheehan pressed.

"But I'm hiding nothing," Henry cried, still waving his hands and most of the rest of his body as well. "I'm hiding nothing."

This guy is getting more effeminate by the minute, Sheehan mused, watching the excessive body language. And he's scared. He's definitely lying. Okay, time to put on a bit of a show. He sat forward and with great deliberation pressed the pause button on the recorder. "I didn't want to go down this route," he said to the suspect, "but you're forcing my hand." He gestured to the sergeant beside him. "Doyle here is ex-military, trained in interrogation techniques. Was highly respected in Afghanistan." He turned to Doyle and asked affably, "What was your success rate, Doyle?"

Doyle's reply was a terse, "Hundred per cent, sir."

"Ah yes, a hundred per cent." He looked at the suspect, now staring at Doyle in horror. "I don't know how he does it." Then he smiled. "But of course, I wouldn't. I always leave the room before … Well, anyway …" He looked at his watch.

"How long do you think you'll need, Doyle? Half an hour?"

"Hardly that, sir," came Doyle's dead-pan response. "He doesn't look very strong."

Henry was breathing heavily, close to panic. "You can't do this. You can't do this. It's an infringement of my human rights. It's … it's …"

"What are you talking about, sir? What infringement? I'm simply leaving the room to deal with some pressing matters. I'm only asking Sergeant Doyle to keep an eye on you until I get back." He leaned forward and started the recorder again. He spoke into the machine, "Chief Inspector Sheehan leaves the room at …" He glanced at his watch. "… four twelve pm. Interview is temporarily suspended." He turned the recorder off and stood up. "Keep it quiet, Doyle, okay?"

He walked to the door but before he reached it, Henry, in tears now and terrified, cried, "All right, all right. I have an alibi. I have an alibi. Please … please …"

Sheehan paused. He had expected something but he wasn't expecting this. An alibi? He returned to the table and, picking up the recorder, rewound it for a second or two. He listened to the playback until he heard, "I'm hiding nothing."

Then he pressed the recording button again and said, "I believe you're hiding something, Mr. Henry. It would be best if you told us everything now before this situation gets out of hand for you."

Henry was almost blubbering. He had his head in his hands and began to mutter, "When I left the principal's house, he was still alive."

"Speak up, Mr. Henry, please. For the recorder."

Henry stared at the machine and continued with scarcely much more force. "But I did not go straight home. I spent the night at ... at a friend's house."

"At a friend's ..." Sheehan almost exploded. "Then why in the hell didn't you ..." He paused, staring at the defeated man. "It was a male friend, wasn't it?"

Henry nodded miserably. "A young colleague. If word ever gets out about us. Catholic teachers in a Catholic school ..." He looked at Sheehan, his eyes begging for understanding.

Sheehan gritted his teeth and returned the man's stare for several seconds before saying, "How long were you with him?" There was truth in this; he had no doubt about that.

"Most of the night, from about nine-thirty." He paused, again pleading for secrecy. "Sir, is it necessary for this to come out?"

Doyle had little doubt about the answer. "You need to read your bible, sir. Try Leviticus: 'If a man lies with a man as one does with a woman, both have committed a detestable act and they shall be put to death'."

Henry looked astounded. Sheehan said, "Okay, leave it, Doyle. Society has moved on a wee bit since Leviticus." But that did not make him feel any better. "How long have you been in this relationship?" he said to Henry.

"A couple of years."

"I take it that your colleague has deep feelings for you?"

"Yes."

"He'd support you in this, then? Confirm your alibi?"

"Of course."

"You have no doubt about that?"

"None. He's very protective of me."

Sheehan stared at the broken man. "You've just given us a motive for the murder," he said.

Henry looked up, stunned. "What?"

"Like you said, Catholic male teachers in a Catholic boys' school ... in a homosexual relationship. Mr. O'Donoghue found out, didn't he? He threatened to expose you to the school authorities, didn't he? Bang go all your ambitions, your career, your hopes of a headship, your very livelihood. You had no choice. You went to his house to try and get him to change his mind but he wouldn't. You fought ..."

Henry was aghast. "No ... no ... no ... it was nothing like that. I went there with the figures. My colleague ..."

"Aye, right. Your colleague will want to protect you. He'll say anything that makes you look innocent. You fought and ..."

Henry was incoherent now, in tears. "No, no, he didn't know. He couldn't have known. We were so careful. Nobody knows."

There was a knock on the door. Tom Allen poked his head in. "Sir ..."

Sheehan was annoyed. "I told you no interruptions, Detective. Can't it wait?"

"I don't think it can, sir. I think you will want to come over to the incident room."

Sheehan grunted his annoyance, bent over the

recorder and intoned, "Interview temporarily suspended at four twenty-nine. Chief Inspector Sheehan leaves room."

As he followed Allen to the incident room, he said, "I had that perp dead to rights, Allen. This better be important."

"It is, sir," Allen replied, standing aside to let Sheehan precede him into the room. "Over here, sir." He indicated some photographs that had just been sent up from the morgue. "Dr. Campbell's autopsy report has just come in, sir. It's more or less what we expected but ..." He selected a photograph from several spread on the table. "... Look at this photograph here, sir."

The photograph was a full glossy of the back of O'Donoghue's head and neck.

Visible just under the short hairs near the bottom of the neck were some spidery scabs growing over some marks that had been cut into the skin. It was clear that what he was looking at was a letter and three numbers: E148. "Oh, crap!" he muttered. "Oh, crap! Oh, crap!"

"Looks like there is a connection between the murders, after all, sir," Allen said. "Thought you should know before you went on with the interrogation of Mr. Henry. This seems to let him off the hook."

"Y' think?" Sheehan was trying to fight a wave of anger. What the hell was going on? "Or maybe it puts him in the frame for both of them," he said. "Get away down to Doyle and find out if Henry has an alibi for the night of the bishop's murder." Allen made to leave. "And Allen, I don't want to hear any shit about him spending the night with his lyin' partner."

He studied the photograph again, looking also at

some of the others and at the autopsy report. The report confirmed that the rope had, indeed, been little more than ornamental and that O'Donoghue had been killed by a blow to the throat with the rigid fingers of the assailant's right hand. *What the heck was the rope all about?* he wondered. He looked again at the photograph with the numbers. *What are these numbers? What is the killer telling us?*

Allen came back into the room. "I think he's in the clear for the bishop's murder, sir. He was at an overnight conference in Bangor. All the male teachers in attendance had to share double rooms to save on expenses. He shared with a teacher from another school. He says that can easily be confirmed, too. We still have to check it, sir, but I'd guess his alibi's tight."

ELEVEN

Catherine Higgins left the meeting dejected. She had given up her Friday evening for what she should have known was a totally futile endeavour. But she had had such high hopes for her proposal, one that had caught the attention of the Chair of YouthAid, no less. She had read a paper at a recent conference for youth and community workers from the Belfast City and District Council and, apart from a number of plaudits from all and sundry, she had been particularly pleased to have been invited by the Chair of YouthAid to address a small but select group of senior government personnel representing both education and youth work.

She pulled her anorak more closely around her and walked smartly, head down, into the chilly, evening breeze. Although she had spent the whole weekend working on it, the essence of her proposal was simple. Forty per cent of Northern Ireland's school leavers enter society with no qualifications, many of them, indeed, functionally illiterate and innumerate. Her argument was that there was need for a coherent and integrated vision between the formal education system and the non-formal world of the youth worker. In terms of the development and education of the deprived youngsters, her idea was sound but the representatives from the teachers' unions, who were also present, got so fixated on status, effect on teacher salaries and issues of discipline, that the meeting ended scrappily without a single proposal being made.

For Catherine this was a serious disappointment. She experienced a *frisson* of concern. Her situation was becoming precarious. She needed this coup to restore her status and regain the respect of the locals. Disconsolate, she turned into the side street where she had parked her car, wondering if her proposal would ever again see the light of day. Those arrogant teachers. They saw their "profession" as being so superior to youth work, that any serious partnership between the two would be forever unworkable. Their territoriality meant so much more to them than the futures of these unfortunate young people.

But something tugged at the back of her mind, something she tried to dismiss. The thought, the concern, pushed its way through her defenses. Could the rumours surrounding her private life have reached the ears of some members of the meeting, thus accounting for her lack of any success? A surge of guilt raced through her. *Dear God*, she thought for the thousandth time, *how could I have allowed this to happen?*

Head bowed and lips tight, she continued to press

forward into the cold wind, trying yet again to come to terms with what her life had become. She had befriended Joanne because she was vulnerable, one of life's victims. How could she have known that they would fall in love? A shy, reticent, fourteen-year-old child. What could they possibly have in common? She was thirty-three years old, for heaven's sake. And yet …

They had been so discreet but someone, somewhere, had found out and her life had recently been plagued with anonymous midnight phone calls accusing her of paedophilia and child abuse. Her colleagues, the young people, and even local parents would soon become aware, if they were not aware already, of her folly. But there was maybe still time to fix it. She'd explain the situation to Joanne. *God, the child will be heartbroken.* Her parents, victims to the drink and drugs culture, had neglected the child's social development leaving her to fend for herself since early childhood. It had been clear to Catherine that their relationship was the child's first experience of any real kindness.

She turned into the side street where she had parked her car, two rows of red terraced houses on a road littered with scraps of paper, throwaway carry-out containers and more than a few empty beer cans. Her car was barely visible now in the evening dusk, but she became aware of dark markings on the passenger-side door. She squinted and saw that a single word, written in graffiti-style writing, was sprayed across the length of the vehicle. The word was 'DYKE'.

Annoyance assailed her. No doubt this vicious prank was the work of the same anonymous creeps who squawked and screeched down her phone in the early hours of the morning. Perhaps not so anonymous, she thought, as she lifted her head and saw three hooded youths leaning against the wall on the opposite side of the street.

Insolent yobs. She knew who they were. Up to their usual Friday night villainy. She had had them expelled from the community centre some months before because of bullying and vandalism. She had since learned that all three seemed to spend more time in the magistrate's court than they did on the streets. Joyriding, drugs, burglary with menaces, paramilitary involvement ... their list of criminal behaviours was endless and none of them was yet out of his teens. They were dangerous youths, almost feral in their utter lack of social conscience and awareness, but she was so angry at the wanton damage to her car that she shouted over to them, "You did this, and don't think I don't know it. I am reporting the three of you to the police."

One youth raised his arm with his middle finger pointing to the sky. "Sure you will, scag. We know what you're hidin'. Take that to the cops."

The other two cackled shrilly at this scintillating repartee, high-fiving on the pavement and making further lewd gestures. Catherine bit back tears and opened the door of her car. Before she had settled in her seat, however, she heard the gang's spokesman yell after her, "Hey, lesbo. See that stuff about the naked murders in the paper? Guess who's next?"

She pulled the car door shut, cutting off the raucous hoots that followed this witticism, and drove off.

TWELVE

Sunday morning and Sheehan, unusually, was seated at the edge of a pew about halfway down the middle aisle of the St. Peter's Pro-Cathedral in the Falls Road of Belfast. He had earlier been standing across the street for some twenty minutes, staring at the towering twin gothic steeples which, for many decades, had dominated the changing landscape of the city. Something had stirred in him as he had approached the impressive main entrance of the church on the morning of Bishop Loughran's funeral service. The building's magnificence was naturally arresting but its aura, touching something buried in his soul, had given him pause. Had it not been for the fact that he would hear Margaret play, perhaps even speak to her after the service, he might well have turned and walked away.

The coffin, holding the body of the late bishop,

with his red biretta and breviary placed on top it, was lying on the undertaker's wheeled trolley at the top of the aisle, directly in front of the steps leading to the wide, spacious altar, with its high ceiling and huge ornate crucifix suspended several feet above the tabernacle. Sheehan felt dwarfed by the massive arches and pillars that flanked the middle aisle and somewhat ill-at-ease as he sat in a chapel for the first time in as many years as he could remember.

When a bell sounded, he stood up with the rest of the congregation to watch as rows of diocesan priests in white surplices and black soutanes processed on to the large altar. The altar was filled with extra pews and chairs to accommodate the many priests who would sit there. On one side of the altar, isolated from the other seating, was a single *prie dieu* with an ornate cushioned chair behind it. That had been placed there for the Primate of All Ireland who, accompanied by two acolytes, followed the priests on to the altar. His soutane, bright scarlet, contrasted strongly with the more muted purple of the lesser prelates behind him, all of whom turned right at the foot of the altar and began to fill the first twenty rows of pews that had been left empty for them on the right side of the middle aisle. Already seated in the front rows of the left side were the bishop's extended family and dozens of invited lay dignitaries, politicians, and even, Sheehan noted, a number of Protestant Moderators. The rest of the huge cathedral was already packed, with crowds standing at the doors.

The procession had been conducted in silence. Sheehan might have expected funereal organ music to accompany this significant gathering of clergy had Margaret not mentioned during their conversation of a few nights before that her playing would be limited to accompanying the hymn singing. He had told her that he was looking forward to hearing her booming out something massive by Bach or Handel but she had smiled and shaken her head. Apparently recent directions from the Holy See required that the organ remain silent during funeral Masses except to accompany singing. Thus, Margaret had told him, almost regretfully, no organ preludes or postludes.

It came as no surprise to Sheehan to see Monsignor Byrne, accompanied by two concelebrants on either side of him, begin to say the Mass. The talk was that he was in the running to succeed Bishop Loughran. He stared around the packed cathedral. Doyle had been right. Attempting to observe this crowd for unusual signs would have been about as useful as attempting to identify passengers on a railway platform from the window of a speeding express train.

Monsignor Byrne spoke briefly, commiserating with the members of the bishop's family gathered here to mourn the passing of their beloved brother, and thanking all those who had come to pay their last respects to a much-loved bishop. Then he raised his hands shoulder high, palms outwards, and began to read from the altar lectionary. Kneeling down again with the congregation, Sheehan stared at the monsignor, listening vaguely to the half-forgotten but familiar opening prayers of the Mass. It had been a long time since he had attended Mass. Even when any of his Catholic colleagues or friends passed away, he would attend the wake at the house the evening before rather than go to the Mass.

In what seemed like seconds, he heard the organ strike out the opening notes of the *Kyrie Eleison* followed almost immediately by the *Gloria in Excelsis Deo*. The music was almost understated but the choir was well trained and the singing had a spiritual quality that began to tug at something long lost in Sheehan's psyche. He stood with the rest of the congregation for the gospel but heard little of it, focused as he was on what was happening to him.

Seated again, he did hear the first few words of the monsignor's homily and was struck by them. Monsignor Byrne had opened his eulogy by referring to a phrase from the gospel – 'a lonely place'. "This phrase," he said, "reminds us of our own mortality and forces us to confront realities that we normally choose to evade."

The monsignor's reflections on the bishop's life faded as Sheehan grappled with the opening words. Realities? *What realities? What is it we normally choose to evade? Thoughts of death, certainly. Those are real enough.* But that wasn't what the monsignor was talking about. He was talking about the 'realities' of eternity, of heaven, of hell, of salvation, of damnation. Realities or myths? *The monsignor certainly seems to believe that they are realities. But eternity? A post-mortem dimension? Another life after death?* These thoughts he had long ago dismissed from his belief system. But hearing the monsignor, a man whom he had begun to admire and respect, talking about them so matter-of-factly, in this place, with this music …

Monsignor Byrne's voice, quoting Jeremiah, penetrated his consciousness again. "Ah, Lord, look. I do not know how to speak. I am a child." Sheehan stared at the tabernacle. *Ah, Lord, look. I do not know how to speak. I am a child.* He stopped short. *What am I doing, praying now?*

Monsignor Byrne continued to proclaim, "As a serving priest during the thirty odd years of the troubles, Charles Loughran was deeply affected by the violence and suffering that was the lot of many of his parishioners in those seemingly godless times. The discouragement of those years weighed heavily upon him ..."

Again the monsignor's voice faded. Sheehan had been a child and a growing adult in those awful days and the terrible cruelty that had characterized the so-called 'acts of war' had never failed to shock him. How many funerals were there then? Evening after evening, month after month, the evening news reported some new death, some awful atrocity. Names raced off the headlines and blurred into the ether, remembered only by the small coterie of grieving relatives who felt their pain anew with each new tragedy. He stared at the tabernacle again. *Where were you then, God? Hundreds, thousands, of deaths. And for what? Realities? The reality is that nothing has changed. Continuity IRA, Real IRA, Dissident IRA, Ulster Volunteer Force, the Ulster defence Association. Still they fight. Still they riot. Still they hate.*

Monsignor Bryne's voice penetrated his thoughts again. "Today the Church finds itself in another struggle, its reputation deeply damaged by numbers from its own line of kings, aware of its profound limitations and failures, unsure where to turn. Our people are confused, angry, hurting, because of the actions of some of their pastors. To whom do we now turn, they ask. Whom can we trust? But we, as individuals, we know where to turn. The Risen Lord invites us to turn to him with confidence and humility ..." Sheehan's eyes were drawn again to the tabernacle. Guilt racked him. He closed his eyes but still he heard echoes of the monsignor's voice, "... but we know where to turn. We know where to turn ..."

The Credo was being sung, words well known and loved during his childhood in his parish choir, *"Credo in unum deum ..."* The choir sang and in his mind he sang the Latin phrases with them, almost word perfect after all these years. *Credo in unum deum;* I believe in one God.

The choir was silent again and Monsignor Byrne and his concelebrants intoned the Offertory. Sheehan barely heard them. He felt restless, confused. He had come here to hear Margaret play the organ. What was this unease? A bell was ringing. Instinctively he knelt for the consecration and stared at the Host as the monsignor raised it aloft. We know where to turn; we know where to turn. *I do not know where to turn, Lord.* He stared at the tabernacle and heard again, 'turn to me in confidence and humility'.

Lost in thought, he scarcely noticed time passing. Suddenly the crowd was processing up the aisle for Holy Communion. The choir was singing the beautifully melodic *'Ubi Caritas'*. He heard the words as the choir repeated them soulfully during the distribution of the Hosts. *Ubi caritas et amor, ubi caritas, deus ibi est.* "Where there is charity and love, where there is charity, there God is." The refrain, repeated over and over by the choir, filled his mind, filled his ears, filled his soul. Something was happening to him, something that was making him feel intensely uncomfortable. He did not join the crowds receiving Communion. Even in his lapsed state, he never could have allowed himself to receive the Host unworthily. Something of his childhood spirituality clung in tendrils to his soul and, now that he was back at Mass again, the Lord seemed to be pulling on them.

He became aware that the Mass was over. What had happened to the time? He had no consciousness of its passing. Did he have some form of mental lapse? Freudian psychology might conclude that he had experienced a mild dissociative disorder, a psychogenic amnesia as an act of self preservation. Self-preservation from what? Unwanted memories? Unwanted beliefs? Resistance to … to … the urgings of grace? Maybe it wasn't any form of cognitive disorder. For those brief, uncluttered moments, he had been totally at peace, unknowing, unthinking, unburdened. Had he been lost in contemplation? *Contemplation? Me? Aye, right.*

But time had passed since his last conscious thought. The coffin was now being carried down the aisle to the waiting hearse at the bottom of the cathedral front steps. He stood respectfully with the rest of the congregation as the coffin was carried past his seat and the choir sang, "Nearer my God to Thee". He sat again and remained in his pew, puzzled, disturbed, until the singing was over and he could hear the choir members leaving the gallery.

As he left his seat, he genuflected to the altar, feeling again that odd strangeness at this unaccustomed act of worship. His aching hip did not help and he was unable to get his knee anywhere near the floor. He went to the bottom of the gallery stairs and saw Margaret exiting, carrying pages of music in her arms as she chatted with one of the choir members. She saw Jim waiting for her and her face lit up. She excused herself to her female companion and walked over to the policeman.

"Hi," she smiled. "I wasn't sure you'd come."

"I said I had to hear you play," he replied, his expression gentle as he stared into her eyes.

Her eyebrows came down slightly although her smile did not falter. She stared back at him, searching.

94

"You seem different," she said, now wearing a quizzical expression. "I don't know wha ..." She shook her head, still smiling but puzzled. "You just look different."

He emitted something between a bark and a laugh. "I washed my hair before I came out this morning. Come on and have a cup of coffee with me somewhere."

THIRTEEN

PART 1

The young girl's voice is frantic, garbled. "Please … please … send somebody … she's not moving …"

"It's all right. It's all right. Someone will be with you immediately." The 999 operator speaks calmly, businesslike, trying to sooth the caller's panic. She notes the date, Thursday 28th October, and the time of the call, nineteen twenty-five, and says, "Just tell me your name and where you are."

"I'm Joanne. I've been banging on the door for ages but she won't answer …"

"Please, we'll come to that in a minute. Where are you? Who is not moving?"

"It's Catherine. She's supposed to take me to the Community Centre, but she won't answer the door."

"Where are you?" The operator's voice, calm, efficient, penetrates the girl's panic.

"I'm at Catherine's flat in Rockdale Street, beside the Falls Road."

"Thank you, Joanne. What's the house number?"

"I dunno. It has red brick, there's a wee wall and a wee hedge."

"All right. Thank you. Now, who isn't moving?"

"It's Catherine. I knocked and I knocked. Then I looked in the window ..." She begins to sob, panicking again.

"It's all right, Joanne. Someone will be there in a minute. What did you see?"

"I can see her foot behind the couch. She's just lying there ..." The girl's voice trails away in a wail.

The operator, writing furiously now on a pad, signals the dispatcher who takes the paper from her and goes to his office. He radios two police patrol cars and an ambulance and sends them to Rockdale Street while the operator continues to speak quietly to the caller, advising her not to touch anything and to wait at the front of the house for the ambulance to arrive.

PART 2

The first patrol car arrived at the scene scarcely ten minutes later, followed by an ambulance from the nearby Royal Victoria Hospital. Although it was dusk, the police driver spotted the girl, no more than thirteen or fourteen years of age, waving frantically at them at the front of a narrow red-bricked, terraced house. The WPC who accompanied him went to the child and brought her into the back seat of the car, talking quietly to her. The driver uttered some brief words into a mouthpiece attached to his shoulder and, one hand on his still-holstered revolver, joined the two paramedics who were already at the front of the house. One was pushing at the door but it was holding firm. By now the second patrol car arrived and the two officers joined the group at the front door.

"It's locked," the first officer told them.

One of the paramedics was peering through the front window. "There's someone dead or unconscious behind a sofa in there," he said. "I can see a bare foot sticking out."

One of the officers said, "We're going to have to push the door in, unless any of you guys know how to pick a lock?"

Blank stares greeted him. "You're watching too much TV, mate," one of the paramedics said.

"Okay." The officer, a burly sergeant in his fifties, positioned himself close to the lock and threw his weight against it. The lock gave easily and the policemen, guns drawn, entered the house. A quick search of the small flat confirmed that there was no immediate danger and they beckoned the paramedics to enter. They rushed into the front room where they found the pallid, naked body of a woman sprawled on the floor in front of a worn sofa which had its back to the window.

The policeman stared in horror. "Good God! What sort of demented psycho would leave a poor lass lyin' like this?"

One of the paramedics felt for a pulse but found none. Hardly surprising, given that there was a six foot length of orange plastic clothesline tied around the woman's throat and attached to a large, cement breeze block. "This woman's dead," he told the policemen.

"Looks like she's been dead for several hours."

His partner, young and new to the job, looked green. Scarcely able to get the words out, he said, "Hangin's not good enough for the bastard who did this." He looked around helplessly. "Is there not a sheet or a coat or somethin' we could throw over her?"

The sergeant's lips tightened. "Better not touch anything until the SOCOs arrive. They'll chew us to bits if we do. But we'll get everybody to fuck outa here. She doesn't need anybody gawpin' at her in that state." He stared for a moment in mystification at the clothes-line and the breeze block and then, becoming businesslike, he said loudly, "All right, gentlemen, the victim's obviously beyond medical help. Don't move her; don't touch anything." He spread his arms as if he was herding sheep. "Everybody out, myself included. We may already have contaminated the crime scene but we better get out of here now and protect it as best we can. Aidan, you guard the door. I'll radio dispatch."

As they left the house, he spoke into his shoulder radio, asking the dispatcher to send a forensics unit, a Forces MO, and someone from the Serious Crimes Unit.

PART 3

When Chief Inspector Sheehan arrived at the scene, the Deputy State Forensic Pathologist was already in the house examining the body. The Forensics team was still standing-by outside the house, waiting permission to enter. Two paramedics, one leaning against their ambulance smoking, were chatting quietly while they waited to take the body away. As Sheehan got out of his car, he noticed Sergeant Doyle arriving. The sergeant jumped out of his vehicle and joined his superior. He was wearing a duffle coat slung over jeans and a polo shirt. Sheehan fixed his eyes on his sergeant's attire.

Doyle, following his boss's gaze, looked down. "Oh, I was off duty, sir. Apparently everybody else is tied up. I was told it was urgent. I didn't have time to change." He stared at the busy scene, officers taping off access to the house, the waiting teams, the guard on the door. "What's up, sir?"

"Some woman's been murdered. Get your bunny suit on. We'll go in and have a look."

As he donned his coveralls, Doyle noticed the teenager in the patrol car talking to the WPC. "Who's the wee girl?"

"A friend of the victim, I believe. She made the 999 call. We'll hear her statement later."

They went to the front door, Sheehan nodding at the policeman on duty. They had met more than once before under similar circumstances. They entered a dark, narrow hall, with an even narrower staircase against the left wall. There was a door just to their right leading into a small, sparsely furnished room. A worn sofa faced a tiny fireplace and a twenty-inch TV sat on a small occasional table in the corner. Dr. Campbell was kneeling in front of the sofa beside the body of a youngish female, probably middle thirties, who was sprawled on a threadbare red and green mat that covered part of the wooden floor. He was fiddling with an orange clothesline tied round the victim's throat. He looked puzzled.

Sheehan studied the scene, fixing it in his memory. A pair of jeans, a tee shirt and some underwear had been thrown carelessly over the side of the couch. The woman was naked, lying on her back but with her bottom half pulled to the right. Her right knee was pulled up over her left knee which was also bent. Her left arm was stretched above her head and, while her right arm was also pulled above her head, it was bent at the elbow permitting the right hand, seemingly, to clasp the left arm. Sheehan' gaze drifted to the breeze block at the end of the plastic rope and his face expressed his puzzlement.

Dick Campbell looked up at the two detectives. "Ah, Jim, and your ever faithful sergeant. Credit crunch got you working overtime again?"

"What have we here, Doc?" Sheehan asked, ignoring the medic's blithe greeting.

"A little puzzle, I think," Campbell replied. "This clothes line, it's tied tightly around her neck but I'm pretty sure it was post mortem. I don't believe the lady died of strangulation."

Sheehan raised his eyebrows. "Oh? How did she die then?"

The pathologist looked back at the body, touching the skin, peering again into the mouth and throat. "I'm not sure. I detect signs of froth sputum in the mouth here, carefully wiped away for whatever reason, presumably by the killer. The skin is very pallid, a bluey-grey colour which indicates depleted oxygen in the blood at the time of death. Looks like pulmonary edema. No way had the breeze block and plastic rope anything to do with her death."

"So what, then?" Sheehan persisted.

"I can't be sure till I've done the autopsy. I'll need to check the lungs for damage and the bone marrow for diatoms, but if I was pushed to guess, I'd have to say that death was caused by excess of fluid in the lungs. The victim, apart from being dead, looks healthy enough …" He beamed up at the two detectives. "… so no obvious disease." He looked down at the body again, making some uncertain waggles with his hands. An element of doubt entered his tone. "I think, and believe it or not there are no proven pathological tests to confirm this, but my gut instinct is telling me that she may have been drowned."

"Drowned? In her front living room?"

"I would doubt that. There's patchy lividity on the body. It was moved a while after death, but not long after and not far. I'd guess from the bathroom upstairs."

The inspector was pensive for a few moments, staring at the body. Then he said, "Keep a lid on the drowning, Dick. I'd like to keep that out of the press. In fact, say nothing to anybody about it for the time being." He glanced at Doyle. "Check the bathroom, will you?"

"On it, sir," Doyle said.

Sheehan turned to the doctor again. "So what's with the plastic line and the brick?"

The doctor shrugged ignorance. "No idea. Can't figure them out at all." He struggled to his feet and said, "It's like that situation last week. There was a rope round that victim's neck, too, although he wasn't drowned like this one. But he was naked. Still, these two deaths might be connected."

"I'll think about that," Sheehan said. "Any idea of the time of death?"

"Well, as you know, naked bodies can cool faster than clothed ones. And smaller bodies cool faster than larger ones. And this body, it's sort of spread-eagled. That affects temperature too. Crumpled bodies retain heat longer, and the nights are cold now ..."

"Doc, if I want a lecture I'll go to the University of Ulster for night classes. Just give me an approximation."

"Humphh! Well, that's all it'll be, so don't hold me to it. Probably some time during last night, middle of the night, early hours, something like that."

"What about the … uh … was the body violated at any time, pre- or post-mortem?"

"No. Our killer's abstemious. Whatever his motivation, it wasn't sexual."

"Okay. You about finished here?"

"Yes, she's all yours," he said, snapping off his latex gloves.

Doyle came back into the room. "Bathroom's immaculate, sir. Bath, floor, basin, toilet, windows. Bit old and worn, but totally spick and span."

Sheehan nodded. "Okay, get the forensics unit in here." He walked from the room, trying not to disturb anything. "I'll go and have a chat with the wee girl." He paused to examine the broken front door and shouted back, "Any word on how the killer got in?"

Doyle said, "No sir. The windows are all securely fastened, no sign of any break in. A couple of uniforms had to break in when they saw the woman lying in the front room. They say that the door had been locked before that."

"Maybe she knew him?" the inspector surmised. Outside, he threw his coveralls in the boot of his car. "The victim is relatively young. Her parents are almost certainly still alive. See if you can find out who and where they are. They'll need to be notified."

"I'll see what I can find out when I get back to the station, sir," Doyle said.

Sheehan went over to the patrol car where the young girl was sitting. She was crying softly now but obviously still very upset. He opened the door and bent his head in, saying, "Hello, Joanne. I'm Jim Sheehan. I'm a detective. I'm just going to have a few words with the constable here but then I'd like to ask you a couple of questions. Would that be all right?"

The girl nodded tearful acquiescence but did not speak. The young woman constable climbed out of the car and Sheehan said, "Well?"

"From what I can gather, sir, the victim was in the habit of giving Joanne a lift to the Community Centre in the evenings. The victim was a Senior Youth Worker there. Seems to have befriended this wee girl. She's pretty broken up."

"She have anything useful to say?"

"Well, it seems that the victim met with her a couple of nights ago, very upset about something. Her car had been vandalized, graffiti sprayed all over it. And threats had been made."

"Oh? What kind of threats?" Sheehan said.

"I don't know, sir. The victim apparently didn't want to worry the wee girl so she told her that it was just some young hoods mouthing off and not to be worrying about it."

"But she did worry about it?"

"Yes, she says that the victim seemed very upset about the whole business even though she was trying to make light of it."

"Has she any idea who the hoods were?"

"She says she doesn't, sir, but I think she's hiding something."

"All right. Thanks, Jean." He made to enter the car but stopped to say, "Could you just wait here a minute. I'll go and have a wee word with her but I want you here when I've finished." He got into the car and sat beside the tearful girl. "Have they told you what has happened, Joanne?" he said.

The child looked at the man who had come to join her. He looked like one of her uncles. He had a nice friendly-looking face. She felt that she could trust him. Nodding slowly in answer to his question, she asked, still tearful, "Is she really dead?"

"I'm afraid so." He waited while a fresh bout of sobbing seized the girl. Then he said, "Do you know of anyone who might have wanted to harm Catherine?"

"No, she was lovely; she was great. All the kids at the centre loved her."

"Who all goes to the centre?"

"Most of the kids from around here go. It's something to do in the evenings."

"What ages go?"

"All the teenagers. There's all sorts of things to do there."

"Do the big boys go there as well?"

"Yes, nearly everybody goes. There's games and classes for all sorts. The big boys can play pool or table tennis or tae kwon do."

"Do any of the big boys give Catherine any trouble?"

The girl fell into silence.

"Joanne?"

Head down, her voice muffled, the girl said, "Catherine doesn't have nathin' to do with the big boys. Patsy looks after them."

"Who's the boss at the centre?"

"Catherine is."

"Wouldn't she have to discipline any boys who didn't behave themselves?"

"Sometimes."

"How would she do that?"

"She'd give them warnings and if they didn't stop messin', she'd have to ban them."

"Did she have to ban anyone lately?"

Again that strangely reluctant silence.

"Joanne?"

"There was three very bad boys, they was wreckin' the place. Even Patsy couldn't control them. She banned them."

"Can you remember their names?"

"They're terrible liars, Mister. You can't believe nathin' that comes out of their mouths." This in a rush of passion that took Sheehan by surprise. He decided not to push the child any further. It would be easy to discover who had recently been banned from the Community Centre without forcing the girl to reveal the names. He found it odd, though, that she was so secretive. Surely if there was any chance they had anything to do with her friend's death, she would be anxious to tell what she knew. Kids nowadays. Who could figure them?

He opened the door of the car. "Thank you, Joanne. You've been very helpful. WPC Jean here will drive you home, okay?"

The girl nodded and Sheehan went back into the house. The forensic crew had already taken all the photographs they needed and combed the body for any unusual signs or foreign matter. The clothes had been bagged for forensic examination back at HQ. Sheehan shouted to the officer on the door to tell the paramedics they could now take the body to the mortuary, and as he turned back into the crime scene, he recognised the ample figure of an SOC officer that he had met at crime scenes many times before. The man was dusting the door frame for prints.

"That you in there, Mick?"

A hollow voice emitted from behind the mask. "Hi, Chief, how's about ye?"

"Ah, y'know, same old, same old." He stood aside as the paramedics stretchered the body to the ambulance and then said, "Find anything interesting?"

The hooded figure shook his head. "No. Surprisingly clean. Couple of wee things that I'd say came from the patrol officers breaking in. Other than that ..." he shrugged. "Perp was ultra-careful."

"Knew what he was doing?"

"Unquestionably."

"So who would know how to clean up like that, apart from somebody in law enforcement?"

"Are you kiddin'? Have you seen those American shows on television, CSI, CSI Miami, CSI New York? They're all about forensics, although I have to say that some of the forensic details owe more to imagination than fact. But anybody who watches those shows would probably know the basics about keeping a crime scene clean, keeping their head covered, wearing latex gloves, maybe in exceptional cases some protective gear. Access to a vacuum-cleaner and they're off and runnin'. A wee bit of patience could leave any crime scene clean as a whistle. Sorry, Chief, but this perp clearly had plenty of patience, and some nerve to hang about as long as he did."

"So we're looking for a TV addict?" Sheehan said drily.

The SOCO chuckled. "Might be your best bet," he agreed.

"Doyle says the bathroom's clean, too."

"Immaculate. If the victim was drowned there, there's no way to tell. Not now anyway. Maybe the doc'll find some particulates in the lungs during the autopsy that'll match up with whatever's in this water."

"All right, thanks, Mick." Sheehan took one last look around the room and turned to leave. He met Doyle approaching the door and said, "Nothing much to learn in there. Get the door-to-door started. Get something on the six-thirty local news appealing for witnesses. I'm off down to the Community Centre to see what I can find out about three youths that were giving the victim a hard time."

FOURTEEN

D C. I. Sheehan sat in his office studying a sheaf of reports that had been sent up from Juvenile. He had easily acquired the names of the three youths who had been harassing the Community Centre Supervisor and, as he read the catalogues of burglary, joy-riding, affray, vandalism, drugs abuse, suspected paramilitary and other anti-social behaviours, he could understand why Catherine Higgins had no option but to ban them from the Community Centre. Their crimes, in the main, however, were the petty, disorganised misdemeanours that were so much a feature of the lives of many disaffected youths in any number of pockets of deprivation in and around the city. Marginalised, under-achieving in both social and educational terms, they led generally disruptive, unfulfilled lives, ground down by the generational hopelessness that was their inheritance. But murder?

There was nothing in the files that he was studying that would indicate that Alex Gibbons, 18,

Dermot Patterson, 17, and Jackie McCann, 17, had turned to, or were capable of, criminal activity of that magnitude. And yet, thirty plus years of 'the troubles' had desensitised the city's marginalised youth and hardened their behaviours into violent aggressiveness and other extreme forms of deviance. Many who had fallen victim to paramilitary influence in estates where there were high levels of poverty and unemployment had passed easily from petty crime to murder and other serious offences. Why would these three be any different?

Twenty years on the force, fifteen of them as a detective, had left Sheehan with few illusions. But he hated the cycle of brutality that never seemed to end, that seemed to leave the children of the sink estates with no hope, no future, no way out. He stared at the wall in front of him, unseeing. He had attended a crime scene some dozen years before where a husband had battered his wife to death. He would never forget the horror and distress on the faces of the two young boys, aged only seven and eight, whom he had found in a hall cupboard at the scene, clinging to each other in terror. He looked after them that night, lovely little lads, and was later to find an aunt who promised to bring them up. Sadly, she too lived in one of the most deprived areas in the city and the two boys, men now, were serving life sentences for aggravated assault and murder. What a bloody country!

He turned to the reports collated from the enquiries made by the detectives assigned to the case. Miss Higgins had been a capable supervisor who had run the Centre for the past four years and who had been a force for good in the community. She had a strong sense of social justice and was well-known to have a burning urge to end the cycle of what she had called 'victimhood'. It was her aim to empower the young people in her charge with the intellectual, affective and vocational skills they needed to break out of their disadvantage.

But somewhere along the line she had given in to her sexual leanings. Just before her death, it had become a fairly open secret that she was conducting a supposedly clandestine affair with an underage female child. Sheehan now knew the child to be Joanne, the one he had spoken to in the patrol car. Joanne had told him that the youths who had been banned from the Centre were liars. No doubt she had anticipated accusations of her improper relationship with the Centre Supervisor and was getting her denials in early.

Sadly, most of the good work that Higgins had been doing had suffered as a result of her improper relationship with the child. Tongues had started wagging and in the black and white values system of the deprived and uneducated, there was little hope that she would find understanding or empathy once the full truth became known. Some parents had already begun to prevent their children from attending the centre, discipline was breaking down among those who were still attending, and her subordinates had been wrestling with the obligation to report the situation to their superiors at the City Council.

The first Joanne's mother knew about the liaison, however, was when she heard it from a WPC making enquiries about it. Nonetheless, it is unlikely that much more time would have passed before the information would have reached her. Or had it reached her already? Or members of the extended family? One would not have to search too deeply into any of the families in the area before coming across members with paramilitary connections who would think nothing of murder as a solution to a problem. For many, indeed, murder was often the solution of choice. Was the community worker's deeply inappropriate relationship with the child the motive for her murder

The fact that the victim had been naked earned Sheehan a call from the Assistant Chief Constable who seemed to think that this killing was in some way related to the two cases that Jim Sheehan was working on. But it was early days yet. He had told the ACC that he already had a couple of suspects for this killing and that he was gathering evidence before making an arrest.

"All right, Jim," the ACC had said, "but if it doesn't pan out, you need consider this case related to the other two. That's my take on them."

Two days had now passed since the murder of Catherine Higgins but wanted more reason to call the youths in than the simple fact that they had been banned from the Centre. He was convinced that the parents of Joanne, or some of her relatives, would prove a more fruitful line of enquiry. He had three detectives checking them out but so far, they had little to show for their efforts. It appeared that the family and a number of relations who had been interviewed had known nothing of the illicit relationship. Streetwise these locals might be but his detectives did not credit them with the kind of acting skills that would be required to feign convincing ignorance. This line of enquiry was looking precarious indeed.

Right now, however, he had to deal with the victim's parents. They had come to the mortuary to identify the body and both were inconsolable. It was a part of the job he hated. They were clearly a church-going couple whose faith meant something to them. The mother was weeping as much for the fact that her daughter had been dispatched from this life at a time when she had distanced herself from her childhood faith as she was at the death itself. The father had been pale, shocked and incapable of speech. They lived on the Glen Road and still went to the same church where Catherine had made her first Holy Communion. "We still had hopes that she would find her way back to her faith," the mother had said to Sheehan, "but now ..." And again the tears had flowed.

Sheehan shook his head as if to dismiss the memory. *Dear God, what am I doing in a job that has so much misery attached to it?*

There was a knock on the office door. "Yes, come in," he shouted.

Doyle put his head in. "Lady here I think you need to talk to, sir."

"Who?"

"Witness. Saw our appeal on the Ulster News."

Sheehan put down the papers he was holding and followed Doyle out of the room. There was a nervous looking, middle-aged woman, wearing a maroon, woollen overcoat, standing at Doyle's desk. He stopped. "Doyle, bring her into my office, will you. Go and get her a cup of tea and come in and take notes."

The woman entered Sheehan's office, peering from side to side as she edged towards the chair he had placed in front of his desk. Sheehan beckoned her to sit and said quietly, "Please sit. No need to be nervous. My name is Chief Inspector Sheehan. Could I ask who you are, please?"

The woman sat down gingerly, apparently too frightened to meet his eyes. "I'm Mrs. Josephine Rocks. I saw the thing on the News, y'know, about the murder of that community worker."

Doyle entered with a tray containing a cup of tea and a small jug of milk and a plate of biscuits. Struggling to twist his stolid countenance into something approaching welcome, he said, "I brought you some tea but I didn't know how much milk you take. You'll have to pour it yourself. There's a couple of biscuits here as well."

"Thank you, Detective," she said, gratefully. Tea she understood.

Sheehan allowed her time to pour, sip and nibble before he said, "Do you have something to tell us about the community worker?"

The woman wiped her mouth with her fingers and said, clearly afraid, "You won't tell anybody I was here, will you?"

"We won't tell anyone anything about your visit without your permission," Sheehan assured her. "I can promise you that."

After another moment's hesitation, she said tentatively, "The woman who was killed; I knew her."

Sheehan nodded for her to go on.

"The other night, Monday around nine o'clock, she was in Beechmount Street. Her car was parked there. So was mine. I was coming round the corner and I heard her shouting at three wee hoodies who had damaged her car or something ..." She looked at Sheehan, fear still there. "If they ever hear it was me who told you ..."

"It'll be fine, Mrs. Rocks. Please, go on."

"Well, they were very nasty and I was scared, so I hid round the corner until they would go away. When Miss Higgins was getting into her car to drive away, one of them, the biggest guy, shouted after her ..." She sat up and stared at Sheehan in fearful earnestness. "Please, sir, don't ever let them know I reported this, but I have to. He shouted something about the naked murders in the paper and that she would be next."

She sat back, terrified now that her secret was out in the open, staring at the two policemen.

Sheehan was stunned. He glanced at Doyle whose ball-point was frozen above his notepad. "Mrs.

Rocks," he said, "you did absolutely the right thing reporting this to us. And don't be worrying. These three will never be any threat to you. I'll see to that. Now, you didn't happen to recognise them by any chance?"

"They were all wearing those coats with the hoods on but they were under a lamp and they were jumping around banging each other's hands. One of the hoods fell down and I recognised the boy under it. He's caused a lot of trouble in our area. Everybody knows him."

"Do you know his name?"

Mrs. Rocks stared at him, reluctant to speak further.

"Please, Mrs. Rocks. If they're responsible for one death, you don't want another on your conscience."

"He was Alex Gibbons. God forgive me, I used to know his mother. What'll she ever say if she finds out that I ..."

"Don't worry about that, Mrs. Rocks. We'll do everything in our power to keep your name out of it." *Until you have to appear on the witness stand. Dear God, the lies we tell.* "Don't say anything to anybody about this."

"Are you joking? I didn't even tell my husband. If he ever found out I was here ..."

"I understand. Do you need a lift home?"

"Oh no, no, no, no, I'll get home on me own, thanks. Last thing I want is a patrol car appearing at the house."

"Very well, Mrs. Rocks. Thank you for coming in. You've been very helpful. We'll take it from here."

FIFTEEN

DC I Sheehan fidgeted in his office while Doyle arranged for the three suspects to be picked up. It had been a couple of hours since he issued the command but he was not expecting an immediate response. This was Northern Ireland. Single patrol cars with a couple of officers did not drive up to a house in the working class estates and bundle residents out into the back seat of the car, especially on a Saturday afternoon. Protection had to be arranged. Armoured land-rovers with armed officers would have to accompany the detectives. Recent rioting in some of the loyalist estates was not making the situation any easier. Only yesterday evening, some two hundred or so youths and children had been rioting in the Rathcoole estate, ostensibly, according to a local spokesperson, because of recent police searches in the area. A bus driver had been assaulted and his bus burnt. The nationalist areas on the west side had been relatively quiet but his detectives would still be lucky if they got back to the station with nothing more than a few stones thrown at them.

He stared at the phone on his desk, pondering on whether or not he owed the ACC the courtesy of a call. If the three youths had anything to do with the murder of the community worker, and there was every reason to suspect that they had, it was unlikely that there could be any connection between this killing and the others he was working on. But the ACC had been very insistent there was a link. He shook his head, dismissing the idea. Bit early for that.

A knock on the door was followed by Doyle's head peering in at him. "They've McCann and Patterson in one of the interview rooms, sir."

Sheehan sat up. "Separate them immediately," he ordered, "before they get time to collude on some fabricated story. And where's Gibbons?"

"Scarpered, sir. He must have got wind of the other two being lifted. They can't find him anywhere."

"Get down and separate those two right away. Send me the detectives who brought them in."

"Yessir." Doyle's head disappeared.

The DI sat drumming the fingers of his right hand on the desk until Sergeants McCammon and McCullough knocked and came into the room.

"Where's Gibbons?" Sheehan asked.

"We couldn't find him, sir. He's gone to ground." McCammon sounded apologetic.

"What is he, a master criminal with a network of connections?" Sheehan said, irritaated "He's only a cretinous hoodie, for crying out loud. If you can't figure out where he's likely to hide before he figures it out himself, you don't deserve to call yourselves detectives. Here!" He almost threw Gibbons's file at McCammon, the senior of the two men. "The answer's in there. He can't be too far away from the Upper or

Greater Falls; he has no resources for an extended flight. He's holed up somewhere fairly close. Check his known associates, relatives."

McCammon began to leaf through the file, McCullough, on his toes, trying to peer over his shoulder.

"And don't forget to check with the Neighbourhood Police Team," Sheehan continued. "They'll have established links with community representatives and local residents. Not too many of them will have any great love for Gibbons. Somebody will know something. Now, go and get him." The chastened detectives turned to leave. Sheehan called after them, "And for God's sake, make sure you've some protection with you when you pick him up. Get Doyle to organise it."

He sat back on his chair, his eyes ranging the clutter on his desk - the files, the pens, various reports, the phone, the laptop - seeing none of it. One case or three? If what the chief had surmised was true, there was only one one. Truth to tell, he was leaning that way himself. *Dammit. Let's see what the wee buggers downstairs have to say.*

He reached for the phone and dialled Doyle's desk. "McCammon and McCullough en route yet?"

"It's organised, sir. They're waiting for the land-rover."

"Right. What about the two we've got?"

"Cooling their heels, sir. Separate rooms like you ordered."

"They're minors, right? Parents here, or solicitors, or some adult support?" He should go down there and wring the truth out of the two wee thugs but Sheehan felt the need to work by the book..

"Nobody yet, sir. But they haven't been cautioned or anything. Maybe they might just talk to us voluntarily, y'know, help us with our enquiries? Some of these lads are happier without parents knowing what they're up to. And, sir, it'll be easier to find 'the lie' if there is no solicitor present either."

The lie! The time during the interview when a witness damns himself with a lie. So much easier to engineer during an interview when the witness does not believe himself to be under arrest. Sheehan pondered this for a moment. Doyle just might be on to something. "Okay," he said. "Wait there. I'll be down in a minute."

SIXTEEN

DC I Sheehan found Doyle standing at the door leading into the corridor where the interview rooms were situated.

Sheehan said, "Who's where?"

"We've Patterson in Room One and McCann in Room Two."

"What's your assessment?"

"McCann's trying to brazen it out, sneering, putting his feet up on chairs, generally acting tough. Seems to have a sly intelligence. Patterson's a nervous wreck. Scared out of his skull. I'd guess that any trouble he's been in was due to peer pressure, probably scared to do the things recorded on his sheet and probably too scared of his mates not to do them."

"All right, we'll talk to him first. How do we handle it?"

"Jump all over him from the word go, sir. He'll crack like a peanut."

Sheehan nodded and the two detectives went

down the corridor and into Interview Room One. The seventeen year old behind the table was a sorry sight, huddled on his chair with his hands joined between his knees, pale, shaken, eyes almost out of his head as he stared from one to the other of the two detectives who had come into the room. Both men sat opposite the suspect, Doyle sitting back on his chair with arms folded, Sheehan, grim-faced, setting a small tape recorder in front of the youth. He switched on the machine and stared into the eyes of the trembling boy for some seconds before barking, "Name?"

The youth jumped about six inches on his chair at the sudden crack of the Chief Inspector's voice. He seemed too paralysed with fear to answer. Sheehan found it strange that a youth with a record of misdemeanours as long as Patterson's should be so cowed. Perhaps there was something to what Doyle had surmised. "Name?" he snapped again, leaning forward belligerently.

"Uh ... Dermott Oliver Patterson," the boy croaked.

"Address?"

"Twenty-seven B, Whiterock Road."

"Do you know why you are here, Mr. Patterson?"

"N ... n ... no."

"You're simply here to help us with our enquiries, right?"

The youth stared his ignorance.

"We have a problem. You might be able to help us out. You're happy to do that, aren't you?"

The youth stared again.

"Aren't you?" Sheehan growled.

"Y ... yes, sir. But I don't know nathin' about nathin'..."

"Oh, but we think you do ..." Sheehan let that hang as he watched the boy's slow brain trying to make sense of it. Then he said, "Why did Gibbons scarper?"

The youth recoiled. "What?"

"Gibbons went into hiding when he heard that you were invited into the station to help us with our enquiries. Why do you think he did that?"

Patterson's sluggish brain was in overdrive and the pressure was showing on his face. *Who knows what misdemeanours are charging around in his head*, Sheehan was thinking. *He doesn't know which ones we might know about. Or maybe he knows exactly which one we know about.*

The boy's lips were in constant motion as he sought to answer. Eventually he said, "I dunno."

"You don't know? Do you think maybe he thought you were under arrest?"

"I dunno."

"Are you under arrest?"

"I dunno."

"You are not under arrest, okay? You know why you're here? To help with our enquiries. All right?"

The boy nodded, ill-at-ease.

"How long have you been pals with Gibbons?"

The answer came slowly, like an admission of a crime. "Since primary school."

"Since primary school? And now you're trying to tell me you don't know how he thinks?"

"I don't. Gibbo does what he likes. We never know what he's going to do."

"We? Who's we?"

"Me and Jackie McCann."

"Oh? Gibbo's the leader of your gang, is he?"

"He's the smart one."

"Oh? He's the one who comes up with all the ideas?"

"Yes."

"Uh huh! And was it his idea for you all to kill Catherine Higgins?"

The youth's mouth flew open and he stared, stunned, at the inspector. Sheehan felt a spasm of uncertainty. There was no way this reaction was feigned. The accusation had come as a complete surprise to the boy. Patterson gasped and tried to frame a coherent answer. "Wha ... no ... that wasn't us. We niver ..."

Sheehan stared at him. "And I suppose you are also going to tell me that you three did not threaten her a few evening ago on Beechmount Street."

Fear flashed in the youth's eyes. He struggled to deny the accusation. "No ... no ... we ..."

Sheehan waved a sheet of paper in the boy's face. "We have a full statement from a witness who saw and heard everything that happened that night." He looked down at the paper and read slowly, "*Did you see about those naked murders in the paper? Guess who's next.*" He stared at the boy. "Do you deny shouting that?"

"That wasn't me. I didn't ..."

"If it wasn't you, who was it?"

The youth's head went down. "It wasn't me, mister. It wasn't me."

"Well, who was it then?"

The boy's face was screwed up in fright but he did not reply.

Sheehan leaned forward and roared, "Who was it?"

The youth recoiled, hands raised in front of his chest to defend himself. He stared at the detectives for a moment and then whispered, "Gibbo."

Sheehan leaned back, a surge of satisfaction coursing through him. "Ah, Gibbo," he said. "Gibbo told Catherine that she was next?"

Patterson nodded, on the edge of tears now.

"And why did he say that?"

"She was corrupting and abusing one of the wee girls outa the neighbourhood. She was a slut and had to be punished," the boy said, with a degree of animation. It sounded like something he had learned by rote.

"So, you murdered her?"

"No, no, we niver. Gibbo was just mouthing off. It was on'y a joke."

"A joke? And yet, a couple of days later, Catherine is found murdered, and naked, just like Gibbo said. You're telling me that's a joke?"

The youth stared at him, confused, his mind wrestling with possibilities. "I didn't do it. It wasn't me. Maybe ..." He fell silent.

"Maybe what?" the Inspected pressed.

"Sometimes they tell me I'm useless. Maybe they ... somebody ... done it but wouldn't tell me because I wouldn't do that."

Sheehan eyed Doyle who was staring speculatively at the youth. This had caught them both by surprise and yet, looking at the wretched figure huddled before them, Sheehan had to admit to himself that the pitiful surmise was credible.

"Where were you on the night of the twenty-seventh of October between nine o'clock and three am?"

The youth's face screwed up. "I dunno. What night was that?"

"Last Wednesday night, the night Catherine was murdered. You remember that night, don't you?"

"Yes. I was at home. I wanted to see the match on TV."

"Who else was there?"

"My da. My bro'r ..."

"You know that we'll be asking your father to

confirm this."

"He will, mister, he will. Honestly, he will."

"Where was Gibbons that night?"

"I don't know. He might have been lookin' at the tele in his own house, I think."

"So he wasn't with you?"

The boy made to reply, hesitated, sensing a trap of some kind.

"Well, which is it. He was watching the match with you or he wasn't. And don't lie, boy. This is a murder enquiry."

Patterson slumped, defeated. "He wasn't at my house."

Sheehan sat back. He knew that he had reached a dead end with Patterson. Further questioning would be futile. He stared at the boy for a few seconds longer and then, turning, signalled to the sergeant with his eyes. He spoke into the recorder. "Interview ends, seven ten, pm."

The two detectives left the room. Sheehan said, "What do you make of that?"

"No way he's that good an actor, sir. I think he's telling the truth. He wouldn't have the nerve to cope with anything like murder."

"You think his two mates carried it out on their own?"

Doyle's eyes drifted to Room Number Two. "One way to find out, sir."

Sheehan nodded. "All right. Lead the way." Then he added wearily, "You take the lead this time."

SEVENTEEN

Decades of conflict have left their mark on the predominantly nationalist Falls Road, situated on the west side of Belfast. Although it is today a relatively safe place, many sightseers and tourists still feel more than a *frisson* of tension as they follow tour guides down through its length, down past its many political murals and boarded buildings. Eyes stare in awe at the murals depicting men in paramilitary battle gear, carrying machine rifles, their heads covered by balaclavas. They stare, silenced, at the huge metal gates that separate the Catholic 'Falls' from the Protestant 'Shankhill', one of many so-called 'peace walls' that are dotted all over the city to separate warring communities. Police cars still patrol the area nervously but the west side has pretty much signed up to the peace arrangements.

Political agreements aside, however, there still remains that instinct to lawlessness found in the gangs of feral youths who nightly roam the maze of side streets and estates that are found bordering the main Falls Road along the whole of its length. Affray, rioting, joy-riding, stoning ambulances and police vehicles, are among the more common forms of evening amusement enjoyed by these young citizens. This fact had not slipped the consciousness of detectives McCammon and McCullough as they drove in front of an armoured police vehicle, passing the huge mural of Bobby Sands, the hunger striker who had died at the Maze prison during the height of 'the troubles'. While the two detectives did not anticipate any trouble, their senses were on edge and McCullough's tension was evident from the tightness of his grip on the steering wheel.

"They'll be getting ready for Hallowe'en," McCammon said, his eyes focused on both sides of the road, "but there'll be plenty of fireworks tonight as well. Try to ignore any squibs some smart wee fecker will throw at us. In and out, okay?"

McCullough nodded. They were heading now for Iveagh Crescent, situated far inside the warren of side streets, drives, parades and crescents that fall away from the main road. The chief had been right. Gibbons' file revealed that, among other things, he had been arrested along with an older cousin some months earlier for an attempted break-in at a chemist's shop in Andersonstown. The cousin, Aidan Rooney, lived alone in a small rented terrace house in Iveagh Crescent. Intelligence from the Neighbourhood Police Team had confirmed, however, that someone else had been seen earlier that day going into the house.

It had taken a couple of hours to secure and validate this information and dusk was fast approaching as the patrol car, followed by the armoured land-rover, prowled through the side streets. The Saturday night jackals were gathering. Gangs of youths stood at street corners, jacket hoods covering their heads and faces. All eyed the police vehicles, their silence and stillness unnerving. Individually, each youth would have exuded little of threat. Gathered, however, in gangs like these, anonymous, faceless, alien, their aura was sufficiently menacing to test the stoutest heart.

As McCullough drove along Iveagh Drive, across Iveagh Street, looking for the turn that would lead them into Iveagh Crescent, Sergeant McCammon said, "In and out, McCullough. No hangin' about." He stared out through the side window. "Look at the wee bastards, just itching to start something." A crack from an exploding banger sounded and another one, spitting orange sparks, landed on the road in front of them. "Ignore them," McCammon said tersely.

The armoured vehicle behind them flashed its headlights, signalling that they had passed their turn. McCullough reversed and turned into Iveagh Crescent. This street was empty. They quickly found the number they were looking for, a narrow red-bricked house with a small iron gate in a tiny hedge about four paces from the front door. The detectives remained in the car, waiting for their armed colleagues to ease themselves from the land-rover and position themselves front and back of it with their machine rifles aimed loosely at both ends of the crescent. The small terrace house was in darkness and showed no signs of life. When the protection detail was established the two detectives got out of their car and approached the front door, nerves jangling with tension.

McCammon banged on the door. "Aidan Rooney," he tried to shout. It didn't come out right, more a croak than a shout. He cleared his throat and tried again. "Police." There was no response.

McCammon banged on the door again. "If you do not come out now we will break your door down. We have reason to believe you are harbouring a fugitive." He stood back and tried to look in through the front window.

McCullough added his voice. "If you do not come out immediately, you will be arrested."

Shadowy figures began to appear on the street, standing well away from the scene but watching closely. The armed officers at the land-rover began to stiffen, their eyes locked on the small knots of spectators. One hissed to the two detectives, "Kick the bloody door in and get on with it, for God's sake."

McCammon raised a booted foot to kick the lock when the door suddenly opened and a shadowy figure stood there with his hands raised. McCammon, startled, lost his balance and fell back a couple of paces. McCullough caught his arm and steadied him.

The figure at the door could now be discerned as a stout, bald, forty-year-old man, wearing a grimy singlet and jeans. "I'm Aidan Rooney," he blustered. "What do you want, threatening me like that? I have rights."

McCammon, angry at the embarrassment of stumbling, grabbed the man by the arm and frog-marched him to the armoured vehicle. "Stay there," he rasped. He went back to McCullough who was still standing by the door. "Find the hall light," he said, "we're going in."

McCullough fumbled along the wall of the narrow hall and found a light switch. He flicked it on and nervously followed his partner who was now too incensed to be apprehensive.

"Gibbons," McCammon bellowed into the house. "If you're here, you better come out now. Make this difficult for us and you're in all sorts of trouble, ye wee bastard." There was silence. "D'you hear me, Gibbons?" McCammon roared. "Don't make me have to come looking for you."

There was a sound from the back kitchen. Both men tensed, hands diving instinctively to truncheon handles, as a pallid youth, skinny, wearing a hooded fleece, jeans and sneakers, inched into the hall, hands above his head. "Don't shoot. Don't shoot. I'll come out."

McCullough stared at him in disgust. *This is what we were afraid of?* His own ire rose and he caught the youth under an arm and propelled him along the hall and down the path to their vehicle.

"Hey, who're you pullin', pig?" the youth shouted, attempting bravado.

"Get in there," McCullough snapped, pulling the back door open and practically throwing the youth in one-handed. He turned to Rooney. "And you," he growled, waving a finger in the man's face, "consider yourself lucky we're not taking you in with him."

EIGHTEEN

M cCann was sitting with the chair balanced on its back legs, his feet on the table, crossed at the ankles. "Who're youse?" he asked, as the two detectives entered the room. Sheehan closed his eyes, torn between irritation and his usual depressed wondering about the kind of upbringing that could have inculcated such appalling insolence in this youth. Doyle, unburdened by liberal qualms, kicked the chair from under the youth, sending him sprawling to the floor.

"We're your elders," he rasped. "That's who we are. Get back in that chair and show us some respect."

Less cocksure, but still bristling with attitude, the youth pulled the chair to the table and sat back in it with his legs defiantly spread in front of him. "That's intimidation," he said, "I'm reporting you for that."

Doyle leaned his huge bulk across the table and, with his face about two inches from that of the startled youth, he roared, "You're gonna do what? You're

130

gonna do what?"

McCann was leaning as far back as the chair would let him. Still attempting bluster, he said, "Hey, pull your face away, you."

"Pull my face away?" Doyle continued to shout, veins showing on his neck. "Pull my face away? If you don't sit properly in that chair and start answering questions, it'll be your face I'll pull away. Sit up ... NOW." He sat back and watched with a measure of satisfaction as the youth, thoroughly unmanned, did as he was told. It was, however, as far as that interview was concerned, the only satisfaction he was to experience.

The interview progressed in much the same manner as the one with Patterson. Alternating between swagger and reluctant acquiescence, McCann told a story that differed little from Patterson's. His shock at being accused of murder was genuine; his ignorance of the details of the murder could not have been feigned. He admitted to having heard Gibbons say that they "... should do the bitch in" but denied any involvement in the subsequent murder. Like Patterson, under Doyle's persistent questioning, he betrayed an anxiety about the likelihood that Gibbons might have been involved. But, again like Patterson, he sought to distance himself from involvement by saying, "Maybe it was them other two what done it and they niver told me."

When it became obvious that they were wasting their time, Sheehan signalled Doyle to terminate the interview. Outside the room Doyle said, "I don't know what we'll get from the Gibbons guy but those two have no involvement in this."

Sheehan was forced to agree. "Yes, we're going to have to let them go, but that doesn't mean Gibbons is in the clear. Those two could never handle themselves in the aftermath of a murder. They'd give themselves away in no time. Gibbons could easily have figured that and might well have gone solo on the killing."

NINETEEN

PART 1

Jim Sheehan's apartment was situated on the Ormeau Road, a safe residential district. On his way home, he would pass St. Malachy's Church in Alfred Street, not far from the City Hall. Always he passed it. This evening, however, seeing light emanating from the church door, he stopped for reasons he could not fathom, parked his car and went to the entrance. There was something autonomic about his movements, about the state of his will. He did not know why he had stopped. He did not know why he was going into the chapel. He could still think, however, and he kept asking himself, "What's this all about? Why am I going into this church?"

The Saturday evening Vigil Mass was in progress as he entered and sat in one of the back pews. The church was newly renovated and it had recently hosted a visit from politicians and luminaries from across all denominations in the city. Sheehan stared at the gleaming white marble altar, at its impressive furnishings, but his gaze slipped quickly off the tabernacle as if it were covered in ice. He raised his eyes to the vaulted ceiling. He remembered having heard somewhere that it had been built in imitation of the Henry VII chapel at Westminster Abbey. He experienced awe at its architectural magnificence but again he asked himself, "What the heck am I doing here?"

Mass was almost over. People were returning to their seats after having received Holy Communion. Sheehan watched them with no thoughts of his own. His eyes strayed again to the tabernacle and, as before, flitted immediately away from it. Moments passed in that strange state of unawareness until suddenly he heard the priest giving the congregation the final blessing. Everyone stood up as the priest left the altar, and began to file out. Sheehan continued to sit in the back pew, staring at the people as they passed by him, acutely aware of each one, of the elderly lady who wore an oddly flamboyant pink scarf with a simple plain coat, of the well-dressed, thirty year old yuppie-type who seemed as out of place as himself, of the two nuns who walked together, silent, heads bowed. His observation skills were still intact. He could have offered anyone who might care to ask full descriptions of all of the people who had passed him. But what he could not do was to hazard even a guess as to why he was sitting there, in the back of a church, afraid to look at the tabernacle yet reluctant to leave.

The church quickly emptied and the sacristan went about the business of preparing to lock up, blowing out candles, clearing the credence table of the gold chalice and other vessels, checking the confessionals to ensure that they were empty of opportunistic homeless, locking the side doors, standing somewhat impatiently near the main door, waiting for this last recalcitrant penitent to leave. Jim realised with a start that he was keeping the man back. He left his seat hurriedly, with an awkward bob towards the altar as a sudden twinge of pain hit him mid-genuflection, gave the man an apologetic glance on his way out and stood, again mystified, on the steps outside. *What was that all about?* His mobile phone rang and reality intruded.

PART 2

Inspector Williams was cursing himself. He was cursing that propensity that drove him to tortured introspection if he was tempted to ignore a superior's orders. Was it a trait that spoke of honesty and integrity? Was it a trait that labeled him a coward? He shifted guiltily, convinced that honesty had nothing to do with it, that it was his fear of the consequences that would not allow him to make autonomous decisions, to disobey orders when decisive action might result in a serious collar. He sat glumly at his desk, his mind stuck in well worn grooves. Every time he went down these tracks, his self-image took a trouncing.

He yearned to close the social worker's murder, to bring a clearly documented, unassailable result to the ACC. And he was convinced that he would have a result if he could lean hard enough on this Gibbons guy and force a confession from him. But the dread of the ACC's inevitable comment, "I thought I asked you to bring DCI Sheehan in on this?" was giving him pause. He knew that he could field the question if Gibbons was proven to be the murderer. He had no problem with that. But what if Gibbons had an alibi? What if he had, in fact, only been "mouthin' off", as young Patterson had claimed? And that other wee thug, McCann, he was as annoying as hell but there were elements of truth in his denials. He was guilty of all sorts of petty misdemeanours but he seemed genuinely clueless about the details of the social worker's murder. That didn't mean that Gibbons wasn't guilty, of course, but initially all three were hot suspects. Now we're down to Gibbons himself. What if he, too, was as innocent as his cronies? How was he going to stand in front of the ACC and tell him he had nothing when the ACC had been sure that there was a connection between this case and the two that Sheehan was working on?

He shook his head in self-disgust as his hand, almost of its own volition, reached for the phone.

PART 3

Sheehan was standing at the entrance of St. Malachy's, still wondering what he was doing there, when his mobile phone rang. He reached for it automatically. "DCI Sheehan."

"Fred McCammon here, Chief. We have Gibbons is custody."

"Great. I'll be right there."

TWENTY

"It'll be interesting to hear what he has to say about this," Sheehan said, when he met McCammon at the station. . "There's a certain sophistication about the way all of this has been done. Does your suspect have that kind of moxy?"

"Moxy?"

Sheehan grinned. "My da used to say that all the time. Never actually asked him what it meant. I think it means some kind of mixture of brains and courage."

McCammon looked dubious "Gibbons? I'm not sure," he said, adding with more force, "Tell the truth, I can't see it. He's stewing in one of the interview rooms. Want to go and hear what he has to say?"

"Sure. Lead on."

When Sheehan stepped into the interview room, he felt deflated. Despite his reservations, he had entertained vague hopes that by some serendipitous fluke they had stumbled upon their killer. One look at the pale, skinny youth, his blotchy, spotted face, the rings in his nose and lower lip, told him that his hopes were vain. Whatever tenuous profile they were developing about their killer, nothing in it would point to the waste of space that was sitting in front of him.

Sheehan eased himself into a chair beside McCammon who began informing the recorder of the time, the date, the name of the suspect and the fact that DCI Sheehan and Sergeant McCammon were conducting the interview.

Gibbons was sitting at the other side of the table, hands folded in his lap, his expression neutral. *He's been around the block a few times, this one,* Sheehan was thinking. *He's not going for the aggressive, 'don't dis me' attitude. Probably learned some time ago that it doesn't work.* He stared at the youth who was studying his folded hands. There was a feral stillness about him. He may not have carried out the murders they were preparing to question him about but the day would come when he would be guilty of serious crimes of his own.

"So why did you run away?" McCammon said, without preamble.

"Run away?" The youth's expression simulated genuine puzzlement although both detectives knew that he fully understood the question.

McCammon remained patient. "You went into hiding with your cousin when we picked up your two mates. Why did you do that?"

"Hiding? I was only staying with him for a few days. We're good mates."

This could go on for hours, Sheehan thought impatiently. He raised an eyebrow at McCammon who nodded assent.

"We've got your fingerprints and DNA on the weapon," Sheehan stated flatly. "Are we going to spend all day pretending that you did not commit this murder?"

He got a strong reaction but not the one he had been hoping for. "DNA? Fingerprints? But I've still got … I mean, I don't have no weapon, so how could my prints be on the murder weapon?" The mystification this time was genuine as the youth struggled with the complexities of what had been said. It was obvious that he still had his weapon, whether it was a knife or a gun. That gave him the certainty that the DCI was lying. It was also obvious that he was presuming that it was either a knife or a gun that had been involved in the social worker's killing, in which case he could not have been involved. He clearly knew nothing about the rope or the drowning.

The youth's face cleared, mystification replaced by a cunning awareness. "Ah, I see. Some sort of a trap. You're lying, mister. There's no way you could have my DNA or prints because I wasn't there."

"Wasn't where?" Sheehan said.

"Wherever you found the weapon and the murder you're talking about."

"Where were you around nine o'clock on the night of the twenty-fifth of October?" **McCammon** interjected.

The youth looked blank. "I can't remember. What night was that?"

"It was the night that you and your two cronies, McCann and Patterson, threatened Catherine and told her that she would be next to be found naked and murdered," Sheehan snapped. "Are you trying to tell us that it was a pure coincidence that she should turn up naked and murdered a couple of nights later?"

The youth paled. This was information, very damaging information, that he did not know the police had. He stared at Sheehan, silent, trying to decide whether to go with denial or explanation. His eyes then began to flick from one interrogator to the other, panic beginning to overcome him. Even though he had nothing to do with Catherine's murder, this kind of evidence could land him in court facing a life sentence. He was scared now and it showed. He opted for truth, knowing he could never hold on to a lie in these circumstances. "Right, I did shout that. I admit it. I shouted it. But it was on'y ... we was on'y tryin' to scare her. She was abusin' one of our wee friends. I was on'y after hearin' about them other murders and I just shouted that to scare her. But I niver went near her house. I didn't kill her, I didn't." He looked stricken. His eyes widened as a further thought struck him. "And I don't know nathin' about them other two murders, neither." He was babbling now, truly terrified. "This has to be a stitch up. I don't know how my prints got on that weapon. I wasn't near the place ..." A new thought stopped him. "I want a solicitor here," he said. "I am entitled to a solicitor."

McCammon glanced at Sheehan who looked at the youth and said, "That is your right, of course. But you are not under arrest at the moment. Weren't you aware of that? You are simply helping us with our enquiries."

The youth could not keep his eyes or his hands still. Even his lips were moving agitatedly before he was able to say, "Does that mean I'm ... I'm free to go, if I want?"

"Of course," Sheehan said, indicating the door. "You were always free to leave."

The youth hesitated a few seconds as he sought confirmation from their expressions that the cops were telling the truth before bolting for the door.

"If we do need to arrest you," Sheehan called after him, "we'll always know where to find you." He turned to McCammon shaking his head. "We needn't pin any hopes on him. One look at that wee creep ... I mean, our man is calculating, controlled, methodical, leaves no clues and is physically strong. He goes in like a ghost and comes out like a ghost. That wee thug doesn't match the profile on any count."

McCammon nodded. "Didn't fancy him for it myself when we pulled him in. Wee loudmouth. Nothing more."

"I'm going to take a look over the crime scene. I know the SOCOs have checked everything but I'd like to get a feel for it myself."

"Sure. Do you want me to go with you?"

"No, I'll be fine on my own. I'll probably leave it until Monday morning, anyway. No point in stirring up trouble. Darkness does funny things to the youth of these neighbourhoods. And tomorrow, well, it's Sunday."

TWENTY-ONE

PART 1

A miasma of poverty hung over the streets, clung to the houses, the roads, the very walls. It was unmistakable, tangible, depressing. Its aura was everywhere, penetrating right through to the minds and spirits of the people who lived there. Sheehan hated the ease with which some young thugs in these areas could spring into violence against any of the formal representatives of service or authority – ambulances, fire-trucks, buses, police vehicles. For reasons he never could fully comprehend, vehicles from any of these services called to aid someone in the community became the targets for stonings, bashings with iron bars and sticks and, often enough, set alight with petrol bombs. But as they drove through the narrow streets and the 'crescents' and the 'drives' searching for Rockdale Street, he could not help

142

wondering how his own life might have turned out had he been born into this never-ending cycle of hopelessness.

"Dismal," he said to Doyle who was driving.

"Grim," was the sergeant's response.

Sheehan sighed. His country was universally recognised as one of the warmest and friendliest in the world, particularly welcoming to foreign visitors with our *'cead mile fáilte'* and the great Irish smile. *Yet we are best known now for our violence and our sectarian hatred. What a contradiction. What are we now? Who are we now? Are we a naturally a hostile and intolerant people or have we been driven to that by politics?*

They turned into the victim's street and spotted the house immediately because of the yellow crime tapes sealing off the gate and the front door. Doyle pulled up outside and Sheehan glanced right and left to see if he had attracted any attention. It was after ten in the morning and, while there were some neighbourhood women, carrying plastic shopping bags, walking to or from the main Falls Road in the dry but strong breeze, there was little to worry him. All seemed quiet and there was no sign of the lawless youths who would have little compunction in seeking to cause trouble for a couple of lone policemen in an unprotected vehicle. *Early yet,* Sheehan thought. *Monday morning? They're probably still in bed or maybe at school. Aye, maybe.*

"Keep your eye on the car, Doyle," he said. "I'll try not to be too long but I will be a while." He did not wait for a reply, knowing that there would not be one. He pulled the tape from the gate and from the door and let himself in. He stopped for a moment in the hall, his back to the door, and closed his eyes. The house had been searched and restored to a tidy condition but it was still redolent of death. He felt momentarily like the traveller in De La Mare's famous poem, half suspecting that there might be phantom listeners crowding the narrow stairs at the side of the hall, observing him, resenting him, trying to fathom his purpose.

He shook the image from his mind and went into the living room, familiar to him because of his study of the crime scene photographs. Trying to ignore pain to his hip, he lowered himself into a kneeling position on the floor and began to examine the worn carpet closely, looking for anything that might seem like pen-marks. His examination of the floor was slow and meticulous. On both knees now, he inched carefully along the area where the body had lain, pulling back the worn carpet fibres to search for any marks that might have been recently made there. He found nothing. He expanded the search to the whole floor. Still he found nothing. He moved his focus, with the same painstaking care, to the back and sides of the sofa, to the walls, to the TV, to the small occasional table on which it sat. Still nothing. Clambering to his feet, he emitted a frustrated breath, staring again around the small room. A thought caused him to jerk his head towards the ceiling. His eyes ranged it from corner to corner but apart from the fact that it could do with a good coat of paint, maybe two, he learnt nothing else from his scrutiny.

He went into the narrow hall, dark there despite the morning light outside. He tried the light switch. The light came on. Power NI must not yet have got round to switching the power off. He studied the walls, peeling brown paint with several names and scrapes that were probably clues to a succession of tenants who might have rented the place. He felt its desolation again. Catherine must have loved her job to live in a place like this. She could have afforded better. Did she want to be near and be part of the community she served?

Marks on the wall, half-way up the stairs, caught his attention. He climbed the couple of steps closer. They seemed relatively fresh, definitely a capital E, then something indecipherable because a fleck of paint had fallen off, and then some numbers. He could just about make them out. His heart twitched. Was this what he was looking for? Peering closer, he slowly deciphered the numbers … 2 … 0 … 0 … 9. He studied the marks. "E … something … 2, 0, 0, 9," he muttered.

His heart was beating faster now, not that he was any the wiser but simply because he felt that he had moved a step closer to his killer. Then chagrin hit him.

You've moved nowhere, y'eejit! That's somebody's initials and last year's date. He stood up, his arms folded in frustration, and wondered incongruously if those damned listeners on the stairs were laughing at him.

There was only the bathroom left. He was prepared to bet that he would find nothing in the bedroom because that simply did not fit the pattern. The numbers, if there were any, would be near the place where the body was left or maybe where she was killed.

The bathroom was small, worn linoleum on the floor, stained bath and sink, but clean. He gave every inch of it his fullest attention but, as before, he found nothing. His brow was creased as he left the room, drying his hands on the back of his trousers after having briefly washed them in the sink. Could it be that this is not my killer at all? Maybe he made assumptions without sufficient evidence, something he hated to do, simply because of a very tenuous 'profile'. He should have known better. Police profiling was nowhere nearly so informative or as functional as its fictional counterpart on television.

But his instinct rebelled. Not Gibbons. No. He just doesn't … he had to stop himself from thinking 'fit the profile.' But if Catherine's murderer was the perpetrator of the 'naked killings', there had to be another set of those numbers somewhere. Maybe. But they were not in this house. Sheehan was prepared to bet a week's salary on that. His examination had been thorough. But if not here, then where?

He went back down stairs, and stopped one last time to stare at the body-trace on the living room floor. Without conscious thought, he muttered, "God have mercy on your soul, girl!" and left the house. He made a half-hearted effort to stick the tapes back again and got into the car.

Doyle gave him a 'where now?' look.

"Back to the incident room for another look at the photographs and the evidence," Sheehan said. A thought jolted him. *And for a look at that breeze block.* It was sitting in the evidence locker. It might be worth additional scrutiny.

PART 2

He paced around, his impatience palpable, while Doyle took care of the red-tape required to get the stone to the incident room. He returned to the evidence board, examining again the photographs of the crime scene, the truncated annotations here and there, different views of the body, and the separate photographs of the plastic rope and the breeze block.

146

The officer in charge of the evidence locker entered. He was a tall man, bony shoulders sharply defined in his regulation dark green wool sweater, lanky legs lost in heavy trousers. Only a few strands of grey hair lay across his bald pate but a countenance that might well have been cadaverous appeared warm and open, and the man's eyes crinkled with good humour as he smiled the visitor a wordless greeting. Sheehan knew him by sight but couldn't name him. "You wouldn't have a magnifying glass?" he said to the man.

"Yes, sir, there's one in that desk." The officer crossed the room, opened a drawer and handed the glass to the chief inspector. "There y'are, sir."

"Thanks," Sheehan said. "Do you mind if I take down a couple of photographs from your board, just for examination here at the desk?"

"Of course, sir. Not a bother."

"Thanks."

Sheehan took down all of the photographs of the breeze block and pored over them, scrutinising every inch under the magnifying glass. But if there were any marks on the stone, he could not see them. He did note, however, that, although the breeze block had been photographed from a number of different angles, it had not been moved from its original position. *It'll be interesting to see what's underneath it*, he was thinking, when Doyle came into the room with the block in his arms. He was slightly flushed. It was only one block but he had had to climb a flight of stairs and carry it along two corridors. He placed it on the desk in front of the chief inspector and said, "I'm going down to the canteen for a cup of coffee. Do you want any?"

"No, you go ahead. I'll come down and get you when I'm finished here."

Seeing the breeze block in the reality, Sheehan was struck anew by its total incongruity. The girl had been drowned. The rope had left virtually no trace on her neck and the stone had been just sitting there. What in heaven's name could it mean? Or was it an insane irrelevance in the killer's mind that had no meaning? But the rope had been tied around the block and attached to the girl's neck. It had to have some significance. He picked up the glass and studied the pitted surface. Nothing on the top side. Nothing on the sides either. He turned it over and tensed when he saw some gouges scraped into the cement. He could not quite tell if the marks were uniform. They were crudely done, possibly because the surface was porous and brittle. "Do you have any fingerprint powder handy?" he called over to the Office Manager.

"I'll get you some, sir."

The policeman left the room and returned in a few minutes with the powder.

"Could you just stand there ..." Sheehan said, "Sorry, what's your name again?"

"Jones, sir."

"Of course, Jones. I want you to witness what I'm doing."

Jones nodded mystified acquiescence.

Sheehan spread a thin dusting of the powder over the markings on the rock and gently blew it into the crevices. He repeated the process. A pattern began to form. Jones leaned forward, interested now. Sheehan's stomach was taut. He was pretty sure that he was about to prove that Catherine was the third victim of the killer they were hunting.

"Can you read that?" Sheehan asked him.

"I think so, sir. It looks like an E and maybe a year or something ..." He bent closer. "Sixteen forty seven." He gave Sheehan a lop-sided grin. "Charles the First was beheaded in sixteen forty-nine, if that's any help, sir."

"What was he doing in sixteen forty-seven?" Sheehan muttered, not demanding an answer, focused instead on the realisation that his hunch had been right.

But Jones was rather enjoying himself. "If I remember rightly, it was about that time that Charles was getting up Cromwell's nose, bringing in the Scots to fight the Parliamentarians and attempting to impose Presbyterianism on England. That was a couple of years or so before he was beheaded."

Sheehan stared at the numbers. 1 6 4 7. "Cromwell, huh? Doesn't get us very far."

"Not a whole awful lot, sir," Jones agreed, grinning.

"Could you photograph this?" Sheehan asked.

"Yes, sir. I'll go and get a camera."

Sheehan was mystified. The Office Manager had been talking tongue-in-cheek. Both of them understood that. But Presbyterianism ... religion again. And he was pretty sure that Charles had been married to a Catholic and that his children were Catholic. Could there be anything to Jones's impromptu history lesson? Could his flippant remark have fluked a connection that might otherwise have been missed? He pulled out his notebook to check the other numbers. The bishop's was 3 4 1 0. If that was a year, it was a bit far into the future. Jones came back and took some photographs of the numbers on the block. Sheehan said, still staring at his notebook,

"Know anything about what might happen in three thousand, four hundred and ten?"

Jones peered over Sheehan's shoulder. "Not sure I could stretch to that, sir," he replied cheerfully, "but maybe it's a modern date, like third of April, 2010."

"Maybe. What happened on that day that was interesting?"

"Soon find out, sir," Jones said, sitting before a laptop on one of the desks. "Anywhere in the world, sir, or just Belfast?"

"Keep it local."

Jones's fingers worked the keyboard. "Well, you had the start of the 'Titanic Made in Belfast' week on the third of April."

"Fascinating. Anything else?"

"The Wolfe Tones were performing at Andersonstown Leisure Centre."

"How did I miss that?" Sheehan looked at his notes again. "One four eight mean anything to you?"

"Fourteenth of August?"

"Okay. Do your thing."

Jones jiggled the mouse and clicked a couple of times. He turned to look at Sheehan, an amused grin on his face. "Expo-Nations Celebrations any good to you, sir?"

Sheehan stared back at him. "This is all as clear as mud, Jones."

Jones's grin widened. "Ah, but sure you'll have it all sorted before midnight, sir."

The grin was infectious. Sheehan was smiling despite his frustration as he put the notebook back in his pocket. He headed for the door. Over his shoulder, he said, "Thank you for your input, Jones. Very interesting. Totally useless, of course, but very interesting." As he closed the door, he heard the Officer Manager emit something between a grunt and a strangled laugh.

Sheehan's own lips were twitching as he went to find Doyle in the canteen. The sergeant was sitting at a table with Fred McCammon but got up when Sheehan arrived.

"Doyle, would you go and sign that breeze block back in again, please? We don't want anyone accusing us of distorting the chain of evidence."

Doyle nodded and left.

McCammon staring after him, said, "Wear your ears out, wouldn't he?"

Sheehan grinned. "That's Doyle. Doesn't talk much but he's reliable and steady. Nobody I'd rather have with me if I'm heading out to trouble."

"What's his story?"

"Not sure. I worked with an old sergeant a while back, he's retired now, who knew the Doyle family. Said that the young Doyle was hardly ever allowed out to play with other kids on the street. Probably never got much practice at talking. The father was apparently very puritanical, very controlling."

"Ah, that probably accounts for Doyle's sense of humour."

"What sense of humour?"

"Exactly."

Sheehan grinned again, then said, "Just before I go, Fred. There's something I want to tell you; but keep it under your hat for the time being." He told the sergeant about the numbers found at each of the three crime scenes.

"What do you think they mean?"

"No idea. I had a good chat about them with the guy in evidence … oh, could you make him aware of the need for discretion about them, please? I was so engrossed with what I found on the block, I let it slip that there were two other numbers."

"Okay. What about the Community Worker's killing?

"Hard to say, we're totally guessing now. We need to do a thorough background check on the victim … same as the other two. Maybe something will crop up, maybe it won't. You know police work. We're probably going to have to depend on our perp to make a mistake. His tracks are extremely well covered."

"Maybe there's some sort of connection between the three victims?"

"Aye, right," Sheehan grinned, sure that it was unlikely. Then serious, he added, "but it would be good if we could find one."

Doyle appeared at the canteen door and held up a finger. Sheehan nodded and, rising, turned to McCammon and said, "Could you nip down to Jones in evidence now, Fred, and tell him to keep schtum about those numbers."

Fred rose, too. "On my way. Chief."

TWENTY-TWO

As Detective Declan Connors was about to pull the door of his apartment after him, he glanced once more into the sparsely furnished room that was now his home. His lips tightened. Nothing of his earlier life was reflected there, not his forty inch plasma television, not his favourite armchair, not his music centre and his collection of CDs. The injustice of it washed over him, and he tasted again the same bitter bile that seemed to reside almost permanently in his throat. She was the one who betrayed him and yet he was the one consigned to a miserable poky flat with little but an electric kettle and a few cups to show for the fifteen years of building a home and a life for his family. He banged the door rather more loudly than he should and walked, anger simmering in him, to a nearby bus-stop. *She even took the bloody car. How can that be just?*

The evening, dank, dark and dismal, reflected his mood, a mood which had become more or less permanent. He was heading back to the station. The DCI had called the squad together that Tuesday evening for another debriefing. Connors' anger began to blaze when he jumped off the bus and saw a crowd of media journalists and cameramen milling around the front of the Police Service Northern Ireland station. He had once visited the Spanish town of Pamplona to see the Running of the Bulls. He flexed his muscles and for one insane moment was tempted to charge into the midst of the reporters like one of those bulls and send them scurrying for cover.

Inhaling a deep breath through his nose, he fought the impulse and prepared himself for the barrage of daft questions, many coming from ridiculous assumptions that bore no relationship to the facts. Staring straight ahead, not even bothering with 'No comment', he forced his large body through the throng, eliciting a number of angry 'Heys' and 'Watch it, mates'. From these he derived a sour satisfaction and headed up the stairs to the incident room.

Sheehan was talking to the squad, confirming that the third body, too, had been naked. He was about to outline the details of the killing when Connors came into the room, looking flushed and harassed. "Bloody reporters," he said. "I had to beat my way in here through a whole gang of them, asking loaded questions, trying to write their own fabricated stories. They're lucky I didn't scatter the bloody lot of them."

The others nodded agreement, having run the same gauntlet.

"They're not half stirring it up," Fred McCammon said. "All that crap about the city being 'under siege' and 'people terrified in their beds' and the endless criticism of the police investigators. The TV is every bit as bad. I know there's a nutter running about but the press are starting a panic and doing everything in their power to make us look bad."

"And that guy on the radio with his 'biggest show in the country', constantly going mad trying to get one of us on his show to be interrogated," Miller said. "Did you hear him this morning?" Adopting a passing imitation of the radio host's hectoring voice, he mimicked, "'Three people brutally murdered and what have the police done? Nothing. People scared to go on the streets at night and what are the police doing to reassure them? Nothing. Several times this show has asked DCI Sheehan to come and explain himself to you, the people of Belfast. Where is he? I don't know but he's not here. Do the people not have a right to know …?'"

This lightened the mood somewhat and there were some chuckles. Several of them, listening to their car radios on their way to work that morning, had heard that rant, in exactly those tones.

"There'll be no stopping those reporters now," Doyle said. "And you can be sure we'll have the English Nationals crawling all over us as well." All eyes were upon him. It was not normal for the taciturn sergeant to sound off about anything. Doyle must have been feeling the strain too because, uncharacteristically, he went on speaking. "Think about it. A naked bishop killed in an apparently frenzied stabbing that turns out to be a carefully crafted crucifix on his chest. A naked school principal with a rope around his neck, his stomach hanging out, but not hanged, Kung Fu'd to death. A social worker seemingly garrotted with a clothes line; but not garrotted, drowned. That's sensational stuff. We're

155

going to be tortured by every paper in the country, cameras and microphones up our noses, doorways blocked everywhere we go …"

In anyone else's mouth, the words would have possessed some element of feeling, annoyance perhaps, maybe frustration. Coming from Doyle's mouth, they had all the emotional force of the British Telecom speaking clock.

McCullough eyed him. "Calm yourself, Doyle. You'll do yourself an injury."

This earned him a few grins.

Sheehan said, "That'll do, McCullough." Addressing the whole team he went on, "Doyle's right, so let's not give the nosey bastards anything to work with. We want to keep a lid on as many of the details as possible." He glared at them. "No leaks, right?"

This was met with an uneasy silence as each officer searched his memory, and his conscience, for any injudicious remarks that might have slipped past his lips during the previous few days. Young Tom Allen broke the silence "What are the details of this third murder, sir?"

Sheehan gave them a run down on the murder, the position of the corpse, details of the death, the nature of the crime scene, the futile interrogation of the three adolescent suspects, and his own search of the house and evidence board culminating in his discovery of the letter and numbers on the breeze block. "So, it's definitely ours."

"We're pretty thinly stretched, sir, to be undertaking another whole new set of enquiries." It was McCullough's nasal whine.

Sheehan didn't look up from his notes. He simply said, "DI Williams wants to help. The killing did happen on his patch. He has offered us manpower and resources to help nail this nutter." Then he stared at McCullough. "And we're going to get him no matter how many hours or days or weeks it takes, right?"

"Yes, sir. Of course, sir," McCullough agreed. He was probably sinking back into his chair but his ample bulk simply rippled.

Allen again jumped into the uncomfortable silence. "Three different methods of killing, that's a bit unusual, is it not?"

"Aye, you're right," Fred McCammon agreed. "Usually when a killer finds a method that he's comfortable with, he sticks to it." He turned towards Sheehan. "You're sure it's the same killer, sir?"

"Pretty much. The numbers we found at each scene more or less confirm it."

"Unless you have a couple of killers working together, you know, the alpha male and the submissive one." This from Connors.

"Nothing to indicate that, although the total lack of forensics doesn't indicate anything," Sheehan said.

Bill Larkin was posting the new photographs on the white board and writing truncated notes. He turned away from the board to say, "Maybe it's a male and a female. Maybe that's how the killer gets into the homes. Most people would have few qualms about opening the door to a woman."

"Not you anyway, Larko," McCammon laughed.

"I've been thinking about that …" Allen started.

"What? Opening your door to a woman?" Miller threw in.

Allen grinned. "No, about how the killer keeps getting into the premises without having to break in.

You could be right about a woman partner; she'd certainly know how to clean the place up. But I was thinking more about a priest's collar ..."

Sheehan looked up sharply. "Meaning?"

"Well, if somebody wearing a priest's collar knocked on your door, you'd probably invite him in."

A number of heads nodded and turned towards Sheehan.

"Are we sure that that monsignor's alibi is airtight?" McCullough said.

"The guy in charge of the desk said that nobody could have got past him at that hour of the morning," Gerry Loftus said, flushing a little, making his freckles darker and more defined. The question threw doubt on his ability to check an alibi.

"Yeah, I know," McCullough said, "but maybe ..." His voice trailed away, bereft of an alternative explanation.

Allen's imagination was made of sterner stuff. "No disrespect, Gerry, but you were asking the guy about the monsignor, black suit, clerical collar. You couldn't miss that at seven o'clock in the morning. But what if he wasn't dressed as a priest? There was a big wedding party staying there that night. What if the guy at the desk was busy dealing with early leavers? Would he pass much remark on somebody dressed up in jogging gear and trainers with maybe a wool cap pulled low on his head on a chilly October morning? I'd say there'd be a few joggers that hour trying to clear their heads. The monsignor could have dressed like that and slipped in along with one or two of the others when he got back from Belfast."

The other detectives stared at him, impressed. McLoughlin was nodding but he said, "Aye, but then he wouldn't have been wearing his collar to get into the bishop's house. You wouldn't let a jogger in at midnight or whatever time it was."

"Maybe had a woman with him," Larko offered.

"You've got women on the brain, Bill," Sheehan snapped. "He wouldn't have needed either the collar or the woman, McLouglin. He'd have a key, y'eejit. He lives there."

Larkin turned quickly back to the white board and McLoughlin made a grimace but persisted, "Well, if it was him, he'd need the collar or the woman to get in to the other two houses."

"There's been no mention of any woman in connection with the monsignor," Loftus said.

Sheehan's stomach clenched, suffering sudden doubts. Bad enough if he was wrong about the monsignor but the only woman he connected with him was Margaret.

It took all of his self-discipline to say, "Well, he is friendly with the organist from St. Peter's."

Loftus nodded. "Okay, I'll check her out."

Sheehan signalled agreement but inwardly he was panicking. *What am I doing? Margaret had no more to do with those killings than I had. Why land her in it like this?* But another voice said, *if you had no feelings about her you'd throw her name into the discussion without a qualm. You have to be professional.* Surrendering to the voice, he forced himself to say, "She was with him one time when I called in to see if anything else had cropped up about the bishop. But I have to say …" He shrugged the implicit accusation away. "… she seemed like a nice friendly lady." *Lord, if they find out that I had coffee with her. Why the hell are you hiding it?* "Nothing there that would cause the least suspicion. And the monsignor as well. He seems very above board." He paused to let that sink in and went on, "And what would be their motive? These killings look like the work of a sicko. Maybe they're just random killings." His stomach churned with guilt. *If you thought that one of the squad was squiring a suspect, you'd have his guts for garters. What's going on with you here?*

He forced himself to listen to Doyle who was saying, "Everybody has motive for what they do, no matter how sick it might look to others. They'd have their own clear rationale. Chances are that if we look in the right place we'll find a connection between the victims or between the victims and their killer."

Young Allen had been listening intently. "Maybe these killings … maybe these people had to be killed in these ways for a reason. Sergeant McCammon says that killers like to use the same method all the time, but maybe our killer had no choice about method. Maybe he has his crazy reasons for killing in these particular ways. Maybe there's something to do with ritual in it …"

His words hung in the air. *This kid's going to go far* Sheehan was thinking, dismissing thoughts of Margaret from his mind and forcing himself to focus on the discussion. "Good point, Tom," he said. "And the posing, I'm convinced the bodies were posed, would tend to substantiate that thinking."

"You mean, the bodies were killed in those ways and posed like that to tell us something?" Connors asked.

"It's a theory. One I quite like," Sheehan said.

Allen looked pleased. He'd been thinking a lot along these lines and was emboldened now to

160

continue. "The element of ritual and the element of religion, they seem to match. Maybe if we could get a handle on what exactly the killer is trying to say, we could uncover the motive, and maybe the killer. I've a strong feeling that it has something to do with religion."

"With the bishop, maybe," McCullough said. "But what about the community worker? What has she got to do with religion?"

"It'll be in the killer's head," Allen replied. "And we haven't even started our enquiries about her yet."

"How're your enquiries about the bishop going?" Sheehan asked.

"Myself and Geoff have been checking into that Tridentine Mass thing. There's been one running in St. Paul's on the Falls Road a few times since 2005. There's the occasional Solemn High Mass as well, plenty of Latin in those. There's been a fair wee bit of interest. We've been talking to some of the people who support it."

Geoff McNeill chipped in. "They're all very earnest people and het up ab … ab … about getting the Latin M … M … Mass reinstated, but there's no malice in any of them. I'd stake my life on all of them b … b … being totally innocent."

"Geoff's right," Allen agreed, "but there's a name that's been cropping up, somebody we've yet to see. He's an oldish guy, Jerome Connolly. He runs a weekly prayer group and from all accounts, it's blood and thunder fundamentalism. We're going to have a talk with him later. But he's not a priest; he's an ex-cop."

A sudden pulse electrified the room. Shock? Disbelief? The detectives had been listening

161

attentively to Allen. What he was saying had sounded like a promising lead. But now their attention was total. A cop?

McCammon was the first to speak. The words came out slowly as if they would have preferred to remain unspoken. "A badge and a uniform would get you into people's houses."

"Yeah, we th ... th ... thought of that," McNeill agreed. "That's why we're anxious to t ... t ... talk to him. And he's also got a background in the forces, don't know where, exactly, but c ... c ... combat experience. We still have to check that out."

"Don't pin too much on that," McCammon said, giving the detective a hard look. "A lot of cops have military experience. I served in the army for two years myself. So has Connors."

McNeill's eyes went down and Allen chipped in quickly, "As an ex-cop he'd sure know how to clean up a crime scene, too." Catching McCammon's still smouldering gaze, he added, "Might be nothing, of course. But we're still gonna have to talk to him."

Something shifted in Sheehan's memory. "Connolly? There was a Sergeant Connolly operated out of B District when I was a rookie. Tough man, from all accounts. Maybe it's the same guy. Bloody hell, I hope he hasn't gone rogue."

Doyle said, "If he's that old, would he be capable of the kind of killings that ...?"

"This guy might," Sheehan interjected. "He was an Olympic boxer, as I recall, big guy, a keep-fit fanatic. Maybe he's kept up exercising. But a cop? No disrespect to your thinking, Tom," he said to Allen, "but I hope to God this is a false alarm. A cop? God, we don't need that."

That silenced the room. Then Fred McCammon threw his notes on the desk in front of him. "I'm wrecked. I'm away round to The Crown for an hour or two. Who's coming?"

"Count me in," McCullough said reaching for his jacket.

Sheehan noted McCullough's alacrity and wished sourly that he could see a bit more of it when the squad was working. He was also worried about Fred. These visits to the Crown were becoming uncomfortably regular. Some of the others, Connors, Smith, McNeill and Allen, all indicated interest. McCammon looked at Doyle. "Coming, Doyle?"

Doyle shook his head. "No thanks, Fred. Don't drink."

"I know, but come on round for the craic. Take an orange or somethin'?"

"Thanks Fred, but I'm going to evening Mass."

McCammon turned to Sheehan. "What about you, boss?"

"Not tonight, Fred. I've got plans."

"Oohhh! Do tell!"

Sheehan grinned. "Get outta here, the lot of you. Back to the grindstone in the morning."

TWENTY-THREE

PART 1

Margaret dropped her handbag and briefcase on a low table in the hall, kicked off her high heels and went into the front lounge. She put on a pair of woolly slippers that were lying beside the sofa and went into the kitchen. It had been a long day at school, followed by a rehearsal for the forthcoming school concert. It was well after seven-thirty and she hadn't eaten since lunchtime. She went into the kitchen, wondering, as she always did, whether making a substantial dinner for one was worth the trouble. She looked around. The kitchen had not been tidied since last night, the hall, the bedrooms needed vacuuming and the lounge was a mess. *Why do you hold on to a house this big?* she asked herself for the millionth time. But she knew the answer. Sell the house and she'd lose what was left of her memories of Ed. She

164

sighed. Ten years and his presence still filled the house they had shared together during the few years of their married life.

She shook herself. *Come on, snap out of it. You've been down this road too many times before. No tears tonight. Get cooking.* She looked in the fridge for the packet of chicken nuggets she had bought the day before. A couple of roast potatoes, some chili sauce, and a few deep-fried nuggets and she'd soon sort out her hunger. *Better peel a carrot as well,* she decided in afterthought.

She was washing the potatoes when the phone rang. "Hello?"

"Hi! It's Jim."

"Oh, Jim. Hi!" There was a silence at the other end. "Did you just call to do some heavy breathing or did you want to say something?" she said, grinning.

There was an embarrassed cough and a half laugh. "Oh, sorry, I was just about to ask how you are doing."

"Doing? I'm doing fine. How are you doing?"

"Oh … fine. Fine."

"Good." She knew Jim was struggling but something mischievous in her would not allow her to help him. She waited.

Jim said tentatively, "What are you doing?"

"Goodness, always the policeman. I'm making myself some dinner."

"Oh, God, I didn't mean that how it sounded. I meant, would you like me to join you?"

"You're inviting yourself?"

"No, no, I meant, would you like me to join you,

or rather, you join me, in a restaurant downtown somewhere. I'm inviting you."

She laughed aloud. "Oh, Jim, you are so easily teased. I've dinner half ready. Why don't you come over here and share it with me. As always, I still have the habit of putting on enough for two instead of one. You'd be doing me a favour if you came over here and helped me get rid of the extra."

"I didn't mean to put you to that kind of bother."

"No bother, Jim. I'm already in the middle of it. Are you coming over?"

"Yes, I'd like that. Where do you live?

"Connsbrook Avenue, not far from Sydenham Bypass."

"How do I get there?"

"It's easy. Just drive along the Sydenham Bypass until you come to Kyle Street. Drive along there and on through Connsbrook Drive. That'll take you out on to my avenue. I live in a bungalow in a small cul-de-sac down at the far end. There's a light outside over the front door with red and green glass in it. I'll put that on. You can't miss it."

"That's great, Margaret. I'll be there in about half an hour."

"Good, see you then." She hung up. Yikes! She did some mental arithmetic. She would just have time to get that container of home-made soup out of the freezer, and the apple tart that's in there as well, ready for baking. She looked in the cabinet. Oh God, no wine. Don't panic. No way Jim's going to land in here empty handed. Just time to give the lounge a quick once over and then she had better get cracking.

PART 2

Jim found the avenue easily enough and, as he coasted slowly along its length, he could not restrain a quiver of nerves. He had unintentionally wangled an invite into her home. He was nowhere nearly ready for that kind of intimacy. But she had been so casual. *She only sees it as two friends sharing a meal. Don't try to make it into any more than it is. 'Do you mind if I join you'? What kind of an eejit are you?* He looked at the bottle of wine lying on the front passenger seat. *I hope she doesn't think I'm trying to get her tipsy. Don't be stupid. You can't turn up for a meal at somebody's house and not bring a bottle with you. There's the cul-de-sac.* He turned into it and saw the green and red light on a substantial, up-market bungalow. His insides fluttered. He took a deep breath and parked outside her door.

"Come in, come in," she invited, smiling and standing back to allow him into the hall. She closed the door and led him into the lounge. "Almost ready. Just sit there and listen to the music." Jim held out the bottle. "Oh, is that wine? Good. I'd run out."

Jim stood at the door of the lounge, smiling down at her like a country yokel. She grinned back. "It's not a church, y'know. You're allowed to talk."

"Oh, yes." He looked around. "Nice house." He became aware of the music. "Nice music. I think I recognise it. It's …"

"Bizet, the Pearl Fishers."

"Ah, yes, I like that."

"You into classical music?"

"Light classical, some opera, old pop classics from the forties and fifties …"

167

"Oh, that's something we have in common, then. Here, give me your coat, sit down there and I'll be with you in a few minutes. It's only a snack. If I'd known you were coming ..."

".... you'd have baked a cake," he finished, grinning.

"Exactly. Back in a couple of minutes."

He sat on an armchair and looked around. The room was tasteful, polished wooden floor, some rugs strewn here and there, leather suite, one wall shelved from floor to ceiling and filled with books, a music centre in a corner, and a warm fire in the fireplace. *Right, if this is how she lives, no way I'm ever inviting her to my dump.*

A few minutes later, Margaret came back and said, "Come on into the dining-room."

She has a dining room? Definitely no way she sees my place. She led him back across the hall to a smaller room in which there was a large oval mahogany table with six elegant chairs around it. It was set for two, but both places at the middle and opposite each other. "Go you on round to the far side so that I can run in and out when I need to," she said.

Jim sat and took the ring off a napkin that was sitting on a side plate. Margaret went out and returned with a bowl of soup which she set in front of him. He felt oddly ill-at-ease but said, "This is nice," as he spread the napkin across his knees.

She went and got soup for herself and sat. "Now we can talk."

And they did; small talk, casual references to the weather, local politics, events in the news that had caught their attention. Margaret was happy to let the conversation take this course until she saw signs that

Jim was beginning to thaw. They moved through the small courses, the nuggets, the apple tart with fresh cream, the coffee and then Margaret said, "Let's take our wine into the lounge."

The room was quite warm although the fire was dying. Margaret encouraged Jim to take his jacket off and ordered him to relax. Margaret had been aware for some time during the meal that Jim had something to say to her. Now was as good a time as any. "You didn't just ring up out of the blue, did you?" she said. "Was there something you wanted to say to me?"

Jim was startled. *Is this woman clairvoyant?* But in truth, he had been looking for the opportunity to broach what was troubling him.

"Yes, Margaret. I need to warn you about something."

Her eyebrows went up. "Warn?"

"Aye! The squad had one of our briefing meetings today about these murders, we're still chasing our tails, I'm afraid. But some of the guys were trying to figure out how the killer gets into the homes of the victims without having to break in."

"Obviously the victim must let them in," Margaret said, wondering where this was going.

"Yes, but why? There have been three murders but the same killer. Does he know all of the victims that well? That's the question that's bothering us. One or two of the guys think the killer might have a woman partner, and others are looking again into the monsignor's alibi."

"Monsignor Byrne? Jim, that's ridiculous."

"I think so, too. But in cases like this every lead has to be followed until all doubt has been eliminated."

Margaret's hopes for the evening were foundering on jagged rocks. In a tight little voice, she said, "What's all this got to do with me, Jim?"

Sheehan could not meet her eyes. He had fought with himself all evening whether or not to broach this thorny subject at all but he concluded that Margaret deserved to know. "It's just that your name has come up in connection with the monsignor, y'know, working with him in connection with the parish and the cathedral choir and so on ..."

Two small red patches began to appear on Margaret's cheeks. "Your squad has the monsignor down as a mass killer; and me, what am I? A gangster's moll?" She looked distressed and worried. "Jim, how could you have allowed this?"

He tried to placate her. "It's not like that, Margaret. The detectives are trained to follow leads. They are quite autonomous. I only hear about these things at the debriefing meetings."

"And the monsignor and I are suspects?"

"No, no. They just need to confirm both your alibis and eliminate you from our enquiries."

Margaret's look of hurt grew as did the small flushes high on her cheeks. "I thought you came round here to see me, Jim. Are you only here to check out my alibis for the night of the murders?"

"No, I'm sorry if it looks like that. I did want to spend time with you. But I was very uncomfortable when your name came up today. I just thought I should warn you."

"My social life, as you know, Jim, can hardly be described as hectic. Every night for the past couple of weeks has been spent here, marking schoolwork or preparing music for the choir. Oh, sorry, I had choir practice on two weekends but the murders were mid-week, weren't they? I was here, Jim, on the nights of the murders. I was here alone, so, I don't have credible alibis."

"Margaret, please, don't be like that."

"Don't be like what, Jim?" Margaret was near to tears. She wanted to discuss the issue frankly and coolly but the thought that she might be a suspect and that Jim had allowed his squad to … to what? She had been so looking forward to a night of warm intimate conversation and now, this?

No, she couldn't be cool. She was hurt. She was surprised by how hurt she was. She had been developing feelings for this policeman and here he was … what? Telling her that she was a suspect in a serial killer murder case? "Am I to expect your men to come traipsing all over my house searching for daggers or guns? And come to think of it, why are you consorting with a suspect? Surely that's not allowed?"

Jim rose from his seat and made to move towards her. Margaret rose too and moved away from him. "Margaret, please, it's just a routine enquiry. I just wanted you to be prepared for it if anyone came knocking on your door."

Margaret stood behind her armchair, her arms wrapped around herself, her head down, trying to stem tears. Jim stared at her, helpless, knowing neither what to do nor what to say. She had got it all wrong but even with the thought he could understand her distress at the idea that her name might have been bandied around the incident room as a possible suspect in the murders. "I'm sorry, Margaret. There's no way you're a suspect."

Margaret looked up at him. Gone was the

mischievous sparkle in her eyes that had so drawn him to her, gone was the teasing smile from her lips. Instead, all he could see was misery and the beginning of tears. "Jim," she said, "perhaps you should leave now and give me time to get my head around this."

"Margaret …"

"Please, Jim. I'll get your coat."

PART 3

It was the middle of the night. Sheehan's eyes flew open despite the fact that he had just wakened from sleep. He stared at the ceiling, not seeing it. Something sudden and important had pulled him awake. Was it that scene at Margaret's this evening? He experienced a dead, defeated ache in the pit of his stomach at the memory. He'd blown his chances there, that's for sure. And so pointlessly. No way was Margaret, he half-grinned at the memory, a 'gangster's moll'. How could he have hurt her like that? And why had he not disabused the team of the ridiculous idea that any suspicion of the monsignor or the organist was rubbish? *Aye right. The same way you told them that you were sorta seeing her.*

He continued to stare into the darkness, feeling her hurt, but he knew that that was not what had dragged him to wakefulness. It was something to do with the case. He had missed something significant during the day. He knew that as surely as he knew his name. But what was it? He closed his eyes again, rushing mentally through the day, wondering what he had missed, wondering if he could even figure out where he had been when he missed it. God, he hated it when his subconscious did this to him. What the hell was it? It was important, he knew it was. Ah, Sheehan, you pathetic idiot. Why didn't you notice it at the time? God, what was it?

He lay still, searching through the previous day for some connection between his activities and the feeling that was now electrifying him. His subconscious was buzzing with it, a significant point that could probably break the case wide open. This kind of thing had happened to him before and always the missing point was a vital element in the breaking of a case. But he always knew the vital point. This time he couldn't remember what it was. It would come to him eventually but it might take days. Usually something would trigger the subconscious memory and bring it to the forefront of his mind. But what if he missed the trigger this time? Dammit, how does this happen? Was he getting Alzheimer's?

Again he struggled to remember. *Was it something to do with the interview of that Gibbons punk? Something McCammon said? Something in the incident room?* He felt a mental tremor. The incident room? Did somebody say something significant? *Young Allen? He's a bright lad that, astute.* His reasoning had been inspired but it was easy to follow. Sheehan did not think he had missed anything. Unless there was some implication in what Allen had said that all of them missed?

His eyes were clenched, his teeth were clenched, his fists were clenched, as he tried to recreate the conversations that had taken place in the incident room that evening. His brain yielded nothing. But the impression was still there. Something meaningful had been said. He was positive about that. He had definitely been thinking about it just before he woke up. Lord, what the hell was it?

He forced himself to relax. *Don't think about it.*

Think about something else. It might come to you suddenly if you do that. It's like when you can't remember somebody's name. It comes to you as soon as you stop trying.

He closed his eyes and emptied his mind. Or tried to. He drifted off to sleep. The elusive thought remained elusive and thoughts of Margaret's hurt plagued his soul.

TWENTY-FOUR

Allen and McNeill sat in a parked car on Gransha Parade, not far from the Glen Road. It was towards evening the next day. They were studying a large red-bricked, semi-detached house which, because it was at the end of a terrace, had substantial front and side gardens. There may well also have been a rear garden, but they could not see one from their particular vantage point.

"How are we going to handle this?" McNeill said, straining to see of there was any movement at the windows of the house. Comfortable with his younger companion, he showed no sign of his stutter.

Allen was studying his notes. "We have to be very careful," he said. "We've no justification for even questioning him. Any evidence we find today, if there is any, we have to ignore and try to get it some other way. We don't want some smart alec barrister wiping us in court on a technicality."

"Do you really think it's him?"

"Can't say. We're flyin' blind." Allen studied his notes again. "Retired in 2002, still a sergeant? Funny that. He's got a good record. Mustn't have been interested in putting himself forward for promotions. Or was there something not right with him? We'll have to check that. Wife died a few months ago. Took it badly. No children. Holds a prayer meeting every Tuesday night in the parish offices. Suppose he has to do something to get out of the house." He looked up. "This is Tuesday. He'll be out tonight if you want to take a wee look around his house?"

"Don't even joke about that," McNeill said.

Allen went on, "The prayers are generally fervent but he gives a little talk each week and that's when he goes nuts."

"Have you that written down?" McNeill said, craning to see Allen's notes.

Allen grinned. "No, I'm just summarising. From what I've been told, he is very conservative. When he starts to speak, he brings up all the politically correct liberal events that take place during the week and that seems to bring out the worst in him. Apparently modern liberals are all going to hell. He's always ranting on about lax morals, abortion, and homosexuals and civil partnerships and that sort of thing."

"Gosh, you'd need to be careful when you're talking to him if he doesn't like gays."

"What? What are you talking about?"

"Well, everybody knows that you d … d … don't have a girlfriend and … and …"

"Oh, hah, hah! Very funny."

McNeill was grinning. Everyone also knew that Allen had been trying, unsuccessfully, for the past few weeks to connect with a new secretary in the front office.

Allen had been reading a paper he had extracted from an envelope he had earlier stuck into the notebook. "Good grief, listen to this. 'Sergeant Jerome Connolly served for over twenty-eight years as an officer of the Royal Ulster Constabulary, Belfast. He was awarded the Queen's Police Medal twice for services in protecting local communities during public disorder situations, and during his time in the Belfast A District he successfully liaised with community representatives and mediated across sectarian divides. He has been Commended and Highly Commended on numerous occasions for his role in public order situations. During the period of 'the troubles' in Northern Ireland, Sergeant Connolly constantly risked personal safety, a hazard he was willing to face as he served the community. He is renowned within the organisation for being a dedicated, industrious and highly professional police officer.' "

"Geez!" McNeill's eyes widened as he turned to stare at his partner. "Where'd you get that?"

Allen placed a forefinger along the side of his nose and said with a grin, "I've a friend in the front office who has access to computer records."

"Are we sure we want to go after this guy? That's some record."

Allen's own expression expressed doubt but he said, "We're still going to have to check him out but we'll do it with kid gloves."

"Feck! How?"

Allen shrugged. "We'll just tell him the truth and ask him if he can help us. No harm in that. Come on." He got out of the car and paced towards the house. McNeill, caught by surprise, had to jump out of the car and run a few steps to catch up. Allen glanced at his partner when they reached the door, put his expression into neutral, and rang the door bell. They heard the chimes but there was no other sound from the house. After a couple of minutes Allen rang again.

"All right, all right, no need to waste all my electricity," said a gruff voice from behind them, causing both detectives to start. The speaker was a tall, heavily-built man, plenty of white hair, early sixties, dressed in an old green woollen pullover, the collar of a red check shirt sticking up above it, and worn jeans, currently covered with what looked like cement dust. He was carrying a trowel in his left hand and had come to the front from somewhere round the side of the house. He was now staring at the two young men, his face grim, suspicious. "What do you want?"

Allen was first to react. He stepped forward quickly, right hand extended in greeting while he searched for his warrant card with his left. "Detectives Allen and McNeill, Sergeant Connolly," he said, hand still extended although Connolly was eyeing it with the same suspicion he had earlier accorded its owner. "We're just making some routine enquiries and your name came up as someone who might be able to help us."

Connolly's expression may have mollified but, if it did, it required sharper sight than possessed by either of the two detectives to discern it. He did, albeit reluctantly, take Allen's hand and gave it a brusque squeeze. He made no effort to extend the same courtesy to McNeill. *Well, Sheehan did say he was tough*, Allen was thinking, and nothing in the report suggested that he might be sweetness and light.

Connolly looked at the trowel in his hand and at his dusty grey boots. "I can't go into the house like this," he said. "Come on round the back. There's a couple of chairs on the patio."

He led the two policemen round the side of the house and onto a covered patio that looked out on a narrow garden. Allen noted that Connolly was in the process of building a waist-high wall down the right-hand side of it, about two feet in from the existing retaining wall. With breeze-blocks.

Connolly noticed Allen's gaze. "Gettin' on a bit," he explained. "Kneelin' down to tend flowers all summer is the devil on the back. I'm going to build a waist-high flower bed down the length of the lawn. It'll be easier to tend." Talking about his garden made him sound almost sociable.

Allen nodded and glanced over the man's shoulder, past a wooden shed that was situated against the left wall, at a line of cement slabs laid down along the left side of the lawn, clearly there to keep dry the feet of anyone hanging out clothes on the clothes-line above the makeshift path. Allen's eyes stuck open for a second. The clothes line was orange plastic. His insides were quivering and he could not even look at McNeill as he sat on the chair Connolly was pointing to. McNeill sat as well. Connolly chose to stand, his shoulder leaning against one of the patio supports, arms folded. His expression looked no different but his voice seemed less intimidating.

"Well, how is it I can help you chaps?" he said. If he experienced any concern about a police presence at his home, he revealed no sign of it.

179

Allen cleared his throat. "Sir, you probably have heard about the murder of Bishop Loughran ...?"

The old sergeant emitted a loud snort. "I'm retired, son, not dead."

"Of course, sir. Sorry, sir. The thing is, we have been instructed to look into the bishop's background."

"As you would. You needed instructions to do that?"

Allen ploughed manfully on. "We can't be sure, sir, but there seems to be some kind of religious dimension to the killing. The bishop has been ..."

"I know what he has been," the old sergeant interjected. "He's been starting to lose the plot. That's what he's been."

"So we're led to believe, sir. We know that he had turned his face against introducing the Tridentine Mass into your parish. I'm sure that must have angered a number of people. We were wondering if you could suggest where we might ..."

Connolly straightened and glared down at Allen. "You're trying to say that he angered some of our members and one of them killed him? What a load of nonsense. Our group may not have agreed with the bishop's liberal tendencies but none of us would have killed him. What a preposterous idea." He glared again. "Is that what you came to ask me?"

Allen looked at McNeill who appeared uncomfortable. He returned his gaze to the older man and said, "Sir, basically we hoped that you might be able to point us at someone who ..."

Connolly did not wait to hear where he was supposed to point. "Well, basically you and your ... your chatty mate can get out of here. Who's your boss?"

"DCI Sheehan," Allen said, rising. "Sir, we're sorry if we offended you. We're just trying to open a few leads."

"Try doing some detective work. That's how you get leads. Away you go, the pair of you. Your boss is going to hear from me."

The young detectives exited the Connolly gate at some speed, not looking at each other nor looking back to see if the angry owner was still glaring after them.

"Geez! Would you have wanted him for your boss?" McNeill said, half laughing, as they climbed onto the car. Allen risked a glance over his shoulder. There was no sign of Connolly. He must have stayed at the back of the house.

"DCI Sheehan, all is forgiven," Allen grinned, as he started the car and reversed into a nearby gateway to turn back towards the Glen Road. "Did you see the breeze blocks?"

"Did I what? Feck! You could have kn … kn … knocked me down with one of them," McNeill responded, his excitement bringing back his stutter. "And the orange plastic line, too. Can we accept c … c … coincidence here?"

"Coincidence? Get outta here!" Allen was tense with contained excitement. "I'll bet a month's salary you'll find a length of sisal rope in that potting shed and it'll match the rope that was round O'Donoghue's neck."

"How do we g … g … get access to it?" McNeill shared Allen's conviction that they had found their killer. His excitement was obvious. "And we're going to need pieces of that clothes line and a block for f … f … forensic analysis." Words were spilling from his mouth now with uncharacteristic haste. "Geez! We don't want to do anything that'll nullify that evidence. Do we have just cause for a search warrant? Shit! If we get this wr ... wr ... wrong, Sheehan'll kill us."

"No, he'll not."

"He'll not?"

"No, because we're taking this and laying it in his lap. We've done our bit. He can make the decisions about it."

He glanced at his partner. McNeill's face was contorted with glee and, despite the lack of space, he was continually pumping a clenched fist down towards his lap.

"Let's go round to the Crown," Allen suggested. "We deserve a celebratory jar."

"Too right," came the response.

PART 2

The Crown Bar, situated on Great Victoria Street, is one of the oldest and best loved bars in Belfast. And not without reason. In 1885, after the emancipation of Catholicism in Ireland, there was a sharp increase in the building of Catholic churches. Skilled craftsmen from Italy were brought into the North of Ireland and the owner of The Crown persuaded some of these tradesmen to supplement their income by moonlighting on the refurbishment of his saloon. These Italian craftsmen were responsible for the tiling, glasswork and rich ornamental woodwork which turned dream into reality, and gave The Crown its distinctive character. It is little wonder that at times when the sun beams strongly through the stained-glass windows, customers are often imbued with the feeling that they are in a church. This impression is enhanced by the wonderful combination of snugs which look at times like confessional boxes. It is often said that no visit to Belfast would be complete without calling in for a pint or two because The Crown Liquor Saloon still retains an indelible flavour of yesteryear. It is a place full of character and of characters and, as the management is frequently at pains to point out, it is a place where "... there are no strangers; only friends who have yet to meet."

Allen parked in a nearby side street and, as he and McNeill approached the portico of the saloon with its two ornate marble columns, they noticed Sergeant McCammon staggering to a car parked illegally at the pavement in front of the building. Allen said, "Dear God, Fred's bombed already."

The sergeant was struggling with the lock when the two younger detectives approached him. "How's about ye, Sarge?" Allen said.

The older detective peered at him. "Ah, young Allen. How's about ye?" He stumbled a step or two backwards and peered at McNeill. "And McNeill. How's about ye? Are youse comin' in for a wee drink?"

"Ah, maybe you've had enough, sir," Allen said, glancing at McNeill, not quite sure how he should handle this situation. "Are you thinking about going home?"

"Home? Aye, home. Thash where I was goin'."

"Are you driving?" Allen asked.

McCammon stepped closer to the young detective and said truculently, "Yis, I'm drivin'. What's it to you?"

Allen decided that there was no point in arguing

with the man. He said to McNeill, "Get the car, Geoff, and follow us." And to the sergeant, "Come on, sir, let me get you into the passenger seat." He took the keys from McCammon and half led, half dragged him to the other side of the car. McCammon tried to protest but, although he was wiry and strong, he was too far gone to offer any real resistance. He seemed to surrender suddenly and slumped into the front passenger seat, waiting while Allen settled himself behind the steering wheel. He swayed a little as Allen pulled away from the curb and the young detective said, "Seatbelt, sir."

The older man's response was instinctive and, as he fiddled with the belt, Allen could hear him muttering, "The drink doesn't kill the rage, son. I jush want to go somewhere and wreck ringsh round me." He lay back in the seat, silent as Allen drove. After some minutes he said, "You got any children, son?"

Allen laughed. "I'm not even married, Fred."

McCammon was silent again, his breathing heavy and irregular. Then, almost inaudibly, "Wise man. Wise man."

Allen knew where McCammon lived, having once had to deliver some papers to the house, and soon he was parking the sergeant's car in his front drive. He helped the sergeant to the door and, using the Yale key on the key-ring, let him into the house. He handed the sergeant the keys and said, "Have a good night's sleep, Sergeant. See you tomorrow."

McNeill was just pulling up as Allen left the drive. He climbed into the car and said, "Let's get that drink, Geoff."

TWENTY-FIVE

PART 1

The short, chilly November days were stealing the colour from the trees and the hedges. The dull Wednesday afternoon was already running swiftly into evening. Sheehan had sent Doyle off to search for any links that might exist between the community worker and the other two victims and was now sitting at his desk, his head in his hands. He was depressed. His brain was running madly along tracks worn smooth by constant repetition of the same thoughts all afternoon. *This is what happens when you get involved with a woman. It just never works out. You've had umpteen years with a clear head and total independence. You could work your cases with no distraction. Now your head is full of misery. I thought you had learned your lesson? Here you are, stuck in one of the most confusing cases you've ever had to deal with, and all you can think about is Margaret.*

He sat back in his chair, sighed, and stared at the ceiling. He wondered if he should try to phone her but dismissed the idea. He wouldn't have a clue what to say to her. And if past experience was anything to go by, it would be the wrong thing anyway.

A noise in the squad-room caught his attention. Declan Connors' huge bulk had just come through the door followed by the more dapper Simon Miller who was now striding purposefully towards Sheehan's office door, his hand searching the inside pocket of his jacket. Connors fell in behind him and Sheehan waved them both in.

"Sir," Miller said, "Declan and I thought it would do no harm to go back to St. Matthew's School to see if we could dig up anything we might have missed." He pulled a piece of paper from his pocket. "Connors here was chattin' up, I mean …" He grinned at his partner, "… interviewing one of the female staff and she happened to mention that O'Donoghue had caused a lot of bad feeling towards the end of the summer term in the previous school year."

Sheehan eyed Connors. He still had that pale, distracted look that had haunted his features since his divorce. He raised an eyebrow and said, "Chattin' up? Didn't think you were ready for that yet."

"Miller's just spoofin', sir." Connors sounded more weary than amused.

Sheehan took the paper from Miller's hand. "What am I looking at here?"

"It's a Catholic School, as you know," Connors explained, "and most of the staff are Catholics, quite committed by all accounts. Anyway, O'Donoghue sent this memo out to all heads of department before the end of the summer term and it was very badly received by some of the staff. There were a few who didn't care one way or the other but the whole school was buzzin' with it before they broke up for the summer holidays. The woman had it in her files and gave us a copy."

"Yes," Miller added, "and we were wondering, given the religious angle that keeps cropping up, if maybe it was significant."

Sheehan's hip was bothering him again. Surreptitiously he shifted his butt on the hard chair as he bent his head to study the paper. "Well, is it?"

"We're not sure, sir," Connors said. "That's why we're bringing it to you. Read it, sir, till you see."

Sheehan focused on the paper, quite long for a memorandum.

MEMORANDUM

To: Management Committee and Heads of Department

From: The Principal

Date: 7th June 2010

SUBJECT: Government Guidelines re Inclusivity of All Faiths

Recent Guidelines re Inclusion of Other Faiths in Secondary Schools demand that all schools honour and respect the faiths of our increasingly growing multi-cultural student body. The Guidelines, however, are merely that. The final decision as to how this problem is to be dealt with is to be left to the school authorities.

I have given this difficulty considerable thought.

1. First, I must point out that the logistical

problems posed by attempting to retain a Catholic ethos while being all things to all faiths, makes demands that our institution has neither the time nor the resources to cope with.

2. Second, a number of our non-Catholic parents have expressed concern about the possibility of the proselytising of their off-spring by overly zealous teachers. Such actions would be disrespectful to the growing diversity within our school and would be contrary to the guidelines.

It has been decided, therefore, that the approach that offers the fairest solution to all is to abandon specifically Catholic practices and to offer a Religious Education curriculum that is a broad and inclusive study of all principal religions.

Sheehan looked up at the two detectives who had been silent while he read. "That's pushing the boat out a bit," he said.

Both men were nodding. Connors said, "The teacher I was speaking to said that some of the staff feel that the memo was coming from pure cowardice, that the principal had caved in to the growing secularism of the Department of Education, and that some others seem to think that O'Donoghue himself has lost his faith and was glad of the excuse to get rid of religious practices in his school."

"Either way, you can see how it would annoy some of the ordinary Catholic teachers there," Miller offered.

"Yes, I can see that, all right," Sheehan said, "but why do you think it means anything? Do you think somebody killed him for writing this memo?"

Both detectives shook their heads. "Wouldn't go that far, sir," Connors said, "but if we're looking at a religious angle, it would be fairly significant from that point of view."

Sheehan was nodding. His comment had been a bit facetious. The memo may not have been a motive for murder but he had felt his own hackles rise as he was reading it. Part of his brain questioned this … hypocrisy? After all, he himself had not engaged in any Catholic practices either for the past several years. Must be a reaction to what he imagined the principal's job description should be. There was no doubt that the memo could be interpreted as a dereliction by O'Donoghue of his responsibilities as a Catholic headmaster. There would certainly be many who would react badly to it. Connors was right. It was something that could not be ignored, at least at this point in the investigation.

"Good work, men," he said, winning pleased smiles from both of them. "To be honest, I can't quite see right now where it might fit in but I agree that it is something we should pay some attention to. Get Bill to pin it to the white board. We'll see what the squad thinks about it at the next briefing meeting." He glanced at the two subordinates. "You two can talk to it but I don't think the rest of the guys are going to be too happy about it."

Connors raised his eyebrows in a question.

Sheehan's answer was another question. "How many staff are there? Fifty? Sixty? All their backgrounds are going to have to be thoroughly checked."

"Oh, hell …" Miller grimaced, and pleaded as he turned to leave, "You'll divide it up, sir, I hope."

"Organise the uniforms," Sheehan said. "They can do the bulk of it."

When the detectives left the office, Sheehan could not help feeling that the memo might indeed have some bearing on O'Donoghue's murder. Problem was, it opened up the pool of suspects significantly. And it also led them further down the speculation that both the principal and the bishop were killed because of their tendencies to secularism or liberalism. Could there be a real motive for murder there? Perhaps there might be one for some sort of fundamentalist who was carrying out 'executions' or something? There could be any number of members of staff with fundamentalist leanings who could function more or less unnoticed in a Catholic school. But what then was the connection to the bishop? It was clear from the investigation reports that the bishop's avant garde writings had annoyed more than a few ordinary Catholics as well. Was there someone who had something in common with both camps? But what about the community worker? Would Doyle's investigation throw up any connection between her and the other two?

His head was back in his hands again. What a case! Usually the squad would be tripping over all sorts of clues, some maybe worth nothing, but at least they were tangibles to work with. This bizarre set of killings offered no clues and was leading to all sorts of, probably futile, abstractions. The men were getting fed up with it, except maybe Allen. He seemed to be enjoying the speculative nature of his enquiries. But the others were less cerebral and wanted some meat to chew on. And now he would have to pile extra work on the squad, forcing them into the backgrounds of the teachers and the bishop's connections as well. How likely was it that they would come across someone who was directly linked to both victims? And that doesn't even take into account the community worker.

They were casting their net further and further afield, expending more and more time and energy, and all the while the killer might well have no connection to any of the victims. What if he was picking them at random? What if he was just reading about them in the newspapers and identifying them as victims from that source? Sheehan knew that the bishop and the principal had appeared in the local press several times over the past couple of years but did the community worker? Had she been involved in anything that got her name in the papers? He had no memory of it if she had.

On the other hand, he felt strongly that there had to be a connection between the victims, a connection to each other and a connection to the killer. Random nearly always disappeared in the hindsight of any case. People tend to be constrained by the boundaries of their own little worlds and when a killer goes on a spree, the victims are found somewhere within his world's parameters.

What if? What if? What if? God, when are we going to have something specific to work with? Maybe Allen will bring something to the table. At the memory of Allen's lead something in him recoiled. God, no, not a cop. Not Connolly. Okay, he was a bit of a tough nut in his day but, if memory served, he was a solid cop. There had been no breath of scandal attached to him as far as Sheehan knew. Still, he had been a serving cop through the worst of 'the troubles', a terrible time to be a policeman.

He recalled the Omagh bombing. It was Sheehan's everlasting misfortune to have been briefly seconded to Omagh in 1998. The carnage he had witnessed there would haunt him forever. Horrible! Horrible! Like other policemen in the town that day, he had rushed to the scene of the bombing to see how he could help, trying to patrol the crowded, stunned street, listening to the wails of the bereaved, stumbling over tons of rubble, trampling and sliding through torn flesh and bloodied, bodiless limbs, gagging at the smells, and all the while scared shitless that there would be another explosion aimed at the security forces who were trying to deal with the first one. He shook his head to chase images that still plagued him a dozen years later.

How many policemen left the force after that day, severely traumatised? Lots of serving officers all over the province lost it in those days. How many stories had he heard from wives of traumatised cops on sick leave who would spend their days in darkened rooms, crying like children, refusing to come out? How many pensioned-off cops tried to find work in civilian pursuits but were unable to survive in the jobs more than a couple of weeks because of anger issues? Different guys responded in different ways to the horrors of those times. Many caved completely. Connolly, too, would have his nightmares. He would doubtless have been shot at, would have faced bombings many times, would have been physically injured, would have found himself under severe threat in the middle of vicious and violent riots. That was the lot of the policemen of 'the troubles'. Was it possible that Connolly had now suffered some sort of post-service breakdown that had tipped him over the edge?

Sheehan leaned back in his chair, ran the fingers of both hands through his hair and then clasped them behind his neck. He stared unseeing at the ceiling until the last vague tendrils of the flashback to those dark days began to dissipate. He tried to return to his analysis of the case. But he couldn't focus. There was nothing to focus on. He sat forward again, exasperated.

For crying out loud, would you quit with the pointless speculations. You've no facts, no clues, no viable suspects. Your brain is wrestling with smoke. Give it a break.

His head was splitting. His hip was aching on the hard chair. Little sleep the night before, a disintegrating love life (or what might have been a love life had it got off the ground) and now, questions, questions, questions … and not an answer to be found. *"Go home. Go home and get a shower and relax in front of the television". Aye, right.* Like the T.V. could stop the flood of thoughts that was driving him to distraction.

PART 2

On his way home, Sheehan called again into St. Malachy's. The chapel was empty apart from an elderly woman lighting a candle at one of the side altars. He made his way into one of the back pews and sat there, ill-at-ease, puzzled. These visits to St. Malachy's were becoming more and more frequent, yet he had no understanding of why he was there. He didn't pray, he didn't meditate and, as far as he knew, he didn't even think. He would just call in for a few minutes, feeling out-of-place and uncomfortable. There he would sit, restless, refusing with all his will to imagine that God was involved in this, refusing even to acknowledge God's presence on the altar. Something had awakened in him that day at the bishop's funeral, something unexpected, something inexplicable, a by-product of his intention to hear Margaret play. And here he was, "paying" what the priests of his childhood days used to refer to as "a visit to the Blessed Sacrament." He shook his head and rose to his feet. *This is crazy.*

As he left, he genuflected to the altar, yet without looking at it. The action was an ingrained response from his childhood, almost a conditioning that he was still incapable of shaking off. Limping from the pain that the attempted genuflection had brought to his sciatic nerve, he returned to his car. His brow was furrowed. There was something going on in his head but it must have been at some emotional or atavistic level because, whatever it was, he could not hang any kind of conscious thought on it.

Back in his apartment, he prepared a plain meal of scrambled eggs, tea and toast, able to focus clearly on what he was doing but still experiencing that same mental blankness where thoughts would normally be tumbling over themselves to find expression.

He switched on the ipod standing in the kitchen window. Strains of a forties ballad filled the small room. Sheehan's taste in music was catholic – old ballads from the forties and fifties, instrumental music, popular classical pieces, operatic arias, the very occasional modern pop song if it was musical and original. He had about five hundred songs on his playlist and just let them run and run, only very occasionally adding anything new when he came across something that caught his fancy.

He finished the meagre meal and went into the living area. He sat on one of the armchairs and flicked the remote at the television. After a few seconds, the screen was filled with an announcer's head talking about a "policeman's family in a grenade drama." Sheehan's brain clicked into gear immediately. The announcer went on, "A PSNI officer and his young family were forced to leave their home in the early hours of this morning after a grenade had been thrown into their home …"

Sheehan's lips tightened. He tried to remain dispassionate. He had learned to curb the acidic futility of anger at these appalling attacks by the so-called 'dissident republicans.' Peace had reigned in Northern Ireland for several years now but these faceless idiots, without any kind of mandate even from their own republican communities, were trying to start 'the troubles' all over again. He listened with half an ear while a succession of politicians from all parties condemned the attack, warning these 'dinosaurs' that their time was over, that there was no place for them in today's Northern Ireland.

His thoughts drifted to Margaret again. There was still that empty space in his heart that wouldn't go away. Again he fought the temptation to phone her. *Waste of time, Jim. Face it. There's no point in torturing yourself about something that's not going to happen. You shattered her trust by leading her to believe she was a suspect in a murder case. No. No. Not so. You did try to soften it but, from her point of view, there was no other possible interpretation. She'll run a mile the next time she sees you. Just stop thinking about her and get on with your life.*

A new item on the News programme arrested his attention.

"Controversial MLA, Edward Corrigan, today launched what some MLAs have described as 'a vitriolic attack' on Cardinal O'Driscoll. Jim McNicholls has the details."

The picture on the screen changed to the grounds of the Parliamentary Buildings at Stormont where a reporter, wearing a duffle coat and heavy woollen scarf, spoke into a hand-held microphone. "Earlier today, the Primate of All Ireland, Cardinal O'Driscoll, stated that the recent judgement of the European Court of Human Rights regarding the legal position on abortion would require careful analysis and reflection. Mr. Corrigan, responding on the floor of the Assembly this afternoon, appeared incensed at what he called 'the Church's unwarranted interference in matters of government.' He went on then to claim that the Cardinal's remarks, seen by many as temperate and measured, were 'outrageous' and he accused the Cardinal of 'fundamentalism.'"

The reporter's face was replaced by a clip of the day's proceedings at the Parliamentary Assembly at Stormont. MLAs were shown listening to Edward Corrigan, a tall man, well-dressed man with a full head of dark hair, delivering what could clearly be seen as a strident attack on the Church in general and on Cardinal O'Driscoll in particular.

"This has taken my breath away. We have failed for years to get any movement from the Church leadership to protect abused children and to deal with perverted clerics, but one mention of pregnancy termination and the Church leadership is galvanised into action. I call on the Speaker to send a memorandum to Armagh on behalf of all MLAs, outlining where we stand. They can do the praying down there and we will do the legislating up here. If we want to legislate for Sharia law or whatever kind of fundamentalism they want to peddle to us, we will give them a call when that arises. It is outrageous that Armagh should attempt to influence how the state should legislate on issues of human rights."

The reference to Sharia law triggered in Sheehan a memory of a news bulletin he had heard a couple of weeks before. "You bloody fraud," he said aloud to the face on the television. "That's almost word for word the same stuff that that Irish TD was ranting about in the Dáil a couple of weeks ago. If you're going to attack the Church, at least use your own ideas. That's pitiful. And you a Catholic, too." As he raised the remote to change channels, he heard the reporter add that MLA Joe Donaldson had stated that Mr. Corrigan was not speaking for the majority of the MLAs and that the language he had used was disgraceful and intemperate.

TWENTY-SIX

Eight-thirty on Thursday morning and some of the men in the room were bleary-eyed and yawning. Sheehan had called this early briefing session before the detectives headed off for their daily grind of researching, questioning, chasing up minor leads. The principal's memorandum was important enough but Allen's phone call yesterday evening had been filled with possibilities. He wanted Allen to share his discoveries with the group as soon as possible. He was saving that for later in the meeting, however. There were other reports to be delivered as well. He called on Loftus to speak first.

Loftus spoke from his table, sitting back but speaking clearly. "I went back to the Lough Erne Hotel and had another wee look at the monsignor's alibi. I told you earlier that it was tight but Allen's talk about a disguise rattled me. And now I'm not so sure …"

"You mean he could have committed the murder?" McLoughlin seemed pleased at the possibility.

"All I'm saying is that his alibi is not a hundred per cent airtight. It might have a hole in it." He paused unsure how to proceed.

"Is this some sort of new parlour game, Loftus?" McCammon said, often on a short fuse these days. "We throw possible answers at you and you tell us if we're right or wrong?"

Loftus' freckles deepened as he flushed and he hurried on. "Sorry, it's just that I was talking to the day-time receptionist at the Lough Erne Hotel. He told me that he arrives for work every morning a few minutes before seven o'clock. The thing is, you can see the staff car park from the reception area and apparently the night man always drops everything as soon as he sees the day guy driving in. He usually goes out for a wee chat at their cars before the day guy goes on in. So there's a three or four minute gap at that time, sir, when the front desk is left unattended. It would be easy for someone to slip in or out of the hotel unnoticed at that point, particularly if there were any others moving around as well."

"Doesn't mean the monsignor's lying," Doyle said. "It just means that his alibi is not as tight as it was."

"It just means we can't trust his alibi at all," McLoughlin said.

"Does he have alibis for the other two killings?" Sheehan asked.

"No, sir. Home alone. No witnesses," Loftus said.

"All right. Good work, Loftus. All we can do is file that along with everything else and keep an open mind about it. For myself, I can't see the monsignor as our man but don't let that stop you following up any leads that you find." He paused and went on casually, "Did you have time to check out the organist, Mrs ..."

"Sands, sir. Yes, I'd say she's clean. She doesn't have alibis for the nights in question but anything I've heard from talking to those who know her, neighbours, the school she works at, would indicate that it is normal for her to be at home alone. And my own assessment of her is that her attitude shows none of the usual indicators of any kind of guilt."

"I hope you were polite?"

Loftus threw him a quizzical glance but said, "Oh, I was. It was easy to be, she's a very nice woman. She did seem a bit stiff and tended to be uncooperative at first. I could see that she felt as if she was being accused of something. But when I explained that she was one of a substantial number of innocent people whose names had to be eliminated from the enquiry, she seemed a bit more relaxed."

"Good."

"Funny thing, sir," Loftus added. "She asked if it was you who had sent me."

"Me?"

"Yes, I thought that was a bit odd, sir, But I told her that we all followed lines of enquiry that we normally cleared with you but that you had not actually sent me. And then, that's when her frostiness melted. She seemed very pleased about something and chatted away after that, happy as Larry. Bit odd that."

Sheehan found himself inwardly jubilant but simply said, "Wonder why she mentioned me?"

"I asked her about that, sir. She just said that she

believed she had seen you at the bishop's house talking to the monsignor."

"Oh, right. Doyle, you're up next."

Doyle removed his ever-present notebook from his jacket pocket and began to read with no attempt at inflection. "Catherine Higgins, Community Worker, was born and reared Catholic but during her time at Queen's University abandoned her faith and espoused atheism. She was chairperson of a gay rights group at the university and was prominent in several rallies and protests that sought various legal rights and entitlements for the gay and lesbian community. She was also something of a Marxist in her student days and was always protesting against any laws that seemed to be based on essentially Christian principals. Her espousal of these causes, however, seemed to peter out after she graduated." Doyle looked up to stare at his audience and said woodenly, "Perhaps she got some sense and realised that railing and wailing wasn't going to get her a job." He bent his head to the notebook again and continued his report. "When she was employed by the Belfast Council as a community worker, she moved quickly through the ranks to a supervisory position. During her time on the job she seemed to have become passionate about finding new and more relevant approaches to the education and development of the disadvantaged young people from the ghetto areas of the city."

He looked up again and spoke directly to Sheehan. "There's nothing there that could give us any serious line of enquiry but there was no doubt, however, that she was having a near-pedophile affair with a fourteen year old girl and the word was beginning to filter out into the community."

"Thank you, Doyle. Very comprehensive. Any

questions before we move on?"

"Just wondering, sir," Oliver McCoy asked, "if anything came from the investigation into the family members of the young girl and whether or not there's any possibility they might have been involved in the social worker's murder?"

No. McCammon and McCullough have virtually exhausted that line and have come up with nothing so far." Sheehan looked around, waiting for any further questions. None were forthcoming. "Right. Connors? Miller?

It was Miller who spoke. He revealed details of the memo O'Donoghue had written and said that it could reasonably be seen as a trigger for a 'fundamentalist nutter'.

There was some agreement about that but the enthusiasm waned somewhat when Connors told them that all members of staff and Catholic parents who had children at the school would have to be looked at. Even with help from the uniformed branch, they were looking at hours of boring slog.

The moaning went on and Sheehan said, "Find the killer, then, and we won't have to do all this leg-work. You know as well as I do how necessary it is. We need one piece of luck and that nearly always means combing through haystack after haystack until the bloody pin sticks itself in one of us."

Allen said, "We might be able to help with that, sir." That grabbed the room's interest. "Myself and Geoff checked out the retired cop, Jerome Connolly today. He was building a wee wall for plants and brought us round the back so that he wouldn't dirty the house."

"He had b ... b ... breeze blocks and an orange

202

clothes l … l … line back there," McNeill jumped in, earning a glare from his partner.

There was a palpable reaction from all in the room.

"Orange clothes line and breeze blocks?" This from McCammon. "He has to be our man."

McLoughlin was in on his heels. "What are we waiting for? Let's go and get the bastard."

Sheehan tried to calm the growing excitement. "Guys, you know as well as I do that we have to follow procedure."

"No chance of getting a justice of the peace to issue a search-warrant, sir?" Allen asked, having to shout over the top of the buzz of conversation that had followed his revelations.

"Okay, quieten down," Sheehan called to the room. In response to Allen's question, he continued, "I'd be doubtful about that with what we've got at the moment. It'd be great to get a piece of that clothes line and a block for forensic comparison but we've no reasonable grounds."

"Sir," Allen said, "there's material on the premises that could be of substantial value to our investigation and likely to be relevant evidence." He had wondered if the DCI would be cautious and had checked out the legislation regarding authorisation of entry and search of premises.

Sheehan was amused by what he recognised as a direct quote from the police manual. The young detective was trying hard. But his expression remained serious. "You're right about that as far as it goes, but the key word in the legislation regarding grounds is 'reasonable'. We only have speculation and surmise. I mean, the guy's name only cropped up because he likes to go to Latin Masses." He spread his hands and went on, "And the words that you are instinctively using yourself, Allen, are 'could be of value', 'likely to be evidence'. We don't know anything, literally. How can that be 'reasonable'? I mean, go into any branch of B&Q and the place is coming down with orange plastic clothes lines. I'm sure half the houses in the Gransha estates have them. We need to be careful here. Connolly is entitled to his legal rights. We need something more solid against him before we could convince a JP to give us the warrant. And besides, we don't want him to know we're on to him and send him to ground before we can build a solid case against him."

Allen slumped. So did McNeill. The others were ambivalent. They still did not want an ex-cop to be the killer but Allen's reasoning was having its effect. The orange clothesline and the breeze blocks. How could anyone see past those?

"Dig into his background a bit more," Sheehan said to Allen. "How did the death of his wife affect him? Any of his prayer group notice anything different or odd in his behaviours lately? Do some cross-checking into the backgrounds of the victims and see if Connolly's life overlaps with them anywhere. There has to be something that connects the victims to each other and to their killer."

TWENTY-SEVEN

PART 1

The dank, depressing November mist was turning to rain that Wednesday evening but Edward Corrigan was feeling pleased with himself. Sitting at a table in the canteen at Stormont, drinking a solitary cup of coffee as he studied some statistics, he reflected on the day's 'success'. His speech in the Assembly that afternoon had incurred the ire of quite a few of his Assembly colleagues but that fazed him not the slightest. Publicity! Good or bad, publicity was the fuel that kept his political ambitions burning. What was it somebody said a while back, something like '... what used to be humiliation is now simply publicity'. He grinned. He liked that and vowed to remember it for use at some notable gathering in the future. Publicity, and self-promotion, too. He had fought his way on to some of the most prestigious committees in

Stormont, was his party's spokesman for Education and Learning (always good for a sound-bite or two), and he made a point of appearing on television every chance he got to champion human rights and all forms of equality legislation. He had recently tabled a private members' bill for the legalising of Civil Partnerships. Got up a few noses, that. Bit too modern for the puritanical majority in Northern Ireland but it put him at the fore of the campaign. He knew how the wind was blowing across the water and, latterly, down in the South as well. It wouldn't be long before he would be called again to speak to his bill, and this time, people would listen.

A small voice, almost inaudible now having been dismissed so many times during his active years in politics, reminded him that he was a Catholic and that the causes he was espousing were against Catholic doctrine. His response to the weak voice had become a mantra. *Religion has its place and politics has its place. Politics is about fighting hard for the rights of all people. Specific and antediluvian religious mores that have not kept pace with modern psychological thought have no place in the political arena.*

Irritated, he looked at his watch. The thought had dented his good form. He focused on the watch's face. Six-fifteen. Just time to call into the office to check his appointments for the following day before he headed home. He was only a few miles east of his constituency office and even with the evening rush-hour traffic, the West Link motorway could have him there in less than half an hour. He drained the cup he was holding and left the canteen with a nod to the young lady who had served him. He was wearing a navy top coat, with a white scarf casually draped around his neck. He knew he looked good, elegant. No doubt the young waitress was pleased he had noticed her.

He drove out of the car park and along the one mile length of the Prince of Wales Avenue that led from the Parliament Buildings out to the Upper Newtownards Road. The rain wasn't heavy yet but he needed the intermittent wipers. He waited at the gate for a space in the traffic and eased out, not noticing that an inconspicuous, dark-coloured saloon which had been parked across the road had now pulled into the line of traffic two cars behind him. Corrigan drove steadily westwards, not hurrying but wasting no time. The vehicle that was following had little trouble keeping pace with him.

Some minutes later, the shadowing car's driver pulled a mobile phone from his pocket and, heedless of the law prohibiting such acts, dialled a number. Corrigan's car-phone rang, a lawful hands-free unit. He pressed a button and said, "Edward Corrigan. How can I help you?"

The caller said, "Detective Inspector Michael Gordon here, sir."

Corrigan didn't recognise the name although the caller's confident tone made it clear that recognition was expected. He said, "Inspector Gordon? Could you tell me how you got this number, please?"

"Excuse me, sir?" The caller sounded mystified.

"This is my private mobile. I was wondering how you got the number."

"You gave it to me yourself, sir, the last time we met." The voice was patient, a simple exhortation to remember.

Corrigan had no memory of an Inspector Gordon but he met so many new people in the course of a week and often gave his number to individuals who he considered might at some point be useful to him. It was perfectly feasible that he had done so in this case.

"Ah, yes, of course, Inspector. Sorry, I had forgotten for a moment. What can I do for you?"

"I'm just outside your constituency offices, sir," the caller replied. "I was hoping to find you in. I need to speak to you on a matter of some urgency. Are you likely to be at your offices any time this evening?"

"As a matter of fact, I'm on my way there now. Can you let me know what's so urgent?"

The caller hesitated. "It's delicate, sir. The truth is, we have received a threat on your life." Then with a cheerful rush, he added, "No need to worry unduly, sir. We get these things all the time and they rarely amount to anything. But it does no harm to take precautions, right sir? I just need a word or two about security arrangements. Shouldn't take long."

Corrigan experienced a tremor of panic. "Ah, right, of course, Inspector. Would you wait where you are, please? I should be there in about fifteen minutes."

"Thank you, sir. It'll be good to get this done this evening. I'll be here when you arrive."

PART 2

Grosvenor Road, once known as Grosvenor Street, straddles a large swathe of the western suburbs, leading in a virtually straight line from the Falls Road to the city centre. A long road, it has seen more than its fair share of disruption and violence during 'the troubles'. Plans for new motorway links during those thirty years of mayhem often had to be abandoned because of the riotous and destructive behaviour of the warring factions. But in the early 2000s a new junction, what the Minister for Roads and Transport described as "... another important milestone in the one hundred and four million pound upgrade of the M1/Westlink", was completed and the result was greatly improved access to the city centre and the Royal Hospitals.

Now a long, sedate city road, it is home to numerous thriving businesses, retail outlets, and medical and dental surgeries of various kinds. It also accommodates the constituency offices of some of the MLAs who serve the people of that region. One such office is that of Edward Corrigan, housed in a large building with an old-fashioned, ornate exterior, and which provides work for three members of staff. At close to seven o'clock in the evening, however, the offices are locked and in darkness, and the staff have gone home.

As Corrigan parked his car in front of the office and made to get out, he noticed a smallish, nondescript car just parking across the road from him. A tall, heavily built man got out, raised an arm in greeting, and began to walk across the road.

"Inspector Jordan?"

The visitor extended a gloved hand. "Yes, Mr. Corrigan. Good to meet you again, sir."

Corrigan had no memory of an earlier meeting. Perhaps the policeman had been part of security detail that had formed protection for him on a past occasion. Disarmed, and perhaps a little surprised that the policeman had chosen not to remove his glove, he shook the proffered hand and replied, "Nice to see you again, too, Inspector." He looked quizzically at the car that had just parked and turned to the policeman. "Just arrived?"

The inspector smiled, "Oh, when you said you'd

be fifteen minutes, sir, I took the opportunity to nip away and buy an evening paper."

Corrigan produced his keys, opened the door, switched on the entrance light and stood aside to let the policeman in before him.

But the inspector smiled and said, "After you, sir." Corrigan shrugged, led the visitor down a short hall and into his own private office. He took off his overcoat and threw it over a chair in the corner. Then he turned to face the man standing behind him. His eyes initially went to the plastic coveralls his visitor was wearing under his overcoat and the odd looking latex cap that was covering his head and forehead before he found himself staring into two cold, grey-green eyes. Suddenly unnerved, he said, in a voice that was unsteady and pitched higher than normal, "Uh … what's this death threat you were talking about?"

The man's right hand, fingers rigid and extended, flashed forward like a rush of sudden wind, catching the politician on the side of the throat. The stricken man gagged and fell back, grabbing his throat as he struggled to find breath. His assailant answered his question with a single word.

"Me."

TWENTY-EIGHT

He lies face down and naked on the floor in the middle of the room. His arms are stretched straight out from his body, his legs joined together and stretched out behind him. His forehead is pressed to the ground and, with his eyes closed, he prays. Tears stain his face as he moans, caught up in the intensity of his prayer:

"And the Lord was very angry and put him in the hands of those who would give him punishment. I thank you, Lord, that you have seen fit to make me your instrument. It is a heavy burden, Lord, but I bear it gladly for your sake." He continues to moan wordlessly, his face a rictus. Words from the psalms begin to pour from his mouth, *"Let the praise of God be on their lips and a two-edged sword in their hands, to deal out punishment on all the peoples, to carry out the sentence preordained: this honour is for all the*

faithful. The faithful, Lord, the very few who can truly carry out your sentence. *For these are the days of punishment in which all things in the Writings will be put into effect."*

He lies silent, motionless, for some minutes. Then, suddenly, his head shoots up and staring at the ceiling, he shouts, *"You snakes, offspring of snakes, how will you be kept from the punishment of hell? I will execute terrible vengeance against them and punish them for what they have done."* His voice lowers, diminishes, but still with the same terrible intensity he continues, *"In the Lord's name I crushed them. They blazed like a fire among thorns. In the Lord's name I crushed them ... in the Lord's name I crushed them ... in the Lord's name I crushed them ..."* His voice is barely a whisper now. "*... but for all this his anger has not turned away and his hand is stretched out still* and in my hands is your fury, Lord."

He remains staring upwards for several minutes, silent now. Then he rises slowly to his feet and walks over to a crucifix hanging on a wall. He stares at the image of Christ, his face now in repose. "All but one of the sacrifices have been offered, Lord," he whispers, eyes ablaze. "I offer them to you now in mitigation for the sins of those who would lead your people astray, who would flout your laws, who would turn their back on your covenant. *O Lord, you know how to keep the unrighteous under punishment for the day of judgement.* In your name, I have visited judgement upon them and *your right hand will triumph again."*

TWENTY-NINE

The phone on Sheehan's desk jangled. Sheehan pulled it to his ear. "DCI Sheehan."

"Jim, it's Bob Williams. The ACC asked me to contact you."

Williams' voice sounded strained. Sheehan's chin fell to his chest and a sick weariness took hold of him. He knew what was coming but that did not make it any more welcome.

"Bob, how's about ye? You've found a body?"

"I'm afraid so, Jim. Have you heard already?"

"No, but it's Thursday morning. Every bloody Thursday morning for the last four weeks somebody rings me up to tell me they've found a body. What is it with this guy and Wednesday nights?" He sighed heavily into the phone, then said, "Go on, tell me. The body's naked, it's posed, there's some funny stuff that doesn't make sense, and the crime scene is as clean as a whistle, right?"

"You sure you haven't heard?"

"It's an easy deduction to make, Bob. I could be describing any one of three other crime scenes I've seen recently. Where are you?"

"Edward Corrigan's constituency offices on the Grosvenor Road."

"Corrigan? The MLA? Why am I not surprised? I was listening to that guy ranting on the tele only last night. Is it him, or one of his staff?"

"No, it's Corrigan himself."

"Okay, we're on the way over now."

Sheehan had known Inspector Williams for years and was aware of the secret ambitions the DI nurtured. Judging from the defeated tone in the inspector's voice, it was a safe bet that Williams had hoped to pursue this case since it had landed in his patch. Maybe he had hoped to use it to climb one more rung up the promotion ladder but had been ordered by the ACC to hand it over to Sheehan. Sheehan empathised. He did not want to deny Williams any kudos that might come his way from a result in this investigation. Bob was the quintessential 'nice guy', a good, steady cop. But there was no denying that he had already been promoted to his limit of competence. He was good at what he did, in organisational terms, but that was where his competence ended. And, anyway, it was clear from the brief information he provided that the ACC would have seen this case as linked to the others Sheehan was working on.

There were two sets of skills, either one of which might have enabled Williams to progress further, but Bob possessed neither. He did not possess the good detective's capacity to develop and follow up on a hunch, what Sheehan was often amused to see described in the media after a successful result, as 'intellectual brilliance and ingenious deductive reasoning'. Neither did Williams have the pragmatism, Sheehan would have called it the "sycophancy", to play the internal political game. Lord knows, there were enough incompetents already in high places who possessed this skill in spades.

No, Williams was going nowhere. However, Sheehan liked him and determined that whatever the outcome of the investigation, he would keep Bob in the loop and work with him. Not that that would be any great sacrifice. Bob was methodical, plodding, and could always be relied upon to follow-up on and complete the boring elements of any investigation, to ensure that all of the paperwork was complete, to make sure that all information, no matter how seemingly negligible, was properly ordered, recorded and logged.

He replaced the phone and shouted to Doyle who was typing laboriously on one of the incident room's laptops. "There's been another killing, Doyle. Let's go."

Fifteen minutes later Doyle dropped Sheehan at the door of the MLA's constituency offices and went off to find a place to park among the police vehicles already surrounding the scene. Sheehan was led down a short corridor by the officer on the door. They went through a large, bright front office where two women and a young man, probably staff, were huddled together in shocked silence, and into the politician's smaller office. Sheehan reached immediately for a handkerchief to cover his mouth and nose. The smells in the room almost made him gag. Bob Williams was standing just inside the door, his mouth and nose similarly protected. He nodded at Sheehan as he

215

entered but did not say anything. He was keeping his nose well covered.

Sheehan looked around. The environment might have been strange to him but the essence of the crime was all too depressingly familiar. The office desk had been pushed back a couple of feet, the victim's clothes had been tossed behind it and, on the floor, naked, was the now pallid body of Edward Corrigan. He was lying on his back with his hip and legs turned sideways to the right. The knees were bent, one lower than the other and the arms were reaching straight down but pulled out at an angle from each side of the body.

A foul-smelling drool, mixed with vomit, had slipped down from the victim's mouth on to his neck and chest, and what was clearly diarrhoea stained the floor beneath him. Beside him on the floor was a cup half full of what looked like water, and a plate containing some foul smelling, overcooked vegetables.

The usual CSI officers were moving about in their tyvek overalls, dusting for prints, taking photographs and examining every inch of the floor, walls and furniture.

The Deputy Forensic Pathologist was already at the scene, bent over the body, sniffing at the mouth, feeling the hair, studying the fingernails.

"What are you looking for, Dick?" Sheehan asked.

The pathologist looked up. "Oh, it's you, Jim. And a good morning to you, too."

Sheehan sighed. "Okay, good morning, Dick. Now, what are you looking for?"

"Hope I'm not being too cold and dispassionate but I have to say your killer provides interesting puzzles."

"Dick!"

"All right, all right. I'm looking for smells, for traces of poisoning, perhaps arsenic."

Sheehan stared at the body, still breathing through his handkerchief. Dick seemed utterly immune. "Take me through it from the beginning."

Doyle had entered fortuitously at that point and was already reaching for his notebook and pen.

"Good morning, Sergeant," the doctor effused with his customary cheerfulness.

Doyle gave him his usual impassive nod.

Sheehan said, "Dick?"

"Well, your victim was initially felled by a blow to the throat, you can see the marks here, but they're a bit … diffused. Not naked fingers." He pointed. "The killer was wearing gloves, probably leather. That cushioned the blow a bit, so I don't think it killed him. Probably deliberately administered to disable without killing. Your man is definitely good." He pointed to the cup and the repellent plate. "I think he had something more interesting in mind for his victim."

"What's that on the plate?"

"Now that is puzzling. There is no poison in it, of that I'm sure."

"So? What is it then?"

Dick got up with his usual awkwardness, folded his arms, then released one hand to raise a pedagogical finger. "What you have there, detectives, is a plate of cruciferous vegetables. Cruciferous or Brassica vegetables are so named because they come from plants in the family known to botanists as Cruciferae or alternately, Brassicaceae. Many commonly consumed cruciferous vegetables come from the Brassica genus, including broccoli, Brussels sprouts, cabbage, cauliflower …"

"You're saying we have a plate of broccoli, sprouts, cabbage and cauliflower?" Sheehan interrupted.

"And some mustard greens, too," the doctor said, almost petulantly. He had been enjoying his lecture. "If you must have the genus in more mundane terms, these foods come under the general classification of bitter vegetables."

Sheehan stared at the plate, baffled.

The pathologist raised his finger again. "If I might add, cruciferous vegetables are unique in that they are rich sources of glucosinolates, sulphur-containing compounds which, when the vegetables are overcooked, produce a bitter taste and emit a pungent aroma , a smell like rotten eggs."

"And I need to know this because …?"

"I have no idea. I'm simply telling you all I know about what's on that plate."

"They couldn't be there just to make a smell, could they?"

"No idea."

"What's in the cup?" came Bob Williams' muffled voice, still well away from the sources of the smells.

"The sixty-four thousand dollar question," the pathologist replied. "It looks like water but I have my suspicions that there is a heavy metal poison in it, maybe arsenic, found in common rat poison and therefore easily acquired. Can't be definitive though.

Arsenic is odourless and colourless."

"Is that what killed him?" Williams asked.

"Not sure. I don't think that the dosage in the cup would be of sufficient quantity to kill overnight. He would have needed a lot of it. But I can't say anything definitive until I do the tests."

He struggled to his knees again and started peering at the body. "I was just about to search for other evidence of poisoning. I'm fairly sure that death was due to poisoning but I suspect that it was injected via a syringe rather than taken by mouth."

"So what's with the cup, then?" Sheehan asked.

The doctor turned his head to stare back up at the detective. "As I have to tell you so often that it has become almost a mantra, I give you the facts, you make the deductions." Then he raised his finger yet again and said emphatically, "But …"

Sheehan's lips remained resolutely closed.

The pathologist's eyes twinkled as he waited a beat or two longer before saying, "I might perhaps be able to make a suggestion."

Sheehan continue to stare at him.

The pathologist grinned and said, "I think some of the contents of the cup and the plate were fed to the victim as a symbolic gesture of some sort. Hence the drool and the vomit. But they're props, like the rope and the clothesline and the breeze block. They're part of some larger scenario in the killer's head …" He paused and then said, "… I think. Far be it from me to do your job for you."

He turned back to the body and pored over it, spreading the skin here and there with probing fingers. Eventually he lifted an arm and found what he was looking for, just below the inner bicep. "Aha!" he said.

Even Williams had approached the body and all three detectives now peered over the doctor's shoulder to see what he had found.

"Voila!' the doctor said, holding up the arm and gesturing to a small red puncture wound like a magician who had just executed an impeccable feat of prestidigitation. "Whatever was in the syringe that made this mark, is what killed your victim."

"What do you think it was?" Williams asked.

"Oh, I couldn't say at this point. There are certain poisons I can rule out. The eyes don't show the characteristic narrowing that would result from a morphine overdose. I can't detect the bitter almond smell of cyanide. Maybe the killer used heroin." He shook a raised hand back and forth as if to deny what he had just said. "I say that simply because it is so easily acquired nowadays. Might have been a large dose of sodium pentothal. I'll not know until after the postmortem."

"Time of death?" Sheehan said.

"I can't give you any idea when the poison was administered, too many variables in terms of the quantity, nature of the poison used and so on, but I have already estimated the time of death to be somewhere between five o'clock yesterday evening and about two or three a.m. this morning."

Sheehan turned to Doyle. "Try to find out what Corrigan was doing yesterday afternoon and evening, when he left Stormont, where he went, where he was until midnight. You know the drill."

Doyle nodded, put his pen away and made to leave. He turned and said. "How are you going to get back to the station?"

Sheehan looked at Bob. "I'll get a ride with DI Williams."

When Doyle left and the doctor was upright again, peeling off his latex gloves, Sheehan said to them both, "I don't suppose there's any chance that this one is not really what we think it is? Could it be politically motivated?"

The doctor shook his head. "Too many similarities to your other naked killings. Some of the elements of the MO may be different but the overall feel of the thing is exactly the same as the others."

Williams nodded. "I agree. I was talking to one of the SOCOs who was present at some the earlier scenes you mentioned earlier. He says it's the same as before. The scene is forensically immaculate."

"Cool customer," Sheehan muttered. "He must hang around a good wee while after he kills in order to clear up after him." He looked at Williams. "What about the three in the front office?"

"Found the body when they came in to work this morning. Shocked, of course. Worried about their jobs. But they weren't able to offer anything helpful. They're going to compile a list of recent visitors to the office but I wouldn't hold out much hope that there'll be anything useful there either."

"You've got uniforms going door to door?"

"Yes, but no hits yet. We'll have to get out a media appeal for anyone who saw any kind of movement in or around these offices last night, especially around closing time."

Sheehan emitted an exasperated groan. "Blazes! This guy really is a ghost. Four murder scenes and he has left neither hide nor hair at any of them. He drifts in and out of each location unseen and unheard. I'm beginning to wonder if he's some sort of phantom that can pass through walls."

Dr. Campbell had closed his briefcase and gave each a small salute. "Well, I'm off. I'll try to get you some answers within the next couple of days. But I'll be constrained by the speed of the lab on the poisons, so you're going to have to wait a while."

Sheehan nodded. "Thanks, Dick. I'll be in touch."

The doctor went off grinning. "I have no doubt you will, Jim. Cheers, Bob."

When he had gone, Sheehan said to Williams. "Don't suppose anybody mentioned finding some weird numbers?"

"No. Sorry. Were you expecting something?"

"Ah, not really. Just an aul' notion I have. It's not important." He stared at the door. "I'll just have a quick word with the staff next door."

He went into the front office, a large airy room with a window that occupied most of the street wall. The three members of staff were still sitting where he had first seen them. The younger of the two women was nervously pulling at a handkerchief with which she occasionally dabbed her eyes. The other two showed less emotion but were clearly shocked by what had happened.

Sheehan walked over to them and remained standing. "I'm sorry for your loss," he said, "but I need to ask you a couple of questions. I'll only keep you a minute."

Three heads nodded in unison.

"Mr. Corrigan was a very outspoken politician," he said, "and I have no doubt that you've had plenty of complaints about him?"

222

The older woman, wearing lipstick that was much too red for her wrinkles, said, "Yes, he liked to support some causes that were a bit liberal for the Northern Irish people. We get plenty of crank calls about him."

"But he did a lot of good work, too," the tearful one broke in, "and worked very hard for his constituents."

"I'm sure he did. Apart from the usual cranks, did you happen to notice anyone slightly odd hanging about or perhaps a visitor who came to see him but would not tell you what his business was?"

All three stared at each other wordlessly, seeming to communicate telepathically. The older woman spoke again, "No, nothing like that. We always knew who Mister Corrigan was seeing and why."

"Did he ever receive any threats of violence, from paramilitaries or anything like that?"

The young man, skinny, long hair, stud in his nose, said, "We occasionally get stones thrown through the big window there. Costs a fortune to keep it replaced. I sometimes wondered if the stone-throwers were making any kind of political statement. But there were never any notes or messages."

"So, no obvious enemies?"

"Well, he had enemies, all right," the youth said. "But they were members of other parties. The DUP voters couldn't stand him. They used to argue and row with him all the time, but I don't think they would have killed him."

"Just the usual Northern Ireland politics, then?"

The youth managed a faint grin. "I guess so."

"All right. Thank you. You can leave now, if you wish. The ambulance is here to take the body away.

But would you please give your names and addresses to the officer at the door in case I need to speak to you again."

The two detectives went outside to breathe some clean air while the body was being removed. One of the CSI's was carrying out the plate and the cup when Sheehan suddenly stopped him. "Hey, hold on a sec."

The officer stared at him, bemused.

"Could I have a wee look at that plate?"

The officer handed it to him and Sheehan raised it above his head to look underneath it. There were one or two manufacturer's marks, stamped in faint gold lettering but nothing else. Disappointed, he asked for the cup. Underneath it were tiny numbers preceded by a capital E, written with a fine indelible marker. They could easily be mistaken for a manufacturer's series number. "Tell forensics to be careful with that cup. It's as important as its contents," Sheehan said. "Ask them to see what they can learn from it."

He turned to Williams and noticed the puzzled expression on his face. "Do you feel like going back in there?"

Williams shook his head.

"Me neither. Let's go for a coffee somewhere and I'll explain about these numbers. Then you can give me a lift back to the station."

THIRTY

Back at his own office that afternoon, Sheehan sat at his desk, forlornly studying the forensics and some of the early reports on the Corrigan investigations. Doyle was at a lap-top in the incident room checking out Corrigan on the internet, looking for any connections there might have been between him and any of the other victims. Sheehan threw the sheets on the table and leaned back, running his hands through his hair. He was learning nothing from what he was reading and intuiting even less. So much for his fabled 'hunches'. There was so little to go on that he couldn't even make wild speculations except of the most general kind. His desk phone rang. "Hello!"

It was the front of house receptionist. "Sir, there's a Monsignor Byrne here to see you."

Sheehan didn't respond immediately. He was wondering if the monsignor had found anything in the bishop's files or, somewhat guiltily, if he was here to talk about Margaret. There was still the query hanging over his alibis, too. How far should he allow that to influence his interaction with the priest? "Send him up to my office, will you, please. Tell him I'll meet him at the top of the stairs."

He had scarcely reached the outer door of the incident room when he saw the monsignor, despite his top coat, sprinting up the last few steps. The monsignor grinned when he saw Sheehan. "Good morning, Chief Inspector." He gestured at the stairs. "I like to keep fit. I take my exercise when and where I can."

Sheehan smiled back and led him quickly through the incident room and into his office. "Please, take a seat." He sat down himself and continued, "Well, Monsignor, what can I do for you ... oh, would you like tea, coffee?"

"No, no thanks, I'm fine." The monsignor reached into the inside pocket of the overcoat he was wearing and took a folded A4 sheet of paper from his pocket. "I've been going through the bishop's files as I promised. There's very little there that would be of any interest to the police, at least I thought so until I came across this last night." He handed the page to Sheehan.

Sheehan took the sheet and looked at it. It was a lengthy letter, obviously printed from a computer file. It was headed:

A WARNING TO BISHOP CHARLES LOUGHRAN

Sheehan straightened and glanced up at the monsignor who was watching his reactions. He went back to the letter, reading aloud, "*My Lord Bishop ...*

Well, a polite and formal greeting … *It is with regret that I am obliged to write this letter. Your recent behaviours, your writings, and the increasing ambiguity of your Sunday homilies, all reveal a disturbing disconnection from the Magisterium. Rome has made it increasingly clear that she views with distrust those bishops in the United Kingdom who are becoming increasingly liberal in their thinking, who profess increasing sympathy for the arguments from the homosexual and feminist lobbies. You, Bishop Loughran, are one of those failing prelates. You, Bishop Loughran, in your writing and in your example, are morally corrupt."*

Sheehan looked at the monsignor again, slight accusation in his tone. "I didn't get an impression of anything like that when I talked to you about the bishop a while ago."

The monsignor shrugged. "I believe I told you that what was going on with the bishop was more about tone than about content. But this guy's exaggerating. This is his own opinion he's spouting, not necessarily fact. He's obviously very conservative, even fundamentalist."

Sheehan nodded and read the next paragraph. *"The Soho Masses in London are one of the worst scandals imaginable. Here the London archbishop openly invites practising homosexuals to most Holy Communion. And yet you, Bishop Loughran, have shown your approval of this sacrilege by deliberately attending at least two of these monstrous functions, openly disgracing your mitre and crozier. How dare you lend your name, our diocese's name, to a disgraceful service where you must have known that grave sacrileges would be committed?"*

Sheehan's expression revealed his puzzlement.

"What's that all about?" he asked.

The monsignor was nodding grim-faced. "Big bone of contention," he said. "These are Masses held every first and third Sunday of the month in the Church of Our Lady and St Gregory in Soho, London, for gay and transgendered people. The argument justifying support for the Soho Masses is that they are celebrated for the benefit of gays who accept the teachings of the Church and who therefore refrain from any form of sexual activity. There are many who see that argument as no more than a pious hope." The monsignor sat back and sighed deeply. "I always had reservations about these Masses myself and was disturbed, I must admit, when Charles told me he had been attending some of them to show solidarity with the archbishop over there."

"What are your objections?"

"Well, Catholic teaching obviously is that homosexuals must be accepted with respect, compassion, and sensitivity but, and it is an important 'but', they are also called to chastity. The whole ethos of these Soho Masses, from what I have been hearing, seems to ignore this teaching. I'm told, and the sources are reliable, that practising homosexuals are encouraged by the Archdiocese of Westminster to present themselves for Holy Eucharist. That's disastrous, if it's true. The writer of this letter has obviously got wind of what Charles was doing. What he is saying in his letter is that it is not morally acceptable to describe these Masses as pastoral care."

"So you agree with this guy?"

The monsignor gave him a hard stare. "Nobody ever gets their side of an argument a hundred percent wrong, Chief Inspector, not even crazies."

Sheehan broke away from the direct grey green eyes that were penetrating his. *This man can be hard as nails if he needs to be,* he thought. Aloud he said in a mollifying tone, "No criticism implied, Monsignor." He turned back to the page. "*These Masses rank with another scandal, the distortion of Catholic teaching which passes for religious instruction in most Catholic schools. This is a direct result of your lack of watchfulness over your flock.*" He stopped reading and said, "I've seen a memo written by that principal who was murdered, deciding to abandon Christian practices in his school. Could that be what he's talking about here?"

"I'm not sure. There seems to be a strongly secularist current in Catholic education nowadays. Mr. O'Donovan was probably just part of it. This writer might be talking more generally. There are other principals in the diocese who are starting to neglect their schools' Catholic ethos."

"So he's right again?"

The monsignor spread his hands. "About the creeping secularism, maybe, but no way the bishop deserves that amount of blame."

Sheehan continued to read. "*All this in the name of inclusiveness. Woe to you, Shepherd, who has allowed his flock to scatter, prey to the enemy. You will face the day of wrath.* Well, that bit's come true. I wonder if the writer of this is also the killer."

The monsignor spread his hands. "It's possible, but I don't know if you can deduce that without supporting evidence."

"Yes, indeed. I know a little bit about that. *And finally! You have tried to block those faithful who seek a return to the true version of the Holy Mass. The*

Novus Ordo Missae, the so-called 'New Mass', is little more than another version of the Anglican Protestant mass. Hundreds of martyrs in England during the Protestant revolt shed their blood, endured great hardships and trials, and even lost their lives because they refused to attend the Anglican mass. You have declared, by your refusal to restore the Tridentine Mass, that these holy martyrs have shed their blood in vain. I say to you that such a betrayal demands blood for blood.

"Blood for blood? That's quite explicit," Sheehan said, lips pursed as he continued to stare at the letter. Then he asked, "How do you feel about the Tridentine Mass, Monsignor?"

"I have to confess that I didn't understand Charles' attitude towards it. Rome is perfectly happy to allow these Masses where people want them. I've said a few myself and I find them inspiring and prayerful. We're asked, of course, to take care that any such Masses should be harmoniously integrated into the already existing parish liturgical schedule."

"So what was the bishop's problem?"

"I think he thought that these Masses would start a slide back into a too-conservative Church. I did tell you that he was liberal in his approach to things."

Sheehan nodded and began to read again. The final paragraph was chilling. "*It seems that Rome is reluctant to pass judgement on you. It seems that your own diocesan clergy do not have the strength of faith even to question much less put a stop to your apostasy. Know, however, that I have no difficulty in drawing attention to your corrupt abuse of the Magisterium. Know that I have no difficulty in condemning your betrayal of the Catholic martyrs. Know that as the Lord's instrument, I am fully prepared to abide by the*

Lord's judgement of you. Know that this is not the last you will hear from me. You know not the day or the hour, but hear from me you will.

"*A Traditional and True Catholic.*

"Gosh, that's pretty threatening. And the bishop didn't show this to you at the time?"

"No. I've been wondering about that myself. There are a lot of crank letters in his files, fair enough, and I can understand why he ignored them. But this one, it stands out. That's why I brought it to you. The only thing I can think of, and I could be way off base here, is that there is a stinging element of truth in the letter that Charles was a bit ashamed of and he decided to hide it away. Had he shown it to me, it certainly would have led to some frank discussions that Charles might have found unpleasant."

Sheehan thought for a while, still perusing the page. Then he said, "Don't suppose there was an envelope with it?"

The priest's brow furrowed as he tried to remember. "The page was simply filed with other mail," he said. "If there was an envelope there, I didn't notice it. But I can search the cabinet again, if you like. Do you think there'll be fingerprints?"

"Well, between the Post office and anyone else who might have handled it in the meantime, it's hardly likely that there'll be any useful prints on it. But there might be a possibility of getting a DNA sample from under the flap if the writer licked it."

"Goodness, if we could find it, you'll know your killer."

"I'm afraid not. It'll only give us who wrote the letter. He may also be the killer but we'll need other evidence than the DNA on the flap. But don't worry too much about it. The sample might be degraded, or corrupted by the gum on the flap, or there might be no sample at all. But thanks for bringing the letter to us, Monsignor. It does seem to support a line our enquiries are following."

"Oh?" The monsignor's brows were raised in question.

Sheehan felt obliged to give him something. "That there's a strong religious undercurrent to these murders, although we're still struggling to get a handle on it."

"If the letter-writer has anything to do with them, you're probably looking at a murderer who thinks he's the hand of God."

Sheehan stared at him. The hand of God? The monsignor might have been speaking flippantly but was this just another way of saying 'fundamentalist nutter'? He rose to indicate that their business was concluded and, as they were passing back through the incident room, the monsignor stared around with a degree of fascination. Noticing Doyle working at a desk in the corner, he smiled and said, "Good morning, Sergeant."

Doyle raised a hand shoulder high but did not look up.

Continued his inspection, the priest said to Sheehan, "So this is an incident room," he said. "Remarkable. I've never been in an incident room before." He stared at Larkin's boards. "And these are the crime photographs …?"

Sheehan was not keen to have the monsignor spend too much time examining the evidence board but, even as he reached out to touch the monsignor's elbow as a polite invitation to keep moving, he noted that the priest's expression was no longer simply interested. It was transfixed.

"Monsignor?" The priest did not seem to hear him. He tried again. "Monsignor?"

This time the priest responded. "Is this how the bodies were found, in these positions?"

"Yes." Sheehan wondered what the monsignor was seeing. "Is there something you see there?"

The monsignor seemed to turn to answer the question but his eyes could not leave the board, keeping his face pointed that way, making the turn look strangely awkward. "There's something very familiar here," he said, "something I should recognise." He moved closer to the photographs. "It's these bodies," he said, almost inaudible in his concentration. Then he did turn directly to the policeman and said, "Could I take some of them down and look at them on a table for a minute?"

Sheehan was torn between protocol and the possibility that the monsignor might add new insight to the evidence. Trying to hide his reluctance, and hoping that the monsignor's interest in the crime scene photographs was much more than prurience, he said, "Certainly, Monsignor. Which ones?"

The monsignor chose four photographs, full body pictures which most clearly showed the positions of the bodies at each crime scene. He placed them on a nearby desk and began to move them around until the four pictures combined made it appear as if the bodies were tumbling over each other. After staring at them for some minutes, he said, "I cannot be specific about this but I am convinced that the bodies are deliberately posed to represent the damnation detail of a Doom painting."

"To represent the what of a what?" Sheehan said, staring at the photographs but seeing nothing new.

"Well, a Doom painting is a painting of the Last Judgement. They were extremely common in churches in the Middle Ages. There were hundreds if not thousands of them, many very crudely painted. But there are a number of very significant ones, none more famous than the Last Judgement painted by Michelangelo in the Sistine chapel. That one is pretty frightening. And there are other famous ones, of course. Fra Angelico, for example, comes immediately to mind. Look, there's a book dealing with many of the more celebrated ones in the bishop's library. I could study it tonight, if you like, and see what I can find out." He studied the photographs again. "I don't know if I recognise these actual body positions but they have the same general tendency found in Doom paintings."

"Forgive my ignorance, monsignor, but could you explain what you're getting at? You lost me somewhere back there in the Middle Ages."

The priest grinned. "Sorry, I got a bit carried away there. But seriously, dear God, I shouldn't be saying this, those bodies have been wretchedly maltreated, but if this is the work of a criminal mind, it has a certain intellectual fascination."

Sheehan's face remained blank. "I'm still not getting anything, Monsignor."

The monsignor grinned again and apologised again. "Sorry, Chief Inspector. The Last Judgement paintings are all very original to their artists, obviously, but they have the essential theme of the Last Judgement in common, Jesus in judgement of souls on the last day. Nearly all of them, therefore, have Jesus as the centerpiece. Often they include the pope, St. Michael weighing souls, the Virgin mother, sometimes St. Peter. But the most common feature is that on Jesus' right hand are a number of good souls progressing to heaven, the salvation side. On his left, that is, the right hand side of the painting, is where the Hell Mouth is and often souls are painted tumbling down into the Abyss. I think these bodies here are posed to represent something like that. Maybe your killer is copying these positions from a Doom painting. I'll know more when I've had time to study the book tonight."

Sheehan was all ears now. This was new and, he suspected, something of a breakthrough. No longer reluctant to share, he pointed at the other pictures, the principal's rope, the plastic clothesline and the breeze block found with the community worker, the cup and plate found near the MLA. "Do any of these say anything to you?" he asked.

The monsignor examined them, lost in thought. He seemed particularly focused on the photograph of Catherine Higgins. After some reflection, he said, "Did anything in your investigation of this victim's background bring up reference to scandal with children or anything like that?"

Sheehan stared at him, surprised. *Has this priest heard something about the community worker's secret and is trying to impress me with his Sherlock Holmes impersonation?* He simply said, however, "Actually, yes, there was some issue about her having a lesbian affair with an underage girl."

The monsignor nodded, tightlipped. He did not look surprised. His next question, however, caused the blood to freeze in Sheehan's veins. "Did drowning, or perhaps some imitation of drowning, play a part in her murder?"

Sheehan was too stunned to answer immediately.

Only the killer could have this information. What does that say about the man in front of him? Is he the killer, toying with him, playing games? Was Loftus right about the hole in his alibi for the bishop's murder?

The monsignor correctly read the suspicion in the detective's expression. "Don't look so shocked, Chief Inspector," he said with a grin. "My assumptions are just that, assumptions. I have no knowledge of what happened to this unfortunate young woman. But we're clearly dealing with religious themes here, my area of expertise. The possibility that this poor woman may have drowned is an easy conclusion to arrive at. See Matthew's gospel, chapter eighteen, on scandals. One of the things Jesus was reported as having said was, 'He that shall scandalise one of these little ones that believe in me, it were better for him that a millstone should be hanged about his neck, and that he should be drowned in the depth of the sea.' Given the religious significance of doom here and the clothesline with the stone tied around the victim's neck, it was any easy deduction to make."

Sheehan's excitement levels were rising fast. This priest was seeing far and away more in these pictures than any of the team had. "What about the other rope," he asked. "Any ideas on that?"

"The only other rope that comes to mind is the one Judas hanged himself with. When he was in despair after betraying Jesus, he couldn't seek forgiveness. He obviously thought he deserved to hang and, as Matthew tells us, 'he went away and hanged himself.' I gather from our earlier conversation that this principal was abandoning religious practices in his school? That could easily be interpreted as a denial, a betrayal of Christ. In a deranged mind it might easily be considered a hanging offence."

"But what about the exposed entrails hanging out?"

"Yes, awful that, isn't it?" His expression registered distaste. Then he went on, "There are some who argue that there is a contradiction between Matthew's version of Judas's death and the version found in the Acts of the Apostles. In the Acts we're told that Judas 'obtained a field with the reward of his iniquity; and falling headlong, he burst asunder in the midst, and all his bowels gushed out'." The priest shrugged, "Sorry about the graphic language. Actually this is something I have spent some time studying. Properly understood, there need be no conflict between the two versions. It is probable, given evidence from other sources, that Judas suspended himself from a tree on the brink of the precipice overhanging the valley of Hinnom. It appears likely that no one removed his body for some time and eventually it fell under its own weight into a field below and the decomposing corpse burst open."

"Good grief!" Sheehan said. "Compelling stuff, this religion."

"It has its moments," the priest grinned.

"You're pretty impressive at this, monsignor. Do you have a police background?"

The question was not elegantly disguised but the enquiry team was convinced the killer had a police background and Sheehan was anxious to eliminate the monsignor from suspicion. The more time he spent with the man, the more he was coming to like him.

"No, of course not!" The priest laughed. "Years of study for my Ph. D. You really have to examine and weigh evidence there and, believe me, if you get it wrong, there are plenty of intellectual luminaries to jump all over you."

That made sense. Sheehan was no longer in any hurry to have the monsignor leave. These new insights were extraordinary. He had no idea where they might lead but the weird stuff on the board was suddenly starting to make sense. He pointed at a photograph of the cup and plate found beside Corrigan. "What about these?"

The monsignor shook his head slowly. "Nothing leaps to mind, but I can check it out tonight. What was significant about them?"

"We can't understand the significance of what was on the plate. I'm told they were cruciferous vegetables, rotten smell, bitter flavour. The cup had arsenic or something like that in it."

The monsignor shook his head. "No, doesn't mean anything at the moment. I'll check it out this evening and see what I can find."

"What about the stab wounds on the bishop?"

"The cross? The symbol of Christ. I suppose you could also say that a bishop is the symbol of Christ in his diocese. If your killer was the person who wrote that letter, he was none too pleased by the bishop's performance in the role. Maybe he was trying to brand the crucifix into the bishop as a way of saying, 'This is what you represent. Now you'll carry it with you forever.'"

Sheehan nodded. "Good as any explanation we had so far. And the tongue?"

"The Old Testament contains a number of references to deceitful tongues. I certainly recall something about that in one of the psalms. I'll have to look that up for you as well."

Sheehan offered his hand to the priest. "Monsignor, I can't thank you enough for these insights. We really were running round in circles. You've given us a whole new area for investigation."

"Think nothing of it, Chief Inspector. I'm rather enjoying this. I'm looking forward to seeing what I can discover this evening."

"You'll get back to me right away if you find anything?"

"Of course."

As the monsignor turned away, Sheehan decided to take a further chance on him. "Oh, there's one other thing you might be able to help us with. We found letters and numbers concealed at each of the scenes. You remember me asking you about the numbers on the bishop's desk?"

The priest's brow furrowed. He said nothing but something was clearly going on in his head. Then he said, looking furious with himself. "For heaven's sake! How could I have missed that? What an idiot!"

Sheehan looked at him, bemused. "What's up?"

The monsignor was still inwardly berating himself. "I know what those numbers represent. How did I miss it before?"

"You do?" Sheehan's earlier suspicions began to reassert themselves. This man knew far more than he should. But the priest's explanation eased his fears.

"Since your killer seems to be operating from scripture, it's a pretty safe bet that your numbers are scripture references. I suppose we missed it because of the nastiness of the killings. Brutal violence like that … the last place we'd have turned our minds to would have been the scriptures. But I think I get it now. The one on the bishop's desk was E something, right?"

"They all begin with E," Sheehan admitted.

"Book of Exodus, maybe, or Ezekiel, or Ecclesiastes, or even the Letter to the Ephesians. If you give me the numbers I'll take them home and try to make some sense out of them this evening."

"We should have had you in as a consultant weeks ago," Sheehan said, allowing himself to trust the man again. "The numbers are … hold on. I'll write them down for you." He grabbed a page from a nearby desk and wrote the numbers. Handing them to the priest with a grin, he said, "You're going to get no sleep tonight."

"Years of study, nearly always at night, have left me unable to sleep much anyway," the priest said, taking the paper and putting it in his pocket. "Burning the midnight oil is the norm for me."

THIRTY-ONE

Sr. Brenda Sullivan had been a nun most of her adult life. In her early twenties, she had joined the Sisters of the Contemplative Heart and, apart from a two year novitiate at the convent in Florida, she had spent her entire life as a religious in the mother-house in Belfast. She had even spent six of those years as Abbess to the entire Congregation, spending that time visiting all of the Order's convents in America, Europe and the British Isles. It had been her role to lead the Order at that time, to preserve its integrity and to shape its path. She was therefore convinced that she had a clear understanding of their founder's inspirations and the charism that was supposed to guide their life, its patterns and its rules. Together with the sisters who shared the life with her, Sister Brenda had drifted happily within the ambit of the Rule for some forty years, experiencing little dissension or disharmony within the community.

But as she sat in the assembly room on an evening early in November 2010 with all of the other sisters, listening to a talk given by their charismatic new Abbess who had come to stay at the mother-house, she was filled with misgivings. Sr. Maria Alexander had arrived from America some eight months earlier. Outgoing and seemingly friendly, popular with all of the sisters, she was invariably the centre of attention at any gathering that she might be part of. She was forward thinking, filled with new ideas about how the Congregation should review its Rule and spirituality in response to twenty-first century enlightenment, and was already being hotly tipped both in Europe and America to serve a second successive term as Abbess.

For some months now, she had been making a point of seeking out each individual sister, spending earnest time with them, educating them in what she called 'the new vision.' One or two of the older sisters did not embrace this vision because they could not understand it. Sr. Brenda could not embrace it because she understood it all too well. As she listened to the American on the dais, Sr. Brenda stared at her sisters, right and left. All but a few seemed rapt. Their new sister was presenting them with a modern view of spirituality that was extraordinarily far-seeing and the younger sisters, in particular, were hanging on every word.

"The scriptures, we can all see it if we look, sisters, are androcentric. Man is the centre, the beginning, the end. The female is little more than a chattel. But the emergence of the women's movement in the late twentieth century allows us now to view with some suspicion the traditions handed down by these texts." She smiled at her audience, her face radiant with the glow of the inspired. Many unconsciously smiled back. "We are beginning a journey now that is taking us beyond the bounds of institutional religion. Our search for the Holy may have begun rooted in Jesus as the Christ, but deep reflection, study and prayer have opened it up to the spirit of the Holy in all of creation. With a new viewpoint, rooted in a completely new way of being holy that is integrative, non-dominating and inclusive, women are also beginning to see the divine within nature, the value and importance of the cosmos. Like the deer that yearns for running streams, like those who have thirsted for too long, they pine for the emerging new cosmology that will encourage their spirituality, that will feed their souls. As one of our American sisters described it to me, 'I was rooted in the story of Jesus, and it remains at my core, but I've also moved beyond Jesus.'

"We're on a journey, sisters; we are sojourners. We are courageous women about to embark on a new vision of the religious life. We are leaving the religious domain of our earlier sisters and are travelling in a foreign land, mapping our way as we go. We search, sisters, and what we find may very well provide a glimpse into the new thing that God is bringing about in our midst. We will pursue the spirit of ecumenism in its purest form. And who's to say that the movement beyond Christ is not, in reality, a movement into the very heart of God?" Sr. Maria stood to her full height, her arms spread, her eyes ranging across all the members of the community seated in the room. "We will continue to be religious women, but we will no longer be women religious as it is defined by the Church. We will choose as a Congregation to step outside the Church in order to step into a greater sense of holiness. Ours will be a choice of integrity, of insight and of courage."

There was a rustle of approval and many nods of

agreement. Sr. Brenda sat transfixed but not for the same reason as her sisters. She was aghast. She was listening to a pitch from a snake charmer that was bordering on heresy and her sisters seemed blind to it. The American sister's next words, confirmed Sr. Brenda's worst fears. "And so, sisters, it is my intention to make a proposal for our next Chapter. I would so love you to support it. With our new realisation that salvation is not limited to Christianity, that wisdom is not only found in the traditions of the Church but also beyond it, in Judaism, in Islam, in Buddhism, I propose, that as a Chapter, united on both sides of the great ocean, we change our name from Sisters of the Contemplative Heart to 'The Congregation of the Divine Sojourners'. We will choose the way of the sojourner and leave the land of religious familiarity. In so doing we will become leaders for the New Age, models for women and men who hunger for leadership, insights and inspiration."

Sr. Maria beamed and bowed. The sisters in the hall began to clap loudly, many rising to their feet. Sr.Brenda felt sick. How could her sisters embrace a spirituality so dangerous, so bereft of truth, so lacking in coherent philosophy or central dogma? She glanced at her friend of years, Sr. Pamela, a couple of seats behind her. Sr. Pamela returned her gaze and in her eyes Sr. Brenda saw the same tortured concern that she knew must show in her own.

As the assembly moved forward to throng around the charismatic American, to shake her hand, to be in her presence, Sr. Brenda left her seat and moved towards her friend. Quietly she said, "Let's walk."

They went through the door at the back of the room, into the cloistered corridor that ran the entire length of the ground floor. Sr. Pamela was almost in tears. "How can this be happening? How can she have subverted so many of our sisters?"

Sr. Brenda could only shake her head. "She has been working very hard to gain support over the past few months and she has been doing it with great subtlety. I have to say that her success has been startling. With her charisma and that crazy New Age rubbish she's spouting, she could singlehandedly destroy the entire Congregation. We must do something to stop her."

"What can we do?"

"I don't know but we must do something."

THIRTY-TWO

True to his word, the monsignor was on the phone just after ten o'clock the morning following his visit. When Sheehan took the call, the priest said, "Good morning, Chief Inspector. My midnight endeavours have borne some fruit. Are you busy now or could I call round and see you?"

"Please, come now by all means," Sheehan assured him. "I'm anxious to see what you've discovered."

"Be there in fifteen minutes," the monsignor said. Then before he hung up, he added, "Oh, had a bit of a search for that envelope. Couldn't find it, I'm afraid. But I rather think you'll like what I did find." He sounded pleased with himself.

Sheehan sat at his desk, trying to read some reports but unable to keep his mind from drifting to the monsignor's impending visit. Yesterday's conversation had him see-sawing between suspicion of the priest's guilt and excitement at the new insights he was bringing. What would this morning's meeting bring? What would he learn? Would the monsignor's findings lead them any closer to the killer? Would they simply provide insights into the killer's motivation and very little else? Or, indeed, would they be so full of information that only the killer could know, that suspicion would have to fall on the priest again? Is he playing some cat and mouse game that only he understands?

Sheehan tried to remain calm. *You're jumping away ahead of yourself, Jim. One step at a time. We'll see what he has first, study it, and then decide what we learn from it.* There was nothing calm, however, about the way he snatched the phone when it rang.

"Sir, there's a Monsignor …"

"That's okay. Send him up right away, please," he interrupted and rose to greet the priest on the stairs. Monsignor Byrne was carrying a brief case with him and when he sat down and placed the case on his knees, Sheehan could hardly take his eyes off it. The monsignor noticed the detective's interest, smiled and patted the case. "I have to say I learned quite a bit about where your killer is coming from." As he was opening the case, he looked around and said, "Where's your sergeant today?"

"Oh, Doyle? He's at Mass. First Friday of the month."

"Good for him." He lifted out a few A4 sized pages. "I'm not sure how it will help you find your killer but I have a fair bit of material for you." He lifted a page from the top of the pile and handed it to Sheehan. The others he set on one side of the desk. "I thought we'd start with the Doom first," he said.

"What you have in your hand there is a very much reduced version of this particular Doom. In the end, it wasn't that hard to find although, to be honest, I almost missed it at first."

Sheehan studied the printout in his hand. It was a colour photograph of what seemed like a two-tiered painting broken into a number of panels. Many of the details were unclear, with the result that he found it difficult to focus on any of it. Christ in the centre was an obvious figure but he could make little out of the rest. "I can see why you might have missed ..." he said, still peering at the page. "Lot of stuff in here. Tell you the truth, I can't make much out of it."

"Exactly. That's why I almost missed it. The details are hard to make out. I had already seen and dismissed this one during my search. I had to do quite a bit of frustrated poking around that led me nowhere before I came back to it again. It was only then that I realised that the detail on the extreme right was what I was looking for."

Sheehan raised the sheet closer to his eyes and peered at the detail. He still couldn't see much.

"That's only a four inch version of an original that is enormous, roughly seven feet by nineteen feet," the priest told him. "You'd have no trouble making out the details on the original."

Sheehan looked up. "So you think this is the Doom the killer is working from?"

"Oh yes. It was painted around fourteen-fifty by one of the most influential painters of the fifteenth century, especially throughout the Netherlands. His name is Rogier van der Weyden and this Doom was called, logically enough, 'The Last Judgement'. As I say, it's huge. It was originally painted on oak panels, fifteen panels of different sizes, and was hung in the "great hall of the poor" in a hospital in Beaune in France called the Hôtel-Dieu. I think the hospital is a museum now and the painting is still there, believe it or not. It's still famous and about three hundred thousand visitors arrive in Beaune to see it each year."

Sheehan stared at the photograph again. *Would I go all the way to France just to see this?* he wondered.

The priest reached to his bundle of papers again. "As I say, it took a wee while but once I went on to the internet and found this pair of details ..." He waved the page in the air and answered Sheehan's unspoken question. "Ah, when you have a photograph of a part of a painting, it is called a 'detail'. Anyway, when I found this, I knew I was on the right track."

He handed Sheehan the second sheet. It was headed, "Corner Details of the Last Judgement *[Rogier van der Weyden, c.1450]*" and depicted enlarged versions of the two panels at either end of the painting he had been looking at earlier, one panel entitled 'Salvation' and the other 'Damnation'. Here the figures were much clearer and as soon as Sheehan looked at the Damnation detail, he knew immediately that this indeed was the killer's inspiration. He had spent many hours studying the crime scene photographs and had no trouble recognising the postures in the painting. Four of the souls, tumbling down to hell with flames lapping at them, were identical in their bodily positions to the scene-of-crime positions of the four murder victims, one with the tongue lolling out in excruciating pain. He noted with concern, however, that there were five souls on the detail, three male, two female.

He was about to comment on this but the priest spoke first. "I see you count five damned souls?"

Sheehan waited, staring at him.

"I spent a fair bit of time thinking about that last night." The priest's expression was grim. "Your murderer is locked into this scenario, mentally and emotionally. He's fixated on this Doom. It's his inspiration; it's his guide. There are five souls here, or 'bodies', if you like. I'm convinced that your killer is psychologically incapable of stopping after the fourth victim. He'll have to replicate this detail in its entirety. I believe that you will have another murder soon and that it will be another female."

Sheehan felt his insides squeeze. Tension filled him and instinctively he raised a hand to his mouth, almost as if to prevent himself uttering assent. But as he studied the detail again, he knew that he could not argue with the priest's reasoning. "Good grief," he muttered. "Where do we even start to find this woman before the killer does?"

The priest had been observing his reactions carefully. Now he said, "Yes, that's going to be a problem and you'll blame yourself if you're too late." He reached out and placed a friendly hand on Sheehan's shoulder. Holding the detective's gaze, he said, "I advise you now, don't make that mistake. The murderer is the only one to blame."

Sheehan nodded but he was remembering other times, other places, where the killer was to blame but that had not stopped him suffering guilt and remorse.

The monsignor had continued to watch him and, apparently satisfied that Sheehan had heard and absorbed what he had just been told, he removed his hand and said, "There's nothing we can do about it right now. Let's move on."

He lifted another page. "I also tried to decode

your numbers for you. Ran into a few brick walls at first. Started with the bishop's E3410. Tried Ezra first but that book didn't have thirty-four chapters. Then I tried Exodus and I got something that was coherent enough but didn't seem to be very relevant. Exodus, Chapter 34, verse 10 says something like, 'I am making a covenant with you in the presence of all the people. I will do marvels never yet done in any land.' Makes sense, as I say, but I couldn't see how it applied to the bishop's situation. I knew Ephesians didn't have thirty-four chapters either so I went to Ezekiel. I should have known to go to him first. He's a great old prophet of doom. Chapter 34, verse 10 says, 'I am going to call the shepherds to account and reclaim my sheep from them. No longer shall they tend my flock.'"

Sheehan nodded. "Yes, that makes sense. I can easily see how it would apply, or how the killer would apply it, to the bishop. He sees him as a bad shepherd. So did you look up that thing about the tongue?"

"Yes, apart from the fact that the tongue in the Doom is already protruding, I believe your killer is sending an additional message. Psalm fifty, verse nineteen offers the following judgement, 'You have a mouth of evil and a deceitful tongue.' I think that more or less tells us what he thinks of the bishop and it tallies with what is written in the letter."

"I see. I see. What did you find for the others?"

The priest grinned at the detective's almost childish impetuosity. "Oh, you're finished discussing this one then?"

Sheehan responded with a sheepish grin of his own. "Sorry, Monsignor, but when you've spent as many fruitless hours as I have wrestling with these things, it's hard not to rush on to find out what they all mean."

"I understand." The priest's grin was still there but he went on, "Well, all of the quotations are from Ezekiel and all are doom-laden. Take the one found on the principal. O'Donoghue tried to turn his face away from the Catholic religion while retaining his post as a Catholic school principal. Echoes of that can be found earlier in Chapter 14 of Ezekiel where Yahweh speaks scathingly about prophets who stray away from him yet go through the motions of consulting him while their hearts are separated from him."

"The principal wanted to work in a Catholic school but didn't want to be bothered with the Christian ethos?" Sheehan said.

"Exactly. The quotation that was applied to the principal was Chapter 14, verse 8, and tends to follow on from that. 'I will turn my face against this man. I will make him a proverbial example. I will strike him from the midst of my people and you will know that I am Yahweh.'"

"So you were right about this killer thinking he is the hand of God?"

"There can be no doubt about that now. This guy is convinced that he is God's instrument and that he has to strike down the ungodly in Yahweh's name."

"Bloody hell … uh … excuse me, your eminence, or … your highness, or whatever I'm supposed to call you."

Monsignor Byrne laughed heartily. "Look, just call me Niall. That's easy to work with."

Sheehan grinned. "Okay, Niall. *Chief Inspector*'s a bit of a mouthful, too. I'll settle for Jim."

"Right, Jim it is. So, I then checked out the

numbers you found on the stone. As I told you yesterday, there was already, through the clothesline and the stone, a clear reference to the horrible fate of those who scandalise children. Ezekiel, Chapter 16, verse 47, comes after some seriously angry ranting by Yahweh about Sodom in which he threatens all sorts of dire penalties upon its people." He looked up. "You know that the word Sodomite comes from Sodom?"

Sheehan nodded.

"Some of the practices they were guilty of, well, your killer would have equated those behaviours with what you tell me your community worker was doing."

"Well, I don't know exactly …"

"I understand. I'm rushing on a bit, trying to see things through the killer's eyes. Funny enough, when I was looking for 1647 …"

Sheehan cut across him, "One of Williams' sergeants thought that had something to do with Cromwell's Roundheads making life difficult for Catholics in the seventeenth century."

The priest grinned. "Wasn't a bad guess but it wouldn't fit in with any of the others. Anyway, reading Chapter 16, I noticed that in verse 39 the Lord declared that he would '… strip them of all their splendour, leaving them naked and bare'. The killer would have seen that as further confirmation that stripping the victims was part of Yahweh's judgement for them. He would think Yahweh was actually speaking to him through the words of scripture. Anyway, the quotation he applied to the community worker is, 'You have followed their ways insanely and have given yourself to the same abominations. You have been more corrupt than they in every way.'" The priest looked up from the page. "I didn't know the girl so I am making no judgements, but your killer certainly felt strongly about what she was doing."

"Doesn't justify what he did, Niall."

"Absolutely not, Jim. I'm just trying to show where the quotations apply to the victims from the killer's point of view."

Sheehan nodded wearily. "I know, I know. He might be insane but there is reason in his madness. Doesn't take away the horror of what he's doing, though."

The monsignor handed Sheehan the page and lifted the final one from the desk. "Your last victim, the MLA, was targeted because he was espousing and promoting modern causes and attitudes that more or less drove a horse and cart through Catholic doctrine. I take it you were aware that he was Catholic himself?"

Sheehan nodded. "They were all Catholic; I'm beginning to think that's part of the problem."

"Yes, Jim. That was the conclusion I came to last night."

"So what does he have to offer for Corrigan?"

The priest said, with a small smile, "Again, I have to say that the killer knows his scripture. There's a passage earlier in Chapter 13 which threatens *woe to senseless prophets who mislead the people, who follow their own inspirations, and whose discourse is trickery and lies.* I've seen Corrigan a few times on television. The killer might well have used that one."

Sheehan nodded. "Yeah, that would apply. He was certainly trying to win the secular vote."

"Actually, there's a word in the quotation the killer did use that might, in other less tragic circumstances, be considered amusing because of its relevance. E139, that is, Chapter 13, verse 9 says, 'My hand will strike the prophets whose revelations are delusion, whose predictions are lies. They will not be accepted among my people's assembly.'"

Sheehan couldn't restrain a grin. "I see what you mean. 'My people's assembly'. I take it they didn't have Members of Legislative Assemblies in those days?"

"Well, sort of, but that's not what they were called." He looked up grinning. "Oddly enough, if you can cope with a small digression, the Greek word 'ekklesia' was somewhat controversially translated to mean 'church' in apostolic times, that's where we get the word ecclesiastical, but it could be more accurately translated as 'assembly' or 'congregation'. Wonder what some of our more secular MLAs would make of the idea that they belong to a 'congregation'?"

"Aye, indeed." Sheehan was less interested in philological niceties than he was in learning more about his crime scenes. "I don't suppose you were able to figure out what the plate and the cup were all about?"

"Actually, I did," came the enthusiastic response. "It eluded me for a while because the answer wasn't in Ezekiel. But then I remembered that the rope was Matthew and the poor girl's murder was Matthew and The Acts, so I figured a wider search was necessary. I finally found what I wanted in Jeremiah, Chapter 9, verses 13 and 14. Chapter 9 has a number of references to tongues that are addicted to lying and traitors who live amid deceitfulness. There's a whole bunch of stuff also about following the Baals, about tongues like deadly arrows, uttering deceitful words. I'm trying not to be uncharitable about the dead here, but all that stuff made me think about Corrigan and his anti-Christian politics. Anyway, that was where I found the reference to your plate and your cup. 'It is because they have forsaken the Law that I gave them that I will make this people eat bitter food and I will give them poisoned water.'"

The priest handed the last page to Sheehan and said grimly. "Corrigan was seduced by the modern Baals of liberalism, secularism, and moral relativity. There's a new and aggressive dark culture that is striving to change Catholic values. Corrigan was part of that culture and I believe that is why the killer targeted him."

Jim sat back, overwhelmed by what the priest had brought him. "My goodness. I have to thank you, Niall. You've done a tremendous amount of work on this. We never would have got there by ourselves. But where does it all get us?"

"There's a lot there to try to absorb in one go but you know a bit more about your killer now and what drives him. Maybe when you've had time to chew on it, you'll find the inspiration you need. I could hazard a wee guess, if you like."

"Please."

"Well, taken together, the murders seem to represent a critique of the disintegration of Christian values in modern western society. Each victim seems to represent some aspect of the modernism that's infecting the Church, moral relativity, secularism, liberalism, disintegration of family, and so on. It seems to me that your killer is on a one-man crusade, trying to hold the line by attacking significant Catholics who seem to exemplify what's harming the Church today."

Jim's eyes were slightly glazed as he said unconsciously, "Aye, right."

The priest rose and offered Jim his hand. "I'd better get on. I'm glad I was able to help."

Sheehan blinked his mind back into gear. He accepted the hand and said, "Thanks, Niall. I might have to call on you again."

"Feel free. You know where to find me." Sheehan made to move round the desk to accompany the priest to the door. "No, no, it's okay. I know my way out." He raised a hand and left. Sheehan followed him as far as the incident room. Bill Larkin was trying to tidy the whiteboard, fitting connecting sections together, re-writing information more cogently.

"Bill," Sheehan called and walked over to hand him the bishop's letter and the A4 copy of the Doom details. "Get this letter photocopied and locked up in evidence, will you, please. Pin the photocopy on the white board along with this picture. And then come back to my office. There's a few wee quotations I want you to type and post under the pictures of the victims."

THIRTY-THREE

Another evening briefing. Bill Larkin had already received the photographs from this morning's crime scene and was reshaping the white board. He was doing some excellent work, filling in the new photographs of Corrigan, positioning the Doom details, pinning the copy of the bishop's letter near the photograph of his dead body and under the key photographs of the four victims he had stuck neat little slips of paper on which he had typed the scriptural quotations. The original of the bishop's letter was now safely stowed in the evidence locker.

Sheehan watched the men file into the incident room, watched the small groups from the various teams engage in desultory conversation, watched others who were not conversing but were sitting at their tables looking resigned. Some officers leaned on desks as they chatted to those seated around them, others leaned back on chairs having shouted conversations behind the backs of colleagues who were themselves engaged in noisy chatter or studying reports.

Fred McCammon was sitting alone, staring at the floor, dark shadows around his eyes, his gaunt face more pale and taut than Sheehan ever remembered seeing it. Hardly surprising, though. Fred was fast approaching some form of clinical depression. He had taken to nightly drinking at the Crown, afraid to face the night terrors occasioned by horrific visions of what might be happening to his son at the tough London prison. Slight young men, and his son was slight and young, had to face ruthless treatment. But the beatings were the least of McCammon's worries. Slight young men were an attraction to brutal, long-term prisoners. Sheehan suddenly felt the man's pain. How could any father cope with such thoughts?

His eyes ranged the room again. He was happy to allow the men these few moments of grace. The overtime earned was feeble compensation to many of the family men who had been working for days and evenings on end without seeing their kids. He sensed an air of, not resentment, exactly, but a grudging acquiescence to yet another evening of reports, analysis (probably futile), and guesswork. This latest killing was going to do nothing to lighten the mood. Nonetheless, there was still that small coterie of men, energetic, wound up, talking and gesturing animatedly as they traded newly conceived courses of action, or offered for each other's consideration wildly speculative explanations for the murders. These were the men who would keep the investigation alive and active, who would inject regular doses of enthusiasm into the weary, the disillusioned and the defeated.

Slightly later than most of the others, Doyle, too, entered the room, head down as usual. He looked up and gazed casually around the room, checking out who was present. When his eyes reached the white board, they stopped short. His face remained impassive but something about his body language hinted at an inner disturbance. He recovered quickly, however, and walked to his usual place behind Sheehan. Sheehan leaned backwards in his chair and whispered, "What was that about?"

"What, sir?"

"I know you too well, Doyle. Something caught your attention or upset you when you came in."

Doyle stared at him for a beat or two and then shrugged. "I'm just coming in from evening Mass, sir. I lift my head when I walk in here and the first thing I see is all those dead bodies on the white board. It sort of sneaked up on me a bit. They're gory, sir. Sorry about that."

"Sorry? No need to be sorry, Doyle," Sheehan said over the noise of the chatter and bustle around them. "We see far too much death and destruction in this job. It's easy to become inured, even callous. Be glad you still have your sensitivity, Sergeant. Shows you're still human. Too many of the guys lose that."

Doyle melted back into the wall, expressionless as ever.

Sheehan sat forward again and called the meeting to order. "Right, men, we've a fair bit to get through tonight." He glanced around. "I'm sorry to be dragging you from your homes for yet another evening ..." He paused to allow some of the men to mutter a few inarticulate growls and moans and continued, "Most of you will already have heard that we have had yet another killing this morning, this time one of our MLAs."

"You're sure that it's one of ours, sir, and not a politically motivated copycat?" asked Oliver McCoy, his round face serious. McCoy had twenty-five or so years on the force and many of those had been served at the latter end of 'the troubles'. The mind-set of those fearful days was never far below the surface. Any mention of politics in a crime situation had him diving for explanations that involved paramilitary activity, revenge killings, or sectarian hatred.

"We're pretty sure that that isn't the case, Oliver," Sheehan said. "There are too many similarities between this killing and the other three."

"Yes, but the papers have battered the other three stories to death. Even the dogs in the street know all the details of them by now. It would be very easy for some loyalist gang to fake up the killing to look like a copy of the other three."

The door had opened as McCoy was speaking and the Assistant Chief Constable entered the room, immaculately dressed as usual, wearing a dark woollen overcoat, his hair shaped and styled like something from a hairdresser's magazine. ACC Peter Harrison was not a particularly handsome man. His face was too large, his lips rather too thick, but he was tall, heavy but not fat, and carried himself well. He exuded an air of such confidence and authority that any defect in his features was made irrelevant. This image, however, was dented by an arrogance that rendered his pronouncements so pompous that few people gave any serious credence to what he had to say.

He had heard McCoy's final remarks and, as he walked through the room to join Sheehan at the top, he said, "Very astute, detective. There are many among the higher echelons of the force who would echo that line of thinking." He set his black leather gloves on the top table and turned to Sheehan, offering his hand. "Good evening, Chief Inspector." He gave the room a small wave of greeting. "Good evening, men. Thought I'd drop in and offer some words of encouragement."

The ACC was now playing a favourite role, a leader of men, stepping down to visit the ranks, motivating them with some charm, some exhortation, some strong injunction, to greater effort and eventual success. He affected an expression that was calculated to portray earnestness and fellowship. "It has been a difficult few weeks, men, and I am aware of the efforts that you have been making to solve these terrible and senseless murders. Your DCI has been keeping me informed about your progress and, while there are those who might say that little has been achieved, I know of the work that is being done."

Sheehan was severely tempted to raise his eyes to the ceiling but struggled instead to emulate Doyle's impassivity.

"I trust that you will soon break those first three killings but my concern this evening is with this morning's horrific murder of one of the most respected members of the Legislative Assembly."

Corrigan's political machinations must have extended to the ACC, Sheehan thought. *The man seems almost prepared to put the other three killings on hold in order to solve this one.*

The ACC continued. "I compliment Detective McCoy on what he was saying as I came in. The voice of experience, I would say." He beamed at McCoy who flushed but said nothing. "The thing is, and I know that there will be some disagreement about this, but I believe the force would be best served if we pursued some form of paramilitary involvement in Mr. Corrigan's murder."

Sheehan moved but the ACC held up a hand.

"Yes, Chief Inspector, I fully appreciate that there are certain superficial resemblances between the MOs of the previous killings and the murder of the MLA but I have no doubt that Detective McCoy has hit the nail on the head. This is a sectarian murder, disguised by the perpetrators to resemble the so-called 'naked murders' …"

"But sir," Sheehan interrupted, "there are also present at the crime scene some elements of the previous crimes that have not been revealed to the public …"

The ACC smiled benignly and said, "I appreciate your point, Chief Inspector, and if there had been only one murder before this one, I would probably have to agree with you. But after three murders, you know as well as I do that the elements we try to conceal somehow find their way to other ears. It's unfortunate that that should happen but it's a fact of life. I am convinced that this is what has happened here. I am aware, and I don't mind sharing this with you, that Mr. Corrigan has been the subject of threats to his life in the past …"

"As have many other MLAs," Sheehan said.

"Of course," the ACC was suddenly frosty, "and we do not take those threats lightly. But the threat has actually been carried out on Mr. Corrigan and I would be concerned if time was wasted on a misdirected pursuit of an unhinged fundamentalist or, I should say, an alleged fundamentalist. As I understand it, there is as yet no evidence to support that theory."

He drew himself up to full height and gave the detectives his carefully practised 'serious leader' expression. Time for a motivational talk. "There can be no doubt that in this particular case we are looking at some paramilitary or sectarian motive. Northern Ireland has had more than its share of this contemptuous lawlessness. We've had thirty plus years of it. We will not allow loyalist paramilitaries or dissident republicans any foothold in the derailment of the peace process." Somehow a few lines of the speech he had recently delivered at the newly established Department of Justice had found their way into this address. "It is towards those groups that I want you to direct your energies, men. Go to all your off-the-record contacts, your informants and what have you, and see what you can learn from the grapevine. It is vital that Mr. Corrigan's killer or killers be found and brought to justice … toot sweet." He picked up his gloves, clearly interested in hearing no opinion other than his own. "Needless to say, the chief and I expect an early result on this and I would advise you, men, to pursue the angle that makes sense. That's the way to a fast result."

He waved the gloves he was holding in his right hand to the assembled detectives, gave Sheehan a grandly condescending nod, and exited the room. His departure was followed by silence, a silence filled with a variety of reactions ranging from wry amusement to open contempt.

Sheehan was convinced that the ACC's attempt to steer the investigation into sectarian or political lines was completely misguided. The word his mind formed was 'rubbish'. This was definitely the work of their 'fundamentalist nutter', an appellative he was hearing more and more frequently used in the incident room. He was not about to permit in his presence, however, any disrespectful comment on a high-ranking superior, so he said quickly, "The ACC has given us something to think about but we'll go through the agenda for tonight's briefing first and see where that takes us."

He pointed at Larkin's board. "Some startling new evidence has come in, the letter you see beside the bishop's photographs, that picture at the end, the little typed scriptural quotations that you see underneath some of the photos, all courtesy of Monsignor Byrne." Some of the detectives were half way out of their seats, peering at the board, trying to get a clearer look at what their boss was talking about. Sheehan held up a hand. "Sit down, men. You'll have all the time you want to study them after I have explained what I have learnt. I have had two visits from the monsignor and he has been extraordinarily helpful."

He then spoke at considerable length, acquainting the squad with what the monsignor had told him. His audience, for once, was rapt and there was not a single interruption while Sheehan meticulously detailed each item of information, sticking to the facts, leaving interpretation to the discussion that would inevitably follow. Even McLoughlin was fascinated. He was leaning forward, his brow furrowed, as he tried to assimilate the scriptural and religious overlay that Sheehan was applying to each crime scene.

All eyes were still fastened on the evidence board when Sheehan finished speaking. For a time, an intense silence prevailed. Some of the men were bemused, others were trying to frame and focus the pictures Sheehan had planted in their minds, and yet others, less literate in scriptural history and modern ideology, struggled with confusion.

"Another one?" McNeill whispered. "A w ... w

… woman? Where d … d … do we even start to try to find out huh … huh … who she might be?"

Sheehan had given the matter some anxious thought with, however, little practical result. He said, "Well, we can guess that she'll be Catholic, she'll have some sort of prominent position in her work, and she'll be up to something that is disgracing her faith. She probably won't be a teacher, a social worker or a politician. Our perp has been there already. Any ideas?"

"Is there some sort of diocesan committee with a woman chairperson who's causing grief?" Allen was first to break the silence.

"Good idea," Sheehan said. "You and McNeill find out. Anyone else?"

"Maybe a Eucharistic Minister in one of the chapels around the city?" Connors offered.

"Possibly. Tall order to isolate anyone."

"Well, if she's up to something that doesn't fit, maybe having an adulterous affair …"

Connors' mind is never far from the cause of his divorce, Sheehan was thinking; but he simply said, "Yeah, might be something there. There'll be gossip about it if there is. You and Miller take that on."

"I wonder if that woman in charge of the choir could be a target?" Loftus said.

Sheehan's insides cramped. Loftus's words hit him like a blow. Trying to reveal nothing of his sudden inner turmoil, he said, "I wouldn't think so. You couldn't find any scandal …"

Loftus nodded. "Yeah, you're probably right."

"Any other ideas?"

266

"A nun," Doyle suggested.

Sheehan paused. "Hard to imagine what a nun might be up to. Still, we can't afford to ignore the possibility. Can't be too many convents in the Belfast area, are there?"

"Actually there's close on two dozen Orders," Allen said. "Remember that stolen car we found dumped on the Falls a couple of years ago? There was a nun's prayer-book in it but no mention of her Order. Number plates had been ripped off so we had to search the convents for the owner. We found twenty plus Orders during that search, Poor Clares, Presentations, Dominicans, Daughters of Charity …"

"All right, all right. I'll take your word for it. We're only interested in nuns with authority, mother superiors or the sisters who train the young ones, what do you call them, novice mistresses or something. You follow that one up, Doyle, will you?"

He addressed the group again. "Anyone else?"

"What about a female journalist?" This from McCammon. "There are a few of them, on the radio and in the press, who used to be Catholics but are now pushing a hard modernist agenda?"

Sheehan gave him a long glance. Modernist agenda? What had Fred been reading?

Aloud, he said, "That's a good idea, Fred." Then, after a short pause, he continued. "Actually, it's a very good idea. It feels sorta connected to everything that our perp has been at before. Yes, you and your team take that one on. Give it all you've got."

He stared hard at the assembled detectives. "This is Friday evening, we're all exhausted, and we've only got five days, Wednesday afternoon at the latest. If the killer sticks to his pattern, he'll strike again on

Wednesday night. We have to find this woman before that."

Sheehan waited for more suggestions but none were forthcoming. He looked at McCoy. "Oh, Oliver, would you look into the ACC's sectarian motive for Corrigan's killing. Use some of your old contacts. I don't think you'll find much, but just to be on the safe side."

McCoy said, "Will do, boss."

After some moments, Loftus cleared his throat, almost afraid to break the contemplative aura that had descended on the room.

"Sir, getting back to the real killer ..." Loftus unwittingly was dismissing the ACC's take on the killings. "... do you not think that the monsignor seems to know an awful lot?"

"Your point, Loftus?" Sheehan said.

"Do you seriously believe that he could have come up with all that stuff simply by deduction? I mean, how many thousands of mediaeval paintings are there in existence? How was he able to come up with that particular one in just one night? Looks very suspicious to me, sir."

"Well, he did say at the outset that it was a Doom painting and that he had a book about those. That would cut the research away down."

"But sir, an awful lot of what he says is very detailed and, I would have to guess, accurate. How could anyone not involved in the killings suddenly produce all that stuff, I mean, answers in a couple of hours for everything that's been baffling us for weeks?"

"Well, obviously I had the same thoughts, but his

reasoning and his explanations of how he arrived at his conclusions were very convincing. And why would he tell me all of this if he was guilty? Why would he risk exposing himself?"

"You said he's clever. Maybe he gets some sort of egoistical thrill out of pitting his wits against the cops," Miller offered.

"Our man is not about thrills, I think we can see that. He's cold and careful. He doesn't take risks. He's only interested in doing the Lord's work in accordance with his perverted perspective."

"Well, sir," Loftus said, "the thing is, there's something more that I've discovered."

"Well?"

"Sir, I still had a few leads to follow about the monsignor ... I know, sir, you think I'm wasting my time. But, sir, I discovered that he's ex-forces."

"The monsignor?"

"Yes, sir. He was a forces chaplain with the British Army for five years in Bosnia. Wasn't supposed to involve himself in the fighting but he spent a lot of time training with the squaddies, hand-to-hand combat, weapons training, pack-runs, was fitter than most apparently. Won several of the boxing competitions that the soldiers have ..."

McLoughlin seized on this. "Big, strong, clever, combat-trained, knows weapons, up to his eyes in religion, and can explain everything that's going on. We can't ignore him, sir. He's got the means, combat trained. He's got motive, wants the bishop's job, or maybe wants to clean up the Church. He's got opportunity, he's a monsignor, anybody'd let him into their house ..."

Others were nodding. McCammon looked perplexed. "My head's spinning," he said. "Who is it? Connolly? The monsignor? Paramilitaries as the ACC seems to think? Somebody else?"

"At least we're narrowing it down," Connors said. "It has to be one of those two. I don't give the ACC's take on it much credence." He glanced at Sheehan. "Sorry, sir."

"Sir, Sergeant McLoughlin's just after giving me an idea." Miller's voice entered the discussion.

McLoughlin looked more surprised than flattered.

"It's just that he was trying to fit the monsignor into a profile a minute ago. We have a lot of information here now. Maybe we could use it to try to develop some sort of profile on our killer. If we get a usable profile, we can maybe use it to have another look at those two, the monsignor and Connolly"

Sheehan's expression indicated that he wasn't convinced. "Profiling looks great on TV but it's notoriously unreliable in real life. Worse, if we believe the profile, we could get stuck in a rut where our perp doesn't even exist. I think it's important to keep an open mind."

"That's true, sir," came endorsement from the almost invisible Arthur Smith. The old detective did not normally say much but he did listen to all that was being said. "I remember the Yorkshire Ripper case. We were all fascinated by it at the time. The profile they developed then almost lost them their collar."

"What was that, Arthur?" asked Allen.

"Well, the SIO, what was his name …?"

"DCS George Oldfield," Sheehan supplied.

"Oldfield. That's right. Chief Superintendent Oldfield. He was the Senior Investigating Officer at the time. Well, he got tapes from somebody pretending to be the Ripper and Oldfield got stuck on the idea that the killer had a Geordie accent. That went in the profile. So when one of his detectives made solid and convincing representations that the real Ripper, Peter Sutcliffe, was a strong suspect, he was ignored because Sutcliffe didn't have a Geordie accent and so didn't fit the profile. So you're right, sir."

"That's true, Arthur," Sheehan said. "I remember the case. And the other point about that is that Sutcliffe did not really fit in to any of the other standard indicators of this type of killer. What they had in the way of a profile was useless."

Allen put in tentatively, "Yes, sir, but the standard profile indicators tend to be pulled out of the air by psychologists, and sometimes after the murders have been committed. What we have here, thanks to the monsignor, is a whole bunch of facts. We should be able to extrapolate some genuine information about our perp from those."

"Good point, Tom," Fred McCammon said. "Do you have any ideas?"

"Well, I've been reading a wee bit about serial killers …" McCullough's chair creaked heavily at this but he remained silent. Allen threw him a quick glance but went on, "They tend to have a few things in common, like psychopathic personalities, dysfunctional family background, poor at forming relationships, but there are several kinds of serial killer and I've been trying to work out which sort our perp is."

"Are you talking about Ronald Holmes' classification?" Sheehan asked.

"Yes." Allen looked impressed.

"Well, have you figured out which type our guy is?"

"Type?" McCammon's lean face looked sceptical.

Allen looked at Sheehan who gestured that he should answer. "Well, Holmes figured that there are probably four types of serial killer. He talks about the 'visionary' type who is psychotic and kills certain kinds of people in obedience to voices in his head."

"That could fit our man," Connors said.

"Then there is the 'hedonistic'."

"The wha …?" McCullough snorted.

"Hedonistic, pleasure-seeking," Allen explained patiently. "Kills for the thrill, perhaps even becomes sexually aroused by the act of murder."

"Not our man," Doyle said. "He goes about his business too methodically."

"Yes, I agree," Allen said. "And there's another type doesn't fit the bill either, the 'power-oriented'. He kills to exert control over his victims. He's obsessed with capturing and controlling his victims and forcing them to obey every command. Our killer seems to be in and out. He wouldn't have had time for that. Again, simply business."

"So what are we left with?" McCammon asked.

"The mission-oriented. These killers usually target a specific group of people without whom, they believe, the world would be a better place."

"So what's your take on this, son?" McCullough's inadequacy kept driving him to remind the kid who his superiors were.

272

Allen glanced at Sheehan again. Sheehan simply looked interested. "Well, I am kind of torn between the visionary and the mission-oriented, from the point of view of motivation. The visionary is more psychotic whereas the mission-oriented would be colder, more calculating. Our guy is clearly cold and calculating but then again there are all those props, the ropes, the stone, the cup and plate. The monsignor says that they are clear pointers to God's warnings to sinners. That's very much visionary. It's hard to know which way to go."

Sheehan looked thoughtful. "Our man seems to think he's acting on God's instructions, according to the monsignor, so there's a strong possibility that he's the visionary type. I hope he is."

Allen stared at him, puzzled. "Sir?"

"Mission-oriented killers accentuate their behaviours over time, they begin to see single killings as inadequate to their aims. If our man is one of those …"

"You mean, he might start killing people in groups, two or three at a time?" Miller's words mirrored the shock on the faces of the team.

"Well, he still has to finish this phase. There's one more killing to go, according to the monsignor. But if he decides to start a new mission, who knows?"

"Either way we're gonna have to stop him," Allen said.

"You got that right," Sheehan agreed.

"So, he's a mission-oriented serial killer, or a vision oriented … what was it, visionary?" McCullough said, unashamedly scratching his belly. "What good exactly does it do for us to know whichever it is?"

"Know the enemy, Sergeant," Sheehan said. "You should know that. The more we know about this guy, the better we'll be able to figure what he might do. Most serial killers are caught by two things, a mistake of some kind by the killer and solid police work in recognising that mistake and following up on it."

"Fair enough," McCullough said. "But anything we know has been coming at us in dribs and drabs. Maybe we should pool our knowledge like Miller says and see what sort of profile or whatever that we can come up with."

"That's what we were about to do before you interrupted us. Bill, get your black pen ready. Okay, men. Let's brainstorm this and see if it leads anywhere. Right, what have we got?"

Larkin began to write frantically on the whiteboard as the words flew from all quarters of the room. "Methodical … clever … strong … understands forensics … seems to have access anywhere … combat trained … ruthless … driven by some compulsion …"

When the input dried up, Larkin spent a minute or two changing, erasing, adjusting and finally produced two lists side-by-side on the board:

Personality Traits	Descriptive Factors
methodical	*has access to info about vics*
organised	*understands forensics / police background?*
fearless /ruthless	*combat trained/military?*
strong	*probably local*
careful/controlled	*Christian/probably Catholic*
mission-oriented/d	*white*
fundamentalist	*mature/indeterminate age*
psychopathic	*can be a convincing liar – vics let him in.*
cold/no obvious fu	
calculating/creative	

At Allen's suggestion, simply because they formed part of most standard profiles, Bill added two further descriptive factors but, at Sheehan's request because they were speculative, he separated them from the two lists:

- *may have dysfunctional family background*

- *may be a loner/poor at forming relationships*

The detectives stared at the lists, silent, impressed. The brain-storming had produced a very convincing list of descriptors.

"Gosh, we know a fair bit about this guy," McNeill said, his wonderment allaying his stutter.

"Do we know anyone who might fit this profile?" Sheehan asked. "Anybody on record? Can't be too many files with these kinds of details. Should be an easy search."

"I know a couple of people who might fit it," McCullough said. Everybody looked at him, intrigued, although they couldn't understand his smarmy grin.

"Well, there's Connors there for a start. He's big, he's Catholic, and he was in the army for a while …"

There were some snorts of disgust. Connors was glaring at him. The team did not share McCullough's sense of humour or his prejudices. "For God's sake, McCullough, will you give it a rest," McCammon said.

Sheehan, too, was displeased. "You'd better include me and Doyle on your list of suspects. And Allen and McCammon as well, and Larkin here. We're all Catholics."

McCullough was no longer grinning, but he sat there shrugging his shoulders as if to say his conclusion had been perfectly logical.

Arthur Smith attempted to lighten the atmosphere. He shouted to Larkin, "Hey, Larko, you have forces experience, don't you?"

Larkin's eyes bulged behind his glasses. Quick to deflect accusation, he said, "Steady on, Artie, I was only a cook. Never saw anything remotely resembling combat."

There was a release of nervous laughter. Bill's service record was common knowledge but not the fact that it had been behind the canteen counter. But somehow, the revelation seemed to fit.

"I think we already have our suspect," Allen said seriously, "and it's not the monsignor. He's too nice, too friendly, doesn't have the hard edge that the profile shows, and what would he know about forensics? It's Connolly. Has to be. Breeze blocks in the garden and orange plastic clothes line are damning enough but he fits a whole bunch of the profile elements. He's an ex-cop, big strong man, white, Catholic, fundamentalist to a degree, lives alone, showed no fear of me and McNeill at all, hard to get on with, actually threw us out. If we knew a bit more about him, there'd probably be a whole lot of other fits."

The room was silent but the levels of mental energy had cranked up considerably.

Allen's argument was persuasive. The detectives hated the idea of going after a cop but if it was a choice between him and the monsignor or, indeed, of assuming that it might be one of the squad as McLoughlin seemed to be suggesting, then Connolly walked away with the nomination. But they needed proof, evidence.

The men were mentally sagging as they tried to absorb everything that had transpired at the meeting. Most were sagging visibly in their seats as well. Sheehan was as tired as the rest of them but one small thought leapt into his mind and grew into a fully fledged idea in an instant. The teams noticed the DCI's sudden alertness and waited in expectation. Perhaps he was having one of his insights.

"Allen, what church does Connolly go to?"

"Don't know, sir."

"DI Williams was telling me that Catherine Higgins used to go to St. Anne's on the Donegal Road with her family during her schooldays. That's a church many people on the Glen Road might use. Check out with the parish priest if Connolly and any of the other victims went there too. Might provide us with a connection between the victims and the killer."

Allen brightened. "McNeill and me'll get on it right away," he said.

Sheehan shook his head. "Leave it until Monday

morning. The parish priest might not be too happy having to check into church records this hour of the night." He rose from his chair. "Right, men, I don't know about you, but I'm beat. Everybody go home and get a good rest over the weekend. Sort out your on-duty hours with Bill before you go. Although it's Saturday tomorrow, I'm going to try to arrange a meeting with Professor Greenwald at Queen's University to see what more I can learn about the way our killer thinks."

"Is he that criminologist, sir?" Allen asked.

"Well, he's the guy you're thinking about but he's not a criminologist. He gets called in a lot to help us understand the minds of perps in serious crime, not because he understands crime but because he is a brilliant psychologist." He shoved a pile of reports into his briefcase to read at home. "All right, that's what I'll be doing tomorrow. The rest of you can devote some of the weekend trying to figure out some way we can find that woman."

THIRTY-FOUR

PART 1

On his way home, Sheehan found himself again on the steps of St. Malachy's Church. He was tired and he was hungry. *What am I doing here?* he wondered. A small voice in his head told him that that was what he always said when he found himself going into the chapel. *Maybe I do, maybe I don't, but it still makes no sense. I should be at home, eating, thinking.* Again the little voice. *"You can think in here."*

He tried to shake the voice from his head and walked towards his usual pew near the back. He vaguely noticed a woman wearing a black Spanish mantilla over her head, praying in a pew further up the aisle but he paid her no attention. As always, he was focused on trying to make some sense out of these visitations that had become so consistent a part of his life.

A surreptitious glance at the altar and he quickly bowed his head, settling back on the pew, not far from sleep. His mind drifted to the recent revelations from the monsignor and he found himself wondering about the last judgement. In the eyes of the killer, the victims of the 'naked murders' were sent tumbling down to hell, a judgement meted out by the hand of God. A line learnt by heart during his school days, came to his mind unbidden, '... sent to my account with all my imperfections on my head', words spoken by the ghost of Hamlet's father. A slight tremor shook Sheehan's spirit. These were thoughts that had not troubled him in years. But tendrils of his childhood faith, buried for so long in the hard crust of cynicism that had smothered his spirit, were beginning to pull again on his soul.

It's this damned case, and damned is what it is. All this talk of hell, of judgement, of doom. It would unnerve anybody. The vision of the 'Damnation' was frightening. To be cast out into the pit without any opportunity to be saved, steeped in the slime of unforgiven sin. Sheehan found the thought troubling in the extreme. More words from the ghost's dreadful lament filled his head, "O, horrible! O, horrible! Most horrible!" Sheehan was disturbed by the strength of his reaction to these thoughts. *What's the matter with me? Who believes in hell any more? Who believes in sin? Isn't it all about God's loving mercy these days?*

His mind blanked. Then came the small voice. *"So what are you saying? You're saying there's a God?" I'm not saying that. All I'm saying is that the spin since Vatican Two is all about love, not sin and damnation. It doesn't mean I believe or don't believe. I'm just saying what I heard.* The small voice wasn't convinced. *"Aye, right."*

But thoughts of hell and eternity had awakened strongly held childhood beliefs and he found himself somewhat anxiously examining his own life, his own state. *What would happen to me were I suddenly to be sent to my account? How would I fare? 'Jim Sheehan? Who are you? I haven't seen hide or hair of you for twenty odd years.'*

A light touch on his shoulder startled Sheehan into wakefulness. It was Margaret, the lady with the mantilla. She looked as surprised as Jim felt. "What are you doing here, Jim?" she whispered

"Uh … uh …" Sheehan did not have an answer. "Margaret? What are you doing here?"

"I was visiting a friend on this side of the city. I usually call into St. Malachy's on my way home. My father's name was Malachy and he had a great devotion to the saint."

She turned her eyes to the altar. Still whispering, she said, "Let's talk outside."

Sheehan rose quickly from his seat and attempted to genuflect. A sharp pain seized his hip and he stumbled. He might have fallen had Margaret not caught his arm.

"You okay?" she asked, concerned.

He managed a grin. "Old war wound," he said. "Nothing to worry about. Honestly, goes like that in the cold sometimes."

Once outside, Margaret removed the mantilla from her head and said, "Jim, I'm sorry for the way I acted the other ni …"

Jim touched her arm and interrupted. "No apologies necessary, Margaret. It was totally my fault. I never should have landed that on you the way I did."

"When the detective who visited me explained the situation, somehow it was very easy to understand why he was there and I realised that I had over-reacted."

"Oh, I wasn't able to explain it?" Jim said, with a grin. "My detective is a better communicator than I am?"

For once Margaret was the one being teased but she could live with that, this once. Right now there was something that she needed to say. She had been miserable since that evening she had sent him out of her house, surprisingly miserable. Her work was suffering, her nights sleepless. She wanted his friendship again. "Perhaps it was because my attitude to the detective was neutral. I had no concerns about what he thought of me and therefore it was easy to hear his explanation."

Sheehan's heart leapt. He needed no further explanation and he would not force one from her. If she was not 'neutral' with him, then she was emotionally involved. That was all he needed right now to lift him to cloud nine, to eradicate his weariness, to fill him with delight. "I've been on the go all day and I'm starving," he said. "Will you come with me and get a bite somewhere?"

"Love to," Margaret smiled. "I want to hear all about your war wound. Was that the Second World War?"

Sheehan laughed. "Aye, right." Then he asked, "Are you driving?"

She nodded.

"Look, follow me round to Co-Co's. It's handy there just behind the City Hall. There'll be no problem getting a parking place."

"Co-Co's? But I'm not dressed."

"Don't be silly. I'm not even washed and shaved. It'll be fine. Come on. Follow me over."

PART 2

When Sheehan stood back to allow Margaret to ease past the two black iron tables and chairs and large beige umbrellas that were part of the stylish frontage of Co-Co's, he experienced a mix of feelings that brought a delighted smile to his lips. He felt excited, nervous, happy. He had not been here before but, with Margaret beside him, already he loved the place. The restaurant was relatively new but it was possibly one of the most talked about eating establishments in town. He loved the soft light of the candle arrangement inside the door, a welcoming touch that brought a smile to Margaret's face as she looked at him with raised eyebrows.

"This is nice," she said.

They were met immediately at the entrance by a well-dressed woman carrying large leather-bound menus. She smiled a greeting and led them to a table for two in a corner. Sheehan looked around. A glitter ball gave the bar area an after-dark atmosphere but the dining room was airy, with a lovely wooden floor, black pillars, soft mushroom walls and leather chairs.

Margaret, too, was admiring the surroundings and she nudged Sheehan's arm as she noticed an ibex head mounted on the wall, sporting a pink ski-band. She grinned and said again, "This is really nice."

Sheehan's answering smile was almost proprietorial. He was delighted with the choice he had made. "Yes, it's lovely," he said. He looked directly at her. "And I have to say, it's brilliant to be sitting here with you after … well, I wasn't sure if you'd ever talk to me again."

The waitress came at that point to ask if they would like something to drink, sparing Margaret the necessity of a response. Sheehan ordered a half bottle of the French wine the lady had recommended and said to Margaret, "This is really great. Let's enjoy the evening and make no more references to the other night, okay?"

"Deal," she said.

They lifted the menus. Sheehan did not even glance at his. He was watching Margaret, scarcely hearing a word she was saying, as she mused, "I think I'll start with the chicken liver parfait served with warm toasted brioche and red onion marmalade, and then … ummm … I'll have the roast cod, with potato gnocci, fine beans, asparagus, and salsa rossa."

Sheehan couldn't take his eyes from her as she was reading and when she looked up, he smiled and said, "Right, I'll have some of that, too."

Margaret laughed. "You didn't even look at the menu."

"Don't care. Just being here with you is such a joy after all the cr … cr …"

"Crap?" Margaret offered.

"Yeah, that. These last couple of weeks have been murder, literally."

"Still no clues?"

"Well, we're beginning to figure out what's making this guy tick, thanks in large part to Monsignor Byrne."

"The monsignor? I thought …"

"He was never a suspect in my eyes but he was close to the bishop. That makes him an automatic person of interest to the investigating team until he is eliminated from the enquiries."

Sheehan told Margaret as much as he could about his meeting with the monsignor without straying too far beyond protocol. Their starters arrived and, as they were eating, Sheehan said, "There's something I need you to do, and I'm really serious about this."

Margaret arrested a fork that was halfway to her mouth and looked questioningly at him.

"We're ninety-nine percent certain that the killer will strike again on Wednesday night, or early in the small hours of Thursday morning. I'm convinced this guy is psychotic so I've no idea where he'll strike next. But we are more or less certain that the next victim will be female with a Catholic background and high visibility in the Church."

Margaret looked shocked. She looked around at the other diners. No one was listening. Still she whispered, "You don't think it's going to be me? Not that I'm highly visible."

"No, I don't. But I'm not about to take any chances. I'm going to put two uniforms outside your house on Wednesday night. I want you to lock all your doors and windows and let no-one in, no matter how well you know them. I don't care if it is Pope Benedict himself. He doesn't get in. If someone comes, no matter who, don't answer. Just go to the front room and flick the lights on and off a couple of times. As soon as the two officers see the lights, they'll come running."

"Gosh, Jim …"

Sheehan reached a hand across the table and

285

touched hers for a moment. "Look, this is all only precautionary, more for my sake than for yours. The next victim will have done something that seriously offends the Church. You don't fit into that category." He gave her a questioning look. "Do you?"

"Very funny. So who are you? What have you done with the nice, shy, gauche man I met the other day? I want him back."

Jim grinned. "There's two mes. This's the other one."

"You seemed to have learned a great deal about the killer."

"Yes. Some senior detectives like to work a case alone. I find that I learn far more by having regular meetings with the team and pooling our knowledge. When we meet and talk, all sorts of ..." He stopped speaking suddenly and seemed to stare right through Margaret.

For a moment she returned his gaze and then said, half smiling, "Have I spilled some sauce on my blouse?"

But Sheehan didn't hear her. He wasn't even seeing her. She felt concern. Had he fallen suddenly into some kind of fugue state? "Jim," she whispered urgently. "Jim."

She reached across and touched his hand.

Sheehan blinked and saw the concern on her face. "Oh, sorry, Margaret. Good grief, it's happened again."

"What's happened again?"

"The other night in bed I woke up suddenly, knowing that I had heard or seen or noticed something during the day that had a significant bearing on the case. I was convinced that it was something that would help me find the killer."

"What was it?"

"That's the point. Try as I could, I couldn't figure out what had wakened me."

"So what happened just now?"

"Same again," Sheehan was irritated. "When I was talking to you about working with the team, I had a sudden flash of something that happened this morning, or was said. And it's gone. I just can't grasp it. But I know, I'm absolutely convinced, that it was important. Dammit, that's annoying."

Margaret picked up her knife and fork again. "Perhaps we should just go on chatting and it might suddenly hit you."

Sheehan nodded but remained preoccupied. Margaret ate in silence for a while and then, in a bid to distract him from his thoughts, said, "Why were you in St. Malachy's this evening? Did you know I'd be there?"

Sheehan had started to eat again as well. "No, no, I didn't. Although ..." He smiled at her "... had I known, I definitely would have gone there in the hope of talking to you."

She smiled back. The evening was recovering its earlier magic. "So why were you there?"

He gave her an earnest look. "Want the truth?"

"Of course."

"I don't know."

She waited for more but he was eating now. That was his explanation. She emitted a half-laugh. "You don't know?"

He nodded. "Uh huh."

Their eyes met, hers somewhat puzzled. "Well, that clears that up," she said.

Sheehan laughed. "Sorry, it's just that lately and I have absolutely no idea why I'm doing it …" He checked to ensure that none of the other diners was listening. Then he leaned forward and said in a low voice, "I stop at the chapel on the way home and go in and sit for a while."

"Oh? I didn't have you down for a man of prayer."

"That's the point. I'm not. Haven't been to church for years. And now, suddenly … But I don't pray. I just sit there." He shrugged his shoulders and went back to eating.

Margaret said nothing for some seconds and then, "You should go and talk to the monsignor. He's really brilliant with that sort of thing."

"What sort of thing?"

"Spiritual confusion."

Sheehan took refuge in his meal again and mumbled, "Spiritual confusion? Aye, right!" He cleared his plate, sat back, smiled and said, "Did you happen to notice what there was for dessert?"

Margaret grinned and said, "Well, I wasn't paying a whole lot of attention but I have rather decided upon the apple and autumn berry crumble, baked in an individual gratin dish and served with a boule of well-flavoured, home-made cinnamon ice cream."

Sheehan laughed out loud. "Did you learn that off by heart?"

"Well, I like to cook and that dessert caught my

eye. That sort of thing sticks in my mind."

"Right, that's what we'll have."

They ordered and ate their dessert, chatted intimately about their lives, past and present. Sheehan was astounded when the waitress came to tell them that it was after eleven o'clock and that the restaurant was about to close. They noticed suddenly that they were the only customers left in the dining room, apologised, and rose quickly to leave. At the door they said goodbye, both reluctant to end what had been a wonderful evening. Sheehan told Margaret that he'd be in touch before Wednesday, shook her hand, and settled for two French bises before walking her to her car. He stood on the pavement and watched her drive off, inordinately pleased when her hazard lights flashed a couple of times before she turned the corner and out of his sight.

PART 3

Two in the morning and Sheehan still had not found sleep. He was lying on his back, hands behind his head, staring at the ceiling. He was not even trying to sleep. Despite the fact that he was very tired, past experience, far too much past experience, had taught him that while his mind was in this kind of turmoil, sleep was impossible. And, while his thoughts seemed clear and perfectly lucid, he'd probably review them in the morning and wonder, as he had wondered so often before, what had been wrong with his head.

Memories of the evening meal with Margaret would pop occasionally into his mind and when they did, they would bring with them a small smile of pleasure. But such thoughts were incidental and fleeting. The cause of his turmoil was the case and, more specifically, the events of the past couple of days, especially the monsignor's visits, the findings and the opinions at the team meetings.

McNeill had been right. They did know an awful lot now about the killer. And the profile was not the kind of generalised guesswork so favoured by behavioural analysis specialists. What was on Bill's lists was factual and accurate. He knew that. *So, why doesn't it lead to the killer?* Echoes of McLoughlin's heavy-handed joke about Connors stirred something in his psyche. Was it annoyance at McLoughlin's backward-looking attitudes? He was honest enough to admit to himself that he was indeed irked by the man's bigotry but there was more to it than that. There was a kind of fear. What McLoughlin had said hit too close to home. Despite his angry rejection of McLoughlin's barbed humour, he was forced to acknowledge that several members of the squad matched a number of the elements of the profile lists.

A wave of weariness washed over him and for a few moments he drifted into quiet lassitude. But his brain was not going to permit that for any length of time. Visions of the evening meeting filled his head and he heard again McLoughlin's nasal whine, "… there's Connors. He's big, he's Catholic, he spent a while in the army." *Man that guy just loves to prod the Catholics.* Prod? The slang word for Protestants. *Well now, there's a Freudian slip if there ever was one. Must remember that for a laugh sometime.* He grinned sourly in the darkness. Yep! *You'll remember that in the morning and wonder what the hell was so funny about it.*

What was I thinking about? Oh, yes, McLoughlin.No, not McLoughlin. The scary idea that one of the squad could be the killer, Connors maybe.

Connors had been badly hurt by the divorce and he was still strung up about it but so what? Did that make him a killer? He was still a good Catholic, yes, but his wife had clearly lost sight of her Christian values and walked out on him. Would that kind of hurt tip somebody over the edge? Could Connors be lashing out in an extreme of loss and grief against others who had also betrayed their Christian values, some sort of perverted revenge motivation?

And who knew who else on the team might be harbouring some sort of inner tragedy that they were keeping quiet? What about Doyle? Could his father's death a few months ago have started something? *Gimme a break.* A brick wall could fall on Doyle and even then there'd probably be no kind of reaction. Well, what about Fred McCammon? He was nearly a basket case already. Was that kind of anxiety a trigger for anything? Worth finding out. He would have to ask Professor Greenwald.

He exhaled a heavy sigh. *It's too late at night, Jim. You're getting stupid now.* Fred may be troubled but he couldn't see his troubles finding expression in those terrible killings. *Man, you really are tired if you're thinking like that.* How could it be one of the guys? He would trust any one of them with his life. Well, maybe not McLoughlin. Not that that mattered. He was as far away from fitting the profile as Laurel and Hardy.

He tried to clear his mind and search for sleep. But his weariness left him victim to his mind's vagaries. His intellect chased down avenues and byways that his spirit struggled to avoid. Again his tired brain was forming and reforming questions, and answers were tumbling over themselves in response. *Are there any other likely suspects? Allen? No way, no way. He's big, he's strong, he's Catholic. What might there be lurking in his background? Larko? Now you're having a laugh, Jim.* McNeill? He could just see the headlines: 'The Stuttering Killer". Miller? Too neat. Too slight. Did not have the physical capability.He trawled though each name in turn, and while there were some who had only recently joined the squad and were not all that well known to him, he could not see any of them as the killer. Maybe it was somebody from Bob's district? What about Bob himself? Disenchanted with the way his career and his life have gone, he suddenly flips and goes on a killing spree? *Aye, right.*

His mind strayed back to the moment during dinner when he almost had an answer of sorts. Twice he almost had an answer. He'd have to ask Professor Greenwald about that as well. Maybe he would know a way to access those two insights, or whatever they were.

He turned over on his side and stared at the darkened window, his mind slipping from any focus. Gradually his eyes closed and sleep found him.

THIRTY-FIVE

Queen's University, situated in the south of the city, is one of the great architectural triumphs of Belfast. Its imposing façade, instantly recognisable because it is seen so often on bank notes and tourist posters, was built during the mid-1800s by Sir Charles Lanyon. His design borrows heavily from the Gothic and Tudor character of the great mediaeval universities and the sprawling, red-brick building reflects, in its authority and grandeur, something of the University's much deserved reputation for academic excellence.

Sheehan could not but be impressed by the historic ambience of the Lanyon Building as he made his way down the long front drive to the main entrance. Professor Greenwald, a stout man in his late fifties, wearing a grey sweater and jeans, long silvery hair tied behind him in a pony tail, met him with an enthusiastic handshake and a booming, "Good to see you again, Jim. Come on. Come on. Follow me to my office."

Sheehan allowed himself to be led into the main hall, past the large central statue of Galileo and on through a series of corridors until they came to a halt in front of a dingy brown door. The professor opened the door and stood back, left arm extended. 'Come in, Jim. Sit down and we'll talk."

Jim was not exactly sure how to respond to this invitation. There were three chairs in the small office, one of which was behind an old wooden desk and the other two were covered in books, many opened at specific pages. Noticing the detective's hesitation, the professor chuckled and said, "Oh, sorry. Here ..." He threw a bundle of books from one of the chairs on to the floor and gestured for Sheehan to sit.

Jim eyed the chair with some suspicion and decided that his suit could just about tolerate the dust he saw there. He sat and said, "Thanks for seeing me on a Saturday, Professor."

"Nigel, Jim; Nigel. So what can I do for you?"

"Same as usual, Nigel. I have a killer whose psychological profile is, I think, pretty well defined. I want to know if there are any behavioural clues that I could be looking for to help me identify him."

The professor lowered himself onto his own chair and spread his hands. "Tell me."

Jim spent a considerable time narrating the events of the previous few weeks, the murders, the crime scenes, the monsignor's findings. The professor paid close attention, absorbing everything, saying nothing. Eventually Sheehan wound down his story.

The professor nodded and sat back with his arms folded. "Well, I have to say that I agree with you about the murder of the MLA. It's definitely connected to the others. The ACC is barking up the wrong tree. There'll be expensive overtime there for a lot of wasted man hours. But that's his problem."

Sheehan said, "I agree. I didn't give that line of enquiry any real credence at all. What I really need your opinion on is a question that has been driving me nuts. There were no murders before by this killer, at least, none that we know about, yet suddenly he's a serial killer on a spree. Why now? Why so many?"

The professor said, "Yes, that's a good question, Jim. Clearly something has triggered these actions, some recent trauma that has unlocked memories or emotions that might have been lying dormant in your killer's mind for years. But we'll deal with that in its place." He leaned forward on the desk and joined his hands under his chin. "Let's try to see if we can pin down what's going on here. After your brief hints on the phone yesterday, I was toying with the idea of PTSD ..." He noticed Sheehan's brows go down. "Post traumatic stress disorder. Always a good place to start. But from what you say now, your man is calculating and controlled. Someone with PTSD would likely be disintegrating psychologically by this time and if he was anyone you knew his behaviours would have drawn attention to himself before now."

He leaned back again, looking over Sheehan's head as he tried to clarify his thoughts. "I'm tending now towards some form of delusional disorder." He raised a finger and looked at Sheehan, speaking faster and with more conviction. "You see, unlike most other psychotic disorders, the person with delusional disorder does not appear obviously odd or strange or weird during the active period of the illness. Most mental health professions would agree that unless you happen to discuss directly with the person the aspects of his mind or life affected by the delusions, it would be difficult to distinguish that person from any ordinary member of the public who is not psychologically disturbed."

"So he is able to behave rationally and normally in his day-to-day activities?"

"Exactly. He would have absolutely no idea there was anything wrong with his behaviours and doesn't suffer from guilt or concern about them."

"So, if the killer was in my company when I was talking about him he …?"

"He would behave normally, unless you said something that contradicted his view of himself. He would be aware that the conversation was dangerous to him but he would correct any misapprehensions that you might articulate about why he was doing what he was doing, or he might try to correct some seeming misapprehension you had about the killer by speaking about him in the third person."

"But how can he, I mean, if he is delusional surely he would be talking nonsense half the time?"

"Actually, he wouldn't. The delusions do not interfere with general logical reasoning. The only place where his logic is perverted is within the delusional system, although he would not recognise the difference."

"So he's self-aware and knows how to protect himself from the consequences of his actions."

"Yes, well, depends how he sees them. In the case of your killer, I would hypothesise that he sees himself as God's instrument, 'God-mandated', as we say. He would believe that ordinary mortals would have trouble with someone human executing God's will on earth and he would therefore conceal his actions lest someone should try to stop him carrying out the divine commands. It's an odd phenomenon but the delusions are logically constructed and internally consistent."

"So why has he not been punishing the wicked long before now?"

The professor raised a finger again. "Ah, the trigger. Hard to be specific, of course, with little or no information on the person's background, but there are some general pointers. Often the person who suffers this disorder has been carrying a predisposition of sorts for years, even from childhood. The sufferer might have had abusive or authoritarian parents, or experienced some traumatic childhood event that has been suppressed, that sort of thing. Very often the trigger is some new strong emotional trauma. Something happens that resurrects emotions similar to those experienced years earlier or even in childhood."

"God, I thought my head was sore last night, Nigel, but listening to this …"

The professor laughed. "Trouble is, I can't be anything but vague. That makes it hard to give you anything solid to go on."

"Do you think the monsignor's assessment is anywhere near the mark?"

"Oh, absolutely. He sounds like an intelligent man. There are different types of delusional disorders, erotomanic type, persecutory, somatic and so on but I am pretty sure that your chap falls under the 'grandiose' type. He would see himself as having a distinguished role, singled out for an important responsibility, in this case by God."

"I see. Actually, yesterday evening some of the men were trying to decide what type of serial-killer our

297

man is. We were caught between visionary and mission-oriented."

"Yes, I can see the difficulty. Mission-oriented killers typically justify their actions as ridding the world of a certain type of person that they perceive to be undesirable. Your man seems to be doing that. But all these scriptural quotes, the other God- related clues, point to a more psychotic break from reality. He sees himself, indisputably as, what you referred to earlier, 'the hand of God'."

"So how can I use any of this?"

"Well, if you ever get the culprit into custody, you can challenge his beliefs, rubbish them. These people are over-sensitive about what they believe. He'll show his true colours then. You'll see an inappropriately strong emotional reaction, usually accompanied by a deal of anger and hostility. And, conversely, if you don't get that reaction, chances are you've got the wrong man."

"Well, that's useful, Nigel. I'll keep that in mind." He hesitated, unsure whether to ask the question. "There's one other thing I wanted to talk to you about."

The professor smiled an invitation to continue.

"Twice in the past few days I got these flashes of a memory that I suddenly lost again and couldn't retrieve. What annoys me about them is that in both cases I was absolutely convinced that I had learned something that day which could help break this case but no matter how hard I tried I just couldn't get a fix on what I thought I knew."

"Where were you at the time?"

"Well, once I woke up in the middle of the night and the other time I was having dinner with a friend."

"No, sorry, I meant, where do you think you were when you missed what you thought was important?"

"I'm pretty sure that I was in the incident room with the men both times. Maybe somebody said something, or did something." He shrugged.

"Intuition."

"Excuse me?"

"Intuitive information comes without a searching of the conscious memory. When we receive an intuition, we seem to arrive at an insight directly into the conscious awareness without having to work it out. It just comes. Wham! Out of nowhere. Suddenly it's there."

Sheehan was nodding vehemently. "Exactly. So why didn't these two intuitions come directly to my conscious awareness? I spent a couple of nights trying to recall them."

"Jim, whatever is going on in your subconscious is still going on, so you haven't lost those two insights. But what is happening, I believe, is that you are picking up subliminal or other signals that your conscious mind is blocking."

"Blocking?"

"Yes. Intuition should easily penetrate the conscious mind unless it is blocked. The usual blockages are put in place by the conscious mind because it makes a judgement about the new information, decides it doesn't want to know."

"Doesn't want to know? But why?"

"You say you receive these signals in the incident room?"

"Yes."

"When your men are there, talking or moving about and so on?"

"Yes."

"Well, I can't be definitive, of course, but I would hazard a guess that one of your men might be the killer or have some connection with the killer. He has let something slip, maybe a couple of times. Your subconscious picked it up but your conscious mind won't accept it because he's somebody you like or trust."

Something inside Sheehan sagged, like the last dregs of air leaving an already deflated balloon. He reacted almost with resentment to what Nigel was implying. No way was the killer one of his men. But it was a weak reaction, a reaction born more from dying hope than from any real conviction. Was not this the kind of thinking that had kept him awake last night? Maybe, but he still had a lifeline.

"Hold on, Nigel," he said. "I don't know about that. There's no way it can be one of my men. I trust them all implicitly. I had a good think about that possibility last night and I've rejected it out of hand, especially because we do have a suspect. Thing is, none of us want it to be him because he's an ex-cop. Could my blocked intuition not be something to do with ... uh ... *esprit de corps*, the camaraderie of brothers-in-arms, that sort of thing? One of our younger guys is building an almost unassailable case against him. Maybe he said something significant that I missed?"

The professor seemed unconvinced but he said, "Possibly. Possibly. If you get him into custody, you won't be long finding out one way or the other if you do what I told you."

"Well, we've no grounds yet for pulling him in but we're working on it. I mean, we can pull him in for questioning, surely, but if we pull him in too soon we'll alert him and he might go to ground. We could lose him. At present we have no evidence against him."

"Fair enough." The professor leaned forward, hands clasped in front of him, and said earnestly. "But I feel I need to say one more thing to you, Jim. It's up to you what you do with it."

Sheehan was struck by the seriousness of his friend's tone and waited to hear what the 'one more thing' was.

"You trust your men implicitly, do you?"

Sheehan nodded.

"With your life, you said?"

"Absolutely."

"Well then, Jim, the paradoxical conclusion I have to arrive at is that you cannot trust any of them."

"Uh … run that by me again."

"Notwithstanding your feelings about your ex-cop, I still believe that, in your heart of hearts, you suspect that one of your own men might be a killer. You don't know who because you trust them all equally. Ergo, you're in no position to make a judgement about any of them. So, you have to withdraw your trust from them all until you know who the killer is."

THIRTY-SIX

At eight-thirty on Monday morning, Sheehan was already in his office. He had turned yet again to the Policy Book, reading reports and documents that he had read many times already, in the forlorn hope that this time he might find something he had missed, something that would trigger again the lost intuitions he had spoken to Professor Greenwald about. His mind was not fully engaged in the task, however. He was replaying in his mind the lunch he had had with Margaret the previous afternoon. He had been sitting in his apartment, checking the TV listings for a match or something he could watch, when the phone rang. It was Margaret inviting him to Sunday lunch to repay his generosity of a few nights before. He had accepted with alacrity, of course, and he was now replaying in his mind her every expression, her every smile, her every gesture.

"Sir." Allen and McNeill were standing at the office door.

Sheehan returned to the present with something of a mental lurch. "Yes, what is it?"

The two men entered, Allen, as always, to the fore. "Sir, we've managed to get a hold of the parish priest of St. Anne's. It's been very revealing, sir." McNeill was nodding vigorously but remaining silent.

Sheehan sat looking up at the two detectives, both clearly excited by what they had found. He spread his hands and raised his eyebrows, "Well?"

"Sir, Connolly is a member of that congregation. He always goes to St. Anne's. Two or three days a week he's found there. But we also discovered that the victims all went there, too, at one point or other in the recent past. The school principal, O'Donoghue, was in the habit of going there for Mass every Sunday with the missus. Catherine Higgins was a regular there as well during her pre-university years, always went to Sunday Mass with her parents. They're still active church-goers there. And while Corrigan isn't seen about the place very much now, he was an altar boy there in his schooldays and he turns up from time to time for special feast-day functions."

McNeill, who had been nodding constantly during these revelations like an ornamental dog in a car window, chimed in at that point. "That's how C … C … Connolly knows them all, sir. He must have b … been watching them for a long time, must have f … f … followed their careers and the ways they were falling away from the Church. Clearly wasn't p … p … pleased with what he was seeing."

"The bishop?"

Allen shrugged. "The chapel is part of his

diocese. He'd be well known and would probably have said Mass there a few times at least. He did try to get round many of the parish chapels while he was alive."

Sheehan said, "Good work, lads." He was pleased with the direction this was taking them. Anywhere that led away from suspicion about any of his team was a good direction. "This ties the victims together," he went on with some enthusiasm, "and ties them all to Connolly. That's more than a hell of a coincidence. He has to be our man."

Allen was now nodding along with McNeill. There was a noise in the incident room. Members of the team were arriving. Sheehan craned to look out. It was Connors and Miller followed almost immediately by Fred McCammon who was looking pale and wretched. Sheehan rose from his desk and said, "Let's go into the room and join the others."

McCammon was already seated at his desk, his head in his hands. The other two were chatting, about to sit in their normal places. Others were wandering in, some chatting, some subdued. Doyle, who was part of this latest group, immediately took up his customary position against the wall behind Sheehan's chair. Sheehan gave him a nod which earned him a blink of acknowledgement.

He allowed the men a few minutes to settle, time to exchange post-weekend remarks about sports successes and failures, and then tapped his pen on his desk. "Good morning, men," he said, waving Dick Campbell's autopsy report on Corrigan. "Just to let you know that the pathologist's report on Corrigan's death has just come in but it doesn't contain anything new or useful. It was as the doctor had surmised. The cause of death was a significant overdose of heroin administered by syringe."

"What was in the cup?" Connors asked.

"Forensics say that it was some rat poison, not a particularly significant amount. The pathologist assumes that it was just a prop like the ropes and cement block."

"You have to sign a register or something to buy rat poison, don't you? Any possibility of checking out who's been buying the stuff?" Allen said.

"Needle in a haystack," Smith told him. "I tried that tack a couple of years ago. You can get it on the internet now as well. And I can't imagine our man would make it easy for us by purchasing the stuff in Belfast. I mean how many chemists' registers are there in Northern Ireland alone, never mind the internet?"

"Sounds to me like you'd not just be looking for a needle in a haystack," Bill Larkin said. "You'd be looking at about fifty fields with about twenty haystacks in each one and you'd first have to identify which haystack had the needle before you start looking for it."

That gained him a couple of indulgent chuckles.

Sheehan said, "All right, all right. We get the picture. We won't go down that road unless we've nowhere else to go." He fiddled with his ballpoint and looked down at his notes. Then he said, "Any fruitful results from your weekend endeavours?" He cast a glance at Oliver McCoy who was sitting near the back of the room talking quietly to Arthur Smith. "We'll start with you, Oliver. Are we looking at a sectarian killing?"

"No, sir. I tapped every source I have all over the weekend. I wasted a few good markers, as well. Nada. Absolute zilch. Not only are there no grapes, there's not even a vine. Nobody knows nothin'. If there was any paramilitary connection with Corrigan's murder, somebody definitely would've known somethin'. It's a dead-end, sir. You can forget about it."

"No surprises there, then. Thanks, Oliver. Do you want to report that to your friend, the ACC, or are you happy enough for me to do it?"

There were a few derogatory chuckles. McCoy grinned. "Thanks for the offer, boss, but that's your job. I'm very happy to let you do it."

"Okay. Any clues about the next victim? Doyle?"

"Allen was right about there being a whole bunch of convents, sir. I've been around about ten or eleven of them. Tea coming out of my ears, sir, but no hits yet. I'll get right back on it after this meeting."

"Okay, who else?"

Tom Allen said, "McNeill and I have been round a few of the congregations, quietly sounding out some of the parishioners. You'd be surprised how people will talk when they don't know you're a cop. And you wouldn't believe the simmering animosities and jealousies that are going on in the hearts of a whole lot of the wee Holy Josies that are active in Church life. Our ears are buzzing with it. Right, Geoff?"

"Yes, sir. B … b … but the most of them are g … g … good-hearted enough. There's a few c … c … catty ones who would like to make trouble but we don't think there's any who w … w … would catch the eye of our killer."

"McNeill's right, sir," Allen added. "Nobody stands out."

"This is bit worrying," Sheehan said. "We need to find that woman."

McCammon pointed a thumb at Gerry Loftus,

seated at his table. "Loftus here might be on to something, sir," he said. "Go ahead, Gerry."

Loftus cleared his throat and said, "Well, it was a bit of a fluke actually. I was listening to Sunday Sequence at breakfast yesterday and one of the guests was a local woman journalist. She's always harping on about the male dominance of the Catholic Church and its rigid and inflexible attitudes to sex, etcetera. She was born and reared a Catholic but claims to be humanist now. She was deadly antagonistic to the Catholic Church on that programme."

"What's a humanist?" McCullough asked, probably wondering if this was some new religious group he might be able to vent his spleen on.

Loftus offered the group a somewhat embarrassed grin. "To tell the truth, I didn't know. I had to look it up. As near as I can figure, humanists don't believe in religion or any supernatural being like God or anything like that. They don't think that a divine power is necessary in order for life and humans to have value." He took a small notebook from his pocket and thumbed open a page and read, "Humanists claim that their morality and their life stance comes from respect of the human person for who it is and for what it is. The universe does not need a divine power outside of itself to have value."

He closed the notebook and was about to speak when Connors said, "You've lost me, Gerry. I'm sorry, but what the heck point are you making?"

"It's the journalist on the radio programme. I checked her out. She's very anti-Catholic in her writings; even some humanists think she's way over the top. The concern is that she should be more pro-humanist and less anti-Catholic."

307

"You're saying that she's the sort of Catholic who might catch our killer's eye?" Sheehan asked.

"I think so, sir. She fits his profile. Reasonably well-known, used to be Catholic but now stridently anti-religious."

There were some murmurs of agreement. Sheehan said, "You could be right. I think she's someone we'd need to keep an eye on. Thanks, Gerry." He looked around the team. "So what do we do about her, and our lack of any other possible victims?"

"We'll need to put a couple of men on her on Wednesday night, sir, make sure she's protected."

Sheehan nodded. "Okay. Fred, get a couple of uniforms on that, will you?"

"Right, boss."

"Sir." It was Arthur Smith. "The wife was telling me that there's a bit of gossip among her mates about a female sacristan in one of the chapels near Andersonstown who is married but is in an adulterous relationship with somebody in the choir. It's supposed to be secret but there is considerable gossip about her in the parish. Do you think she might need protection on Wednesday night as well?"

Sheehan gave the matter some thought. "Hard to say, but better safe than sorry, I suppose." He turned to Larkin. "Bill, sort out some protection for her. Make sure she knows to let nobody into her house on Wednesday night under any circumstances."

"Will do," Larkin replied.

Allen coughed, preliminary to speaking again. Sheehan waited. "Sir, Connolly's the real fear here. I think we're all agreed that he's our most likely suspect and that it's almost certain that he'll strike again on

Wednesday night, or the early hours of Thursday morning. I think we need to stake out his house from about early evening Wednesday and follow him if he leaves it. We'll probably need two or three cars involved."

Sheehan stared at him, his mind racing. Allen had just given him a way of keeping an eye on his men without seeming to do so. Anyone who filled any of the elements of the killer's profile could be assigned to partner someone else in one of the stakeout cars. "Yes, I agree," he said. "Where did you say he lives?"

"Gransha Parade, sir," Allen replied, holding up an A3 page with a street map on it. "I've been doing a wee bit of thinking about this, sir. May I?"

Sheehan waved a hand sideways.

Allen went to the white board and pinned the map to it. "Here's the Glen Road running past all these estates." He made a circular motion over one area of the map. "Here are all the Gransha estates ... Drive ... Avenue ... Crescent ... Gardens ... and Parade, where Connolly lives. There are plenty of streets there but they all lead to only two exits out of the estates on to the Glen Road ..." he pointed again, "... here and here." Then he pointed further north. "But if he should go up through Gransha Green and detour into the Norfolk estates, there's another half dozen exits at least on to the Glen Road."

He might have been the youngest detective in the room but he had everyone's complete attention. He pointed again at the map. "So, our best bet would be to set up a stake-out at the end of Gransha Parade, about here, and keep an eye on his house. We could also have another two cars ..." he pointed again, "... here, a few yards from the exit out on to Gransha Gardens and the other one here near the exit to

Gransha Avenue. If he leaves his house, there's no way he can get past us without being seen. We should be able to follow him from there and catch him in the act."

McCoy said, "This guy was active all during the troubles. We all had to watch our backs something desperate in those days. Connolly will have developed an instinct about anybody that might be following him, we all did. It was life or death at that time. He'll spot a tail a mile off."

"Good point, Oliver," Sheehan said. "We'll need a couple of extra cars to parallel his movements and to move in from time to time to let different tails veer away. We're probably looking at a total of five cars. The ACC will go nuts at the overtime, but I think it's necessary."

"Me and McNeill'll do one of the cars, sir," Allen volunteered.

"Thanks," Sheehan said. "Doyle and I will do another one. Right, Doyle?"

Doyle nodded acquiescence.

"Connors, will you do one with Miller?"

Both men nodded.

Sheehan ranged the room, wondering if anyone would notice the preponderance of Catholics on the stake-out vehicles. He stared at McLoughlin. "Are you up to a bit of overtime, Sergeant?"

McLoughlin, who had somehow managed to diminish his flabby bulk to about fifty per cent of its normal size during the 'volunteering' process, sighed a defeated, "Yes, boss."

"Thanks. Take Smith with you. Okay, Arthur?"

Smith said, "Right, sir."

"And Fred, will you and Loftus take the last car?"

Both men nodded. Sheehan stared at them thinking that if there was no killing next Wednesday night it would be because the killer was stuck in one of the stake-out vehicles. *Dear God*, he was thinking, *I really hope we've got the right man in Connolly.*

Loftus raised a finger. "Ah, sir, I know it's a bit of a long shot, but should we not keep an eye on the monsignor's house as well?"

Sheehan couldn't really see the point of it but a few of the men were still convinced by Loftus's argument that the monsignor knew far too much about the murders. "Okay," he said. "I'll arrange to have his house watched as well. A couple of officers should do it."

THIRTY-SEVEN

At first she is aware only that she feels nauseous. Bile rises in her throat and she wants to vomit. With the thought, her eyes open slowly but her brain is still shut down. Her head is bowed over her chest and she feels cramped and restricted. She experiences a feeling of terror and tries to lift her head to see where she is. Understanding comes slowly. A policeman had called at the convent with a report of some serious damage to the grounds at the back of the building. She had accompanied him there to view the damage when suddenly he had seized her roughly … and … and … a cloth, chloroform, was pressed to her mouth and nostrils. Her terror rises again. Where is she? She cannot see. Is she blind? No, it's dark. Where is she?

She strains to move her limbs but finds that her hands and feet are bound. She is bound to a chair in a dark room, a room with no windows. A cellar? She begins to hyperventilate and terror takes hold of her again as she discovers that her mouth is covered with some kind of tape which makes breathing difficult. She is sucking futilely through her mouth and tries to force herself to breath more slowly through her nostrils. But the panic persists. Her eyes roll in her head as she tries to penetrate the darkness. Why is she here?

She wrestles again with the binding on her wrists, whimpering in fright, but to no avail. The plastic cord is too tight. Again she struggles to breathe, choking on the tape over her mouth. She tries again to breathe through her nose, breathing with short, irregular snorts that are not helping her at all.

A noise to her left startles her into stillness and a light comes on. The policeman has come into the room. She has time only to register that she is a in a bare room, unfurnished apart from the chair she is sitting on and a large crucifix attached to one wall. She begins to whimper again, trying to implore him to let her go, that he has made a mistake, that she could not possibly be the person he is looking for. The man takes a knife from his pocket and walks menacingly towards her. She shakes her head backwards and forwards, trying to lean away from him.

"Nnnn … Nnnn … oooo."

"Please be quiet," her captor says, raising the knife to her face. Her eyes focus in terror on its point but the man simply says, "It occurred to me that you might suffocate with that duct tape over your mouth. We can't have that. It's not your time yet." And, raising a hand to hold her head still, he makes a slit in the tape over her mouth with the point of the knife, allowing her to breathe more easily. With that he turns to go. She jiggles her body, urging him to wait, making strangled squealing noises through the tape. He turns to look at her. She pleads with wide, stricken eyes, begging him to release her, asking why he is doing this. He walks back towards her and stands above her. "There is no point in attempting to free yourself. You will only bring yourself pain."

Again she struggles with muffled hisses and grunts, still pleading for release, still pleading for an explanation.

"You have failed in your stewardship. The Lord is king, the Lord is the creator. Universal spirits are myth. You have turned your back on Yahweh and earned his wrath. No longer will there be false visions or misleading divinations in Israel." He turns abruptly, switches off the light and leaves the room.

In darkness again, the terrified woman stares at the point where her captor left, terrified more by the implacable tone of the man's voice than by any threats he might have uttered. She begins once more to hyperventilate, desperately praying to a God whom she has for so long ignored. But since her words are born simply of trepidation and not of faith, she derives little comfort from them.

THIRTY-EIGHT

PART 1

Wednesday afternoon, sometime around four, Sheehan received a phone call.

"Doyle here, sir."

"Yes, Sergeant."

"Sir, I'm at the Convent of the Sisters of the Contemplative Heart."

"Where?"

"I didn't know about it either until today, sir. It's situated over here in West Belfast, sir, off the end of the Monagh Bypass, just heading into the mountains."

"And?"

"There's something going on here, sir. Thought you might need to know about it."

"What's the problem?"

"The Abbess has gone missing."

"That's DI Williams' territory. Why are you phoning me? You know we're up to our eyes today."

The ever-patient Doyle simply said, "If I might explain, sir."

"Right, right, get on with it."

"Sir, I'm talking to a couple of the senior sisters here. Obviously they're worried but during our conversation, one of them let slip that the Abbess is already causing grave concern among the older sisters because she's moving the Congregation towards a New Age type of spirituality."

"What are you saying, Doyle?"

"From what I'm hearing, sir, it seems to me that this Abbess might well be the kind of target our killer would be looking for, an authority figure in her Congregation, going off the rails theologically and trying to bring others with her."

Sheehan was silent. Doyle was definitely on to something. His gut told him that.

"What do you mean, she's disappeared?"

"Well, I was doing my rounds of the convents, only a couple left, and I called at this one a while ago asking to speak to the Mother Superior. They call her the Abbess."

"And?"

"They went to look for her, took a long time. Nobody knows where she is. The office people don't know. The senior nuns don't know. Nobody knows."

Sheehan's insides began to crawl. If the killer has already kidnapped his victim, he could kill her at his leisure anytime during the dark hours of Wednesday night or Thursday morning. But maybe he was over-reacting. "Maybe she's gone to spend time with her folks?"

"She's American, sir. Here about eight months or so. No ties here at all."

"How long has she been missing? Maybe's she's just gone into town or something."

"That's possible, sir. Nobody knew she was missing until I asked to see her. Maybe I'm jumping to conclusions here, sir."

"I'm not sure, Doyle. You might be on to something. Obviously we can't treat her as a missing person for another twenty-four hours but check out the situation. Find out all you can about her, any connections she may have made here in Belfast, the usual stuff. And, make a point of talking to that sister who was worried about the New Age concerns. That might be worth following up. I hope to God it isn't, but check it out anyway. Oh, and Doyle, if she doesn't get back before you leave, get a couple of uniforms to keep an eye on the place this evening. Tell them they're pulling an all-nighter there."

PART 2

Sheehan was sitting in the parked car with Doyle at the inner end of Gransha Avenue. It was just after eleven o'clock in the evening. It could end up being a long night. Sheehan was already feeling the pressure on his hip and he moved restlessly, trying to conceal his discomfort. He pulled his collar up around his neck and muttered, "I thought I'd finished with all this crapola."

Doyle, behind the wheel, continued to stare wordlessly through the windscreen.

"What's this New Age business that Abbess was involved in? Is it witchcraft or something?" Sheehan asked.

"No. Well, there are a whole lot of Wicca people who are also New Age ... I think. I don't know a whole lot about it, sir. Only started looking into it this afternoon. But as far as I can find out there is a whole lot of influential people in the New Age Movement who are trying to reject existing religions in order to allow the development of a single universal religion that could unite humanity. It's a kind of movement rather than a particular religion. But it's moving very fast towards something off-the-wall and a whole lot of Christians are jumping on the bandwaggon, grafting New Age ideas on to their existing beliefs. They've got so-called new divinities, for example, em ... what was her name? Oh yes, Gaia, the Mother Earth, who supposedly pervades the whole of creation. God is no longer a separate, external source of divine authority. He is sidelined into simply being a part of his own creation."

"What does that mean?"

"I'm not sure. I think it has to do with the notion that for New Age devotees, God is simply a state of higher consciousness. Fuzzy thinking, sir. I mean, how can the creator simply be a level of human consciousness?"

Sheehan glanced sideways at him. "How, indeed?"

There was silence for a time during which Sheehan shifted awkwardly again, trying to make some sense of what he was hearing. Then he said, "This is what was annoying the senior nuns?"

"Yes, sir. But one of them also told me that there

is also a significant investigation into convents and monasteries in America being launched by the Vatican. There are thousands of nuns falling for this sort of nonsense. Apparently our disappeared Abbess has brought this kind of thinking over to Ireland with her and, according to the nun I spoke to, a Sister Brenda, the new Abbess was having an unhealthy effect on the young nuns in the convent with her New Age ideas. What Sister Brenda is afraid of is that this woman is mixing Christian ideas with eastern mysticism and other oriental religions and leading the Congregation into some crazy new non-religion."

"Fascinating stuff, I'm sure. Let's hope it has nothing to do with us. Did she turn up yet?"

"Still missing as at seven o'clock this evening."

Silence settled over them once again and, despite the tension he was feeling, Sheehan found the minutes ticking by with wearisome slowness. He lifted a mouthpiece from the dashboard and depressed a button. "Bravo One to Uniform One. Report, please."

The officer on duty outside Margaret's house replied, "Uniform One to Bravo One. All's quiet."

Sheehan repeated the requests for information from the other uniformed officers on duty at the monsignor's house, at the journalist's apartment, and at the bungalow where the sacristan lived. In every case he was informed that lights were going off, that darkness had settled over the dwellings and that there was nothing untoward to report.

Silence reigned again in the car. Sheehan was filled with tension. He was torn between fear that some unsuspecting female was to be a victim of the killer tonight and hope that in Connolly they had the killer and that tonight's endeavours would bring an end to the murders. He looked at his watch for the umpteeth time. Eleven-thirty. If Connolly was going to make any kind of a move, it should be soon.

As if on cue the radio cackled. "Bravo Three to Bravo One. Subject on the move."

It was Allen's car. Sheehan grabbed the mouthpiece in front of him, his every nerve jangling. "Bravo One to Bravo Three. Stay back. Don't let yourself be seen. But don't lose him."

"Bravo Three to Bravo One." Allen's voice was calm, measured. "Subject proceeding to Gransha Avenue. Suggest Bravo One follow."

Even as Allen was speaking, Sheehan could see the headlights of a car emerging from Gransha Parade on to the avenue about twenty yards in front of him. He spoke briefly again into the mouthpiece. "Bravo One to all units. Bravo One following subject on to Glen Road ..." He waited to see which way Connolly would turn. "... turning south on Glen Road. Bravo Two, take over at Monagh Roundabout."

Doyle held back to allow McCammon's vehicle to take over the pursuit. For a while there was radio silence. Sheehan could see the tail-lights of McCammon's car about eighty yards in front. Then there was a sudden squawk on the radio. Despite his training, McCammon's voice had lost its neutral tone. Fuelled by adrenaline, it was almost a screech. "Bravo Two to all vehicles. Subject has run a red light and taken off at speed. Blocked by passing articulated truck. Will attempt to follow."

Doyle increased his speed, driving well over the limit to the lights. Sheehan was cursing. "Bloody hell! Bloody hell!" He pressed the switch on his mouthpiece. "Bravo One to Bravo Two. Have you found him?"

There was no reply for a couple of minutes, then, "Bravo Two to all vehicles. Have lost subject. Repeat. Have lost subject."

Sheehan banged on the padded fascia with the heel of his hand. "For cryin' out loud! How the feck did he spot us?"

"Should have thought of it sooner, sir," Doyle said stolidly. "He might have a police radio."

Sheehan groaned. Connolly should not have had a police radio but it was true that some of the older guys kept their car radios on police frequencies out of habit or simply to feel that they were still in touch. Headlights behind him told him that Allen and McNeill had caught up with them. "Signal Allen to stop," he said to Doyle. He spoke once more into the mouth piece. "Bravo One to all vehicles. Maintain strict radio silence. Repeat. Maintain strict radio silence."

Doyle pulled his car in towards the kerb, with Allen falling in behind him. Sheehan got out, muttering imprecations. He went to the window of Allen's car and said, "We think the bastard's got his radio on our frequency. He's heard everything. Go back to his house and wait for him to get home. I don't care how long it takes. Arrest him and bring him in immediately."

"On what charge, sir?"

"I don't care: running a red light. And get samples of that clothes line and one of those breeze blocks. And check the garden hut to see if there's a rope there. If there is, bring it in, too."

"Have we just cause, sir?"

"Too bloody right. Do as I tell you. I'll get Connors and Miller to back you up when I catch up to them."

He strode back to his vehicle, furious that Connolly could have given them the slip so easily. "Find Connors and Miller. I want to talk to them. After that, I want you to take me back to the station."

"This hour of the night, sir?"

"I want to wait for Allen and the others to bring that bastard in."

"Could be hours, sir."

"Look, Doyle, just find Connors and get me to the station, okay? You go on home after that. If anything breaks, I'll phone you."

Doyle started the car and went in search of Bravo Four.

THIRTY-NINE

At four o'clock in the morning Sheehan was sitting at one side of a table in the interrogation room. Beside him was Allen and on the other side, hands cuffed behind his back because of his belligerent behaviour, sat Jerome Connolly. He was still bristling with indignation and demanding constantly to know why he was here, why he was handcuffed, and why he had been rousted out of his house in the middle of the night. From time to time his eyes would fall on the rope, the piece of clothes line and the breeze block that lay on the table between him and the two detectives but, although his brow would furrow in mystification, he made no comment on them. Sheehan was also resting his folded hands on a stack of photographs from the crime scenes, face down in front of him on the table. He was leaning over on his left buttock, trying to find whatever ease he could from the pain in the sciatic nerve which was throbbing mercilessly now.

Because of the work he had done in identifying Connolly, Sheehan had given Allen the lead in the interrogation. Allen switched on the recorder, intoned the time, place and the names of those present. He started the questioning calmly. "Mister Connolly, where were you headed at eleven thirty last night in your car?"

Connolly was still struggling with his cuffs, his face red with anger and exertion. He stared at Sheehan. "You're Jim Sheehan. I remember you. What sort of way is this to treat an ex-colleague?"

"Would you please answer Detective Allen's question, sir," Sheehan said.

"What's this all about?" Connolly shouted, his rage building again.

Allen just stared at him until he quietened. Then he said, "Please answer the question, sir."

Connolly glared at him and said, "I couldn't sleep. I went out for a drive."

Allen stared at him in disbelief. "You couldn't sleep?" He leaned forward and said more sharply, "Why did you run a red light on the Glen Road at ..." He looked down at his notes. "... at eleven forty pm on Wednesday, tenth November?"

Connolly stared at him, stunned. "Is that what this is all about?"

"Answer the question, sir."

"There was somebody following me. I'm an ex-cop. I'm still a target for paramilitaries. Once I spotted the tail, I got scared and deliberately shook it off."

Sheehan was watching the man closely. Connolly was still glaring at Allen, still vociferous in his responses, but there was no hint of prevarication in his answer, no hesitation. Sheehan could have sworn that the man was telling the truth. But then, he had been a policeman for over thirty years. He knew the ropes. He understood interrogation. He would know exactly what signs the interrogators would be looking for and he could easily supply them.

Allen pointed to the items on the table. "These were taken from your garden."

Connolly stared at them, again with that puzzled expression. But all he said was, "You sure as hell better have had a warrant, son, or your ass is grass."

"Have you any idea why they're here?" Allen said.

"Not a clue. And I haven't a clue why I'm here either."

"Well, I can tell you that forensics is currently establishing that the items here on the desk are a match for the items in these photographs."

Allen glanced at Sheehan who wordlessly spread the photographs, face up, in front of the suspect. Neither policeman spoke but their eyes were focused on the suspect as he stared at the pictures. The man's eyes widened. A look of horror spread across his features. Again Sheehan could not curb the feeling that the man was not acting. "Hey!" Connolly was half out of his seat. "Hey! You're not pinning these on me. I had nothing to do with these … these … terrible things."

"Please sit down, sir."

Connolly's anger was replaced by definite concern. He turned to Sheehan. "You knew me. You must know that I could never have done anything like this."

Allen spoke again, no longer measured in his tone. There was growing anger in his voice. "How do you explain these items from your garden found at the murder scenes?"

"Somebody must have stolen them. My garden is on a corner of the road. It's easy to get into it."

"Right. And how do you explain the fact that all of the victims were members of the church you go to?"

Connolly looked stunned. He seemed unable to reply.

Allen kept pressing, angry now. "Where you between the hours of ten pm and four am on the night of the thirteenth of October?"

"What night was that?"

"Wednesday."

Sheehan, still watching Connolly's every expression, noted a flicker of guilt in the man's eyes. His heart sagged. He experienced no triumph. Something in the suspect's earlier answers had been leading him to believe that they had made a serious mistake, that Connolly was not their killer. That flicker of guilt saddened him. Connolly's next answer, with its sullen lack of conviction, confirmed Sheehan's suspicions.

"I was at home in bed, alone."

"And around the same times on Wednesday the twentieth of October?"

Connolly eyes began to look trapped. But again he muttered, "At home alone, in bed."

"So there are nights when you sleep all right?" Allen said. "Okay. How well were you sleeping on the night of Wednesday, the twenty seventh of October?"

Connolly was angry again. "I'm at home every night at those hours," he blustered. "Who goes wandering around at that hour of the morning creating alibis?"

"Apparently you do," Allen pressed, "at least on the one night we were watching you. Who's to say you were not out on those other nights as well?"

Connolly stared at him, silenced. Again, Sheehan noted that odd shiftiness in the suspect's eyes and a hint, too, of alarm. It was subtle but it was there. Allen was in full flow, now, determined to force a confession out of the suspect. "I put it to you that on the nights mentioned you were out of your bed, murdering members of your parish congregation."

"No. No. I had nothing to do with those murders. I … I …" He turned again to Sheehan clearly frightened now. "For God's sake, Sheehan, you know I could never do anything like this. Surely you're experienced enough to spot a feckin' frame a mile off when you see one."

And again, truth blazed in the man's eyes and Sheehan found himself confused by the mixed signals he was receiving. Then he remembered what Greenwald had told him. 'Challenge his beliefs. Rubbish them. If you get an inappropriately strong reaction, you'll know you have your man.'

Allen meantime, shouting now, was saying, "No point in trying to pull out the old boy network card, Connolly. You're as guilty as hell and you know it."

Sheehan eyed his young colleague with some puzzlement. He was almost spitting and seemed more determined to railroad Connolly into the dock than to ferret out the truth. Then he shook his head. *Bloody hell! Greenwald has me suspicious of even the best men on my team.*

He touched the younger man on the arm to silence him and said to Connolly, "You run a prayer group one or two nights a week? What's that about?"

The surprise in Connolly's eyes was matched by that in Allen's.

"Just a few parishioners get together one night a week for prayers ..." He trailed off, still bemused by the question.

"Do you give talks?"

"Yes."

"What about?"

"Basically about the state of the Church today and the need for reform."

"So you think that today's Church is too liberal or something?"

"Yes, and ordinary Catholics are victim to this liberalism in the media, and television everywhere they turn. They need to be protected. There's no censorship any more." Connolly was still puzzled by the turn the interview was taking but he was on comfortable ground talking about the Church.

"Do you not think you're a bit over the top?"

"What do you mean?"

"Well, this is the twenty-first century after all. Many of the Church's ideas are totally outmoded. I agree with you that the Church needs reform but not in the way you mean. It needs to take into account the findings of modern psychology and update its teachings. People like you want to put the ordinary Catholic in a strait-jacket."

Allen coughed and said, "Sir?"

"It's okay, detective. This is important."

If Connolly was puzzled before, now he was mystified. "Am I under arrest because I lead a prayer group?"

"No, but I have grave concerns about your Old Testament blood-and-thunder brand of Christianity. It does far more harm than good. You're frightening good people with biblical nonsense."

Connolly stared from Sheehan to Allen and back again. None of this made any sense to him. "Look, Chief Inspector, any other time I would love to debate theology with you, but your young colleague has just accused me of some horrific murders. I don't have time for this crap. I want a solicitor and I want out of here."

"You can have your solicitor but you're going nowhere," Allen said belligerently. "We have far too much evidence on you. We'll have forensic confirmation that the articles here match those found at the murder scenes, a connection between you and all of the victims, and we found you running around town in the middle of the night looking for your next victim."

Sheehan was disturbed again. Not only had Connolly failed to rise to the bait, he had not even sniffed at it. There was something else going on here. He leaned forward, his tone earnest. "Look, Mr. Connolly. I do know you. I know your reputation. You were always a good policeman and I do not want one of our own to be guilty of these terrible crimes. But Detective Allen is right. Without an alibi, you're goosed. You were a cop. You can read evidence. Sit on our side of the table and have a look at what we see." He was staring into the man's eyes and he could see that what he was saying was having its effect.

Connolly could not take his eyes off him. "You're not so stupid that you think there's some way out of this without an alibi. Now, once again, where were you going tonight?"

Something seemed to break in the suspect. He sagged in his chair. All truculence left him. His expression collapsed into a mask of shame and defeat. Sheehan stared at him. *What the ...?*

Connolly's head was down on his chest. He muttered something inaudible and Sheehan could see tears on his cheek.

"What did you say?" Allen rasped.

"A man has needs ..."

Allen glanced at his boss, eyebrows down. Sheehan raised a couple of fingers, directing his young subordinate to leave the rest of the interrogation to him.

"If the prayer group should hear of this ..." Connolly raised his head and looked at Sheehan beseechingly. "I had nothing to do with your murders. I swear. Can I ask that my alibi be kept quiet?"

Already Sheehan could read the signs. Connolly wasn't their man. They'd go through the motions of finishing the interview but he knew that they were now wasting time, and at four o'clock in the morning. "So, where were you for those few hours?"

"You know my wife died a while back. There was this woman I helped a few times while I was still in uniform."

"A woman?"

"An unfortunate soul, caught up in something outside of her control."

Allen couldn't contain himself. "What the hell are

you talking about?"

"She was forced into prostitution. I helped her to find her way a few times, not always with any great success. But she was grateful. Now I go to spend a couple of hours with her every Wednesday night."

"You mean you have sex with her?" Allen, in his twenties, was disgusted by the older man's confession.

Sheehan said, "It's okay, Allen. I'll finish this. Mr. Connolly, would you give Detective Allen the address. We'll need to check this out."

Allen wrote down the address the old ex-cop gave him and Sheehan said. "Go on home, now, detective. It'll be time enough in the morning to confirm the alibi."

"Are you sure, sir? The evidence ..."

"Is circumstantial."

"But, sir, even if this checks out, he could have committed the murders en route to the woman."

"Don't worry about it. We'll give Mr. Connolly a room for the night. He's not going anywhere."

The young detective left the room reluctantly, still glaring daggers at the suspect. Sheehan went around the other side of the table and undid the handcuffs. Connolly was rubbing his wrists, still defeated. He said, "Why ...?

"Long story. Let's just say I tend to believe you. But if you have been framed, I have no doubt that it's one of the cleverest frames I've seen in a long time. The evidence is overwhelming. Somebody knows you very well and has it in for you."

"So why aren't you banging me up?"

Sheehan grinned mirthlessly. "Well, you'll be

banged up for the rest of the night. But I know my killer inside out, and you're not him." He pressed a buzzer on the corner of the table and a uniformed constable came into the interview room. He moved behind the suspect and grabbed him behind one elbow. Connolly shook him off and, before the constable could grab him again, Sheehan said, "It's all right, Constable. Mister Connolly can manage to walk unsupported."

The constable stood back and allowed the prisoner to pass him. At the door, Connolly hesitated and turned around, saying, "I suppose I ought to thank you, Chief Inspector. I don't know of any other detective who would have stepped back from this arrest, not with all the evidence you seem to have."

Sheehan gave him a wry grin. "You're not out of the woods, yet. Detective Allen is convinced of your guilt. He's still out to get you."

"That makes two out to get me," Connolly said, turning to leave.

"Appears so," Sheehan said to the retreating back. And the little voice that so often plagued him, said, *Are you sure it's two? Allen seems excessively keen to put Connolly away for these murders. Is there something more to his zeal? You realise, don't you, that everything we have on Connolly came from Allen?*

FORTY

West Belfast is home to some of the most congested roads in the city. As the need for access and freedom of movement became more apparent, new motorways were planned and built. The Monagh Bypass was part of this strategy. However, it is clear that the bypass was never completed. At its northern end, the road suddenly reduces to a two-lane single-carriageway and turns sharply to the right to join the existing Springfield Road. It seems that there had been a plan to extend it further but this would have been difficult because the Monagh Bypass is already quite far into the Belfast Hills and the topography there is increasingly mountainous. No one quite knows why the work suddenly stopped at the mountainside but there are many who express delight that it did because this is a place of great natural beauty and, with the cessation of work on the road, the mountains were saved.

These hills attract walkers during the summer months and, while few are to be found there during the cold days of November, there are those hardy souls who walk in all weathers. Two such walkers, a man and a woman, were tramping their way through the wooded area behind the Convent of the Sisters of the Contemplative Heart when they were arrested by a gruesome sight that would probably haunt them for the rest of their days.

After some moments of panic, neither knowing which way to turn, the man used his mobile phone to call the police.

It was close on noon when Sheehan arrived with Doyle. Allen and McNeill were already there. Allen hardly waited for Sheehan to get out of the car before saying, with some heat, "We're barely fifteen minutes from where we lost Connolly last night, sir. The bastard probably had her in the boot. We should have stopped him before he even left the house."

Sheehan held up a restraining hand. "All right, all right. Just give me time to get my bearings. Where is she?"

"Over here, sir." Allen led Sheehan and Doyle to a small copse near a beaten path in the woods. Just off the path lay the naked body of a female, lying on her left side, her head twisted back as far as it would go, her right arm extended upwards from her head and her left arm lying outwards in front of her. Her right leg was pulled upwards from the other.

Sheehan exhaled a long, despondent breath. His eyes closed and his spirit fought a wave of defeat and guilt. He had recognised immediately, in the positioning of the dead woman's body, the fifth damned soul in the van der Weyden Doom painting. Monsignor Byrne had warned him not to blame himself if this happened but he was experiencing a terrible sense of impotence. Somehow he should have had the wit to realise that there was a senior nun in town who was an obvious victim. He should not have missed that.

Dejected, he studied the body again. Buried in the chest was a branch of a tree, plunged there with considerable force. The branch had not been shaved but there were indications at the entry to the wound that it had been sharpened to a point. As well as its bark, there were a number of small, thinner branches still attached to it, with leaves and berries growing on them. It almost seemed as if the branch was growing out of the body.

Lying around the body, obviously placed there deliberately, were a number of large stones, one of which had blood on it. Sheehan looked again at the victim's head and saw that the skull had been crushed. He noted, too, that a substantial amount of blood had seeped into the soil and on to the vegetation around the victim. On the corpse itself, however, the blood trails were uneven, flowing in different directions as if the body had been moved around after death.

Sheehan glanced at Doyle. "Do you think this is the Abbess?"

"Don't know, sir. We'd need to get Sister Brenda to carry out an identification, but it probably is." He lifted his eyes from the body to Sheehan, "Sorry, sir, if I'd gotten to this convent a day earlier …"

"Not your fault, Doyle," Sheehan said. "We all did our best to prevent this." He stared again at the mutilated body. "Wasn't bloody good enough."

The deputy state pathologist had again beaten Sheehan to the scene and had already examined the body. He had gone to leave his case in his car and had now come back to speak to the detectives. Sheehan sighed when he saw him, depressed that all efforts to prevent this killing had failed. "Well, Dick, what have you to say to me?"

"Good morning, gentlemen. There's no doubt it's your theatrical friend again. I have to say he leaves interesting death scenarios." The two detectives stared at him. The pathologist rubbed his hands together, prior to delivering his findings. "We have here a stone with blood on it. This matches the wound on the victim's head but the blow was delivered post-mortem. Most curious. Was he still angry after he had killed her? And here ... and here ... ligature marks on the victim's wrists and ankles. They're quite pronounced. I'd say she'd been tied up and held somewhere else for several hours before being brought here."

"Was she killed here?"

"Oh, yes. You can see where she bled out. Your killer is strong. This branch has been shoved into the victim's heart with considerable force. I've no doubt several ribs were broken in the process."

"Done, presumably, prior to his trademark posing of the body?"

"Yes. That's why the blood trails on the body are all over the place. She was moved around considerably after she was killed before our friend was finally happy with his work."

"And I suppose like the others she was killed between eleven and four last night?"

"Nooo ... I'd put it a fair bit later than that. I'd say more between two am and about eight am. I can give you a closer approximation after the autopsy."

Sheehan's eyes closed in pain. Despite all of the comings and goings during the previous night, despite his best efforts to ensure that the men were unconsciously observing each other, any one of his men would still have had the opportunity to carry out this killing. Worse, the feeling that one of his men was the killer was stronger than ever now. How otherwise would the killer have known to kidnap the Abbess before Doyle had completed his enquiries? This was a sickening thought that he kept to himself.

Allen, who with McNeill had been listening to the pathologist, noticed a crumpled ball of paper beneath a small bush a few feet from the body. He picked it up and straightened it out. After a moment's puzzled examination of its contents, he handed it to Sheehan "You might want to look at this, sir."

What Sheehan was holding in his hand was a printed flyer headed, 'GOD IS IN ALL'. There was a short paragraph explaining that the Convent of the Sisters of the Contemplative Heart was planning to host an Ecumenical Conference the following spring which would have the intention to "... be accommodating and inclusive to all women, and at which different spiritual traditions would be viewed as equal to the Catholic faith. In addition to rituals by witches, we invite rituals led by Buddhists, Muslims, Quakers and Jewish leaders, as well as Catholic nuns."

There was an application form at the bottom of the page and females proposing to attend were asked to send their name to Sister Maria Alexander at the convent before the end of March. Written in blood at the bottom of the page, presumably the victim's blood, was a capital E followed by the numbers 1224. Sheehan made a mental note to contact Monsignor Byrne.

He handed the leaflet to Doyle who read it, expressionless as usual. "New Age, sir. I'm surprised the other sisters would agree to this."

"You know how it is, Doyle," Sheehan said, retrieving the paper and placing it in a plastic evidence envelope. "A charismatic leader, authority, power, influence. It happens."

"But what's with the branch?" Allen asked.

"Maybe she was a tree-hugger," the pathologist offered, "an environmentalist. Maybe your man hates green politics."

Sheehan's lips went down. He wasn't convinced. "Doyle?"

"Hard to say, sir. New Agers have all these so-called ancient universal spirits, spirits of the air and of the wind and the woods and stuff like that. Maybe this has to do with tree spirits."

Sheehan sighed. He turned to the pathologist and offered him his hand. "Thanks, Dick. There's nothing more we can do here."

"Cheers, Jim. I'll get my report to you as soon as I can." He turned and left, waving a hand when he had his back to them.

Sheehan gave the body one last tired look and said, "Doyle, get the body removed to the morgue and call that sister …"

"Sister Brenda, sir."

"Yes. Get her in to identify the body. Allen, you and McNeill wait and give Doyle a lift back to the station. I need to go and see Bob Williams. This is his patch. He should have been called out, too. I'd better talk to him."

"Right, sir."

Sheehan glanced at the SOCO unit, searching the copse in ever-widening circles from the body. Some were on their knees; others were moving leaves and debris carefully aside with lengths of stick. Every now and then there was a flash as the police camera man was asked to photograph something of interest. Sheehan went over to him. "Could you get the main scene-of-crime photos on my desk ASAP, please?"

The man said, "Yes, sir."

Sheehan said, "Thanks," and went to his car.

FORTY-ONE

PART 1

Bob Williams was sitting at his desk when Sheehan was ushered in by Sergeant Mulholland. They shook hands and, after he was invited to sit, Sheehan said, "You heard about the killing at the Monagh Bypass?"

"Yes, but the ACC told me to let Sheehan get on with it." He grinned. "He seemed a bit miffed about something."

Sheehan rolled his eyes. "He's always miffed about something."

"Was it the same guy?"

"Yes. Different method of death, as usual, but definitely the same guy."

"You're going to have to catch him soon before he decimates the province."

Sheehan gave him a weak grin and said, "That's what I'm here to see you about. I need your help."

Williams looked slightly taken aback. "Oh?"

"I think the killer is one of my squad."

"Holy crap!" Williams' normally dignified persona almost disintegrated in shock. He listened, scarcely able to believe, as Sheehan brought him up to date with his reasoning.

"No disrespect, Jim, but that's hardly evidence."

"But it points the way. Only the squad knew that we were looking for women like this nun. The killer knew to get her out of the way before Doyle found her. He has to be on the team. How else would he have known?"

"You're going to need more than that if you want to get him to trial."

"I know. That's why I need your help. As Professor Greenwald was at pains to point out, I can no longer afford to trust any of my men until I know which one is the killer."

Williams winced. "God, Jim, I still can't believe it. When you say it bald like that, it sounds horrific."

"How do you think I feel? But I know I'm right. I wish I wasn't."

"Okay, how can I help?"

"Well, Greenwald made the point that the delusional element in the killer's psyche has been sitting there for a long time waiting to be triggered. He believes that something recent set the killer off. I need you to go into the backgrounds of my men, well, the Catholic ones, and find out if there have been any traumatic events in their lives recently. Look into their childhoods, too, for anything that might be considered significant. And, Bob, I need it yesterday."

"Gosh! That's a bit ... I'll do what I can but ..."

"Rope in that sergeant I met the other day, Jones. He seems reliable."

"Yes, Jones is a good man. Okay, I'll get on it right away."

"Thanks Bob. But apart from Jones, nobody's to know, right?"

"Yes, I get that."

PART 2

After he left Williams' office, Sheehan returned to the station. The scene-of-crime photographer had been as good as his word. He was just leaving the incident room as Sheehan arrived.

"Just leaving in some of the crime-scene photos, sir."

"Thanks, Officer ...?" He peered at him.

"Gray, sir."

"Of course, Gray. Thanks again. I appreciate the speed."

"Any time, sir."

Sheehan went to his desk and examined the photographs. There were one or two distance shots, full body shots, and some close-ups. He was shaking his head, revolted, even as his hand was reaching for his phone. He dialled a number and waited for a response.

"Hello, bishop's house."

"Hello, Chief Inspector Sheehan here. Could I speak to Monsignor Byrne, please?"

"Please hold."

After a few moments the monsignor was on the line. "Jim, good to hear from you. What can I do for you?"

"Do you have a couple of minutes, I mean, to look at some stuff I want to bring over?"

"Of course, come on ahead. I'll be in my office."

PART 3

The monsignor was as distressed as Sheehan was to hear that his prediction of a fifth killing had come to pass.

When Sheehan told him about the futile efforts that had been made to prevent the killing, he said, "This is shocking news, Jim, really terrible. But you did all you could. I mean, how do you identify one woman out of a whole city who may become victim to a delusional killer? It's impossible."

"Aye, I suppose you're right." Sheehan did not sound particularly convinced. Then he handed the priest the paper that had been found at the nun's crime scene and said, "Could you have a wee look at this flyer?"

The monsignor studied it for a few minutes. "Goodness, she really was losing her way."

"How could she have drifted so far away from her faith? Even I can see that that stuff's rubbish."

"Well, some twenty odd years ago, young people in America and, indeed, in the rest of the world, developed a strong interest in the environment and in ecology. 'Save the Planet' was their watchword. Many Christian idealists shared in this noble aspiration."

"I can get that but where does this ... heresy come

from?"

"It was partly to do with the growing awareness of the need to improve the world. Modern life has become very materialistic and there are many who have become disillusioned with that. Many New Agers in those early days of the movement were determined to mobilise the forces of good for a new world order and over time this led to a movement in which 'the best' ideas from many religions were combined. Once they started going down that road, it was an easy step into the anti-Christian belief that all religions are one."

"You mean Christ and God got left out of the picture?"

"Yes. You couldn't have Christ being a stumbling block for the Muslims and the Wiccas and the Eastern religions and so on. Sr. Maria Alexandra was obviously up to her eyes in this movement. And as far as I know, thousands of nuns in America are falling into the same trap."

His eyes rested on the bloodied numbers at the bottom of the flyer. "Hold on ..." He rose from his chair and went to a bookshelf to retrieve a bible. After flicking through the pages for a minute, he quoted, 'No longer will there be false visions or misleading divinations in Israel'." He looked up from the book. "That's your E twelve, twenty four." He returned to his seat. "I have to say your killer was really on the ball with this one. Wonder how he knew?"

"The killer is almost certainly a member of the congregation at St. Anne's church on the west side. One of the senior sisters told Doyle that the sisters all used to go there as a group for Sunday Mass and many of them could be seen there during the week as well. Very few of them, except some of the older ones, have been there during the past few months. No doubt our killer was aware of this sudden change in their pattern and checked it out." He took some of the SOC photos from an envelope. "What do you make of these stones lying around the body?"

The priest's face registered disgust and horror as he looked at the photographs. "Good grief! Has this guy any idea how sick he is?"

"According to Professor Greenwald, probably not. He would see these horrific killings as simply the way things have to be. He'd feel nothing."

Traces of his distaste at what he was seeing still remained on the priest's face as he said, "The stones? Obviously additional commentary like the ropes and the cup and the other pictures your killer was painting at each scene. These stones make me think of biblical stoning. There was plenty of that in the bible. Wait a minute. I have a notion." He checked the bible again, flicking pages until he found what he was looking for. "Here it is. Deuteronomy, fourteen, seven. Here we have an injunction against those members of family - father, brother, children - who try to seduce anyone in their family into serving others gods. Listen to this '... *gods whom neither you nor your ancestors have known. You shall kill them by stoning because they tried to draw you away from Yahweh.*' That's probably what was in your killer's head when he used those stones, especially when he hit her with one." He put the book down. "Greenwald was right. Didn't he say something about the internal logic of the delusion being totally consistent?"

Sheehan was tempted to let the priest know that he was close to finding the killer but Greenwald's words came to his mind. *You have to withdraw your trust from them all until you know who the killer is.* So he confined himself to a simple nod and said, "Yes, consistently murderous." He gave his head a weary shake, "I'll have to go way back to the office and go through all those reports again to see if there's anything I've missed." He gave the priest a wan grin. "Who'd be a cop?"

"Not me. That's for sure." As Jim was rising to go, the priest said innocently, "What's this I hear about you and Margaret?"

Sheehan grinned at him. "You sound like her father. I suppose next you're going to ask me if my intentions are honourable?"

The priest chuckled. "I wouldn't presume. Just curious."

Sheehan sobered. "To tell the truth, Niall, I have the nervy feeling that Margaret and I are on the brink of something. I haven't been in a relationship for a long time, but I have the feeling that this has the potential to be something deep and lasting. I don't want to do something stupid and mess it up, so I'm … uh … I remember an old Latin teacher we had years and years ago. He had a favourite expression, *'festina lente'.*"

"Make haste slowly."

"Exactly. I'm gonna festina as lente as you ever saw."

The priest grinned. "Margaret deserves a good man like you, Jim."

"Hah! She deserves far better. But if I have any say in it, I'm all she's gonna get."

FORTY-TWO

PART 1

Sheehan was on tenterhooks during that evening and the following morning. He kept himself to his office for the most of that time, head buried in the thick policy book, avoiding any direct contact with his men. He could not curb feelings of guilt and betrayal but the evidence that one of them was the killer was now overwhelming. He could only hope that whatever report Williams came up with would provide the answer he needed to end this uncertainty.

He had to fight the temptation, several times, to phone Williams. He knew that it would be pointless. Williams would contact him when the reports were ready. His stomach was churning. He had been unable to eat any breakfast that morning but he still felt over-full and nauseous. Over and over, his mind trawled through the Catholic members of his team, trying to paint the killer's face on to any one of them. It was a futile exercise. In every instance the face was rejected. Nowhere did it fit. Maybe it wasn't one of the Catholic men at all? Maybe he had completely misunderstood the killer's motivation? Maybe ...

Come on now, Jim. You have not misunderstood the killer's motivation. Neither has the monsignor. Neither have the team members. God has been inflicting judgement on these five sinners and only a deluded, fundamentalist mind could have carried out these killings.

He rested his head in his hands, his elbows on the desk. Even with the action, the phone rang and he almost dropped it in his anxiety to get it to his ear as quickly as possible.

"DI Williams for you, sir," the receptionist told him.

"Put him on."

He waited a second and then heard Williams' voice. "Jim?"

"Yes, Bob."

"We've got those couple of reports ..."

"Good. You in your office?"

"Yes."

"Okay, wait for me there. I'll be less than fifteen."

PART 2

Sheehan made sure the door was closed tightly behind him when he entered Bob Williams' office. Williams was toying with some A4 pages when Sheehan entered and sat down in front of the desk. Without his customary greeting, Sheehan said,

"Well?"

"Obviously we didn't have a lot of time," Williams began, "but I think we've got what you asked for." He shuffled through the sheets on his desk. "There are four of your men who faced some sort of tragedy or trauma within the past six or seven months."

"Which one didn't?"

"Larkin."

"Oh, okay. Give me what you've got."

"None of them is going to come as any great surprise to you. I think you already know about them. We did try to suss out a wee bit more about each of them …"

"Okay, okay," Sheehan waved an impatient hand.

"Well, first there's young Allen."

"Allen? I didn't know about him."

"It was just before he was promoted to detective. He was engaged to be married. Very much in love by all accounts. The girl, well, basically she dumped him. She met somebody else. Allen was devastated. He kept phoning her at all hours and arriving at her house to try and get her to change her mind. In the end, she threatened him with a restraining order. He pulled back after that. From what Jones could find out from friends, we think that he's over it now."

"Anything in his childhood?"

"He was adopted but other than that we could find nothing. Happy enough childhood."

"He seemed hell bent to pin the murders on Connolly but I can't see anything there that might trigger the kind of delusion our killer has."

"Me, neither," Williams replied, handing the first

report to Sheehan who ranged across it with his eyes while Williams lifted the second one. "And Doyle, of course, you know about as well. Father died a few months ago."

"Yes, he asked for permission to go to the funeral. I think it was on the continent, somewhere."

"That's right, France. His father died on the night of the twenty-first of July and Doyle took a week's leave. Couldn't find out a lot about his childhood either. I know you told me that he wasn't allowed out of the house much so I checked the records for any mistreatment or anything like that. Couldn't find anything except that his parents, particularly his father, were very aloof from their neighbours. But they were very church-going and the kid was always with them."

Again he handed the sheet to Sheehan who said, "Nothing jumps out at me there either. Maybe his father was up to something in the home that the public didn't know about."

"Come on, Jim. That's pure speculation. You could say the same thing about Allen. His were adoptive parents. What might they have been up to? It's not like you to grasp at straws. We've no evidence for any of that at all."

"Aye, you're right," Sheehan said, browsing through Doyle's sheet.

Williams lifted the next one. "Connors is a bit of a mystery. You know about the divorce, losing his house, the bad feelings there were. Jones checked him out. He lives like a hermit in that wee flat of his. Never goes out, doesn't seem to have any friends. He's hurting, Jim, and is nowhere nearly over it."

"Anything in his childhood?"

"Well, apparently he was a twin. They were

swimming in a lake somewhere when both of them were seven or eight. His twin was drowned. We didn't get the details yet. But apparently Connors couldn't talk for about a year after that. Had to have all sorts of speech therapy before he could talk again."

"Cripes! There's plenty of trauma there. But I can't see any connection with …"

Again Williams handed him the sheet and began to read the report on McCammon while Sheehan perused the details on Connors.

"Fred McCammon you know about. His son is in prison in London for drugs offences and Fred is having great difficulty coping. He's holding it together at work, just about, but his marriage is caving in and he spends more time at the Crown than he does at home. He's a total wreck." Williams looked up from the page. "Have to say, Jim, Fred's is no state to have …"

He stopped speaking when he saw Sheehan seem to freeze over something in Connors' report. Sheehan sagged in his chair and pain filled his face. "Oh, God!" Sheehan's face was twisted into a rictus. "Oh, God, I don't believe it!"

Williams was half out of his chair. "What is it, Jim? Are you all right?"

Sheehan waved him back into his seat and put down Connors' report. He leaned his elbows on Williams' desk and put his head in them. His brain was churning. One small item that he had not known about and suddenly everything clicks. The forgotten intuitions crowded, fully formed, into his conscious mind. They, in turn, led to other connections that fell into place like winning coins rattling down through a casino slot machine. He could hardly lift his head to stare at Williams. The hurt was visible. "Bob, I know who the killer is." And again he put his head in his hands.

Williams watched him, wondering what he had seen in Connors' report.

Sheehan looked up again, his expression suddenly determined. "Bob, I need you to do a couple of things for me. I want you to go and get Connors. I don't care where he is or what he's doing. Bring him to my office within the next forty-five minutes."

"What if he won't come?"

"Just get him there." He looked at his watch. "It's four o'clock now. Have him there before five. Then I want you to get a text message out to all of my men and repeat exactly what I'm going to tell you now. I want you to say that I know who the killer is, and that I'll hold a debriefing at seven-thirty in the incident room. And tell them … tell them that my back is acting up and that I'm away home to have a hot bath and to get something to eat. Got that?"

"Yes, you know who the killer is. You're calling a debriefing for seven-thirty and you want everyone to be there. Then you'll let them know who the killer is."

"No, Bob. You left out the bit about me going home for a bath and a bite."

"You want that in as well?"

"Yes, I do. Now go and find Connors."

FORTY-THREE

Sheehan sat in an armchair, watching the tail-end of the Ulster News on television. He had a bottle of beer in his hand, opened, but he was not drinking from it. He seemed distracted. The door bell rang. When he opened the door and saw who was standing there, he stood back and with an inclination of his head invited his visitor to enter. "Sergeant? You didn't have to come and fetch me. I could have driven myself."

"Not a problem, sir. I was passing anyway."

"Come in. Come in. Sit a minute. I'm just watching the end of the news."

Doyle sat on the other armchair. Sheehan raised the bottle to his lips. "Oh, sorry, drinking alone. Can I get you something, a beer?"

Doyle shook his head, "No thanks, sir. Don't drink, as you know."

"Of course. But don't make me drink alone. Soft drink? Cuppa tea? Coffee?" He rose from his chair.

"It's all right, sir." Doyle held up a restraining hand. "Sit where you are. I'll get it myself." He went into the kitchen, switched on the electric kettle and poured a spoonful of instant coffee grains into a cup. Sheehan watched him in silence, noticing that Doyle did not remove his leather gloves as he poured a little milk from a jug on the counter into the cup, poured in the now boiling water, and returned to his seat. Doyle sat down again, raised the cup to Sheehan in a gesture of camaraderie and took a couple of contemplative sips. Staring into the embers in the grate, he said quietly, "When did you first know, sir?"

Sheehan used the remote to turn down the sound on the television. "Well, to tell you the truth, part of me had known for some time before I even realised I knew. I mean, my subconscious kept waking me at night, making me aware that I had missed some things but it took me a while to figure out what they were. You were very clever, Sergeant, masterfully clever. But you made one or two little mistakes. I think the first serious error was that time in the incident room when you went on about the press having a field day with the three killings. You tried to show how sensational they were and said that the third victim had been drowned, not garroted. But at that point I had told no-one in the squad, including you, that that was how she had been killed. No one knew that she had been drowned. Williams had kept it back. So only the killer could have known."

"Could have bitten my tongue off two seconds after I said it, sir. I was hoping you'd missed it."

"Oh, I had, I had. At least, I had then. Then there was the time you came into the incident room and

354

turned faint at all the graphic photographs of dead bodies on the notice board. I thought you were just being human. But it was only much later that I realised that a two-tour veteran of Afghanistan, seeing the atrocities you've seen, wouldn't be fazed by a few photographs of dead bodies. That's when I remembered. I had just put up the photograph of the detail from the van der Weyden painting. It was that that had caught your attention, and scared the heck out of you because that was something you never expected to see. You must have thought we were already on to you."

Doyle nodded. "Yes, sir, or very close. It was a shock seeing it, I admit."

"Then there was that time we went to A District to examine the breeze block for numbers. I was so caught up in what I was doing that I didn't realise that you should have been as interested as I was in seeing what was there. Instead you just buggered off for coffee. Were you afraid that you might not know how to act when I found the marks and decided that the best thing was simply not to be there?"

Doyle nodded. "Something like that."

"It's odd but the next thing that caught my attention was probably a shrewd move rather than a mistake. It was that time the team was trying to come up with ideas about the kind of woman who might be the next victim. Each person who offered a suggestion was asked to follow up on it. It was clever of you to suggest a nun. You knew that, as the one who suggested it, you would be asked to investigate that possibility. It gave you total control of where and how that investigation should go. You were able to delay reporting on Sister Maria until it suited you. And, of course, that gave you all the time you needed to kidnap and imprison her until you were ready to kill her."

Two grey-green eyes appraised him. "You always were sharp, sir."

"Aye, right. But it was inevitable, once my mind started down that road, that other little things would start to come together. It all clicked when Bob Williams told me that your father's funeral was in France. Well, not immediately. I nearly missed it. I was actually reading a report on Connors when it came back into my head and suddenly I realised. France. The last time I had been talking about France was with the monsignor. That was the connection. France - the Doom painting. France - the killer. France - Doyle. Your father's funeral had to be in Beaune. And it had been. I checked that out with personnel a couple of hours ago. That's where you came across the van der Weyden Doom, right?"

"A masterpiece, sir. Amazing, inspiring, frightening, wonderful. I spent hours in front of it during that week I spent with my mother after the funeral."

"My goodness, Doyle. You sounded quite enthusiastic, there."

"Some things move me, sir. Not least the dreadful wickedness of those sinners who had to face the Lord's judgement."

"Why did you have to kill them, Doyle?"

"The Lord's work, sir. Yahweh is angered again by the modern world's aggressive secularism. Laws are being enacted that fly in the face of the covenant we made with him. It's the Israelites all over again, turning to false gods, falling into sinful ways. Ezekiel tells us, over and over, '*They had despised my laws and had not followed my decrees; they had profaned*

my Sabbath and their hearts went after their idols.'
And still they do not heed. It has to be stopped, sir."

They sat for a moment in almost companionable silence, Sheehan drinking his beer, Doyle sipping his coffee. Then Sheehan asked, "Very clean crime scenes, Doyle. How did you manage that?"

"Straightforward, sir. I wore my tyvek coveralls under my overcoat. Always managed to immobilise the guilty one before they really noticed what I was wearing. Once I took the overcoat off and left it aside, I became forensically invisible."

"And what about Connolly? How did we get on to him? I mean, you must have had a hand in that? And the physical evidence, the blocks, the clothes-line?"

"Have to give young Allen his due, sir. He followed up on the Tridentine leads like a veteran. Saved me the bother of having to steer one of the team that way. Connolly was a hypocrite, preaching the word on the one hand and consorting with a harlot on the other. He might well have been chosen for judgement but the Lord made me aware that he would be a useful scapegoat, especially since he had that St. Anne's connection to all of the sinners who had to face the Lord's judgement. It was easy to slip into his back garden and procure a bit of rope and clothesline and a breeze block. But like I said, sir, you were always sharp. With anyone else leading the case, it would have worked. He would almost certainly have been convicted of the killings, which he would have deserved."

"I see." Sheehan sipped his beer again and then said quietly, "And are you going to kill me?"

"Regrettably, sir, and I do mean that. But I don't have a choice."

"Do I deserve to die?"

"Collateral damage, I'm afraid, sir. You're a good man but you have inadvertently fallen into a situation where you have become a threat to the Lord's work." Sheehan marveled at how talkative his sergeant had suddenly become. "He has chosen me as his instrument and much still has to be done. You cannot be permitted to stop me, sir. I do not know what my next task is to be but I believe I might be called to the sources of many of our ills, Westminster or Brussels. I wait on the Lord's word." Doyle's voice remained flat. He could well have been talking about the weather. "But if it's any consolation, sir, it will be quick and painless. You are not meant to suffer."

"That's big of you, Doyle."

"It's no more than you deserve, sir."

"Nonetheless, Doyle, killing me won't prevent your capture. We're on to you now."

Doyle responded with a bleak smile. "Good try, sir. But I've phoned round the others to see if any of them knows what you're going to say tonight. All are still in the dark. With you ... removed from the si ... si ... situation, sir, there'll be nothing and no ... no one ... to tie me to ... to ... tie me ... to ... the ... ex ... e ... cu ... tion ... s."

Doyle's voice began to sound strange, garbled. Sheehan noted the change and said, "But how are you going to kill me, Doyle, if you can't move?"

"Wha ... rr? Wha ... Wha ...?" Doyle's speech suddenly became slurred. He seemed to be struggling to move but was incapable of doing so. His entire body sagged, suddenly flaccid. He seemed paralysed. Gone were his reflexes and all motor ability. Gone was the dispassionate expression. His body remained totally still. Only his eyes moved. They were rolling in fury as he struggled to mouth some biblical malediction against Sheehan. But all that emerged was, "Whuuuhh …"

Sheehan gave him a cold smile. "Just a wee drop of something I got from Dick Campbell only an hour ago, Doyle. What he calls a … a curariform neuromuscular blocking agent. You know how he is, he can't keep anything simple. Anyway, I knew you wouldn't have the beer so I put a wee drop of Dick's stuff in the milk. But don't worry. Its effects are only temporary. Basically you'll be semi-paralysed for a few hours and then you'll be right as rain again. Had to keep you manageable while Williams and Connors arrest you and transport you down to the station. Couldn't have a military vet like you putting up a fight in my wee flat. You'd wreck the place, even with Connors here to help us."

"Weh … Weh … lll … lll?" Doyle could no longer speak but Sheehan understood.

"Yes, Williams and Connors. You were expected, Sergeant. I knew when you got the message about the meeting, you'd have no choice but to try to silence me, especially as Williams let it be known that I'd be at home alone beforehand. As you said, we'd no real evidence against you, nothing that would stand up in court, so I laid a little trap. I was a bit concerned that the blocking agent might not work so I brought Connors in to provide muscle if it should be needed. Thankfully it wasn't, but he can help DI Williams make the arrest and carry you down to the car. And as for evidence, well, we've got your confession on tape ..." He looked up at Williams and Connors who had emerged from the bedroom. "… I hope."

"Every word, sir," Williams confirmed, holding

up a small recorder. "All the evidence we need."

FORTY-FOUR

"**D**ear God, I never would have suspected." Monsignor Byrne said, shocked.

"Caught us all by surprise," Sheehan said.

They were seated in the monsignor's study. Sheehan had called in out of courtesy, feeling that he owed the monsignor an explanation about how the case had turned out. The monsignor had listened in silent attention to the detective's story until Sheehan revealed that Doyle was the killer.

"Dear God," he said again. "Poor Doyle."

"Poor Doyle? Try telling that to the investigating officers, or the loved ones of the victims."

"Oh, I'm not condoning what he has done, but his actions were motivated, as you say, by delusion. In that sense he, too, is a victim."

"Victim? The team doesn't see it like that. Even

before we knew who the killer was, they had started calling the killer a fundamentalist nutter."

"Fundamentalist nutter? I can see where that came from. Fundamentalism is a reaction to secularism in modern culture. It tends to be pretty extreme, of course, contrary to the spirit of tolerance that genuine Christianity espouses. Jesus, and Yahweh, is a God of love. Poor Doyle completely lost sight of that. He seems also to have lacked the corrective normally supplied by reason. His thinking became distorted, maybe when he was a child. Who knows what his father taught him, kept in all the time, only going out to go to church. I've come across the type many times. The kid would have experienced any amount of religiosity but probably very little in the way of parental love or, judging from his current delusions, very little in the way of divine love either. All he'd have known about would have been the blood and thunder, the punishment and death. That has to have twisted him. But, I don't quite get why he operated always on a Wednesday night?"

"When Williams told me the date of Doyle's father's death, I took a notion to check which day of the week it was. The father died on a Wednesday evening. Obviously some sort of connection there."

"No doubt. The death probably flooded Doyle's mind with the lessons learned as a child and the day of the death became significant for him. With the underlying delusion already in place, the trauma of his father's death would have been the trigger that drove him to begin his campaign to, I would guess, overcome the corrosive effects of secular culture."

"A bit of a forlorn effort, trying to change the culture of society on his own?"

"He wouldn't see it like that. Doyle was almost

certainly schizophrenic and I have no doubt that psychiatric examination will uncover that."

"Greeenwald told me that he was suffering from a delusional disorder."

"Yes, and I would agree. But there have been many studies that show that there is a deeply manifested relationship between religion and schizophrenia. It's quite well known that delusional patients who believe they have a close relationship with God can have the grandiose belief that they are acting on God's behalf and that they have been mandated to inflict bodily harm on others."

"How do you know so much about this?"

"I came across it a few years ago. I was working with a delusional parishioner and I got it really wrong. I was quite upset about it at the time. I tried to help him find peace and comfort in spirituality not realising that asking him to engage with God only fed his delusion and led to even more pathological conditions. That's why I say 'poor Doyle'. God knows what torture he was going through waging this lonely war against what he would perceive as society's degradation."

"What is the likelihood that there was any real spirituality in Doyle?"

"Hard to say. Who knows what his father put him through as a child. We can easily see, however, that his spirituality, if it could be called that, was very much attuned to the allegedly violent God of the Old Testament. But the bible needs to be interpreted. All Doyle could feel was the anger, probably his father's anger, and that was what was driving him. There might have been prayers of a sort, but they would have been self-justifying. There would have been no real link with the Almighty."

"His fundamentalism seems to have a core of support, judging from the letters the bishop received. I mean, what these people were doing, Doyle is hardly alone in disapproving of them?"

"There are many fundamentalists out there, of course, who would react as strongly as Doyle against the liberal mores of the twentieth century but they wouldn't go around killing people."

"Aye! Doyle was lost, all right. With all that in his background, what chance did he have of seeing things through normal eyes?" Sheehan sounded almost sympathetic.

"You sound sad. I take it you liked Doyle?"

Sheehan sat back in his chair and crossed his legs. He appeared to be more focused on the movement of the suspended foot than he was on the question. When he spoke, he seemed to be searching for words. "We were partners for four years. I don't know if we ever had a real conversation in all that time but yes, I liked him. It's a strange thing to say now but I always thought there was something very straight and sincere about him. It's killing me that he turned out to be the murderer. I can't believe he could have been so brutal."

"Well, he was under the delusion that he was God's instrument. He probably was psychologically at one remove from what he was doing. And then there was Afghanistan. He would have experienced so much death and brutality there that he would have become inured to it. That's probably one of the reasons he was so cold and merciless in the killings."

They sat in silence for a while, each lost in his own thoughts. Then Sheehan said, "How do you feel about the victims?"

"It's sad about the victims, cut off like that in what was probably a sinful state, with no hope of redemption. No … no … I shouldn't have said that. I can't make judgements. God is infinitely merciful, and I pray with my full heart for mercy for the victims. But it's a gamble I wouldn't be prepared to take myself."

"A gamble?"

"The victims' life styles. They could not have been ready for death. I always live my life with one eye on eternity. Jesus warned us often enough that the moment of our death could come like a thief in the night. Always be ready is the message."

"I suppose you really need belief, faith, to think like that."

"Yes, that's true. It's second nature for me, I suppose."

Sheehan smiled. "There are a lot of us who don't think like that." He seemed to look inwardly for a moment and then said thoughtfully, "But I imagine there's a deal of comfort in it." He rose as if to leave, and then hesitated.

The priest noted the hesitation and said, "Was there something else, Jim?"

Sheehan seemed torn, in two minds about something. But even as stood staring down at his still-seated friend, he felt something flood his spirit, a consciousness of a need, a sudden urge that was as shocking as it was unexpected. Something in him was crying out to find his faith, to find the being who had been dragging him evening after evening into St. Malachy's. Scarcely aware of what he was doing, he sat down again and said quietly, "Niall, we need to talk."

Want to read more?

Then click here for Die This Hour, Book 2 of the Inspector Sheehan series :

https://geni.us/diethishour

Enjoyed Angel of Death?

If you did, then please leave a review here:
https://geni.us/angeldeath

Hardly anyone leaves a review, and we will always be grateful that you spared a couple of minutes to write a review.

Thank you
Modus Operandi Publishing.,

We love to hear from our readers. Please feel free to get in touch via email: moperandi2023@gmail.com

Printed in Great Britain
by Amazon